Alison Roberts is a Ne〜 enough to be living in t〜 lucky enough to write f〜 Romance line. A prima〜 life, she is now a qualifi〜 paramedic. She loves to travel and dance, drink champagne, and spend time with her daughter and her friends.

Having tried a variety of careers in retail, marketing and nursing, **Louisa George** is thrilled that her dream job of writing for Mills & Boon means she gets to go to work in her pyjamas. Louisa lives in Auckland, New Zealand, with her husband, two sons and two male cats. When not writing or reading Louisa loves to spend time with her family, enjoys travelling, and adores eating great food.

TWINS ON HER DOORSTEP

ALISON ROBERTS

A NURSE TO HEAL HIS HEART

LOUISA GEORGE

MILLS & BOON

First Published in Great Britain 2018
by Mills & Boon, an imprint of HarperCollins*Publishers*
1 London Bridge Street, London, SE1 9GF

Twins on Her Doorstep © 2018 by Alison Roberts

A Nurse to Heal His Heart © 2018 by Louisa George

ISBN: 978-0-263-26951-2

MIX
Paper from
responsible sources
FSC www.fsc.org   FSC® C007454

Printed and bound in Spain
by CPI, Barcelona

TWINS ON HER DOORSTEP

ALISON ROBERTS

MILLS & BOON

CHAPTER ONE

THIS ROAD WAS ENDLESS.

And winding.

It was also quite spectacular along this particular stretch, with surf crashing onto rocks at the bottom of tall cliffs, but Finn Connelly wasn't interested in the view of the Cornish coastline any more than he had been in any of the sleepy villages he'd already driven through. The GPS told him that the one he was heading for, North Cove, was still about an hour away. Miles from anywhere.

And who knew? He might get there only to have to turn around and come straight back again. It wasn't that he thought this was going to be the answer he was looking for, it just seemed like the *right* thing to do. But after this? He had no idea...

A glance in the rear-view mirror showed him that the children were sitting quietly in their car seats. They weren't looking at the scenery, either, which was understandable, but they were so quiet and that was even more worrying than the fact that they'd barely eaten anything the last time they'd stopped on this road trip.

With every mile that passed, Finn's doubts about the wisdom of what he was doing were increasing, to the point where his head was starting to ache now. There was the slight ethical problem with this plan as well, although that had been easy enough to push aside when he'd had this crazy idea in the first place. He'd want to know, if it were him at the end of this road, wouldn't he? Even if it was going to change his life so dramatically?

'You guys hungry yet?' He turned his head briefly to smile at his passengers. 'I've got apples. And crisps. And those little packets of raisins. You like raisins, don't you?'

'No.'

'Are you thirsty?'

'No.'

'It's getting colder, isn't it?' Finn knew he was on a losing streak but he had to keep talking. To try and make this seem a little more normal, perhaps, when it was anything but. He wasn't hungry, either. It had been an effort to force down even half his sandwich when they'd stopped for lunch some time back. He'd actually felt slightly nauseated.

'Look at those big, black clouds up there.' Was he putting too much effort into trying to sound cheerful? 'You girls warm enough?'

He risked another glance in the mirror to find four large brown eyes staring at him. How could three-year-olds look so suspicious? Maybe it was just wariness, he told himself. And who could blame them?

'Ellie? Emma?' He tried one more time. 'You want me to stop and find your coats? Those pretty pink ones?'

Two small heads shook slowly in a negative response and Finn suppressed a sigh. It was becoming the standard reaction to being asked anything, wasn't it? They didn't want their coats. They didn't want treats to eat. They didn't want to be here, with him, and he understood that. This was confusing. Frightening, even. He might be their uncle but he'd only met them for the first time a couple of weeks ago so he was still virtually a stranger.

Guilt could get added to the worry and the doubts. It wasn't a pleasant mix.

There was only one thing that these little girls wanted—the life they'd had until now. Their family. And he couldn't give it to them.

Nobody could.

Was it the weather outside or the trauma of recent events that made him suddenly shiver?

'I'll put the heater on for a bit,' he said.

'Sophie…how are you, lovie? It's a bit cold today, isn't it? I think we're in for some rain.'

'I'm the one who's supposed to be asking how *you* are, Mrs Redding.' Sophie Bradford smiled. 'I'm the doctor here.'

'I know, love. But I always see your dad.' Maureen Redding closed the door behind her. 'I know you've been here for a few years now but I still think of you as that little girl with the wildly curly hair running past my place to get to school.'

Automatically, Sophie reached up to touch her hair. Those unmanageable corkscrew ringlets she'd been born with were currently saturated enough with product to enable them to be scraped back into a ponytail but she could feel the undulations on her scalp and she knew that, at any moment, a curl could rebel and spring free to make her look unkempt. Unprofessional, in fact. Amazingly, they were standing up to the stress of an unusually busy day and behaving perfectly, for now.

'Dad's still out on his house calls at the moment but he should be back soon. If you want to wait, he can probably squeeze you in.' Sophie closed the screen where she'd just entered the notes on her last patient, clicked to bring up Maureen's history but glanced up with concern a moment later as she heard her new arrival's rasping breaths. 'You're a bit short of puff today, aren't you?'

'Aye…' Maureen Redding sighed heavily as she eased her large frame onto the chair and placed her handbag on top of Sophie's desk. 'I've got the cold that's been going around and, you know, it's the same old story…'

'I know.' Sophie was on her feet. She'd seen enough on screen to know that Maureen's visits were usually due to exacerbation of her chronic respiratory disease. 'Let's have a good look at you and see what's happening with your oxygen levels and blood pressure. Did you walk up the hill to see us today?'

'Oh, no… It's hard enough getting to the corner shop for a pint of milk at the moment. Jim, next door, gave me a ride.'

'That was kind of him.'

'He needed to come in himself, to get his prescription for his heart pills. He's going to wait for me, but I don't want to keep him waiting too long, so I'm happy to see you, love. Everybody says that you're a wonderful doctor.'

'That's good to know.'

'He'll be having a yarn with your mum, I expect. He said he hadn't seen her at the markets for a while.'

'Mmm… We've all been a bit busy.'

Sophie's mother was the nurse in this family-run general practice but, given how full the waiting room had been the last time she'd set foot outside this consulting room, Judy Greene wouldn't be stopping to chat with Jim or anyone else today.

She handed Maureen a handful of tissues as the older woman began coughing and warmed the disk of her stethoscope in the palm of her hand as she waited for the spasm to finish.

Then she paused, frowning. 'Has that happened before?'

'The blood? Oh, once or twice… Your dad says it's usually a sign of infection.'

Antibiotics were likely to be needed, Sophie thought. And a short course of steroids for the inflammation in Maureen's lungs. A trip to the nearest hospital for a chest X-ray might be called for if there was any indication that this could be pneumonia rather than simply bronchitis. And had any mention been made of having home oxygen available for episodes like this?

'I saw your dad coming out of the pharmacy yesterday,' Maureen said. 'He's looking a bit peaky, I thought.'

'Oh?' This might be the only general practice in this out-of-the-way Cornish fishing village, Sophie thought, but she wasn't about to start discussing her father's state of health with one of their patients. It was a close community but there had to be some boundaries.

'It's time he retired, isn't it? I went to school with him so he has to be at least seventy-three.'

'Thereabouts. And he will retire soon. When we've found someone suitable to join us. Now, stop talking for a moment, Maureen. I want to have a listen to your chest.' Sophie had to concentrate on which lung fields were being affected by the fluid and inflammation. Despite the closed door, she could hear the faint wail of an unhappy child in the waiting area, which wasn't helping.

Fifteen minutes later, she was holding the door open.

The wailing had suddenly become a shriek that made Sophie wince.

'Get Jim to take you straight to the pharmacy. He'll be going there to fill his own prescription, I expect. Make another appointment in a couple of days, or sooner if you're not feeling any better, but, if it gets any worse, call us straight away.'

'I will… Ooh, look. There's your dad.' She sailed ahead of Sophie. 'Yoo-hoo! Dr Greene? I wanted to have a wee word with you.'

Sophie's father was crouching by a boy who was holding one arm across his chest with the other and glaring at the doctor. 'Not now, Maureen. Sorry, but we're a bit busy, as you can see.' He looked up and Sophie could see the tense lines in his face relax just a little. 'Ah… Could you take young Toby here through to the treatment room, Dr Bradford? He's fallen off his skateboard and given himself a bit of a fracture. If you can splint it and make him comfortable, his mum can drive him to the hospital.'

'I could call an ambulance.' Judy Greene was behind the reception desk.

'No need.'

Jack Greene got to his feet. Slowly. He *did* look peaky, Sophie realised. Maybe she'd just got used to how tired he always looked these days and hadn't noticed that his colour wasn't so great, either. So pale it was almost grey. He was pushing himself too hard. Working himself into an early grave?

'But I *want* an ambulance,' Toby sobbed. 'With a siren.'

It was Sophie's turn to crouch and be on eye level with the seven-year-old. 'Toby…you're a big boy now. You know that it's important that an ambulance is only called for really serious emergencies, don't you?'

'But…but I've broke my arm. Again…'

'I know.' Sophie's tone was full of sympathy. She flicked a swift glance up at her father, who gave a single nod.

'Baselines are all good. Simple FOOSH.'

A fall on an outstretched hand. The sort that often happened when you fell off your skateboard or out of a tree, as young Toby already knew. He had broken his left wrist last year. This time it was his right. But, if his baselines were good, that meant there was no danger of losing hand function from a compromised blood supply or nerve damage. In any case, Sophie knew she could make him a lot more comfortable with a good splint and some paracetamol, and it would actually be quicker for his mother to take him to the nearest emergency department. Even if there was an ambulance available instantly, it was at least twenty minutes away. Thirty, if there was any traffic or the threatening storm broke.

'I'm going to give you a lovely splint that will help your arm stay very still and not hurt so much.'

'And I'm going to drive you to the hospital,' his mum added firmly. 'Otherwise, how are we going to get home? Daddy can't just turn his boat around to come and get us, you know. And a taxi would cost the earth. About as much as that new game you want for your computer, I reckon, and which one of those would you rather have?'

Reluctantly, Toby followed Sophie, who sent an apologetic glance to people still waiting. Emergencies played havoc with queues but everybody knew that. Old Mr Dobson was getting to his feet.

'I can come back tomorrow if I need to,' he said. 'It's probably nothing a bit of cod liver oil can't fix.'

Maureen and Jim were heading for the door, too, but Maureen paused to touch Jack Greene's hand.

'I just wanted to say that your Sophie's a credit to you,' she said. 'We're so lucky to have the next generation of wonderful doctors here in North Cove.'

'Thanks, Maureen.' But Jack didn't smile as he gazed around the room. 'Who's next, then?'

There was a painful-looking nappy rash on a baby, an adult with a rash and a terrible headache that was probably the early signs of a dose of shingles. Another patient had chest pain and had to jump the queue, but it was easily resolved with a spray of medication. The twelve-lead ECG Sophie took was reassuringly normal as well.

'It's not a heart attack, Colin. You need to use your spray as soon as it happens next time, not wait for me to give it to you. You know it comes on when you start moving furniture around, don't you?'

'I don't like using stuff unless I really need to. And I was right next door.'

'Get those young lads of yours to do the heavy lifting from now on. And, if you start getting pain more often, or when you're just sitting around, let me know. I'm also going to book you in for some more tests at the next cardiology clinic at the hospital.'

The door opened before Colin could touch the handle.

'Sophie? Could you come, please? *Now?*'

Sophie's heart sank. Her mother was a very experienced and calm nurse. She had never seen a look of fear in her eyes like this.

She raced into the adjoining room after her mother.

Was her dad having a crisis with one of his patients? A cardiac arrest, maybe?

But Jack was alone in the room.

Slumped over his desk.

'Dad?' Sophie was by his side in an instant, her hand on his wrist. 'Can you hear me? What's happened?'

She could feel a pulse, thank goodness. A bit faint, maybe, but it was steady.

And her father responded with a groan as he pushed himself upright. 'I'm fine,' he growled. 'Just a bit of a dizzy spell. Stop making a fuss.'

'Did you eat lunch?' Judy demanded.

'Don't move,' Sophie ordered. 'I'm going to take your blood pressure.' She unbuttoned his cuff, pushed the shirt sleeve up and wrapped the cuff around his upper arm. 'Any other symptoms? Are you feeling nauseated? Any chest pain?'

'No. And no.' Jack sighed. 'And no, I didn't have time for lunch. My house calls turned out to be a bit more complicated than usual.'

'Your blood pressure's a bit low,' Sophie said, releasing the valve. 'One ten over sixty. I'm not surprised you felt faint. Now, where's your blood glucose kit?'

His blood glucose level was on the low side as well.

'At least I haven't got diabetes.' Jack pushed his chair back. 'Now, will you two let me get on with my work?' He got to his feet but then closed his eyes and raised his hand to rub at his forehead.

'Headache?' Sophie was watching him intently. 'Still dizzy?'

'I just need a cup of tea. And a paracetamol. Go away, Soph. You've got patients waiting.'

'We're almost done. Mum, take him home, will you?

Give him something to eat and make him rest. I'll have a good look at him as soon as I get back.'

It was only a short walk through the car parking space at the back of the clinic to the gate in the fence that led to the house Sophie had grown up in. Hopefully nobody would notice because otherwise the whole village would be alarmed that there was something seriously wrong with their beloved GP. It was probably nothing more than the fact that he'd forgotten to eat, on top of being a bit run down, but the way that her father had agreed to the plan with minimal grouching was enough to make Sophie even more worried.

Something had to be done about reducing his work load. Soon.

Her last patient of the day had deliberately been given the final appointment because she'd known she couldn't put a time limit on this one.

Shirley needed to talk as much as she needed any review on whether her medication was helping.

'I'm still not sleeping properly. And I still burst into tears all over the place. It's embarrassing. It happened in the supermarket the other day, when I saw the cans of baked beans.' Shirley fished in her handbag for her handkerchief. 'It's was Bob's favourite tea…baked beans on toast…with a poached egg on top…'

Sophie was sitting alongside her patient this time. It meant that she could give the hand she was holding a squeeze.

'I know. It's hard. *So* hard…'

Shirley sniffed and nodded. 'I know you know, dear. That's why it's so good to talk to you. You had such a tough time after your Matthew passed away. We were all so worried about you, what with you losing the baby and all...'

Even after five years, the pain was still there, wasn't it? Not crippling now, though. More like a simple sadness, but one that could still squeeze her heart hard enough to be painful sometimes. At least she'd become an expert in pushing it into a place that she rarely chose to visit.

'I'm fine now,' Sophie said gently. 'I found the answer was to focus on the good things I did still have in my life. Like my family and friends. My work. Being lucky enough to live in such a beautiful place.' She gave the older woman's hand another squeeze. 'You've got both your daughters nice and close. And all those gorgeous grandchildren of yours. Are you spending plenty of time with them?'

'Oh, yes... They're in and out every day, wanting Granny's cake, but...but I just haven't felt up to baking yet.'

'They'll be missing those cakes.' Sophie smiled. 'Everybody knows that no one can make a better chocolate cake than you can, Shirley. And you've got a new grandbaby due to arrive in...ooh...about six weeks, isn't it? I saw Jenny for her check-up just a couple of days ago.'

'Bob was so excited about this new baby.' Shirley's smile trembled. 'He was sure it was going to be a boy, finally. And now he'll never know...' She blew her nose again. 'I haven't even finished the cardigan I started knitting weeks ago. I just can't seem to focus.'

'It's only been a couple of months since you lost Bob,' Sophie said gently. 'It takes time to grieve.' She got up to find her prescription pad. 'I'm going to give you something to help you sleep. And, if you like, I can refer you to a grief counsellor?'

Shirley shook her head. 'I feel better just coming to see you, dear.' She got up from her chair. 'You understand...'

Sophie went to see her out. That way, she could lock the front door to the clinic and there wouldn't be any last-minute obstacles to getting home to see how her father was. Hopefully, he would be feeling a lot better after some hot food and having put his feet up for an hour or two. If not, she was going to be laying down the law about getting a thorough physical check-up from a specialist in Truro—the largest hospital in Cornwall. And reducing his hours here, which was probably the best she would be able to manage until they could find a locum.

Her heart sank like a stone when she noticed the unexpected arrival sitting in the waiting area.

A man who looked to be in his mid-thirties. A man who was good-looking enough for her gaze to snag for an extra heartbeat of time. Probably the father of the two children sitting beside him, she decided. Small girls who were wearing pink, puffy anoraks and little black ankle boots.

Shirley was fussing with the fastening on her umbrella as she headed to the door so she didn't even notice the trio in the corner but Sophie gave them a second glance as she passed. There was something compelling about these people.

The man was definitely not a local, unless he'd just moved here, but the children looked vaguely familiar. No. She shook her head as she closed the door behind Shirley and flicked the lock. There were no identical twins in North Cove, she was quite sure about that. They had to be tourists, but she couldn't turn around and tell them that an appointment was needed for afternoon surgeries at this clinic unless it was an emergency.

After all, there were children involved, and even the brief impression she'd already gained suggested that these little girls were subdued enough to be potentially unwell.

She pasted a smile on her face as she turned back.

'I'm Dr Bradford,' she said. 'How can I help you?'

The man got to his feet. He was tall, Sophie noted, well over six feet, although he looked a little stooped right now. As if he was over-tired. Or sad, maybe. His jaw was shadowed as if he hadn't shaved for a while and his dark hair looked tousled, as if he'd run his fingers through it more than once recently. In the same instant she had the thought, he raised his hand and rubbed at his forehead, exactly the way her father had done earlier and, yes, he completed the action by shoving his fingers through his hair.

Then he nodded.

'I'm Finn Connelly,' he told her. 'I'm…ah…sorry for turning up like this without an appointment.'

The Irish accent confirmed her assumption that he was a tourist.

'That's okay,' Sophie said. She smiled at him, because he certainly looked like he needed a bit of reassurance, and instinct told her that it wasn't something he normally needed. For some reason, this man was way out of his comfort zone and part of her job was to provide a safe environment. Besides, he did look sad, and that never failed to tug at her heartstrings, but there was more than sympathy happening here. There was a pull that she didn't understand and it was putting her slightly out of her own comfort zone.

'We're always available for emergencies,' she added.

Shifting her gaze to the seats behind the stranger, she smiled even more warmly at the children.

'Hi there,' she said. 'What are your names?'

The girls stared at her but said nothing. They looked more than a little frightened and Sophie felt a beat of alarm. What, exactly, was going on here? Children who were scared of going to see a doctor would normally be clinging to their parents, not sitting there like two little mop-haired statues.

That hair…

Clouds of tangled blonde ringlets. Impossible to comb without causing pain. Sophie knew what it was like to have hair like that.

The sudden chill that ran down her spine almost made her shiver visibly. She swallowed carefully.

'So who's sick?' she asked. 'Or has there been an accident?'

'Nobody's sick,' the man said quietly. 'I…um…is there somewhere we could have a quiet word?' The movement of his head, along with the expression in a pair of very dark eyes, was easy to interpret. This Finn Connelly wanted to talk to her somewhere the children couldn't overhear.

'There's no one else here,' Sophie said apologetically. 'I can't leave the children unattended in the waiting room.'

She wasn't sure she wanted to go somewhere private with this man, either. Again, her instinct was giving her a clear message, and this time it was warning her that she wasn't going to like what she might hear. Had these children been abused in some way? Were they in danger?

She actually jumped when a door behind her opened.

'I forgot my bag.' Judy hurried towards the reception desk and bent to retrieve it. 'I was so worried about Dad that I just left it behind.' She straightened up and then froze when she saw that Sophie was talking to someone.

'Oh, I'm sorry. I didn't mean to interrupt.'

'It's okay.' Sophie straightened her back. Fate was giving her a push here and she had a moral obligation to comply. 'Could you spare a minute, Mum?'

'Of course.' Judy came out from behind the counter.

'Could you keep an eye on these children for a minute? Their dad wants to talk to me.'

'Oh…' The different note in her mother's voice advertised that she was instantly aware that something a little odd was happening.

'I'm not their father,' Finn said. 'I'm their uncle. This is Ellie. And that's Emma.'

Judy had stepped closer. She was staring at the little girls and Sophie watched in horror as the colour drained from her mother's face. She moved fast as she saw her start to sway on her feet, but it was Finn who caught Judy before she crumpled completely.

This was unbelievable. Both her parents having dizzy spells on the same day? Was there some horrible virus going around? That would be a catastrophe that could potentially close this health centre on which her community depended.

But Judy seemed to be recovering quickly. She clung to Finn's arm as he helped her towards the chair behind the reception desk, and then she sat, taking several deep breaths before raising her head.

'Sorry,' she murmured. 'But it's like seeing a ghost. Two ghosts…'

'What do you mean?' Sophie had followed them and now had her hand on her mother's wrist, feeling for her pulse.

Judy's mouth opened. And then closed again. Her gaze slid away from Sophie's, back to the other side of the waiting room to where the children were still sitting quietly, and then up, to the man who was towering above her.

'Who are you?' she asked.

'And why are you here?' Sophie added. Her words came out sharply. She'd been aware of her own anxiety about this situation but the fact that it had affected her mother so dramatically made it unacceptable. She wanted the truth. And she wanted it now.

'I think you've guessed,' Finn said slowly. 'Or your mother has, anyway.'

'Mum?'

But Judy didn't seem capable of finding any words. It was Finn who spoke.

'It's Ellie and Emma,' he said, so quietly there was no chance of either of them hearing what he was saying. 'They're your daughters, Sophie.'

CHAPTER TWO

THIS COULDN'T BE HAPPENING.

They had promised her that nothing like this could *ever* happen.

And yet, here it was. Happening.

The shock waves kept on rolling in. There was no point at all in trying to summon denial to deal with this. At some level, Sophie realised, she'd known from that first instant with that puzzling sense of recognition when she'd seen the twins. And her poor mother...

No wonder Judy had almost fainted with the shock of feeling as if she'd stepped back three decades in time and was seeing not only her own young daughter again but seeing double.

How could anyone think it was acceptable to shock people like this? Her mother could have had a heart attack. Sophie was already worried about her father's state of health and now that anxiety had just increased exponentially to include her mother. As for her own state of mind... Well, she wasn't even going to go there right now. This should *not* be happening. For this man to have tracked her down meant that somebody, somewhere—perhaps in the very IVF clinic she and Matthew had used themselves—had broken confidentiality.

Had broken the law?

Okay. Sophie knew how she felt now. Angry. Furious, in fact.

'You shouldn't be here,' she hissed fiercely, keeping her voice as low as possible. 'How did you even find out who I was?'

Finn was still watching her intently after dropping that bombshell, so she couldn't miss the flash of…*guilt*? Yes, that was what it was all right. He knew he'd done something he shouldn't have. But it was gone as fast as it had appeared and what took its place looked disturbingly like defiance. Finn Connelly might know he'd done something that could get him into serious trouble but he was prepared to stand up for himself. He had a reason for doing this and he believed he could defend it.

Judy took a gulp of air in. And then another. Sophie had to admire the way her mother was pulling herself together. She was staring at the two children on the other side of the room and she was also protecting them from hearing any of this conversation. Her voice was a whisper.

'This has something to do with the eggs you donated, Sophie, doesn't it? These girls are your biological children? My…'

The whisper cracked and faded into silence but what she'd been about to say hung in the air as loudly as if it had been spoken.

My grandchildren…

This…this *stunt*…hadn't just detonated an emotional bomb in her own life, it was going to affect other people. Her parents. They'd had to grieve the loss of their son-in-law and then the devastating extra loss of their unborn grandchild. It had taken years for them all to accept those losses and build a new version of their lives but they had done it. Together. With the help of a loyal and close community.

This was such a slap in their faces. A living, breathing reminder of what had been lost. These were someone else's children but they were what her own would have looked like. Who could have known that the genes for her type of uncontrollable hair were so strong? Sophie could feel the sharp teeth of her own grief against her heart, getting ready to bite with a force she hadn't had to deal with for years. Her mother shouldn't have to cope with this as well—it was just so unfair.

But Judy seemed to be coping better than she was herself. She looked up at the two people who were staring at each other over her head and then she pushed herself to her feet. She was still pale, but seemed quite steady as she turned to Finn.

'You know what? I'm thinking you've had a long drive, haven't you?'

Finn nodded slowly. 'We've come from Wexford, in Ireland. Took the earliest ferry.'

'You must be very tired.' Judy's tone held the kind of sympathy that made her patients comfortable to follow any advice she might have to offer. 'And those little girls are probably exhausted.'

She walked towards the twins. Sophie found herself holding her breath. Her mother was the quintessential maternal figure—more than a little overweight, a bit rumpled, with a smile so genuine nobody could resist smiling back—and babies and children adored her.

How would these subdued little girls respond? Could they actually be aware, at some subconscious level, that there was such a strong genetic link?

'You're Ellie, aren't you?' Judy was smiling. 'No… you're Emma. I'm right, yes?'

The twins nodded. They couldn't possibly be aware of any link, Sophie thought, but there was no mistaking that they were falling under Judy Greene's spell.

'Would you like to come with me?' she asked. 'I'm thinking that you're probably very hungry. Am I right?'

Her query earned another nod. Slightly more enthusiastic this time, and Sophie heard what sounded like a defeated sigh escape from Finn.

'Let's put your hoods up. It's raining outside but we don't have far to go.' Judy had a twin holding each of her hands as she came back towards where Finn and Sophie were still standing.

'If it's all right with you,' she said to Finn, 'I'm going to take the girls to the house and give them something to eat.'

Finn seemed to be falling under her spell as well. He just nodded.

'You two need to talk,' Judy added.

'But…what about Dad?' Sophie caught her mother's gaze. Her father had already given them a health scare. Wasn't it a risk to add this shocking development to an already tough day?

'He's fine,' Judy said. 'All he needed was some food and a rest.'

'But…' Desperately, Sophie tried to grasp some element of control in an impossible situation. It might be better if her father didn't see these children. 'He might guess. Like you did…'

'We can hardly keep it a secret, Sophie.' Her mother's gaze was steady. 'It's already too late for that. Talk to—' Her eyebrows rose as she turned her head.

'Finn,' he supplied. 'Finn Connelly.'

'Talk to Finn.' Judy nodded. 'And then you can come and talk to me and Dad.'

The twins seemed happy to follow her towards the back door of the clinic. Judy paused as she opened it.

'And make that poor lad a cup of tea, Sophie. He looks done in.'

The mechanics of making a cup of tea in the tiny kitchenette of the clinic were helpful. The actions of filling the electric jug and pushing the button to make it work, opening a cupboard to take out mugs, opening the old toffee tin to find some teabags—was a curiously normal bubble in the aftermath of the explosion.

Had her mother known that it would make Sophie feel a little calmer?

'Do you take milk?'

'Yes.'

'Sugar.'

'Yes, please. Two.'

Sophie poured boiling water into the mugs and then paused to wait for them to steep. She didn't turn to where she knew Finn was leaning against the wall.

'You can't have done it legally.'

His hesitation said it all. 'Not exactly, no…'

She turned to hand him a mug and then waited for him to lift his gaze again.

'So who broke the law?'

His gaze shuttered. 'I'm not saying. I will say that she's a friend of mine and…and she was persuaded by the circumstances.'

Sophie sipped at her own drink but she was eyeing Finn over the rim of her mug. Yeah…with those looks and that Irish brogue, she had no doubt that he could turn on the charm and persuade women to do whatever he wanted them to.

Well…she wasn't one of those women, even if she had been drawn to give him a lingering second glance when she'd first laid eyes on him.

'You want a biscuit?'

'No, thanks. I'm not hungry. Could we…ah…sit down somewhere for a moment?'

Sophie would have been quite happy to have this conversation standing up. It wasn't as if it was going to be a cosy chat, was it? But her mother had been right in saying that this uninvited guest looked done in. Well-honed instincts suggested that he might even be unwell given that it wasn't warm enough in here to have provoked what looked like a faint sheen of sweat on his forehead. She'd had more than enough people threatening to collapse on her today already.

'Fine…come with me.'

The chairs in her consulting room were still as she'd positioned them to talk to Shirley. Side by side instead of one in front and one behind the desk. Briefly, Sophie considered dragging her chair to make the desk a kind of protective barrier but the unexpected gesture of Finn waiting for her to be seated first made it a step too far. Or maybe it was the hint of a crooked smile—as if he knew exactly how she might be feeling and he was offering an apology.

She did, however, shuffle the chair further away from the one he took. There was definitely no need to be within hand-holding distance this time.

'So…' Sophie put her mug down on top of a medical journal she hadn't had time to open yet. 'What kind of circumstances were enough to persuade this friend of yours to break the law?'

Finn had both his hands wrapped around the mug because it was providing a source of warmth that his body was currently craving.

He hadn't felt this cold since…oh, no…not since he'd picked up that dose of malaria when he'd backpacked through Thailand on his way to Australia. Now the lack of appetite and his headache could be attributed to more than the stress he was dealing with. This could be yet another problem but, right now, there was a bigger issue to address. A whole heap bigger.

'Ten years or so ago,' he told Sophie, 'my brother, Sean, met and fell in love with a nurse. Stella, her name was.'

Never mind that he'd been the one who'd met Stella first. That he had fallen in love with her first. That he'd taken her home to Ireland that Christmas with the intention of popping the question. Sophie didn't need to know the sordid details of his family's betrayal and his subsequent estrangement from them.

'They wanted to have a family straight away,' he continued. 'But it wasn't happening. They spent years trying and having investigations and, in the end, it turned out that it wasn't going to happen naturally at all. Stella had had major problems with endometriosis and it had apparently affected the quality of her eggs. The only way they were going to have kids was by egg donation.'

Sophie made an impatient noise. 'I don't need the back story,' she muttered. 'However touching it is. I want to know why you're here, with these children, on *my* doorstep. What you're expecting me to *do*?'

'I don't expect anything.' Finn closed his eyes.

He was telling the truth. He didn't expect anything, especially in the face of the defensiveness that was radiating from this Sophie Bradford. He'd known she would be shocked but he could actually feel the solid barriers she had put up around her. This wasn't just the last thing she had expected to happen. It was the last thing she had *wanted* to happen. He wasn't about to let the future of his nieces be influenced by someone who didn't even care. It was more than disappointing, however. On some level, it felt as if he already knew this woman. He certainly would have recognised her in the street after the amount of time he had now spent with his nieces. They were gorgeous children. This Sophie Bradford was a gorgeous woman—to outward appearances, anyway...

The coldness that had seemed bone-deep was ebbing fast. Being replaced by heat. He had the medication he knew he needed but it was in his bag in the car. He couldn't exactly excuse himself and go to fetch it, could he? He opened his eyes and focused on the woman beside him. This wouldn't take long. He could tell her what she needed to know and then leave her to think about it. He would go and find the girls and then find somewhere to crash for the night and, if he dosed himself up well enough and got a good night's sleep, maybe tomorrow would bring more than a new day. Maybe it would bring some kind of solution?

'Okay...' He kept his voice matter-of-fact. 'Three weeks ago Sean and Stella were in a car crash. The kids were home with a babysitter. Stella was killed instantly. Sean was badly injured and in a coma. He was put on life support and I was contacted as next of kin. I flew back to find that my role as the closest relative was to give permission to turn off the life support and make his organs available for donation. There was a double funeral for them yesterday.'

Finn could feel sweat trickling down between his shoulder blades and prickling at his hairline. He rubbed his forehead and wasn't surprised to feel the alarming heat on his skin. He was sick all right, and getting rapidly sicker. It was getting harder to focus as well.

'Are you all right?' Sophie's voice sounded oddly distant.

'I will be. It's just a bit of a relapse, that's all. I know how to deal with it. I'm a doctor myself.'

She was silent. Was his brain playing tricks on him already or did the silence feel judgemental? Maybe she thought he was an alcoholic, perhaps? Or a drug addict, or on death's doorstep from something like leukaemia?

'Who's been looking after the children?'

'They were taken into foster care after the accident but I took them back to their own house with the help of a nanny while things got sorted. As their guardian, it was obviously my responsibility to make decisions about their future, along with planning the funerals and everything.'

There was another silence. What had the question been? Oh, yeah…why was he *here*?

'It didn't seem right to hand Ellie and Emma over to Social Services for fostering or adoption when they had a living relative who had no idea what was going on. It's not that I'm *expecting* anything… I just thought you had the right to know, that's all.'

Sophie's breath came out in a huff that sounded incredulous. 'What about you? You're their guardian. And you're alive…' Her tone changed into one of concern.

'Although you're not looking that great at the moment. Maybe I should have a look at you…'

Finn could feel his energy levels dropping alarmingly. He couldn't even start to feel that disappointment morphing into any kind of resentment that he'd come up against a human brick wall who had no interest in her biological children. All he wanted to do was find a bed and curl up. To take his pills and then ride out the fever and chills until he could surface and think clearly again. But he didn't have that choice, did he? Somehow, he had to keep going.

'My life is in Australia,' he told her. 'I'm single and that's not about to change. I work in the Outback with the Flying Doctor service and I have a punishing roster. I live on the base, and I can get called out at any time, and there's no guarantee of when I'll get back. It's no place to raise kids.'

'They're your nieces.'

'I hadn't even met them until I had to turn off their father's life support.'

The silence this time held an edge of shock. Curiosity, too, perhaps, but Finn wasn't about to tell her anything else. With a huge effort he pushed himself to his feet.

'This was a mistake,' he said. Was it his imagination or were his words a little slurred? 'I'm sorry.'

Why had he thought it was remotely the right thing to do? Because he'd felt guilty? He hadn't needed Sophie to remind him that he'd broken ethical codes, if not the law, in getting the information he'd needed to track her down.

What had he thought might happen here? That he'd find a woman who already had her own family but had been altruistic enough to donate eggs to help someone else achieve the bliss of motherhood? That she'd instantly recognise the biological bond and welcome some new additions with open arms?

The way her mother seemed to have done?

Finn shook his head. Where had the mother taken the girls? He needed to find them and get out of here. But shaking his head had been a mistake. It triggered a spinning sensation that rapidly escalated. He tried to catch the edge of the desk to steady himself but only succeeded in knocking over the mug of tea that he'd never finished drinking. He watched the puddle of liquid spreading to reach a stack of medical journals as Sophie leapt to her feet.

'Sorry,' he said again. 'I'm really sorry.'

And then he felt her arm go around his waist.

'I don't *believe* this,' he heard her mutter as she looped his arm around her neck. 'Not *again*…'

He was moving now. Towards the bed in the corner of this consulting room. He was being helped up the step and being turned so that he could sit and then lie down. The spinning hadn't stopped but the pillow felt cool and soft.

So did Sophie's hand against his forehead.

A soft touch, he thought. Nice…

'What's going on, Finn?' There was no animosity in her tone now. She had a patient and she was determined to help him. 'What's wrong with you?'

'Malaria… Had it once before but this is the first relapse. I've got the drugs I need…out in my car…laptop bag…'

'Keys?'

'In my pocket.'

He felt her hand against his hip and then the rattle of the keys being extracted; then, as the shivering kicked in, the weight of a woollen blanket being draped over his body.

'Don't move,' she ordered. 'I'll be right back.'

CHAPTER THREE

THE PACKET OF TABLETS, a combination therapy for the treatment of malaria, was easy enough to find in the bag that Sophie carried back into her consultation room in North Cove's medical centre.

Finding head space where she could even start trying to process this turn of events in her life was rather more difficult.

Impossible, even.

Her daughters? Hardly. The mother of those two little girls was a woman called Stella who'd chosen to bring them into existence. Who'd carried them in her belly for nine months and given birth to them.

It would be a different story if she'd had these babies herself and then given them up for adoption but her only contribution had been an egg donation. She'd given up some biological material to be used by someone who'd had need of it.

Like giving a blood donation. It had been made and that was the end of it.

So why did it feel as if an uncontrollable series of future events was only just beginning?

It was too huge even to know where to start.

And she had something more important to think about right now, in any case.

'I'm not sure I'm happy to hand out drugs without making a clinical diagnosis,' she told Finn.

He looked as though it was taking an effort to open his eyes. Such dark eyes, Sophie noticed, that it was hard to tell if his pupils were dilated or not. And, when his gaze touched hers again, there was something different about it. Because she knew why he was here, now?

No. Sophie suspected it would have been the same if they'd caught each other's gaze on a street somewhere. There was something else here. A sense of connection. Recognition, even?

'You're not handing them out. They're mine. I diagnosed myself. I've kept the drugs on hand ever since I contracted malaria in the first place. In case this happened.'

'What about differential diagnoses?'

Finn sighed. 'Such as?'

'A viral illness like influenza. Sepsis. Food poisoning. Hepatitis…' Sophie racked her brains. Malaria wasn't a common illness in these parts. 'Plague,' she added.

Unexpectedly a corner of Finn's mouth twitched. 'It does kind of feel like plague at the moment, I have to confess.'

So he had a sense of humour? Even more unexpectedly, Sophie felt a twinge of liking this guy, closely followed by a wave of sympathy. He hadn't actually come here with the intention of ruining her life, had he? He was faced with a massive problem and he'd been grasping at straws.

'Even if your self-diagnosis is correct, it's my job to decide whether you're sick enough to be admitted to hospital.' Sophie picked up her tympanic thermometer and fitted a plastic shield onto it. She smoothed back rather damp waves of his hair to find his ear hole. It was a perfectly normal thing to be doing, so why did it suddenly seem a little too personal? Intimate, even? Maybe her words were for herself as much as him. 'Right now, you're a patient in my medical practice.'

Finn submitted to having his temperature taken. 'It was uncomplicated malaria the first time round. I don't need to be admitted anywhere. I just need to take my medication and find somewhere to stay for a day or two. Until I'm fit to drive.'

Oh, yeah... He'd already realised that he'd made a mistake and he'd been intending to rectify it by leaving and taking the children with him. She had to admire that decision given that he'd said he was no more in a position to take on his orphaned nieces than she was.

But why had he only met them so recently? There was more to this story than she'd been given. Possibly because she hadn't wanted to listen and had told him as much in no uncertain terms. She hadn't wanted her heartstrings tugged, to get involved with this story at any meaningful level.

The thermometer beeped and Sophie glanced at the readout. 'Forty point one,' she announced. 'That's quite an impressive fever.'

'Which will probably drop quite soon and then make a reappearance later.' But Finn was pushing away the blanket she'd covered him with. 'Would you have a glass of water available? I'd like to take my pills.'

'Just a minute... I want to have a listen to your chest. And a feel of your tummy, if you don't mind.'

Finn's head dropped back against the pillow again. 'It's not necessary.'

'You're currently my patient,' Sophie reminded him. 'You don't get to fall over in my consulting room and then tell me what is or isn't necessary. Okay?'

He made no response but Sophie almost got the feeling that he was happy to comply. Maybe he was feeling so awful that being forced to get checked was almost a relief?

Malaria could have nasty complications. Fatal ones, such as cerebral oedema, organ failure and coma due to hypoglycaemia. This might be the first case of malaria that Sophie had come across but the professional part of her brain was actually revelling in retrieving information learned long ago.

'Your lungs sound clear. No pulmonary oedema.'

'I could have told you that. I'm not having any respiratory issues.'

Sophie had got past that disturbing beat of feeling that this situation had a personal rather than purely professional edge. She was totally focussed now. 'Would you mind undoing your jeans for me, please?'

She laid her hand on a very flat abdomen, pressing gently to examine a lower quadrant. 'When did you last have something to eat?'

'I'm not sure. We stopped for lunch but I was more worried about whether Ellie and Emma were eating. Which they weren't…'

'Don't worry. If I know my mum, she'll be filling them up with something like fish fingers and ice-cream right about now. Hmm…that hurt, didn't it?'

'A bit…' The admission was reluctant.

'That's right over your spleen and I'd say it's enlarged. It can rupture, you know, in a severe case of malaria.'

'Yeah…thanks for that.'

'I'm going to take some blood as well. I can do a blood glucose here but I'll have to send the rest away to check on your renal function.'

She helped him roll up the sleeve of his woollen jumper and pulled a tourniquet tight above his elbow. He didn't flinch when the needle pierced his skin. A high pain threshold? She'd need to take that into account the next time she was pressing on his abdomen.

'Blood sugar's low normal. Could just be a result of you not eating recently.'

'You happy now? Can I have my meds?'

Sophie handed over the packet of pills and filled a glass of water from the basin in the room. She would hardly call her state of mind any shade of happiness.

What on earth was she going to do now?

'Let's see how steady you are on your feet,' she said, finally. 'I'll take you to my parents' house which is just past the car park. Between us, I'm sure we can sort something out about a place you can stay. Not that North Cove has much in the way of hotels, but there are a few B&Bs and a guest house or two.'

The rain had settled into a steady downpour and the pace that Finn seemed capable of managing was nowhere near fast enough to stop them both getting noticeably wet by the time Sophie led him through the back door of what had been one of the original farmhouses in the area. The door led into a huge kitchen that smelled of hot food and home but it was empty at the moment so she kept going to the living room across the hall. There she found her father, putting another log onto the open fire.

'Dad? This is Finn Connelly.'

Jack Greene straightened. He was still looking a bit pale, Sophie noted, but that could be due to the startling arrival of two children he was biologically related to as much as his earlier dizzy spell today.

Oh, man… Her life was suddenly spinning out of control and she didn't like it one little bit.

'Where's Mum?'

'I'm here…' Judy appeared through the door. 'I was just tucking up the girls.' She met Sophie's stare with one of her own. 'I didn't know how long you were going to be, Sophie. They were exhausted, poor little loves. And there was your old room with its two beds. They were asleep almost as soon as their heads touched the pillows.' She smiled at Finn. 'I hope you don't mind, but I gave them some dinner that wasn't particularly healthy. Fish fingers and ice-cream.'

Sophie's gaze flew to catch Finn's and there was a moment of silent communication.

Told you so…

Yeah… I get it. You're always right…

He spoke, however, to Judy. 'That's fine. You've done better than I have today, finding something they actually wanted to eat.'

'Oh, my goodness. You're soaked. Come over here by the fire. I'll get you a cup of tea.'

'I'm a bit warm,' Finn said. 'I might stay here.' He sank down onto one end of the huge, worn leather sofa.

Jack was staring at the newcomer with a frown on his face. 'You don't look right, lad.' He shifted his gaze to Sophie. 'What's going on?'

'Malaria,' she said.

'What?' Jack pushed his glasses back up his nose.

'That's ridiculous. How did you diagnose that on the spot? When have we ever had a case of malaria in North Cove?'

'Finn's a doctor,' she told him. 'And this is a relapse, not a primary infection. He diagnosed it himself but his signs and symptoms certainly fit the clinical picture. Fever, headache, fatigue. Oh, and a rather tender spleen. I've taken bloods. I'll get them off to the lab myself on my way home.'

She could feel the curious glance coming from Finn. Had he thought she still lived here, with her parents? She was thirty-four, for heaven's sake. Would he still consider living with *his* parents?

No. His parents clearly weren't in the picture if he had been his brother's only relative. And he'd said he hadn't seen his brother in years, either.

Okay. Her father wasn't the only curious one.

'So you're a doctor?' Jack moved to sit on the other end of the couch. 'A specialist? Where do you work?'

'I'm an emergency medicine specialist. I spent five years or so in a London A&E but I've been in Australia for the last few years. I'm hoping to sign a new three-year contract with the Flying Doctors service there.'

Glances were exchanged between Sophie's parents as the implications of his statement sank in. They would both realise how unlikely it was that he would be taking two young children to Outback Australia.

'I'll help you make some tea,' Sophie said to her mother. 'We need to find somewhere for Finn to stay for a day or two as well. He's not in a fit state to drive.'

She hoped that Finn would be filling in the gaps for her father while she was in the kitchen doing the same thing for her mother. She kept it short and to the point and

Judy listened quietly as she put cups and saucers onto a tray and waited for the kettle to boil.

'Well…' she said finally. 'I'm not waking those girls up to get dragged off to a B&B. They'll have to stay here, for tonight at least. Find the biscuit tin, would you?'

A plate was put in front of Sophie with a clatter. A sure sign that Judy Greene was not happy.

A moment later and her father came into the kitchen. He didn't look happy, either.

'That lad needs to be in bed,' he said. 'I'd probably admit him if he was my patient but I don't expect he's going to like that idea.'

'He doesn't need admission. He needs somewhere to rest for a few days with someone checking up on him frequently. What about Mrs Murphy's guest house?' Sophie suggested. 'It's just up the road.'

'You'd put a sick man in a guest house?' Judy sounded horrified. 'And Colleen Murphy? She'd be round here first thing tomorrow morning, and one look at those girls and she'll know exactly what's going on. Like I did.' She shook her head as she poured boiling water into the teapot to warm it. 'That hair…' She swirled the pot and tipped the water out before reaching for the tea caddy. 'And if Colleen knows, the whole town'll hear about it soon enough.'

The teapot hit the bench with a thump. 'He'll have to stay here, in our guest room. Unless you want to take him home, Sophie?'

'Why on earth would I want to do that?'

Judy spoke quietly. 'Because he's the uncle of your daughters, perhaps?'

'They're *not* my daughters.' It felt as if the walls were closing in around Sophie. 'And he's not much of an uncle,

by all accounts. He only met them a matter of days ago.'
She felt her hands curling into fists. 'He doesn't want
them. He wants to get back to Australia and that exciting job he's got with the Flying Doctors. I think he wants
me to have them.'

Her voice had risen with the incredulity of it all, so
the silence after her outburst made the air feel almost
too thick to breathe. It seemed that neither of her parents shared her opinion of how unreasonable this was.

Her father cleared his throat. 'Well…biologically,
they are your daughters, Soph. Which makes them…
our grandchildren…doesn't it?'

'No…' Sophie was cradling her forehead in both her
hands now. 'For heaven's sake, Dad. I donated *eggs*. It
doesn't make me suddenly responsible for what happens
to them, does it? What if I'd donated a kidney to someone? And…and they turned up on the doorstep and said
they were homeless now? Would I have to invite them
to live with me for the rest of my life?'

Dropping her hands, she looked up, and the look on
her parents' faces was enough to break her heart. It took
her back instantly to that moment when their excitement
at the prospect of becoming grandparents had morphed
into yet another grief when faced with the reality of her
miscarriage. When all their lives had changed for ever.

That had been *her* child. Hers and Matthew's. The egg
she'd chosen to have implanted that first time. The baby
she'd fallen in love with the instant she'd seen that tiny
heart beating on the ultrasound screen.

'They're not my children,' Sophie whispered into the
silence. 'Can't you understand? I'm finally at the point
where I'm not missing Matthew and our baby every single day. I love my life just the way it is. I don't want to

be a mother. I'm not ready…and…and I don't know if I'll ever be ready again.'

'You don't have to be.'

It wasn't either of her parents who had spoken. Oh, help… How long had Finn been standing in the kitchen doorway? How much had he heard?

Enough, obviously.

'I'll sort it out,' he said. His face twisted with what looked like regret as he spoke to Judy. 'I'm so sorry,' he added. 'I didn't think. I've created a problem for everybody.'

Judy's shoes tapped on the flagstones as she crossed the room. 'You did what you thought was the right thing,' she said softly. 'We all need some time to think about this so…' She was smiling at him now—that gentle smile that advertised the warmest heart in the world. 'Who knows? Maybe it's a good thing that you're not well enough to go anywhere else right now.'

'I can't stay here…' Finn might look as if he was about to topple over at any moment but he was fighting hard. 'Can you please tell me where that guest house is?'

'You're not going to win this one, lad.' Jack's smile for his wife conveyed an understanding born of a great many years. And a great deal of love. 'Come with me. I'll show you where our guest room is. It's got its own bathroom so you'll be quite private.'

'Find him a pair of your pyjamas, Jack. I'll bring him a cup of tea in a minute. And maybe some soup.' Judy caught Sophie's gaze as she headed back to the teapot. 'You going to stay for some soup, too, love?'

Sophie shook her head. 'I need to get those blood samples to the lab.'

She had to get out of here. Control of her life was being

torn out of her hands and she couldn't deal with this. She needed some time to herself. A lot of time. At least her father would be here if Finn's condition deteriorated so she wouldn't have to add any worry about a new patient to the mess already in her head.

She couldn't help another glance in his direction, however. A glance that was intended to reassure herself that she could, at least, put worrying about the potential complications of malaria to one side.

Finn had one hand on the frame of the door, as if he needed the support to stay upright. He had been watching her, she realised, as her gaze connected with his. For what seemed like a very long moment, they held the eye contact.

She didn't want to feel sorry for this man. Or have to repress the instinctive urge to offer assistance and reassurance but…that look in his eyes was a plea that was impossible to ignore.

He was lost, wasn't he?

Torn.

Wanting to do the right thing but, for whatever reason, feeling incapable of taking the step that they both knew would be the right thing to do here. The only thing to do, in fact.

Protecting two innocent little girls.

Children who'd had everything they knew about their lives ripped away from them.

Children who were, according to genetics, more closely related to herself than to Finn Connelly.

It was a moment of complete understanding. Empathy, even. Sophie found herself taking a deep breath.

'Try and get some sleep,' she told Finn. 'I'll come and see you in the morning.'

* * *

Damp sheets were knotting themselves into ropes and holding him tightly in the grip of a fever-fuelled nightmare.

Dark eyes were staring at him. Four of them.

'He's going to die, just like Mummy and Daddy... We're going to be all alone in the world because nobody wants us...'

No...there were only two eyes now, but they were exactly the same colour, and he could sense the smudge of that crazy, curly hair around them. The voice had definitely changed—an adult now, not a child.

'I only gave you a kidney because I'm a good person... I'm not going to marry you. Why would I want to when it's your brother I'm in love with...?'

Why was she in a plane with him? Where was the pilot? They were somewhere over Outback Australia because he could see the endless stretches of red earth through the window getting closer and closer as the plane spiralled out of control, heading for certain catastrophe.

The strangled sound of his own terror woke Finn. It must have woken Judy as well, because she appeared in his room moments later, fastening the tie of her dressing gown, as he was still trying to catch his breath and untangle himself from the sheets.

'Let me help. Oh, my word, these are soaked. I'll get you a fresh set.'

'No, please... I've caused enough trouble already.'

'Nonsense. It's almost time I was up, anyway. Here... sit in this chair for a few minutes. Unless you feel up to a shower? No...' Judy was taking far more of his weight than Finn was happy with but his legs felt like jelly. 'I don't think leaving you in the shower would be a good idea just yet. I'll get you a face cloth.'

Being incapacitated by illness could make you feel as vulnerable as a baby and Finn hated that. It also intensified the effect of kindness shown by other people and this woman's calm, gentle ministrations were enough to bring a lump to his throat that made it difficult to swallow and almost impossible to respond coherently to anything she said. It reminded him of his own mother back in the days when he'd still been a child. Back in the days when he'd still had the ability to trust in unconditional love...

It was just as well that Judy didn't seem to expect a response. Her occasional quiet words, as she worked, were simply reassurance.

'You'll get better soon but these things take time. Just rest.'

'Sophie will be in to see you soon. Between her and her dad, you're in good hands.'

'And don't worry about the girls. I'll look after them— for as long as it takes. I've already arranged for someone to step in for me at work.'

With the crisp dryness of a fresh pillowcase against his cheek, Finn drifted slowly back into a hopefully more peaceful sleep, his last conscious thoughts being that maybe he hadn't made such a huge mistake after all.

The biological mother of his nieces might not want anything to do with her children but their grandmother was possibly the kindest woman on earth. Such a motherly soul, she couldn't help but take stray chicks under her wing.

If anybody could assist him in finding a way to control the spiralling tumble his life was suddenly taking, surely it would be Judy Greene?

The thought evaporated into a feeling of relief and then that morphed into something very different—the memory of the last eye contact he'd had with Sophie Bradford that had felt like some kind of connection. That she had understood. Or was this just the start of another fever-fuelled dream?

Of course it was. Like the way his skin was conjuring up a memory of the touch of her hand that had felt nothing like the professional touch of a doctor...

With a groan, Finn tried to turn over and pull himself back to reality but it was too hard. His head was spinning again. Any moment now and he'd be back in that small plane, heading towards a crash he could do nothing to prevent...

CHAPTER FOUR

Everything looked perfectly normal.

The waiting room at North Cove's only medical centre contained the normal number and variety of patients waiting to see their doctor. Elderly people mostly, along with a pregnant woman and a young mother with her baby. The door to Jack's consulting room was closed as Sophie went past and she heard the reassuring murmur of her father's voice as he spoke to his patient.

What wasn't normal was that her mother wasn't present, either in the room set aside for the examinations and treatment a nurse could provide, or beside Marion at the reception desk.

'Hey, Liz… How's it going?'

Liz wasn't a stranger here. In her early forties, she was single and worked casually as a nurse in the closest hospital and bigger general practices in Penzance. She'd stepped in at North Cove before, on the odd occasion, like when Judy had caught that bad flu a couple of years ago, and she was clearly thrilled to be back.

'I'm *loving* it,' she said to Sophie, reaching for a file of patient notes on the reception desk. 'You know I'd kill for this job on a permanent basis.'

'It's such a commute for you, though. Must be at least thirty minutes?'

'It's worth it. And, if your mum ever wants to retire, I'd move here in a heartbeat. I don't have any ties where I am and I'm a village girl at heart.'

'She won't retire until Dad does. And he won't retire until we can find a new doctor, which is proving a lot more difficult than we'd anticipated. Unlike you, there aren't that many people who want to live in such a small place.'

'They don't know what they're missing.' Liz turned to smile at the young mother in the waiting room.

'Margaret? Bring Katie through now and we'll get her Well Child checks done.' Liz caught Sophie's gaze again briefly. 'Katie's next on your list for her three-month vaccinations.'

Sophie nodded, picking up the next file on the desk. 'Mr Appleby?' She smiled at the elderly fisherman who was sitting in the corner of the room close to the window. 'Come with me.' She waited as he slowly pulled himself up from the chair and then walked towards her with a pronounced limp that made her think this was probably another flare up of his gout.

Yes. Even knowing her patients well enough to have a good idea of what might be bringing them in for a doctor's appointment was perfectly normal.

Except…

She heard the low rumble of laughter she recognised instantly as she passed her father's door again with Mr Appleby beside her and, with a jolt of surprise, she realised that she couldn't remember the last time she had heard him laugh. Was it only two days ago that he'd looked beyond exhausted and far from happy? Everybody knew how much Jack enjoyed the company of children but surely his young house guests couldn't have lifted his mood this much?

Nothing was really normal, was it?

The firm foundation of the life Sophie had worked so hard to build around her for years now seemed to have turned to sand. And it was shifting beneath her feet.

Not that anybody was saying anything out loud. Yet.

This was the second day since Finn Connelly had arrived in North Cove and he was still confined to bed, fighting his recurrence of malaria. They all knew that they had a lot to talk about but, by tacit agreement—maybe because they all needed time to get their heads around something so momentous—any discussion about what was to happen next was apparently going to wait until Finn was well enough to participate.

Sophie had checked on her parents' unexpected house guest yesterday and taken new blood samples to monitor his renal function. She made a mental note to follow up the results before she went to see him again this afternoon and then, with some difficulty, she shoved the huge issue of his presence and all its ramifications firmly to the back of her mind in order to focus on her patient. Mr Appleby might well need a course of steroids to get this current attack of gout under control and they needed to discuss some lifestyle changes that might prevent it happening again.

Her next patient, at the other end of the age spectrum, was another perfectly normal consultation and should have been easy to focus on. Sophie had dealt with how hard it had been to be around babies long ago and the scars on her own heart had thickened enough to protect her with what she was confident was an impenetrable barrier. As time had gone by, she had coped with those babies becoming toddlers and then young children and, these days, she could get through an entire consultation without any thoughts of how different her life could have been.

Or she *had* been able to. Until two days ago when she'd been confronted with a double dose of what her own child could have looked like. Today, her first thought as she greeted her new patient was a painful reminder of exactly what she'd lost. Of never having been able to hold her baby in her arms and see it smiling up at her like baby Katie. Normally, she would have spent a minute or two admiring the infant and encouraging another smile, but that was too much today. She smiled at Katie's mother instead.

'It's just the second dose of the six-in-one and the rotavirus vaccination today, Margaret.'

'Yes. And I remembered to give her a dose of paracetamol before we came so I hope she won't be as miserable afterwards as she was last time.'

Sophie checked the notes that Liz had made in Katie's health-record book. 'Looks like she's doing well. Right on track for her growth. Breast feeding going okay?'

'So much better. I'm still up several times a night, though.' Katie's mother sighed but then smiled down at her baby. 'Not that I'm complaining. I can't imagine life without her now.'

'Of course not.' Sophie was smiling again as well but it felt different. A bit forced? She was probably more tired than Margaret was, after two nights of sleep deprivation that hadn't had anything to do with getting up for a baby.

Okay…that wasn't entirely true, was it? As she found the vaccinations she needed in the small fridge in her consulting room, she was trying very hard to slam a mental door that had opened on an image of twin babies she had had no idea even existed. The kind of image that had been responsible for her own lack of sleep. Had they been breastfed? she wondered now. Had they been as contented and loved as baby Katie was?

The knowledge that they could so easily have been her own babies was haunting her with increasing force. Someone she had never met had made a choice in a laboratory about which eggs were going to be used for her own assisted reproduction. Two eggs had been fertilised, although only one had successfully implanted, but that had been enough. More than enough. She and Matthew had both been over the moon happy. It had even been a source of comfort that Matthew had died still believing that he was going to be a father. That she was going to be a mother.

She wasn't the mother of those twins.

But, at the same time, she *was*. They had been created from her eggs. They could have been her children. Not Matthew's, of course, and that was something to be grateful for, but fifty percent of those children's genes had come from her.

And she'd felt something when she'd seen them yesterday, sitting on either side of her mother on the couch, listening to the story being read to them. She'd learned to cope with dealing with babies and children both in her professional life and personal life and being near those little girls shouldn't feel any different than, say, being with Katie here.

But it did. There was something there at a cellular level that felt like pressure. Something sharp that held the threat of being able to puncture the protective tissue around her heart. Sophie didn't want to go there. *Couldn't* go there, which was why she'd escaped so fast yesterday, using the excuse of needing to do some house calls. Maybe she could wait until it was likely that the children had been put to bed before she went to visit Finn today. She had to stay in control of this situation because, if she didn't, the life she knew and loved—the *safe* life that had been so hard to carve out of emotional chaos—would simply cease to exist.

And, if she couldn't control how often she had to be near those children, she would just have to somehow step back into the safe space she was in with every other baby or child in the world. Like Katie.

She uncapped the needle on the first syringe.

'Sorry about this, sweetheart,' she told Katie. 'But it'll be all over in just a tick.'

The baby had stopped crying by the time she was dressed again and Sophie followed Margaret back to the waiting area to find that morning clinic hours were over.

Liz and Marion were putting on their coats.

'We're heading down to Joe's Shack for a quick lunch,' Liz said. 'Come with us?'

'I've got a sandwich, and I want to catch up on my paperwork. Another day?'

Her father was clipping shut his medical bag. 'I'm off on a house call,' he told her. 'Did you get the blood results back on Finn yet?'

'I'm just about to ring them.'

'If you're going to go and see him, now might be a good time. He's alone in the house. Now that it's stopped raining, your mum's taking the girls down to the beach for a play.'

'What?' Sophie's eyes widened. 'But…people will *see* them.'

And talk. Those who were old enough to remember what she looked like as a child would have no difficulty putting two and two together and people would start judging her for everything. For donating her eggs in the first place, perhaps. For not being willing to take any responsibility for the consequences. For being prepared to punish her own parents by not acknowledging that they had grandchildren?

'Don't worry…' Her father patted her shoulder. 'We talked about it. She found some woolly hats that hide that hair. And, if anybody asks, she's just going to say that we've got some visitors for a few days. Relatives of an old family friend.'

It was a good thing, Sophie decided a few minutes later as she headed across the car park. It meant she didn't have to see the girls this time. She could check on Finn and then escape.

No. It wasn't a good thing. Sophie could feel herself scowling as she went through the gate that led into her childhood garden. What were they doing on the beach? Finding some pretty shells? Throwing sticks into the waves to watch them being brought back as she had loved to do? Building a sandcastle, even?

Good grief…was that nasty stab of sensation actually jealousy?

She shook it off. It wasn't jealously, it was concern about how involved her parents were becoming in this situation. What if they decided that they were prepared to take responsibility for their grandchildren without *her* consent? Would Social Services deem a woman in her late sixties too old to bring up children, or would they welcome a solution that could be seen as including genuine family?

They wouldn't be so happy about it if Sophie wasn't on board, though. And she wasn't. She was…

Angry, that was what she was. She shut the back door of the house behind her with enough of a shove to make it close to a slam. Getting dragged back into past grief was just so unfair after she had tried so hard to get on with her life. Being presented with an impossible situation that was going to change her life and the lives of people she loved, whatever they decided to do about it, was more than unfair. It was…heart-breaking.

Sophie had to pause for a moment in the kitchen; to close her eyes and take several deep breaths. She knew how to handle emotional turmoil like this. She just needed to focus on the next thing she needed to do and, right now, that was to check on a patient who had malaria. To take his temperature, listen to his chest and make sure that his spleen wasn't getting large enough to be at risk of rupturing. By the time she tapped on the door of the guest bedroom, she was ready to do exactly that.

But there was no response to her knock. Was Finn asleep?

Unconscious?

Sophie opened the door. The bed was empty.

Tilting her head, she could see that the door to the *en suite* bathroom was ajar. She stepped back, planning to give Finn time to finish going to the toilet or whatever he was doing, but then she heard the sound of his voice.

'Judy? Is that you? I…um… I might need some help…'

The low growl of distress in his voice had Sophie

through the door instantly and then into the doorway of the bathroom but then she slammed to a halt.

Oh…*help*…

Finn was standing in front of the basin, his head down, his hands clutching the edges of the vanity unit as if it was the only thing keeping him upright. He had clearly just stepped out of the shower because he was dripping wet.

And totally naked.

And…*oh, my word*…

It was a very long time since Sophie Bradford had seen a naked man in what suddenly felt like a very unprofessional setting—and she had never seen one that looked quite like this. Bronzed skin, apart from those pale buttocks. Hard planes of muscle as perfect as any sculpture. The bumps of his spine that curved all the way up to that bent neck. The appreciation of this male form lasted only a heartbeat, however. The body she was looking at was swaying ominously.

The pause in her movement had barely been noticeable. Sophie grabbed a towel from the rail.

'What's wrong?'

'Dizzy…' Finn managed.

Sophie held the edges of the towel as she wrapped her arms around his body. 'Lean on me,' she instructed. 'Let's get you back to bed.'

But Finn didn't move. He took several shuddering breaths and then slowly lifted his head, his gaze meeting Sophie's in the mirror. He was shocked to see her. And then embarrassed that it was her and not her mother, which was perfectly understandable.

He'd lost weight in the last couple of days. His face looked thinner, paler, apart from the heavy stubble shadowing his jaw. Pale enough to make his eyes seem much darker. Sophie discounted her earlier interpretations of his expression, deciding that it went deeper than embarrassment. It was more like shame. Anger, even.

He was hating this, she realised. Hating being so unwell. Probably hating the fact that his life was in chaos as much as hers was. Oddly, it made her own anger recede. She wasn't alone in this. It was only then that Sophie became aware of how close she was to him physically as she was trying to support him. She still had her arms around him and she could feel the length of his body pressing against her breasts and her belly. She could feel the warmth of his skin and smell the scent of freshly washed male, and her senses were suddenly overloaded to the point where her brain felt foggy. Then she felt the change as the muscles she was in contact with tightened and the misty sensation vanished.

'It's okay…it's going now…' Finn straightened. He pulled the towel from Sophie's hands and wrapped it around his waist as she stepped back. 'Sorry about that.'

'No problem.' Sophie reached for a second towel. 'You might want to dry off before getting back into bed.'

There was an awkwardness now; embarrassment for both of them.

'I thought you were your mother,' Finn muttered.

'She's taken the children out for a bit. To the beach.'

'Oh…' Finn was rubbing at his skin with the second towel. 'They'll like that. She's been amazing, your mum. I don't know what I would have done without her.'

'Yeah…' Sophie's smile seemed to cut through the tension in this small room. 'There've been plenty of times I've thought the same thing.' She eyed the crumpled pyjamas on the floor. 'Do you want me to find you some clean pyjamas?'

'I might try some clothes.'

'But you need to go back to bed. You're obviously still sick.'

'I feel better now. The shower was great and that dizziness has gone.'

'You sure?' Despite wanting to get out of here, Sophie was reluctant to leave him alone in the bathroom. What if he fainted and cracked his head on the toilet or something?

'I'm sure. You could do me a favour, though.' Finn was rubbing his wet hair which made it stick out in spikes all over his head. It made him look younger and...cuter.

'What's that?'

'Find my jeans and a tee shirt in that bag by the bed? Oh, and a pair of underpants?'

The sudden memory of seeing those tight, pale buttocks shot back into Sophie's head. It was just as well the reflection in the mirror had cut off at the point where the lines of his abdomen had just begun that downward arrow, but she could still feel heat creeping into her cheeks. Along with a sensation in her own belly that she hadn't felt in many years—so long ago she had never really expected to feel it again—but she knew what it was and that was as shocking as the sensation itself. She was *attracted* to this man? She still had his scent filling her nostrils and the skin on her arms tingled with the memory of being wrapped around his body. Oh, help...this situation was just getting progressively worse.

'Sure.' The word came out like a punctuation mark. 'I'll meet you in the living room when you're ready. I still need to give you a check-up.'

* * *

Thank goodness she was gone.

Along with that very unpleasant bout of dizziness.

Finn took his time getting his clothes on. Partly because he still felt weak enough to make it seem like a challenging task but he also needed the time to try and process whatever it was that had just happened here.

Something weird.

There'd been that physical awareness of Sophie standing behind him, her arms around his body and the soft, feminine feel of her shape pressing against his back. There'd also been a mix of emotional awareness. Gratitude that he had someone there to help him, but overriding that had been the feeling of shame at displaying weakness. Anger, even, that he was in this situation at all.

And then…then he'd raised his head and found Sophie staring at him in the mirror over his shoulder and somehow it had all coalesced into something he couldn't define. Or didn't want to. Something was happening between himself and this woman that had nothing to do with what had brought him here in the first place. It could have happened anywhere. On the street, maybe. Or across a crowded bar.

A feeling of…connection?

No. Finn found himself gripping the edge of the vanity unit again, staring at his reflection in the mirror. He could still see Sophie's face over his shoulder with those astonishing eyes holding his own. Could still feel the echo of her body against his.

He knew what it had been: physical attraction, pure and simple.

And totally, utterly inappropriate.

Unacceptable.

Had Sophie been aware of it, too? Was that why things had suddenly become even more awkward than they would have been if it had been her mother who'd found him naked and momentarily helpless?

No. He could see what he looked like and no woman would find this attractive. His hair looked like hedgehog prickles, he hadn't shaved for a week and his skin was pale enough to advertise the fact that he was still sick. Not that he had the energy to shave, or even comb his hair with more than his fingers. What he now wanted was to crawl back into bed and sleep, but what he didn't want was to have Sophie Bradford anywhere near any bed that he was occupying. He didn't want any more triggers that could remind him of what had happened in this bathroom.

Summoning all the strength he could muster, he walked though his room, past the kitchen and into the living room. He expected to see Sophie sitting there waiting for him, but she was standing by the window as if she was waiting for someone to arrive. Her mother? Her two biological children that had just been pretty much dumped on her doorstep?

Her glance in his direction was brief.

'You look like you're feeling a bit better.'

'Getting there.'

'You'll be pleased to know that your renal function is still okay. I don't think I need to take any more bloods unless things get worse again.'

'That's good.' Finn was looking out of the window now as well. The back of the house looked out onto the garden and led to the street where the medical centre was situated but this side had the advantage of the view from the top of a steep hill. He could see the jumble of rooftops of the village houses and, beyond that, the sparkle of sunshine on a cove dotted with small boats.

It was a pretty place. About as different to the Australian Outback as you could find anywhere in the world.

'How's your chest feeling?' Sophie asked. 'Any pain or coughing?'

'No.'

'Headache?'

'Not bad. A dose of paracetamol should fix it.'

'And that abdominal pain?'

'Almost gone.' That wasn't quite true but he wasn't about to let Sophie check for herself.

'You had that dizzy spell, though.'

'I hadn't been on my feet for a while. I'm over it.' To prove that, Finn moved again, walking towards one of the armchairs flanking the couch in front of the fire that must have been alight earlier but was now just a warm glow. He hadn't noticed the piano in this room the other night. Or the array of framed photographs on top of it. One of them caught his eye and he paused.

'This is you?'

'Probably.' Sophie hadn't moved away from the window. 'I'm an only child. They're pretty much all me. A record of my entire life.'

They were. It wasn't any baby photo that had caught his attention, however. Or even one of Sophie as a child that made him realise how much of a shock it must have been for her parents to see the twins for the first time. It wasn't the radiant wedding photo, either, although she looked far too young in it to be getting married.

No. It was the photo of her leaning over a wheelchair, her arms draped around the neck of the man who was sitting in it. The same man who'd been in the wedding photo but he hadn't been in a wheelchair then. It wasn't curiosity about what had happened to disable him that held his gaze, however, it was the way the two of them were looking at each other, as if no one else in the world existed. It wasn't often that an image could capture the essence of love like that, but this one had.

It captured everything that Finn had never found.

That he knew he never could now. Not like that, anyway. That kind of trust could never be rebuilt when it had been so effectively destroyed.

It had to be the aftermath of the fever knocking the stuffing out of him that was currently sucking him into this unwelcome space that felt as if he had lost something precious. It was a feeling strong enough to make his throat too tight to swallow.

How long had he been standing here?

Long enough for Sophie to have moved without him noticing, anyway. Somehow, when she picked up the photograph, it came as no surprise that she'd guessed which one had captured him so thoroughly.

'This is Matthew,' she told him quietly. 'My husband. He died five years ago.'

'I'm sorry.'

'Me, too.' Still holding the photograph, Sophie moved to sit down on one end of the couch. Her glance was an invitation for Finn to follow her example. 'You still look like you might keel over any time, you know.'

He had to admit it was a relief to sink into an armchair.

'You might as well know the story,' Sophie said. 'It's part of why you're here.'

Finn said nothing but his gaze was fixed on Sophie. Not that she was looking at him. Her head was bent and that photograph was the only thing she was seeing.

'We grew up together here,' she told him. 'Started dating in high school and got married just after I graduated from medical school. Matt graduated from law school at the same time. We both wanted to come back here to raise our family.'

'You look very young in your wedding photo.'

'I was twenty-four.' Sophie smiled. 'Far too young, but what was the point of waiting? There was never going to be anyone else for either of us. Not that we were going to start a family right away. We wanted a few years to get our careers established and to just enjoy each other's company. We loved walking,' she added. 'Especially along the cliff tops. What we loved most of all was being out in a storm and watching the sea crashing onto the rocks. We knew it was dangerous but we were young and...you know...we felt invincible.'

Again, it was difficult to swallow past the constriction in his throat. Finn remembered that feeling. Life, with all its promise, stretched endlessly in front of him. Love, with even more promise, that could be trusted to make that life endlessly happy.

'Anyway...' Sophie cleared her throat. 'We pushed things too far one time. Matt got blown off the top of a cliff by a wind gust and broke his spine in three places. He was never going to walk again. Or father any children by natural means. We still wanted our family, though, so we looked for help. It turned out that it was trickier than anyone expected so we had to go the extra distance and try IVF.'

Finn was still listening but his mind had gone off at a tangent. How much would you have to love someone for such a catastrophe not to dent a shared vision of the future? He could feel the strength of that love underlying

Sophie's stark words. The love. The loyalty. The *hope*...
It said a great deal about the personality of this woman
and he had to admire that. And he had to envy the man
who had shared it.

He pulled his thoughts back to what was relevant. To
how this story had brought him here.

'You had extra eggs collected? Frozen?'

'Mmm... We didn't know if it would work the first
time. And we wanted more than one child, anyway.'

Finn frowned. He only had a vague memory of the
conversation he'd overheard between Sophie and her parents that first night when she'd been so emphatic about
not wanting anything to do with the twins but he thought
he remembered mention of a baby. 'But the first attempt
was successful?'

Sophie nodded. 'I was about sixteen weeks pregnant
when Matthew got sick. A pneumonia that wasn't respon-
sive to treatment. I miscarried the day of his funeral.'

Oh, *God*...

Finn had no words. But maybe he didn't need them,
because Sophie finally raised her gaze from that photograph and maybe she could see the empathy in his eyes
because, after a long, long moment, her face softened. It
wasn't a smile but it felt like an acceptance that he understood at least some of what she'd been through.

Sophie sighed as she got to her feet, moving to replace
the photograph on the piano top. 'So there you go. I never
gave those extra frozen eggs another thought until I got a
letter a couple of years later. Donating them was one of
the options offered and I finally decided that it might be
nice if something good came from something so horrible.
For someone else. It felt like I was finally letting go of
the past so that I could move on properly with my life.'

The look she was giving him now had an edge of accusation and, as if to underline the fact that he had ruined that moving-on process, the front door of the house opened and they could hear her mother's voice.

'Boots off. No, we'd better leave the seaweed outside, Ellie, darling. You can bring your shells in, though. Oh… is that your favourite one, Emma? Shall we go and show your uncle Finn?'

The animated murmur of children's voice came as a surprise. Finn had never heard these girls utter more than a subdued couple of words at a time.

'I know,' Judy responded. 'We'll have lunch right now. Let me just go and put another log on the fire so it's nice and warm in there for us this afternoon.'

She stopped in surprise as she entered the living room.

'Oh… Sophie… I wasn't expecting you.'

She looked alarmed, Finn thought. Guilty, even. Why?

'Nana?'

The call floated in from the hallway and the sudden tension Finn could sense coming from Sophie's direction was no surprise. The girls were calling her mother *Nana*? And then two small faces appeared behind Judy. Standing close enough to be almost hiding behind her. As if they'd found someone they could trust, at last.

As if they knew they were going to be protected.

One swift glance at Sophie's face and the bigger picture of what he'd done punched Finn in the gut. He'd thought he was doing the right thing by letting her know that she had biological children in the world. By giving her a say in what was going to happen to them. Giving her a choice.

But he hadn't, had he?

She was facing something that had to be tearing her

heart into little pieces and right now, looking at these little girls sheltering behind their grandmother, it looked as though she had no choice at all.

And he was the one who had done this to her.

CHAPTER FIVE

HE COULD FIX THIS.

Maybe.

He *wanted* to try and fix it.

Good grief, when he'd seen that look on Sophie's face…

Not just when she'd realised how much her mother was already bonding with the twins, but when she'd finished telling him the tragic story of so much loss in her life. The urge simply to take her in his arms and try to comfort her—to protect her, even—had been irresistibly powerful.

He'd actually hauled himself to his feet in the living room, without any conscious direction to his body but Sophie was already fleeing. Talking about it being time for afternoon clinic hours soon. About the list of house calls she had to make. About having only popped back to check on Finn.

Judy had been just as flustered. After the door had slammed behind Sophie, she had shooed the twins off to the bathroom to wash their hands and then fussed with the fire, adding more wood and checking twice that she'd secured the guard. She also seemed to be avoiding Finn's gaze.

'So you're feeling a bit better?'

'I am.'

'Stay here. I'll bring you some soup in a minute, when I've got the girls sorted. They're starving after all that sea air and the walk up the hill.'

Despite the muscles in his legs starting to complain at the effort of being upright, Finn still hadn't sat down again. He couldn't let Judy just rush out of the room without saying something.

'Will she be okay? Sophie, I mean… She looked pretty upset. I… I feel responsible.'

Judy stilled. And then sighed.

'It wasn't you. It's because Ellie called me "Nana".' She shook her head. 'But they had to be able to call me something, didn't they? And…and I *am* their nana. Whatever happens, that's not going to change.' She lifted her chin. 'When's all said and done, these girls are my grandchildren, and I'm not about to abandon them to strangers any time soon.'

Her gaze met Finn's. 'I don't think you want to do that either or you wouldn't have brought them here. Is it true what Jack told me? That you probably broke the law to get the information you needed to track Sophie down?'

It was his turn to sigh. 'Let's just say I was given access to information that should have remained confidential.'

'And you did it because it made sense. Because… because you know how important family is.'

Finn blinked. Hardly. This had been about biology not family. He'd cut all his ties with any family *he* had because he'd known that loyalty and support was not a given.

Judy's gaze hadn't wavered. 'Even when you try and

run away from it,' she said quietly, 'the pull is still there when it's most needed. That's what family is all about.'

The pull? Was that what had dragged him back with such urgency from the other side of the world the moment he'd heard the news about his brother's accident? That had kept him sitting beside Sean's bed in the intensive care unit, with so much he wanted to say that couldn't be heard? That had sparked the guilt and the determination to do the best he could for his brother's children? His nieces?

Judy was right. He hadn't been willing to abandon these little girls to complete strangers. Not when there was a possibility that they had any kind of real family out there. But now he had thrown a grenade into the middle of a genuine family where that kind of loyalty and support was abundant. *Two* grenades.

'Sophie told me about what happened,' he said. 'About Matthew. And the baby. About why she decided to donate her eggs.'

Judy nodded. 'It was a rough time but we got through it in the end. Sophie's stronger than you might expect. Too strong, perhaps. Sometimes I think she's shut herself away from life.' She was heading towards the door now, clearly intent on checking on the children. 'You turning up like this has been a terrible shock for her, but we'll deal with it because that's what we do.' She turned her head as she left the room. 'It's something we all need to get used to but you've opened a door for all of us and...' Her voice wobbled. 'And it's showing us a kind of life I think we'd all given up hoping for.'

Finn stared at the empty doorframe for a long moment. Any thoughts that he could fix this situation for Sophie by taking responsibility for his nieces himself and taking them away from here were evaporating rapidly.

He could certainly feel the pull of family that Judy had been talking about. Not his family but this one. The unconditional kind of love that permeated the walls of this old house and must have enveloped Sophie when she'd been grappling with one tragedy on top of another. A family that was already—at least in part—doing exactly what he'd hoped they would and had started accepting his orphaned nieces.

But it still had to be Sophie's choice in the end, didn't it?

He wouldn't be able to live with himself if he thought he'd irreparably damaged her life even further.

How weird was this? He barely knew Sophie Bradford but it had suddenly become very important that he didn't hurt her any more than he already had. He had no business trying to offer her any comfort but he could, at least, try to protect her.

Somehow...

Afternoon surgery hours weren't due to start for another hour. Liz and Marion hadn't returned from their lunch break and her father was still out on his house call so it should have been the perfect time to catch up on some of her paperwork. Or chase up some outstanding results, perhaps, like that exercise stress test that one of her patients had been given by the cardiology department in Truro nearly a week ago.

But Sophie's well-honed ability to shut out emotional disturbance by focussing on her work seemed to have completely deserted her. She was pacing, in fact, even though the space behind the closed door of her consulting room was far too limited.

She needed to be on the beach. Or better still, on one of those wild, cliff-top rambles that weren't that far away. With a good wind blowing that meant you had to fight to keep your balance in the gusts and the tip of your nose would go numb. The kind of walk that she and Matthew had loved so much, that would have had them hanging on to each other for support and collapsing with shrieks of laughter when it wasn't enough.

That was what this was all about, wasn't it?

That photograph. Matthew.

The fact that it felt like a betrayal that she'd experienced a flash of physical desire for another man?

Which was crazy. He wouldn't have wanted her to stay celibate for the rest of her life and it was all part of the plan of moving forward with her life. One day.

Not yet, because she wasn't ready.

And certainly not with Finn Connelly, because this situation was quite difficult enough, and any further complications would make it utterly impossible. But just thinking about him took her straight back into that bathroom and gave her a very clear image of his naked body, and each time she felt an aftershock of that spearing sensation deep in her belly it seemed to become stronger. Fierce enough now to make her catch her breath, in fact.

With a sigh heartfelt enough to be almost a groan, Sophie sat down behind her desk and buried her face in her hands, pressing her fingers against her skull. It wasn't the fact that she'd been physically attracted to another man that was the real problem here, was it?

It was that it felt so different from anything she'd ever felt for Matthew.

So different. Thrilling, even…

With Matt, everything had always been so safe. So solid. So natural. They'd been best friends for so long before their relationship had slowly slipped into something more. Sex had been great. Fun. Exciting, even.

But *thrilling*?

No. Why was that? Because there had never been anything to feel curious about? Any hint of risk or the threat of an unknown skeleton in a closet? They'd always known everything there was to know about each other. The trust had been absolute.

Finn Connelly was a complete stranger. A man who possibly couldn't be trusted? After all, what kind of man would choose to leave his family behind and go to a remote location on the other side of the world? Not to return even once since the birth of his brother's children more than three years ago?

Not the kind of man that Sophie would choose to get closer to, that was for sure. Why would any woman risk emotional involvement with someone who might just change his mind and disappear?

Except…she didn't believe that he wasn't capable of commitment. Or that he didn't care.

He could have said he was in no position to raise children and put the twins into the care of Social Services back in Ireland after the funerals of their parents, but he hadn't. He'd tried to think of an alternative solution and he'd gone to considerable trouble to put his plan into action, even though he'd probably already been feeling unwell by then. He must have known he would be stepping into a very difficult situation as well.

Had he regretted the rift in his family and wanted to do something to try and make amends? Felt guilty because he'd caused it, perhaps? Behind her closed eyes, Sophie could see again the look she'd seen on Finn's face that first evening he'd been here. She could feel that sensation of someone being lost. Of wanting so much to do the right thing but not knowing exactly what that was or how to do it.

She'd felt a connection with him in that moment. Empathy. And that was a rather short step from caring about someone. Throw physical attraction into that arena, and it was a recipe for making life a whole lot harder.

It had to be dismissed.

But not entirely, maybe. The totally unexpected revelation that it was possible to feel that way had to be a positive thing. Eventually. When this current crisis was solved, Sophie would have the knowledge that it wasn't impossible to move on with her life in a very different direction. To find someone new to share her life with in a relationship that sparked mutual attraction and had similar goals for the future. To have her own family— children that were her own, fathered by the man of her choice. Babies that she could bond with before they were even born and then hold in her arms and cherish every moment of their infancy.

She could never bond with the twins like that.

Would it have been a different story if they'd been still helpless babies?

There was no point in even thinking about it. That time was long gone. Her lunch break was gone now as well. Sophie could hear voices from beyond her door. Liz and Marion were back and the waiting room was probably filling up again already, which was a relief. It would be so much easier to focus on her work when she had real people in front of her instead of paperwork.

* * *

The prospect of going to check on Finn's physical condition again the next day was daunting. Sophie needed a break from the emotional turmoil that seemed to be coming at her from all directions. As if it wasn't enough that she had to deal with the fact that she was a mother, whether she chose to take on that role or not, she also had the unexpected—and unwelcome—knowledge that her body had finally woken up again enough to remind her of how compelling physical desire could be.

So, instead of going over to the house to see for herself, she simply asked her father how Finn was doing.

'Improving,' he said. 'Nowhere near a hundred percent yet, of course, but he's getting there.'

'Do you think I should take another blood test to check on his renal function?'

'I don't think that's necessary. He just needs a bit more time to rest and your mother's good food. I might take him out with me in the car for my house calls this afternoon. A change of scene and a bit of fresh air might do him the world of good.'

Afternoon clinic provided the warning signs that a new virus was gaining ground amongst North Cove's population—a heavy cold that was making people miserable with a nasty sore throat, increasing the incidence of ear infections in young children and meant that everyone with any kind of lung disease would need extra care.

Jillian, one of her mother's friends, was one of those people.

'I hate getting a cold,' she told Sophie, her voice no more than a croak. 'It always makes my asthma so much worse. And I'm getting low on my medications and inhalers.'

She got up to leave after a thorough check up and a prescription for everything she needed to avoid complications and make her life a little less miserable over the next few days. She didn't quite get to the door before she turned back, however.

'Oh…my head must be really fuzzy.' She held the carrier bag in her hands out to Sophie. 'Can you give these to your mum, please? They're needed urgently for the school fair committee to price up. I was supposed to drop them off to Isabelle McKenzie a couple of days ago, but I was feeling too grotty, and I don't want to be spreading this cold around if I can help it.'

'Good thinking.' Sophie took the bag. 'And it's no problem. I'll pop over as soon as things are quiet here.'

It wasn't until another hour or more had passed that the waiting room emptied and Sophie had a chance to peep inside the carrier bag. Jillian must have put a great many hours into knitting all these booties and other baby clothes that were just the kind of thing people loved buying at a school fair. Despite it being decades since Sophie had attended North Cove primary school, her mother had remained the head of the annual fair committee.

Her father hadn't returned from making house calls. And hadn't he said that he was taking Finn with him to give him a change of scene and some fresh air? Sophie picked up the bag and left her office.

'Time to pack up,' she told Marion and Liz. 'Thanks for all your help today. Can you lock up? I just want to pop over to deliver something to Mum.'

She hurried through the garden and into the kitchen where she found her mother pouring milk into two small tumblers. A saucer beside the glasses was piled with small, teddy-bear-shaped biscuits.

'Sophie! How lovely. Do you want a cup of tea?'

'No. I can't stop. I just came over to give you this from Jillian. Apparently Isabelle McKenzie needs this stuff urgently for the school fair and Jillian's not feeling too well.'

'Oh, I'm sorry to hear that.' Judy took the bag and peered inside. 'Oh…fantastic. Some of this is needed for a raffle that Isabelle's putting together. She's been fretting about it. In fact…' Judy was heading towards the back door '…be a love and stay here for five minutes. I'm just going to dash down the road and give her this. It'll stop her ringing me yet again this evening.'

'No, I can't… I've got a mountain of paperwork waiting for me in my office.'

But Judy was already halfway through the door, having plucked her coat from the hook beside it. 'I'll only be a few minutes,' she said reassuringly. 'I'll be back by the time you've given the girls their snack.'

The door shut behind her and Sophie's breath came out in an incredulous huff.

Her mother knew perfectly well that Sophie didn't do babysitting, even for her good friends. At first, it had been because it was too hard a space to visit after losing a baby, and then it had just become normal, something that Sophie Bradford simply didn't do. But her mother had deliberately just left Sophie alone with these children.

Her children.

Small children who were currently alone in another room where there was a potentially dangerous open fire. She picked up the glasses, balancing the saucer of biscuits on top of one of them, and went through to the living room.

The girls' eyes widened when they saw Sophie.

'Where's Nana?' one of them asked in a small voice.

'She's gone out just for a minute. I've got some milk for you.'

Sophie put the glasses and saucer down on the coffee table and then perched on the edge of the couch, feeling uncomfortable.

The twins eyed each other and then stared at Sophie. They looked as timid as they had yesterday, peering out from the shelter of being behind her mother's legs— scared of her, almost, and that was a little heart-breaking.

'Would you like me to read you a story?' She picked up the book on top of the pile on one end of the couch. 'Just until… um… Nana gets back?'

Again, the twins shared a glance. And then they reached for the biscuits and milk and Sophie started reading.

'Once upon a time, in a land far, far away there lived a little princess. A princess who had the curliest hair in the world…'

Oh, she remembered this story. Her mother had read it to her so many times and she had loved it, because this princess had the same issues that she had had with hair that didn't want to do anything normal and always hurt to get brushed or combed. As she read the part about the terrifying ordeal with the comb that always made her cry, one of the twins looked over her shoulder. Some biscuit crumbs fell out of her mouth as she spoke.

'Just like us.'

'Mmm…' Sophie smiled. 'Like me, too, when I was little. Like me now.' Her smile widened. 'Except I don't cry any more.'

The other twin—she wasn't sure if it was Ellie or Emma—had a milk moustache. She also had a biscuit in each hand but she was getting to her feet.

'Where?' she demanded. 'I can't see...'

A minute later, Sophie found that she had taken out the hairclips and band that confined her long curls into a manageable ponytail. She also had a small girl on either side of her and, a moment later, she had small sticky fingers playing with her hair.

But it felt as if those fingers were actually playing with her heart.

She'd been wrong about not being able to bond with these children because she hadn't known them as babies.

It would be quite possible to fall in love with the twins.

The feeling of connection coming through those busy little hands was seeping into her own body at a cellular level. What she really wanted to do was to gather both these little girls into her arms and hug them gently, hold them close...

But she couldn't let herself do that. She hadn't thought through enough of the implications of even taking responsibility for these children. Going that step further and becoming emotionally involved with them was too much to consider.

Too terrifying.

Sophie extricated herself from the tangle of small fingers and elbows and legs.

'Finish your milk,' she told the twins. 'I'm just going to get a glass of water.'

To her relief, she heard the back door shutting as she neared the kitchen. Her mother was home, which meant that she could escape.

Except it wasn't just Judy who'd arrived home. Right behind her were her father and Finn and they were all staring at her.

'What happened to your hair?'

'Long story,' Sophie muttered. 'Or rather, a specific story. That one about the princess with the curliest hair in the world?'

'Ah…' Her mother's smile was tender. 'You loved that story when you were little.'

'You did,' her father agreed.

As Sophie's glance shifted to her father, it took in the expression on Finn's face. He was looking rather too pale, as if the outing in the car had been a bit much for him, but the way he was looking at what had to be a mess of curls framing her face was doing something very peculiar to her body. For a horrible moment, she thought her knees might even forget how to keep her upright.

'Mmm…' She edged towards the door. She could still feel the touch of those sticky fingers and the look that Finn was giving her felt like another physical touch. It was all too much. 'I have to go.'

'Stay for dinner?'

'Too much to do, Mum. Another time.'

'Okay, love.' There was a hint of apology in her mother's face as she gave Sophie a hug. Did she realise that she might have pushed a little too hard in forcing Sophie to spend time with the twins like that? 'Soon?'

Sophie nodded and escaped but she knew perfectly well that 'soon' would be way too soon as far as she was concerned.

Thankfully, her parents backed off over the next couple of days, maybe because they could see that she was under too much pressure. The nasty cold had been spreading like wildfire and patient numbers had increased enough for Sophie to be worried about the workload her father was coping with. In an effort to relieve that pressure she was working longer and longer hours herself, which meant putting off some house calls until the evenings, and that meant paperwork was piling up. Even if she had wanted to check on Finn or have dinner with her parents, it simply wasn't possible.

Jack kept her updated on Finn's progress, however, which seemed to be going well, although her father would add a rider such as, 'You can't rush recovery from something like this, you know, or you might find yourself back at square one.'

She knew that her mother would know that she was deliberately avoiding contact with the twins but Judy wasn't pushing her, either, other than to call every day and say that there was plenty for dinner if she had the time to drop in.

'It'd save you cooking,' she'd say. 'I know how busy you are. I can just leave something keeping warm in the oven, if that's better.'

It wasn't just the twins that she was avoiding. It was Finn. Because the disturbance of that moment of attraction was still hovering in the back of her mind and she didn't want to risk anything that might make it more of an issue. Like that look he'd given her when he'd seen her unrestrained hair. Staying away from him was certainly making it easier to deal with but it couldn't go on much longer. Finn was recovering. Decisions had to be made.

It was her father who called time on her avoidance tactics, coming into the clinic on Sunday morning when Sophie had just come back from a house call.

'Your mother sent me over to tell you to come and have lunch with us.'

'I've just been to see Joanne Coombs. I need to write up my notes and then get these blood samples into town for urgent analysis. Her heart failure's getting worse. I'd like to admit her to hospital but she's adamant she's staying at home. I'm going to go and check her again later today and, if it's any worse, I'm going to put my foot down.'

'Good luck with that.' Her father was frowning. 'I'll come with you, if you like. I've known Joanne a very long time. She might listen to me.'

'That would be great. She couldn't argue with both of us.'

Jack smiled. 'Don't bet on it. But if we work together, we'll find a solution.' His gaze softened. 'It's time to start trying to find a solution to our other problem, too, love. Your mum's making your favourite Sunday lunch. Roast beef and Yorkshire pudding. We've tried to give you as much time as possible to get used to what's happened but Finn is almost well enough to leave now. We all need to talk.'

And there it was. Sophie had no choice but to follow her father home. It was with some trepidation that she went into the house. She couldn't be sure that her body wouldn't ambush her with unwanted sensations when she saw Finn again but, more importantly, she had no idea what she was going to say if her parents offered to raise these girls, as she was pretty sure they were going to.

Trepidation morphed into astonishment as soon as she was through the door because the home she had known and loved for ever felt completely different. The kitchen was full of a delicious smell of roasting meat but the table wasn't set for a meal, it was covered with sheets of paper, crayons and some toys that Sophie recognised from a very long time ago.

Her mother was red-cheeked from the heat of the oven but she was beaming as she wiped her hands on her apron and came towards Sophie to kiss her.

'I'm so glad you're here. I've made extra gravy.'

'Are those…my old toys?'

'Yes. I didn't think you'd mind so I got Dad to bring the boxes down from the attic. It was too cold to go to the beach on Friday.'

'Okay…'

But Sophie's heart was sinking fast. Apart from a few toys that had been relegated to the box in the corner of the clinic's waiting room, her mother had always insisted on keeping everything else. Packing it away into boxes. *For the grandchildren,* she'd say with a smile.

She had felt the sands of her life shifting under her feet with the arrival of the twins in their lives but, in the space of a few days, while she'd had her head turned away trying to pretend that she might have some control over this, she hadn't noticed the tide on top of that sand and the current was alarmingly strong. Were those toys ever going to be put back into their boxes and hidden in the attic again?

Sophie did her best to put a smile on her own face. 'Can I help? Clear the table or something?'

'No, no…' Her mother urged her to keep moving with a gentle push. 'Your dad and I have everything under control. Go and put your feet up for a few minutes.'

But there was music coming from the living room and it was nothing like anything her parents normally listened to. It was something bouncy and silly—that kids' song that invited you to clap your hands if you were happy. And there was hand clapping going on.

Had it only been a couple of days ago when she'd seen these children peeping shyly from behind her mother's legs? And being so tentative in her own company when she'd been left to supervise them?

Children could be amazingly resilient and these two girls were bouncing now and clapping their hands. Even more astonishingly, Finn was standing between them and clapping *his* hands. All three of them stopped as soon as they saw Sophie, though, and it felt as if the world was holding its breath, waiting to gauge her reaction. The children actually looked delighted to see her, she realised. Finn looked slightly embarrassed, although nothing like when he'd been caught dripping wet and stark naked.

Oh, no…how could her brain take her straight back to *that* moment?

With a supreme effort, for her own sake as much as anybody else's, she tried to put them all at ease.

'Hey…looks like you're all having fun.' Her gaze was still snagged on Finn's. He was clean shaven, today and… and he was smiling.

She hadn't seen him smiling before and it seemed to be contagious. She could feel the corners of her own mouth lifting. It felt like even more of an effort to pull her gaze away from his than it had been to sound as if she often came across musical games happening on a Sunday afternoon in her parents' living room.

'Don't stop on my account,' she said. 'I could hear some really good singing there.'

But Finn was turning the music down. 'I'm exhausted,' he said. 'I can't dance any more, girls.'

Sophie picked her way past the toys on the floor. Good grief, she hadn't seen that rag doll for decades. And there was an old cane doll's pram, currently overflowing with stuffed animals. And—oh—she'd forgotten she'd ever owned that tiny china tea set. She stooped to pick up one of the cups with its pretty pattern of flowers.

'I believe there's tea in that pot,' Finn said.

'Really?' Sophie's smile was wider this time.

'It's *pretend* tea,' Ellie explained. Or was that Emma? The girls weren't quite identical, Sophie realised, but she hadn't taken enough notice when she'd met them to know which was which. Or even when she'd had that time alone with them. 'But Nana said we're too little to have *real* tea. I'll make it for you,' she added. 'But you have to sit down so it doesn't spill.'

'You, too, Unca Finn,' Emma said. 'Sit down.'

So, moments later, Sophie found herself sitting cross-legged on the floor, facing Finn, the girls taking turns to carefully pretend to pour tea from the miniature tea pot into the tiny cups, followed by imaginary milk from the matching jug.

The sort of thing that young parents would do with their children, she thought. For a moment, she was looking at the scene from somewhere outside herself. As if she and Finn *were* the parents and these little girls were their own children.

The image carried a punch that was disturbing. As she distracted herself by focussing on something actually in front of her, Sophie was aware of a wash of emotion as the image faded.

Longing…?

She focused harder on the little china cups which were the perfect size for those small hands. Emma was balancing one in its saucer with palpable concentration as she handed it to Sophie.

'Thank you, Emma,' she said as she accepted the offering.

'I'm *Ellie*.'

'Oh, I'm so sorry. Thank you, Ellie.'

The small face had a very serious expression. 'You're welcome,' Ellie said.

Sophie focused on that little face. And then she watched Emma present Finn with his cup and saucer. She needed to make sure she could tell the twins apart so she didn't mix up their names again. It was the hair that made it difficult, because they both had that cloud of tight curls.

Like her own hair. Like the hair of that princess in the story she'd read to them. She could almost feel the gentle exploration of those sticky fingers on her scalp all over again.

Their eyes were the same dark brown, too.

Like hers.

Emma's face was a little rounder, though. And Ellie seemed to be the more outgoing twin who smiled more readily. She was smiling at Sophie now.

'Do you like it?'

Sophie pretended to take a sip of the tea. 'Mmm… It's delicious.'

Ellie's smile widened and she hunched her shoulders, as if it was difficult to contain her delight. Maybe it was because she was focussing on these little girls so carefully right now. Perhaps it was that little gesture of sheer pleasure. Or maybe it was because that cellular connection was strong enough to break through any barriers she thought she had shored up the other day. Whatever it was, Sophie could actually feel something melting around her heart and it was so bittersweet it made the back of her eyes sting.

Blinking hard, she looked at Finn. The china cup looked ridiculously small against his lips as he pretended to drink his tea but it wasn't the cup that Sophie was looking at. She was caught by the way his lips were moving, and it was easier to let herself get distracted by that than to think about how she was feeling about these children. Easier to think about how soft his lips looked. To let herself wonder what it might feel like if they were touching her own...

Then her gaze shifted upwards just the tiniest amount. Just enough to find that Finn was looking at her, and she knew that he was aware of what she'd been watching. Worse, he knew perfectly well what she'd been thinking about.

Exactly as she knew that, in this moment, he was thinking about precisely the same thing...

Oh, *man*! That first spear of desire had taken her by surprise but it was nothing compared to the flood of sensation that blossomed this time. It felt as if the sharp sensation deep in her belly had burst something that was unleashing a tingling warmth spreading through her entire body. Right down to her fingertips and toes.

Her cup rattled on its saucer and she hastily put it down.

'That was lovely,' she said. 'But I have to go now.'

'Why?'

'Because I need to help...um... Nana. In the kitchen.'

Not that she looked directly at him, but Sophie knew Finn wasn't watching as she scrambled to her feet, intending to flee. His stillness let her know that the unspoken message had been received.

Yes, the attraction was mutual.

But no. There was no way it was going anywhere.

She turned to find her father coming into the living room. 'Lunch is ready,' he said. 'Come on, chickens. It's time to wash your hands.'

Jack and Judy sat at either end of the old wooden table in the kitchen. The twins sat together on one side, with cushions on their chairs so they could reach their plates. Finn was seated beside Sophie. It wasn't a huge table, probably better suited to four people rather than six around it, which meant that his chair was very close to Sophie's. Even being careful, his leg had come into contact with hers on more than one occasion as he reached to help himself from the platter of roast vegetables and Yorkshire puddings, and the bowls of peas and beans.

'This is so good,' he said to Judy, who was helping the twins cut their slices of meat into manageable pieces. 'Did you grow these beans yourself?'

'That veggie patch is Jack's pride and joy,' she responded. 'Not that he gets much time to do anything in it these days.' She smiled at Finn. 'What's really good is to see you finally getting your appetite back.'

'Mmm…' The mouthful of gravy-soaked potato was indeed delicious, but, even though his leg wasn't in contact with Sophie's right now, it felt as if it was. He was as aware of her beside him as he was of every mouthful of this meal. His appetite for food wasn't the only thing that had come back, was it?

And it was a bit of a problem.

'I'm feeling so much better,' he said. 'Safe enough to drive again.'

Instead of defusing the tension of what seemed to be happening between himself and Sophie by the reminder that he wouldn't be here for much longer, the sudden silence around the table after his words had only made things worse.

Of course it had. This had only ever been about the children, hadn't it? About whether, when *he* left, the children would be going with him. He was finally getting to know his nieces, thanks to all the time they'd spent together in the last few days. More than getting to know them. There was a bond there that was rapidly gaining strength. How could he leave them behind?

But how could he not?

Even the twins seemed to have picked up on this new tension and they both stopped eating.

'I don't like peas,' Emma said sadly.

'I don't like driving,' Ellie said, her gaze on Finn. 'I want to stay here.'

Judy's glance at her husband was alarmed. Jack put his knife and fork down on the side of his plate.

'You don't need to rush off back to Australia, do you, Finn?'

'I…ah… I'm not sure what I'm going to do,' he answered. 'I haven't received an offer of a new contract with the Flying Doctors yet. I might take a locum job somewhere for a little while. Until…well…until things get sorted properly.'

Jack nodded slowly. 'We're looking for a locum here,' he said quietly. 'Or rather, we're looking for a permanent partner, but, in the meantime, a locum would be very welcome. Sophie and I are being run off our feet these days and we only need a flu or a bout of gastro going around to make it impossible to manage.'

Sophie wasn't saying anything. She wasn't looking at anyone, either, just pushing food around her plate that she clearly had no intention of eating any time soon.

Finn suppressed a sigh. 'I was thinking more of a hospital position,' he said cautiously. 'I've never considered general practice. A&E is my thing.'

Was it his imagination or did he feel Sophie relax just a little, as if she was relieved? Jack's nod was understanding.

'It was just a thought. Not a long-term commitment or anything. We've got a couple of enquiries about the position so we'll be interviewing one of them in the near future.'

'Oh?' Sophie finally joined the conversation. 'You didn't tell me that.'

'I just got the email this morning. A Callum Mc-Gregor. Currently working in a general practice in Glasgow but he wants to get out of the city. He's thirty-eight. No family ties.'

'Sounds interesting.'

Finn suddenly found it difficult to swallow his mouthful of food. Why was it so interesting? Because it would relieve the workload or because this potential partner was single? It shouldn't bother him, he thought. But it kind of did.

The sooner this lunch was over, the better.

The twins were adorable, sitting there perched on their cushions and doing their best to eat with cutlery that was too big for their small hands, and currently having a secret competition over who could spear the biggest number of peas on their forks. And the way they both clasped their hands in identical movements of happiness when a chocolate pudding and ice-cream appeared for dessert gave Sophie a squeeze around her heart the way Ellie's shoulder hunch had done earlier and…and it was terrifying.

It was confirmation of just how wrong she'd been when she'd thought that having missed out on the infancy of these children would make it impossible to bond with them. It would be only too easy to start caring way too much for these girls and she couldn't afford to let that happen. To let it cloud her judgement.

She couldn't put her hand up to take on an instant family and raise two orphans. Her career would be severely compromised. The safety of her solitary life in her small cottage would vanish. Everything would change dramatically and the prospect was just too much. Was this how people felt when they were inside an aeroplane, waiting to step out of the door for their first parachute jump? No. That was an experience that would only last a matter of minutes. Taking on children would last a lifetime.

But Sophie knew that as soon as this lunch was over it was inevitable that a discussion was on the agenda. How could it not be, given the tension that Finn had created by suggesting that he was well enough to hit the road again? And what was he planning to say? That maybe he'd changed his mind and finding a locum position that would keep him here wasn't such a good idea? That he wanted to use his power as the twins' guardian to take them somewhere else? To find an adoptive family in Australia, perhaps, so that he could stay a part of their lives? Seeing him dancing and singing with his nieces today suggested that he was certainly bonding with them now.

She didn't want the twins to be taken to the other side of the world, Sophie realised. Not for herself but because she knew that it would break her parents' hearts.

Okay…maybe it was for herself as well. She needed more time. She was edging closer to the idea of accepting these children in her life somehow but she was nowhere near ready to take that leap. She was still fighting the urge to run away and hide.

The opportunity to do exactly that, at least temporarily, came as Judy started collecting dishes as they finished dessert, and it was Sophie who jumped to her feet to go and answer the telephone. She tried not to let her tone reveal her relief when she came back into the kitchen.

'I need to pop back to the clinic,' she said. 'Muriel Bennet's husband is bringing her in with abdo pain that sounds like it might be appendicitis.'

'I could go,' her father offered.

Sophie shook her head. 'If she needs to be admitted, I'll go with her. I've still got those blood samples I want to get to the lab.'

Maybe she wasn't the only one who was relieved that a heavy conversation had been postponed. Judy was lifting Ellie and then Emma from their chairs.

'Who's going to help me do the dishes?'

'Me,' Ellie said.

'And me,' Emma said.

The girls both turned to look up at Jack. 'Poppa, too?' Ellie asked.

Jack was smiling. 'Of course. I always help Nana with the dishes.'

The sense of solidarity in the kitchen was suddenly overpowering. Maybe that was why Finn followed Sophie into the hallway as she headed for the front door.

'Might walk over with you,' he said. 'I could do with a bit of fresh air and there's a couple of things in my car that I need.'

It was Sophie who broke the silence when they reached the gate that led to the car park.

'Are you going to stay?'

Finn caught her gaze but it seemed a long time before he answered her question.

'I don't know. It's…becoming more difficult than I thought it would be.'

'Mmm…'

'I'm their uncle,' Finn continued. 'And that's starting to mean something. And I understand how huge this is for you. I…' His pause became an apologetic smile. 'I had thought I could make this easier for you by taking the girls with me and looking after them myself somehow but…' He shook his head. 'It's beginning to feel like I'd be taking them away from their own family.'

They had reached the point where Sophie needed to turn away to the clinic entrance. Finn's car was still parked where he'd left it that first night, in the far corner.

'You're lucky, you know,' he added quietly. 'You have a *real* family.'

Sophie stopped, surprised. 'Wasn't yours real?'

'Not like yours. And then it got broken.'

Something in Finn's tone told Sophie that that was all he intended to say but she knew this was important. Important enough to stand out in the cold for as long as it took.

'What happened?' she asked gently. 'How did it break?'

'Sean was my older brother by a few years,' Finn said slowly. 'Our dad died when we were quite young and he was the one my mother relied on. She called him "the man of the house". We lived in a small village. Everybody thought he was wonderful.'

Simple words that clearly covered a lot that was being unsaid. Had Finn grown up feeling less important? Less loved?

'I told you that Sean met and fell in love with a nurse called Stella. What I didn't tell you was that it was me who introduced them.'

Sophie waited. She didn't understand what the problem was.

'I'd taken Stella home for Christmas,' Finn added. 'So that she could meet my family. We'd been together for a year by then. I had the ring in my pocket, ready to propose to her on Christmas Eve.'

'Oh…*no*…'

'I could actually see it happening. *Feel* it happening. Her falling in love with my brother. Him falling in love with her. It felt like it happened in the blink of an eye and nothing was ever going to be the same.'

Sophie sucked in a breath. Of course it wasn't.

Finn shrugged. 'I tried to get past it but it got harder to visit home. I guess the last straw was how thrilled everybody was when their IVF was successful and they had the twins on the way. That was when I took the job in Australia.' He closed his eyes for a moment. 'It gave me a good excuse for not coming back when the twins were born. Or when my mother got sick. I didn't even come back for her funeral.'

Another car was pulling into the car park now. Sophie's patient was arriving and she needed to open the clinic doors but she couldn't move just yet.

Finn had trusted her with a story that explained so much, that had broken her heart, in fact. He'd been betrayed by the people he should have been able to trust the most. And yet he'd gone so far in trying to do the best he could for the innocent parties that had been left behind. Children who were the only members left of a family that hadn't felt *real*?

There was something very special about Finn Connelly. Something lost but still courageous. She knew how hard it was to carve out a new life in the wake of something devastating. And he was trusting her, when trusting anyone must be the hardest thing. The connection she felt with him now had absolutely nothing to do with any physical attraction. It was deeper. Even more powerful.

She put her hand on his arm. 'Don't go yet,' she said. 'Please. We'll find a way through this.' She held his gaze. 'Something that's right for all of us.'

'Dr Bradford?' A man was getting out of the car. 'Muriel thinks she's going to be sick. I don't know what to do…'

CHAPTER SIX

HE'D NEVER TOLD anybody that story.

He'd told himself it was because all that was in the past and he wasn't going to let it poison his future.

And because it was nobody else's business.

But that was just an excuse, wasn't it?

The real reason had been nagging at Finn Connelly all night. By the next afternoon it was getting too hard to keep pushing those unwanted thoughts away and he badly needed to clear his head.

'I think I'll go for a walk,' he told Judy. 'I need to start getting back into shape.'

'Good idea.' She smiled. 'You haven't seen our beach yet. Or the port.'

'You're okay with the girls?'

Her glance said it all. She was more than okay being left alone to care for the twins. It said too much, in fact. That she was making the most of every moment she had with these children in case it wasn't going to last.

'We're going to make cookies,' was all she said. 'Chocolate-chip. I'll bet you'll be ready for a cup of tea and a bikkie by the time you get back. Don't get too cold, there's a bit of a breeze out there and it'll be chilly down by the sea.'

There *was* a bit of a breeze and it was just what Finn needed. He could unleash those thoughts and then simply let them blow out to sea, along with the unpleasant emotional baggage they carried.

Like the envy he'd always had for his older brother, who'd never been able to put a foot wrong. The envy that had sharpened into jealousy when the woman he'd loved had decided that Sean was the only man for her. That what she'd felt for Finn was no more than friendship in comparison. That he simply didn't measure up.

The way his mother had always made him feel. No wonder she and Stella had hit it off so instantly, but in the end that had been a blessing, because his mother had had the people she loved the most around her when she got so sick.

There was shame to be found as well. And guilt. That he hadn't come back to see her before she died. That he hadn't come back for her funeral. The way people had looked at him when he'd come back this time hadn't been any surprise, either. He'd proved that he was a lesser man than Sean all his life and he wasn't welcome in his home town.

He'd been made welcome here, though. In this picture-perfect little village. Having walked down the hill, through narrow, cobbled streets with a collection of stone cottages and then quaint-looking shops, he'd reached the beach and could lengthen his stride and push his body against the wind. It seemed a long time since he'd felt physically capable of making his muscles actually work hard and the chill of the sea air on his face was making Finn feel even more alive. A woman walking her dog smiled and said hello as she passed and it was easy to smile back.

Yes. He was welcome here.

And Sophie hadn't made him feel any less acceptable when he'd confessed his sad little story of rejection and betrayal. The way she'd looked at him… As if she admired him instead of judging him or, worse, feeling sorry for him. The way it had felt when she'd put her hand on his arm. When she'd asked him to stay…

He'd known then that he'd been right to trust her with his story.

That he was also right to have brought the twins here. That this was the kind of family they deserved. The kind he'd never had himself. How could he ever hope to provide anything like this for these children when he had no idea what to do? Maybe it had been that family lunch that had opened the door to telling Sophie something he'd never told anyone else, that palpable bond between these people and the way it already included his nieces. Maybe he'd told her because he needed her to understand. To help him make the decisions that still needed to be made.

He'd reached the end of the beach now. Beyond the jetty was the small port crowded with fishing boats. Had it been too rough out to sea today or were they usually all back in port by this time? The bright wooden boats were rolling on the swell of waves but there were people on board some of them. Finn could see nets being checked and decks being scrubbed. As he got closer he could hear the sound of buoys slapping against wooden hulls, despite the cries of gulls circling overhead; an anchor chain dragging against something as the large wave kept rolling through and then the sound of splintering wood. There was a moment of near silence after that, broken by a sharp scream that surely couldn't have come from any of those large seabirds?

Finn's pace quickened as he heard it again, along with shouting by male voices that held an unmistakeable edge of panic. He was running by the time he got past the main jetty, to find another section of the cove's beach where smaller boats were tethered or dragged up onto the pebbles.

'Get help,' someone yelled.

'Call an ambulance! It's Ethan, Charlie's lad.'

'No, call the doctors. They'll be quicker.'

'I'm a doctor.' Finn stepped aside as a couple of men pushed past to run in the opposite direction. 'What's happened?'

'That last big wave brought boats in. That one hit Charlie's boat...'

Finn could see the wooden hull that had been hit hard enough to punch a huge hole in the boards and to tip it onto its side. He kept moving forward, to the other side of the boat, and there it was...

A young man, no more than a teenager, was lying trapped on his side with the weight of the hull on his lower body. He wasn't screaming now but his face was contorted with pain. And fear.

Finn dropped to his knees beside him and reached for his wrist to find a pulse. It was rapid but reassuringly strong.

'We'll get you out, Ethan,' he told him. 'I'm going to look after you until help arrives, okay? I'm a doctor. My name's Finn.'

'I can't feel it any more...my *leg*...'

'Does it hurt to breathe?'

Ethan was taking rapid, gasping breaths. He rolled his head from side to side as a negative response and then made a sound that was almost a sob.

'Where's my dad?'

'I'm here, lad.' A large, bearded man came through the group of fishermen. 'Oh, my God…what's happened?'

He took in the scene at a glance and then ran the last few steps, his boots sinking into damp pebbles, to put his hands against the hull of the boat. Finn could see the strain on his face as he pushed desperately at the weight trapping his son. The other men instantly moved forward as well to add their effort to try and lift the hull but nothing moved apart from Ethan's upper body as he pushed his fists into the pebbles and twisted, trying to pull himself free.

'*Ah*…it *hurts*…'

'Try not to move,' Finn told him. He had pulled off his jacket to put over Ethan's chest. He needed to check as much of Ethan's body as he could reach, but hypothermia was a real risk in these conditions, and it could get worse if the wash of the waves came further up this beach.

'We need more people,' Ethan's father shouted.

'A tractor,' someone else suggested. 'Where the hell is Mitch? He's got the key.'

'He's probably in the pub. I'll go and look.' A man stumbled and almost fell in his haste to move. Someone else caught his arm and steadied him.

'What I need right now is some more coats,' Finn called. 'We need to keep Ethan warm.'

Half a dozen oilskin jackets landed beside him within seconds. Ethan's father pulled off his thick woollen jersey as well.

'Here, use this.'

'Here's the doctor.' The shout was repeated. 'Make way! Here, let me carry that for you…'

For some reason, Finn had expected that it would be

Jack responding to this local emergency but it wasn't. It was Sophie, her face grim as she pulled off the large backpack she was wearing. The man beside her put down the life-pack defibrillator he'd been carrying.

'What's happening?'

'Ethan here is trapped. We don't know how much of the boat's weight he's got on his legs. As far as I can tell, he hasn't got any injuries to his chest or pelvis.' Finn lowered his voice. 'It's been nearly fifteen minutes since it happened. We are probably looking at dealing with a crush injury. Have you got a tourniquet in your pack?'

'Yes, of course.' Sophie was frowning. 'A CAT. Is he bleeding?'

'Not that I've seen. And, judging by the strength of his radial pulse, his blood pressure hasn't dropped significantly. It's a guard against release syndrome. If I can get the tourniquet on, it will give us some control over the release of toxins.'

Sophie's blink was slow. And then her gaze locked on Finn's. 'You've dealt with traumatic rhabdomyolysis before?'

'Yes.' Finn reached for the zipper on the pack.

'Tourniquet's in with the IV gear—section above the airway stuff.' Sophie leaned past Finn and scooped up a sphygmomanometer. 'I'll get some vital signs.' Sophie dropped to her knees beside Ethan. 'Hey, you're supposed to be on top of the boat, mate, not underneath it…' Her tone was teasing but she was scanning the young man's face intently. 'It's hurting, isn't it?'

'Yeah…' Ethan was a lot paler than he'd been a few minutes ago.

'On a scale of zero to ten, with zero being no pain at

all and ten being the worst you can imagine, what score would you give it?'

'Bloody twelve…'

'Okay. I can do something about that right now.' Her hand brushed Finn's as he was extracting the larger tourniquet from the kit. The Combat Application Tourniquet was the best he could have hoped for. This was a well-equipped emergency kit. Sophie grabbed a smaller tourniquet and other supplies for getting an IV line established.

'We need to get some saline running, don't we?' she murmured. 'It's a high rate needed, isn't it?'

'One point five litres an hour,' Finn responded. 'It's intended to dilute the concentration of myoglobin.'

'I'm going to use Fentanyl rather than morphine for analgesia. That okay with you?'

Finn nodded, aware of a beat of something that had nothing to do with delivering a professional opinion. Sophie had just made him an equal partner in managing this emergency. They had become a team.

'It's exactly what I'd choose. Want a hand with the IV?'

'I'm good. See what you can do with that tourniquet.'

Finn lay on his stomach and reached under the curve of the hull to feel for the top of Ethan's leg. Was there any way he could thread the strap of this tourniquet around it? He could hear Sophie's voice behind him.

'An ambulance has been called, yes?'

'It's on its way but it'll be another twenty minutes.'

'What about the fire service? We need some heavy machinery to shift this boat. Okay, Ethan…little scratch on your arm.'

'Someone's trying to find Mitch. He's got the key to the boat tractor.'

'Try the pub.'

'They are.'

Finn could touch the section of the boat that was on Ethan's legs and sensing the weight above it was shocking. The only good thing was the fact that the small pebbles that made up the beach had shifted as the weight had come down to trap Ethan and his lower leg and part of the upper one was almost buried amongst the pebbles which meant that at least part of the weight had been distributed. Finn scooped at the pebbles with his hand. If he could create a gap, he could get the tourniquet on.

Sophie must have got the IV line in and running and had drawn up the drugs.

'This will make you feel a bit woozy,' she was saying to Ethan, 'but it will help a lot with the pain. Okay...' Her voice got fainter, suggesting that she had turned her head. 'Roll it up, Charlie. If someone else supports his head, you could make a gap in the stones and use it as a pillow.'

Finn had managed to burrow his hand beneath Ethan's thigh. The chill of the wet pebbles was another worry. They needed to try and get one of those oilskin jackets underneath the top of Ethan's body to protect him from hypothermia. It should be possible, given that he had got the end of the tourniquet through what had felt like a solid barrier to start with. He looped it over Ethan's thigh and then had to change his body position so that he could use two hands to thread the Velcro strap through the buckles and then twist the stick to cut off blood supply to the leg. There was no way he could reach the lower leg, despite how he could feel his own body sinking into the pebbles with his movement.

As he pushed backwards to get out from under the hull, he saw that someone had made a pillow from a woollen jersey and removed enough pebbles to put it under Ethan's head.

'I've got an idea,' he said.

'What's that?' Sophie was reaching under the layer of coats over Ethan to stick ECG electrodes to his chest. This was good. When they managed to release their patient from this weight, they were going to have to keep a very close eye on his cardiac rhythm.

'We could try digging him out. This boat's not going to sink any further. If we could make a channel we could get him clear.' He looked up at the group of men who were circling this scene, varying levels of fear evident in every face. 'Have you got any shovels? Buckets?'

'Plenty of buckets,' someone nodded. 'And we can use our hands if we can't find enough shovels. Let's go…'

The sound of boots crunching in the pebbles was louder than the waves rolling in behind them but it didn't cover snatches of the men's voices.

'Good thinking, Doc. You're the man…'

'My boat's closest. I've got a shovel somewhere and a lot of buckets.'

The trouble with digging a hole in small pebbles was that the sides of the hole collapsed inwards, but nothing was going to stop this group of men now that they'd been given something to do that might help. They formed a chain, with those closest to the boat frantically digging and scooping stones into the buckets that were then passed down the chain and emptied well away from the boat.

Finn stayed beside Sophie, monitoring Ethan's blood pressure, breathing and heart rhythm and the level of pain control. They were working together seamlessly, he realised, but he was also aware that they were part of a much larger team now. It felt as if they had an entire village working with them and everybody was intent on helping one of their own.

Saving Charlie's lad.

And it was astonishing. Heart-warming. Enough to exorcise the ghosts of another village, in fact, that had closed ranks against Finn and made him a less valuable member of his community than his brother had been. In much the same way that Sophie's family seemed to be the kind of family that he could have only dreamed of having himself, this village had a similarly genuine— and very caring—heart.

He could never take Ellie and Emma away from a place like this.

It was taking too long.

The ambulance arrived but there was nothing more that the crew could do for Ethan than was already being done and, as doctors, Sophie and Finn were in charge of this scene, anyway.

Or Finn was, to be more accurate. It felt as though she was assisting him rather than the other way around. He knew what he was doing. He'd even come up with the brilliant idea of attempting to extricate Ethan instead of waiting for further help to arrive.

No. It didn't quite feel like that, either.

It felt like they were a team. Totally synchronised, to the point that they could anticipate what each other was thinking. And together they had a very real chance of saving young Ethan.

The crunch came as Mitch finally hooked his trac-

tor up to the stricken boat with a chain, and enough of
a channel through the stones had been dug to mean that
the movement of the hull had far less chance of causing
any further damage to Ethan's body. A fire engine was
on the scene now as well, which meant that she and Finn
could focus completely on their patient.

And they needed to.

As a successful conclusion to the extrication drew
near, they were administering various drugs, including
nebulised salbutamol and IV glucose to counteract the
effect of toxins being released from crushed tissue as the
weight was removed.

But Ethan's condition was deteriorating rapidly, even
as the cheer of the men was fading as he was finally
pulled clear. He was pale and sweating and his level of
consciousness was dropping.

'Sodium bicarbonate.' Finn handed Sophie a syringe.
'Slow push over one minute. I've got the calcium chloride to go next but we need a good flush between them.'

Maybe the protection of the tourniquet had been too
late to prevent the release of enough toxins to be dangerous or the action of the drugs to protect cardiac cells
from the effect of too much potassium hadn't kicked in
enough yet. They both saw the rhythm on the screen of
the life-pack change.

'QRS complexes are widening,' Finn said quietly. 'At
this rate, we're not far away from getting a sine wave.'

Which meant that ventricular fibrillation and asystole
were imminent. Had they succeeded in getting Ethan free
only to have him die in front of his father and the whole
fishing community?

Had Finn seen the flash of fear in her eyes? His gaze
held hers for only a split second but she could read his

determination. He wasn't going to let that happen if there was anything he could do about it.

'Draw up another dose of sodium bicarbonate.' His voice was terse. 'And calcium chloride.' He nodded at one of the paramedics. 'We need to make sure that salbutamol is continuous. And we need to transport him as soon as possible.'

They did. Dialysis was the best and quickest way to remove excess potassium from the blood. And a well-equipped emergency department was where they needed to be to manage cardiac or renal failure, as well as the injuries to Ethan's legs. He was going to need orthopaedic surgery. Intensive care was going to be essential as well. Crush injury syndrome was something that could evolve over hours or even days. They needed the biggest hospital available and that meant a longer trip to get to Truro rather than Penzance.

There was no way that Sophie was going to let Ethan get transported without the benefit of advanced medical supervision. Finn was clearly the doctor who needed to accompany him in the ambulance but this was one of her patients. She'd been treating Ethan for various ailments and injuries since she'd first come back to work in her father's practice. And she'd known Charlie for ever—as a small child, her mother had taken her to Charlie's boat every week to buy fresh fish.

'Let's go.' Finn straightened up from adjusting the mask on Ethan's face. 'You're coming too, yes?'

'Yes.' Sophie turned to the nearest man in the silent, sombre crowd that was still watching what was happening. 'Could someone follow the ambulance, please, and bring Charlie to the hospital? And let my dad know where I am? He'll still be finishing the afternoon clinic.'

It was a tense ride, under lights and siren, to get Ethan to the most appropriate emergency department but any relief about getting access to the best care was short-lived. More than once, over the next few hours, it looked as if they were going to lose this young man. Sophie could only wait, sometimes in a private room with Charlie, and then Ethan's mother when she arrived, and sometimes standing in the corner of the resuscitation area where Finn was being included amongst the various specialists who were being called in to deal with this critical case. Finally, as the hours wore on, he was deemed stable enough to take to Theatre for the first of possibly many surgeries on his legs.

Sophie rang home.

'I'm so sorry, Dad. I hope the clinic patients didn't keep you too late.'

'I've just got home but that doesn't matter. How's Ethan?'

'They've just taken him into Theatre. I have no idea how long it will take. I may end up staying overnight.'

'And Finn? Does he want me to come and get him?'

'He's gone in to Theatre to watch the surgery.' Sophie had to swallow past a lump in her throat. 'He was amazing, Dad—on the beach. I don't know that we would have got this far without him.'

'I'll let your mum know not to bother keeping his dinner warm. And I've had more than one person tell me what a great job he did on the beach. Tell him thanks, Soph. From everybody here.'

'I will.'

It was past midnight by the time Finn came to find Sophie.

'It went as well as it could,' he told her. 'The femur

in his right leg needed grafts and plating and the left leg needed pinning for one of the breaks as well.'

'Is he stable?'

'He's going to need careful management but they seem to be in control of metabolic issues for now. He'll be going to Intensive Care. His parents are with him. They asked me to thank you for everything.'

'I've had the same message for you. From everyone in North Cove, via my dad.'

Finn's smile only underlined the exhaustion she could see in his face. 'And there was I thinking that general practice in a fishing village didn't involve cutting-edge emergency work.'

Sophie had to fight the urge to touch his face; the urge to try and smooth some of those lines of weariness.

'You need to get some sleep, Finn. You're only just back on your feet properly and this has been a marathon.'

It had. Both physically and emotionally.

'I'm getting a taxi back to North Cove,' she added. 'They'll contact me if Ethan's condition changes. Want to share the ride?'

'Sure.' Finn closed his eyes, rubbing at his forehead. 'You're right. I need some sleep. I don't want to get a relapse.'

He actually dozed on the trip back down the coast, but he jerked awake as they reached the village and the taxi slowed and then stopped in front of Sophie's cottage.

'I haven't got a key,' he muttered. 'I don't want to wake your parents up in the middle of the night.'

'The door's never locked.' But Sophie knew how light a sleeper her mother was. She would wake the moment Finn stepped into the house. She'd probably get up and insist on making him tea and toast or something. If So-

phie were a guest in someone's house, she wouldn't want
to disturb them like that, either.

'I've got a spare bed,' she said without thinking.
'Crash there, if you like, and then you can go back in
the morning.'

Finn blinked at her. 'Are you sure?'

Sophie was fishing in her wallet to pay the taxi driver,
so she didn't look up. 'I told my dad that we might be
staying at the hospital all night so they won't think it's
odd,' she told him. She reached for her door catch. 'We're
both exhausted and we're only going to get a few hours'
sleep. If you go home, Mum will insist on feeding you
and you'll get even less sleep.'

She heard Finn's door shut as she opened the door to
her cottage. It wasn't until she closed it after Finn had
stepped inside that it occurred to her she had, possibly,
made a big mistake in making that casual offer.

She kept going into the small living room, where she
flicked on a lamp.

'The kitchen's just through here, if you need anything.'
She turned her head to find Finn right behind her. 'Are
you hungry?' Oh, no, she was as bad as her mother, but
Finn was recuperating, wasn't he? 'You must be. I don't
suppose either of us has had anything to eat since lunchtime…' she checked her watch '…yesterday. How 'bout a
quick cup of tea and some toast or something?'

'Sounds nice.'

The kitchen had never felt quite this small before.
Every move Sophie made, filling the kettle and finding
mugs, getting the loaf of bread out and a serrated knife
from the drawer, meant that she had to work around Finn,
who was standing there waiting to be helpful, and the

awareness of this tall man in her small room was becoming increasingly acute.

Oddly, she didn't feel exhausted any longer.

Whatever it was she *was* feeling seemed to make it impossible to look directly at Finn, even when she handed him the butter and then arranged a row of jam pots beside the breadboard.

'You take milk, don't you?' She hadn't forgotten that first cup of tea she'd made for Finn when he'd first arrived at the clinic.

'Yes, please.'

'Sugar?' She couldn't remember that part. It felt like that first cup of tea had been a lifetime ago.

'Two, thanks.'

What was she doing standing in her kitchen in the middle of the night with a man who was still enough of a stranger for her not to remember whether he wanted sugar in his tea?

'Strawberry or raspberry?' he asked as Sophie finished making the tea.

'Raspberry for me.'

'Mmm… Me, too.' Finn handed Sophie half of a thick slice of toast and then took a huge bite of the other half. Sophie glanced up to see him swiping a smudge of jam off his chin and then sucking it off his finger.

Oh, wow…

Yep. This had been a mistake. That awareness of him had just exploded into something uncontrollable. Her knees actually felt weak as she tore her gaze away from Finn's face. From those fingers… She tried to concentrate on her piece of toast but any appetite for food seemed to have deserted her. It took long enough for her to chew and swallow her mouthful to realise that Finn had stopped eating. That he was watching her.

And this time, when her gaze met his, there was no chance of pulling it away.

Clearly, Sophie hadn't been the only one to be aware of that explosion and how it seemed to have sucked all the oxygen out of this small room. Not that the lack was important just yet, because the sheer intensity of the look in Finn's eyes made it impossible to draw in a breath, anyway.

'You've got a bit of jam,' Finn murmured. 'Just there…'

His thumb was on the corner of her mouth and Sophie felt her lips parting as it brushed her lower lip. She still couldn't look away from the intense glow of Finn's stare so she saw the moment when those embers caught and flared into something even brighter.

'Ohh…' The sound coming from low in Finn's throat was one of raw need. Or maybe defeat? Had he been trying to ignore what had sparked between them just as hard as she had? *'Sophie…'*

She let her eyes drift shut as she saw him bending his head. From the first touch of his lips on hers, the rest of the world ceased to exist. The attraction had been there almost right from the start, hadn't it? Simmering away…

And now it had boiled over into something she couldn't hope to control.

She didn't want to.

The thrill of this had teased at her mind and body from that first awareness. This was something she'd never expected to experience and possibly never would again. Was it so wrong just to give in and let it carry her away?

Not that she had a choice. She knew that, from the first caress of Finn's tongue tangling with her own. From the way her body was catching fire under the stroke of the hand that was cradling her head and then ran down her back to shape her buttocks and draw her closer to his body.

Except she did have a choice. Because, as those mugs of tea lost the last of their warmth, Finn finally drew back.

'Do you want this?' The words were no more than a whisper. 'As much as I do?'

'*Yes...*' The word came from a place Sophie didn't even recognise. In a tone she'd never heard before. 'I do...'

CHAPTER SEVEN

WHAT HAD SHE DONE?

Made things a whole lot more complicated, that was what. Harder than they needed to be, that was for sure, and that had already been quite hard enough.

What was wrong with her? Sophie had broken so many rules. The rules that had had to become iron-clad in order to help her put her life back together over the last few years, like staying away from anything—or anyone—that could interfere with her focus on her career and keeping a safe distance from children or babies. Men hadn't even been on her radar, but there were older rules, too—like not having unprotected sex.

She should be feeling very remorseful this morning, Sophie thought as she wound her way up the hill towards the clinic. Ashamed of herself, even. And, given the intense stress of yesterday's incident and the almost total lack of sleep since, walking up this hill should feel as if she was pushing her legs through treacle.

But Sophie was feeling none of those things.

Her feet felt oddly light as they carried her towards her working day.

She wasn't worried about the remote possibility of an unwanted pregnancy because it was the safest part of her cycle. They had both dismissed any risk of an STD at the time as they had both confessed how long it had been since either of them had been involved with anyone.

Even the most astonishing loss of control, in letting someone so close, wasn't going to be a problem. Sophie had planned to talk to Finn this morning and let him know that it couldn't happen again but, when she'd tip-toed into her room just before she left, he'd still been so deeply asleep, she hadn't had the heart to wake him.

If she was really honest with herself, though, that topic of conversation hadn't been on her mind when she'd entered the room. She'd taken in the bare leg poking out of tangled sheets and the hand lying palm-upwards on the pillow with those long, elegant fingers loosely curled. Her body had instantly reminded her of what the touch of that hand could do to her and all she'd wanted to do was crawl back into that bed.

And then her gaze had caught on Finn's face. It had been a little pale, hardly surprising after how hard he'd pushed himself yesterday, and that had accentuated the dark shadow of his jaw, but it was the vulnerability of his sleeping face that had caught her heart. She could almost see the little boy he had once been. Had his mother ever gone into his bedroom and felt this kind of squeeze on her heart when she'd seen the sweep of those dark lashes on his cheeks, or the way the corners of his mouth had a natural tilt, as if he was always ready to smile? A little piece of Sophie's heart was breaking as she decided that it was quite likely that it had been his brother that had received the lion's share of that kind of love.

That had been her wake-up call. Finn Connelly, with that fierce independence that branded him a loner and gave him an edge of danger, was not a man who wanted the same kind of things in life as she did. With understandable reasons, he had abandoned his family, and Outback Australia was the perfect place for him. Sophie had no doubt that his desire to return there would strongly influence any decisions he was going to make about the future of his nieces. Even if he decided to stay, he would be giving up what he really wanted.

Yes, the sex had been every bit as thrilling as she'd imagined it could be, but that was as far as it went. She was not about to let him break her heart and that meant that what had unexpectedly happened last night could not be allowed to happen again. It was one thing to give in to temptation and dip her toe into dangerous waters. It would be stupid to jump in any deeper and go swimming in a current like that. If she got tempted again—and she knew she would—Sophie just needed to remember the way she'd felt when she had looked at Finn's sleeping face, and that would be more than enough of a warning.

The image of his face was filling her mind again now, even as she smiled at Maureen Redding who was standing by her gate up the street, in her dressing gown and slippers. Sophie realised that what she was really feeling, in the aftermath of those extraordinary few hours with Finn, was gratitude.

She'd been so shocked when she'd realised how attracted she was to Finn in the first place but she'd recognised that the ability to feel that attraction was a sign that her future was opening up to new possibilities. What had happened last night had shown her that she was more than ready for that new future. That she'd been missing having someone in her life—and her bed—far more than she'd ever let herself admit.

The sex had been unbelievably good. The warmth

of someone beside her as she'd drifted into a very brief sleep, the weight of the arm holding her close, the sound of another person breathing and, perhaps most of all, the awareness of another heart beating beneath her cheek had been even better. It had been poignant enough for Sophie to realise just how lonely she'd been for so long. This wasn't about Finn in particular but about having a partner in life.

Finn would never know what he'd given her but it felt like a priceless gift, despite any complications that might arise in the future. Sophie felt truly alive again. She felt like her real self, and not just the image she'd created to convince the world that she was okay.

'I heard about young Ethan,' Maureen called as Sophie got closer. 'How is he?'

'He had surgery last night,' Sophie told her. 'No news is good news for the moment.'

'How fortunate it was that that young man who's staying with your parents was there. That he's a *doctor*…'

'Yes…' Sophie kept moving. 'I need to get to work, Maureen. I'm running late. How's that cough?'

'Oh, much better, thanks, love. The antibiotics did the trick.'

'Is he here about the job at the clinic?' Maureen's voice followed Sophie. 'Dr Connelly?'

'No. He's just visiting.'

'What a shame… You could do with someone like that in North Cove.'

Oh, no… That coy note in Maureen's voice told Sophie that conversations between villagers hadn't just toyed with the idea of a new doctor for the community. A handsome male newcomer was interesting for a very different reason. Maureen undoubtedly knew that he wasn't travelling alone, either. That Finn Connelly represented a ready-made family, in fact.

It wasn't just the pressure, albeit unspoken, from her parents that Sophie might have to contend with now. Her feet felt heavier as she climbed the steps to the clinic's front door. Had she really thought that a bright new future was within her grasp? A flash of something like panic made it feel as if the walls of her life were starting to close in on her. She was becoming trapped. If she wanted to break free and gain control, she had a battle ahead of her.

Even more alarmingly, Sophie had no idea exactly what it was she was fighting for.

What had he done?

For a heartbeat, as Finn woke up, he had no idea where he was.

And then he pulled in a breath and he could smell the scent on his pillow. His fingers flexed and his skin tingled as he relived the touch of the woman who'd left the trace of a scent that was delicious.

Even before he'd opened his eyes, however, he realised that he was alone in this bed.

Abandoned...

Sophie hadn't even woken him to say that she was leaving?

Had something happened? Had he slept through a call, perhaps, that Ethan's condition had deteriorated? Wide awake now, Finn glanced at his watch and was horrified to find it was so late in the morning. Almost lunchtime. He'd never slept in like this, no matter how physically exhausted he'd been.

But then he'd never had a physical release like the one

he'd experienced last night, had he? His breath came out with a soft groan as he closed his eyes again for a moment. He'd suspected that making love to Sophie Bradford would be something special, but he'd never known that sex could be *that* good. Mind-blowing.

Or was it simply because it had been so long since he'd been with someone? And that the sexual tension had been simmering between him and Sophie for long enough to result in something so explosive? Not that it mattered. It had been incredible but had also been a one-off. It had to be. This whole situation was quite complicated enough as it was.

Maybe Sophie was thinking along the same lines and that was why she'd left this morning without waking him?

The thought was reassuring but he still needed to talk to her. Finn looked at his watch again as he sat up and pushed the bedcovers back. They'd take a lunch break at the clinic, wouldn't they? Maybe he could catch Sophie for a brief private conversation.

Any hope of that happening, however, faded when he pushed open the door to North Cove's medical centre half an hour later. Or, rather, tried to push it open and then had to wait for whoever was leaning against it to move so that he could step into a waiting room that was so packed that several people were standing. Someone was coughing with what sounded like a nasty dose of bronchitis, a baby was crying and a telephone was ringing. The young woman behind the reception desk was looking flustered as she reached to answer it.

'No, I'm sorry, Gary,' he heard her say. 'Unless it's an absolute emergency there's no hope of an appointment today—with either of the doctors.'

Jack appeared in the doorway behind a patient who was buttoning her coat.

'Stuart?' he called. 'Come on through.' He saw Finn heading towards the desk. 'You're back,' he said. 'How's Ethan doing this morning?'

Fortunately, Finn didn't have to admit that he hadn't just come from the hospital and had no idea of Ethan's current condition, because the receptionist interrupted.

'Dr Greene? I've got Joanne Coombs' son on the phone. He's really worried about his mother. Could you have a word?' She stood up to lean over the counter and hand the phone to Jack.

A large man, presumably Stuart, who had the next appointment, was standing behind Finn now and the woman who had just buttoned her coat was trying to get past. When another patient came from the direction of the consulting rooms, with Sophie not far behind him, the knot of people made the space feel totally overcrowded. It was a situation that could turn into chaos at any moment.

'Gary? What's happening?'

'Excuse me, but I need to get through…'

'Have you called an ambulance?'

'No worries, pet. I'll just wait for the doctor over here.'

As the woman edged past, Finn suddenly had a clear line of vision towards Sophie and the imminent chaos around him was forgotten for a moment as she caught his gaze. He saw the way she went still with the surprise of seeing him and the slow blink, as if she was having difficulty pushing aside a distraction that she didn't need. Finn could understand that difficulty. Just that instant of eye contact and he couldn't think of anything other than what had happened between them a few hours ago.

'Okay, Gary... I'm on my way.' Jack handed the phone back to the receptionist and turned towards Sophie.

'I've got to go,' he said. 'It's Joanne. She's having trouble breathing. The ambulance is on its way but I need to take her some oxygen. Have we got a full cylinder somewhere?'

'In the treatment room. Ask Liz.' Sophie's gaze was roaming the crowded waiting room and then it came back to Finn. 'Are you okay?' she asked. 'Did you need any help?'

'I think it's you that needs the help,' he said. 'How 'bout a locum for the day?'

'Bless you.' Jack's hand squeezed Finn's shoulder. 'That's exactly what we need.'

The waiting room grew curiously quiet as Sophie whisked Finn away to set him up in Jack's consulting room and give him the password for the computer. She caught the wave of curiosity and knew exactly what everybody would be talking about in the next few minutes. That Finn was the doctor who'd saved young Ethan's life on the beach yesterday. That, maybe, he was even considering taking the vacant position on North Cove's medical team. There would certainly be no problem with people being reluctant to see someone they didn't know.

'You're going to be popular,' she warned Finn. 'You might have to be firm to get people to talk about themselves instead of trying to find out about you.'

'I'll cope. How do I access their files on the computer?'

'I'm afraid we're not digital yet for past histories. We've made a start but there's never enough time to make much progress. Marion will have their files on her desk and give them to you when they're called. The prescription pads are here…and referral forms and blood work ones are here. Liz can take bloods, test urine and do a twelve-lead ECG if needed. Just come and find me if you have any questions.'

'Okay.'

But Sophie hesitated for a moment. 'Are you sure you want to do this? I'm pretty sure it's not what you came here for.'

He caught her gaze and, for a long moment, their silent communication had nothing to do with stepping in to help with the workload of a family practitioner. It was all about what had happened last night and there was something sombre in Finn's expression.

'You're right,' he said quietly. 'It's not what I came here for. I think we need to talk.'

Sophie swallowed hard. She pushed away a flutter of something that felt like…hope? A tiny bubble of some kind of teenage fantasy that Finn was going to tell her that he'd fallen madly in love with her last night and now realised he couldn't live without her?

Totally absurd. As if she'd even *want* something like that to happen. The stability of the life she had created for herself was already under quite enough of a threat.

But she nodded briskly. 'Of course.'

It would have to be a very private conversation and that couldn't happen until every patient and the other staff members were long gone. It would be easier, though, to avoid it altogether.

'I'll cope,' she added as she led Finn back towards the waiting room. 'You can change your mind at any time.'

His voice was right behind her shoulder. 'I've made the decision, Sophie. I won't change my mind.'

And he didn't, even as the afternoon wore on and the waiting room never seemed to get much emptier. Sophie tapped on his door at one point, when she knew he was alone, writing up his notes on his last patient.

'Take a few minutes' break,' she suggested. 'You've missed lunch again. Liz has made some cheese on toast in the kitchen and there's fresh coffee.'

'Sounds great. I'll just finish this.'

'How's it going?'

'So far, an ear infection, chest infection, UTI, sprained wrist and a cut that needed a couple of stitches.' Finn was still writing as he spoke. 'Oh, and two sore throats. I've taken swabs but I suspect it's viral.'

Was it her imagination or did Finn sound as if he was finding general practice just as boring as he had imagined it would be?

'And you were right, I'm getting a lot of personal questions. Like whether I like it here. Whether my wife is planning to join me and the children. And if it's true that I might be taking the job.'

'Sorry about that.'

'Not a problem. It's quite flattering, really. I'm surprised that everyone seems to know every detail about what happened on the beach yesterday. They're all worried about Ethan.'

'We're a small community. You can tell them he's doing well. Dad went to see him after getting Joanne Coombs settled into the cardiology ward. He said he's awake, not in too much pain and very happy to be alive.'

'Metabolic issues?'

'Under control. Improving. They've changed his status from critical to stable.'

'Good to hear.' Finn scribbled something swiftly and

then dropped his pen, using his hand instead to push his fingers through his hair.

Instantly, Sophie lost track of what she talking about. She wanted to step further into the room and smooth the tousled mess he'd just made of his hair. And then he looked up and she forgot about his hair as her gaze slid to take in his whole face. The intensity of those dark eyes, that strong nose and even the touch of her gaze on his lips instantly took her mind somewhere else entirely. Back to the moment last night when she'd seen him wipe that smudge of jam off his chin and suck it off his finger and that explosion of desire had detonated.

She saw the flash of surprise in Finn's eyes and, just for a heartbeat, she knew it was hanging there between them again. That desire. And then it vanished, like a switch being flicked off, and it was so conclusive that she knew they must have both hit that switch at exactly the same moment. He got to his feet.

'Cheese on toast, you said?'

'I did. Enjoy. I'd better get back to work. I'm not sure what time we'll get finished but Mum texted to say that she'd be keeping your dinner warm.'

'That's very kind of her. I guess it won't matter how late I am, then.'

The raised eyebrow was a reminder that he still wanted to have that private chat. Sophie turned away.

'No. It won't matter at all.'

It was nearly seven p.m. when Sophie locked the waiting room door as their last patient left. Liz and Marion had left at six p.m., so now it was just herself and Finn who were left. She flicked out the lights in the clinic's reception area and then went to turn out the light in her consulting room. She had taken the last patient for the day, so Finn was probably still in Jack's room writing up his notes. Or maybe he was in the kitchen. She felt her heart rate pick up as she realised she couldn't avoid that conversation any longer and her mouth went curiously dry. She wasn't really procrastinating, she told herself as she headed for her consulting room. She needed to shut down the computer and turn those lights off as well.

Finn was in her room, sitting in the same chair as when she'd brought him in here that first night. The other chair was behind her desk this time but the prospect of a solid barrier between them now seemed wrong and Sophie hesitated for a moment, taking her time to close the door. Finn solved the problem as she turned back by getting to his feet. He took a step towards her and Sophie thought he was going to keep moving. To come close enough to take her in his arms and kiss her.

And, God help her, but she wanted him to do exactly that…

But he stopped and the distance between them suddenly felt like miles instead of inches. She saw his chest move as he took in a deep breath and his Adam's apple bobbed as he swallowed.

'Before I say anything else,' he said. 'I have to tell you that last night was…well…it was amazing.'

Who knew it could be so hard to swallow when your mouth was this dry? Sophie had to lick her lips before she could respond.

'It was.' The words came out in no more than a whisper. 'But…' She was holding his gaze and then they both spoke at the same time.

'It can't happen again…'

For an even longer moment, they kept staring at each

other. It was Finn who began to smile first, a wry twist of his lips that Sophie mirrored unconsciously.

'Who's going to say it first?' she murmured.

'Say what?'

'"It's not you, it's me…"'

Finn's smile faded. 'That's true.'

Sophie nodded. 'For me, too. As much as I like you, Finn, I'm nowhere near ready for any kind of a relationship.'

'And I'm in no position to offer one.'

'I know. You want to get back to the job you love. And I don't imagine that that kind of lifestyle lends itself to making commitments.' She tried to lighten the suddenly heavy atmosphere in the room by adopting a teasing tone. 'I guess you want to get away even more now, after a day of being bored by general practice.'

'It wasn't boring,' Finn said. 'And, even in the busiest A&Es I've worked in, we get our share of the mundane. I had a patient once who turned up because he'd torn a fingernail. If anything, it's made me think that maybe I won't sign up again for the Flying Doctors. I *could* change my job.'

Okay…this really was a flash of hope this time. Was Finn considering being a general practitioner? Staying in North Cove?

'Being in that emergency department yesterday while Ethan was being stabilised reminded me of how much I loved that kind of work,' he continued. 'I could easily go back to a position like that. With set shifts and hours so that my life was simpler.'

'Why would you do that?'

'Because it would be possible to raise the twins that way. With the help of a nanny, of course.'

Sophie's jaw dropped. She hadn't expected this.

Didn't want it...

'You want to take them away? You'd sacrifice the job you love so much for them?'

'I love them now, too,' Finn said simply. 'They're my nieces. The only family I have. It's not just that I feel like I owe it to Sean. I want to protect them, to watch them grow up. To make sure that they know how much they're loved.'

'But they'd be loved here. My parents adore them already.' To her astonishment, Sophie realised that her decision had already been made. She would fight for this if she had to. 'You'd be taking them away from their grandparents,' she added.

'They could visit,' Finn countered. 'We could visit. There are countless children who grow up with their grandparents living somewhere else. And, even though I love Australia as a place to live, that doesn't necessarily mean that I have to go back to the other side of the world. There are plenty of hospitals in the UK where I wouldn't have difficulty getting a job in an ED.'

Sophie had to blink back the prickle behind her eyes. 'You'd be taking them away from *me*...'

'I know...' Finn was silent for a moment. His gaze slid away from hers. 'That's the point...'

He thought he had to take these children away from her? That hurt way more than the idea that he didn't want to sleep with her more than once.

Finn looked at her again and the intensity felt bruising. 'I grew up with a mother who was emotionally distant,' he said quietly. 'I know how damaging that can be.'

He was right. Sophie had been protecting her heart,

keeping a safe distance, even though she knew how adorable these children were. *Her* children.

'I'm trying,' she whispered. 'I think I'm getting there…'

'But you would have to be absolutely sure,' Finn said
quietly. 'You'd have to fall in love with Ellie and Emma
to the point that you wanted to spend the rest of your life
with them in it. So that you couldn't imagine not having
them in your life, and they would become more important
than anything else—even a job that you love.'

Had that happened for Finn? It must have, if he was
considering such a huge career change. Sophie could
feel a tight squeeze around her heart. They were lucky
little girls. Imagine having someone like Finn Connelly
to protect them and love them and be part of their lives
for as long as he lived.

She couldn't claim to feel that way. Not yet, anyway.
It was hovering but she wasn't yet quite capable of letting go and committing herself.

That prickle became uncontrollable. Sophie felt a fat
tear escape and roll down the side of her nose. Her voice
didn't sound like her own at all.

'I'm scared…'

'I know…'

Finn closed the gap between them and put his arms
around Sophie. 'I know,' he said again. 'It's hard. Very
scary. But we have to know that we're doing the best
thing for Ellie and Emma.'

And that could mean that it would be better for them
if they weren't living with—or very close to—their biological mother.

'We've got a bit of time,' Finn said then. 'I don't have
to make any big decisions just yet. Until I'm sure. Until
we're *both* sure. How 'bout I keep doing this?'

What…holding her like this? Making her feel as if, somehow, everything was going to turn out okay? Right now, Sophie didn't want to be anywhere else. He could keep doing this for as long as he wanted.

'Your dad's tired,' Finn added. 'I could give him a break by carrying on as your locum for a while. A week or two, perhaps? Until you find his replacement. You have someone to interview pretty soon, don't you?'

Sophie nodded, her face rubbing against the soft wool of the jumper Finn was wearing.

'In the meantime, I could start looking at some new job options that wouldn't be so far away. That will give me a chance to weigh up the pros and cons of living here rather than in Australia.' His arms tightened around her. 'What do you think?'

Sophie looked up but couldn't find any words to thank him for giving her what felt like a reprieve. Time…

Maybe she didn't have to say anything. They were on this journey together, deciding the future of two small girls, and it felt, in this moment, as if they were making a pact to do what was right, no matter how hard it was.

And then the moment changed as if, having made that pact, it could be put aside for now. And suddenly the moment became about *them*, rather than the girls, her parents or anybody else in the universe. It became infused with memories of being in each other's arms without the barrier of any clothing, but it wasn't about sex, either. It was about being as close as possible to another human being.

Even when Finn kissed her, it didn't inflame desire. It was a slow, gentle, poignant kiss that pierced Sophie's heart.

She honestly didn't know whether she was going to fall in love with Ellie and Emma in the way Finn had but she knew she was in very real danger of falling in love with their uncle.

It was Sophie who broke the kiss and turned away. It couldn't happen. She couldn't deal with that kind of heartbreak again. Finn Connelly wasn't in a position to offer a relationship and she knew that that wasn't just because of his career preferences. He would never commit himself because he had learned never to trust.

'Let's go and find that dinner Mum's keeping warm,' she said, opening the door and waiting for Finn to go through. 'It's Thursday so it's probably my favourite.'

'What's that?' Finn turned his head, his eyebrows raised and a smile playing around his lips.

'Shepherd's pie.'

But Sophie wasn't thinking about dinner as she followed Finn's tall shape through the gate and into the garden. She was thinking about that smile. About how it had felt to be held in this man's arms. About the kind of man who'd change his whole life for the sake of two orphaned children.

She couldn't fall in love with Finn Connelly. It just couldn't be allowed to happen.

But, deep down, she had the disturbing realisation that it might well have already happened.

CHAPTER EIGHT

Pros and cons.

There were always two sides to any coin. Sometimes it was easy to see that one side outweighed the other so much that a decision was a no-brainer but, for big, life-changing decisions, it was rarely that easy. Even when you took emotions out of the equation there were shades of grey that meant that whether something was actually a pro or a con could change depending on attitude.

Take being a general practitioner instead of an emergency department specialist, for example. Finn would have headed a list of cons with the boredom factor but, after a few days of working in North Cove's medical centre, he had to admit that it had positive elements. As a GP, he was in a unique position to identify what could be the first signs and symptoms of a serious problem.

Did that last patient, Brian Taylor, who was complaining about fatigue and other mild symptoms such as intermittent pins and needles in his feet, have a problem that could be flagged as nothing to worry about unless it got worse or could he be showing the first signs of something like multiple sclerosis, muscular dystrophy or lupus?

And what about the woman he'd seen earlier, with her abdominal symptoms? Diagnosing celiac disease in its early stages could make a huge difference to someone's life. Diagnosing cancer early could save a life. Not as dramatically as resuscitating a trauma victim in the ER, maybe, but it was still meaningful. Worthwhile.

Something on the pro list in a practice like this was how well the histories of patients were known. Finn found Sophie in the kitchen as the morning clinic ended.

'What did Brian Taylor come in for today?' she asked.

'He's feeling fatigued. Having trouble concentrating. He's noticed some paraesthesia at times as well. His wife made him make an appointment.'

'That doesn't surprise me. Brian avoids doctors like the plague. I saw him once when he wanted a better bandage for his sprained ankle. Turned out he'd been walking around with a fracture for days.'

'So he's likely to downplay any symptoms, then?'

'The fact that he turned up at all probably means he's really worried.'

'I've given him a thorough examination and taken bloods. I didn't find any red flags, like optic neuritis, but...'

'You've just got a feeling that there might be something more going on?'

'Yeah...' Finn was frowning as he reached for a coffee mug. 'He's going to come back to talk about the results but I might refer him to a neurologist.' He shook his head. 'Walked round for days with a fractured ankle, huh?'

'He's a fisherman. They're tough guys.'

Sophie smiled at him and Finn was suddenly aware of another pro that applied to this particular general practice. He liked knowing that Sophie was working in the same place and that there were frequent occasions when their paths would cross or moments like this when they could share information about patients. Sophie, and especially her dad, knew pretty much everyone in this community and it gave them a connection to their patients that you'd never get anywhere else.

In an emergency department, and even more so working with the Flying Doctors, it was still possible to get involved with patients—with their stories and their families—and feel a connection to them but it was always a brief encounter. They got treated, transferred to the care of others and then they were gone. In a community like this, they were never gone. You'd see them again in the street or the post office. You'd see them again and again as patients over the course of the years, and you'd probably know about things that might have never otherwise been apparent.

Like a high pain threshold and an aversion to medical intervention.

But there was a con here as well. Because there was so much more than a purely professional appreciation of this temporary colleague.

He knew Sophie's story. He knew how courageous she was. How loyal. How good she was at her job and how much she cared about her patients.

He knew what it was like to be allowed even closer. He knew what the secret curves of her body felt like and how delicious the scent and taste of that body was.

And, heaven help him, but it was proving impossible to dampen the escalation of desire to be with her again, even though they'd both decided that that couldn't happen. That it had been a 'one-off'—merely the result of a strong initial attraction coupled with the aftermath of an intense event they had shared, made harder to resist with exhaustion thrown into the mix.

Sophie's smile was fading but Finn couldn't bring himself to break the eye contact. The silence between them was full of something unspoken but so loud it was deafening.

I still want you...

Me, too... Even more than before...

He could actually feel himself swaying towards Sophie. His fingers released the handle of the mug, ready to be lifted and weave themselves into those glorious curls of her hair. To cradle her head so that he could focus on covering her lips with his own...

'Ah, there you are...'

Finn's head jerked back at the sound of Marion's voice.

'Could you fit Jenny Thompson in this afternoon, Sophie? I know you've got a full list but Shirley just rang. They were at the park and Jenny was pushing one of the girls in a swing and she seems to have twisted her back or something. Shirley wants to bring her in and just get it checked.'

'No problem. Dad should be back from his house calls soon and he won't mind giving up part of his afternoon off if we get too busy.'

Finn's sideways glance as he spooned coffee into his mug revealed that Sophie's cheeks were rather pink, perhaps with the effort of having dragged herself back into a professional reality from that spiral of desire that could have had them kissing each other senseless with no thought to their surroundings or any consequences. Had Marion noticed anything when she'd come into the kitchen? Surely she couldn't have been unaware of the electric atmosphere that she had interrupted, but if she had been aware she was covering it well.

'I'll let her know. And then I'm heading out for lunch

with Liz. Want me to bring you guys back a sandwich or pie or something?' She lifted an eyebrow. 'Maybe you'd like to come with us? You haven't tried Joe's Shack yet, have you, Finn?'

'I'm good,' he said. 'I've got a bit of reading I want to do.'

'And I'm good too, thanks, Marion,' Sophie said. 'I'll get something later.'

Marion shook her head. 'You need to eat. There's bread on the counter. Have a bit of toast, at least.'

Alone again, Finn didn't dare catch Sophie's gaze. Just that mention of toast was enough to take him back to being in her kitchen the other night, and every cell in his body was suddenly reminded of what had happened after he'd touched the corner of Sophie's mouth to wipe away that smudge of jam.

'There's probably some cheese left in the fridge, too.' Sophie's voice sounded a little strained. 'Fancy some cheese on toast?'

Like Liz had produced the other day? The day when he'd had that conversation with Sophie about how important it was that the needs of Ellie and Emma had to come above everything else, including the complication of finding himself so attracted to their biological mother?

'I'm not hungry,' he murmured. He wasn't even thirsty any more, he realised. 'I'll go and finish my notes on Brian. There's an article I remember reading a while back on the early signs that can easily be misdiagnosed for diseases like multiple sclerosis. I think I might dig it out again online.'

Sophie stayed in the clinic's small kitchen for some time after Finn had left, grateful for a familiar quiet space.

She needed a moment to grapple with what had happened a few minutes ago. There they'd been, just having the kind of conversation about one of their patients—like she'd had with her father a million times—and something had snapped.

If Marion had come into the kitchen a few seconds later, Sophie had no doubt that she would have caught her kissing Finn. Worse, her father could have returned from his house calls and found them locked in each other's arms, oblivious to the world around them.

Did she really think she had things under control?

For the last few days, it had felt like that. Everybody had been delighted about Finn's offer to be their locum for a little while. Her father had cut his hours at the clinic and he was enjoying doing house calls and then spending more time at home with Judy and the twins. Sophie was spending more time with the girls as well, by heading back to her childhood home for dinner every evening. She was relaxing more in their company. Enjoying it, even, but who wouldn't? They were delightful children.

But it still felt as if they were someone else's children. More and more as if they were Finn's children, in fact. Like last night, when she'd arrived much later than Finn, and her mother had sent her upstairs.

'See how Finn's coping,' she'd said. 'Those girls can make a bit of a mess when they're having their bath.'

The main bathroom of the house was warm, steamy and smelt of strawberries. The quantity of bubble bath that had been used had clearly been generous and all Sophie could see of the twins was their heads and shoulders poking above the layer of foam. Finn was kneeling beside the bathtub, shirtsleeves rolled up, putting final touches to a cone of foam on the top of Emma's head. Ellie already had one that was starting drooping badly.

'There you go, munchkin,' he said. 'Now you've got a hat, too.'

Ellie giggled. She took handfuls of foam as she tried to stand up and reach for Finn's head. '*Your* turn,' she shouted.

But she slipped and would have fallen if Finn hadn't caught her slippery little body. She was still giggling as he lifted her from the tub, turning to grab a towel, which was when he spotted Sophie in the doorway.

'Uh-oh… I think dinner's ready and we're not.' But he was still grinning as he wrapped Ellie in a towel, and she could tell he had been enjoying this as much as the children. That smile lit up his face. He had damp patches all over his shirt that were making it cling to his body and he looked utterly gorgeous. As if he'd been born to be a father and was loving every minute of it. And, just for a moment, it felt as if Sophie could be part of it as well. She had a big grin on her face as Finn spoke to her.

'Could you catch that other slippery little fish for me?'

'No…' Emma slid towards the taps. 'I want *you* to catch me…'

Of course she did. Finn was as much a part of their lives as her parents now were. With a beat that was an odd mix of relief and crushing disappointment, Sophie realised she was still no more than a visitor.

The pull to be more than that was definitely there—in spades. Wanting to be a real part of something like this bath time—like this little family—was squeezing her heart until it felt as if it could burst but, however hard she was pushing against that barrier, it wasn't about to break. Maybe it never would, and although there was relief to be found there, because that meant she would never have her heart totally broken again, at the same time it *was* heart-breaking that it wasn't going to happen. It was conflicting, totally confusing and Sophie had to try hard to find a genuine smile.

'How 'bout I find your jammies instead?' she said.

She discovered later that Finn had also taken over reading the twins their bedtime stories and he seemed completely at home with her parents. More at home than Sophie did that evening, which was really weird. Even being in a place she knew and loved, such as the kitchen of this house, eating food that was just as familiar and loved, she was feeling as much of a visitor as she had in the bathroom. That she wasn't really a part of this new family group. She'd been on the other side of a window, looking in.

Now, as Sophie stood in the clinic's kitchen and pushed away those disturbing memories of yesterday evening, she could still feel that invisible barrier that she wanted to break through so much but couldn't. Had scar tissue hardened her heart to the point where she would never be able to feel the kind of love she had felt for Matt and their unborn baby?

It felt as if she was in love with Finn, but how much of that was simply a physical thing? And, even if it wasn't, he was part of a package and he wasn't going to allow her to be a part of it unless she could offer Ellie and Emma her whole heart. It was possible that she could do that if she could break through that barrier but, if she did, what then? Would she have a man in her life that she was in love with but would never feel the same way? Finn had his own barriers and he might not even want to try and break them. He had deliberately put distance between

them after that intense moment in this space earlier. Was
he sitting in his consulting room, as aware of her presence in this building as she was of his?

No. He was probably engrossed in whatever article
he'd wanted to read, focussed on the job he was here to
do for the time being. Maybe not for that much longer, either. The doctor from Glasgow was coming for his interview tomorrow and it sounded as if he was keen to make
a move as soon as possible if the meeting went well. It
was exactly what they'd been hoping would happen for a
long time now, but Sophie was almost wishing it wasn't
happening. Or that this Callum McGregor would decide
that the position wasn't suitable.

The prospect of a permanent change in the clinic was
adding the pressure of a definite end point to the available time to make big decisions and it wasn't helping.

Sophie's life had been tipped upside down in the space
of a few weeks and her head was enough of a mess without any added pressure. She needed more than a few minutes' peace and quiet. She needed…a miracle? Someone
to wave a wand and give everyone a fairy-tale ending.
Finn would miraculously decide that he loved general
practice and North Cove was the place he wanted to be
for the rest of his life. He would fall head-over-heels in
love with her and they would raise the twins as their own.
Her parents could enjoy a very well-deserved retirement,
blessed with adorable grandchildren who would be in
their lives every day.

But right now that seemed as unlikely as any fairy tale
in real life. It was all too complicated. Sophie had the
horrible feeling that somebody was going to end up getting hurt. Finn was in the best position to protect himself
but maybe it would be herself or her parents who would

be the most affected. It just couldn't be allowed to be the case that the twins ended up being more traumatised. At least they were all on the same page about that.

At the sound of someone walking towards the kitchen, Sophie's heart skipped a beat. That she was disappointed that it was her father and not Finn was disturbing. That her father was looking tired and pale—rather like the day he'd had that funny turn—was also a concern. Perhaps even a few hours' work each day was too much for him?

'Sit down, Dad. I'll make you a cup of tea.'

'No thanks, love. I just came to drop my bag. I'll go home and put my feet up.'

'Are you feeling okay?'

'I'm fine. I've just had a difficult conversation with Dorothy Young. She had another fall. Fortunately she didn't injure herself but it was too long until she was found. It's past time that she went into care but she's adamant that the only way she'll leave her cottage is in a box. Did you know she was my teacher in primary school?'

Sophie nodded. She opened her mouth to suggest something about more home help, perhaps, or an alarm, but she was distracted by the sound of voices in the adjacent reception area. Liz was back, but she wasn't alone.

'Stay here with the girls, Shirley. I'll take Jenny through to see Dr Bradford.'

'No…' Another voice sounded distressed. 'I don't think I can walk any more… I'm… *Arghh*…'

Finn heard the strangled groan of someone in deep distress and leapt up from his chair, the article he hadn't actually been concentrating on still on his computer screen. He'd been thinking about that moment in the kitchen when he'd found himself falling into Sophie's gaze. When he'd been merely a heartbeat away from forgetting where he was and why he couldn't just pull her into his arms and kiss her absolutely senseless.

He reached the reception area at the same moment Sophie and her father appeared from the kitchen. A woman was standing in the middle of the room, doubled over, clutching at a belly in an advanced stage of pregnancy. Two young girls were staring, looking terrified. One was about to burst into tears.

'*Mummy...*'

An older woman was looking just as frightened. 'Oh, my God... *Jenny...*' She reached to offer support but Finn got there first, putting his arms around the upper body of the pregnant woman.

'I've got you,' he said. He could feel the tension of Jenny's body ebb a little but almost immediately increase again, as if one contraction was leading straight into a new one. She was shaking, her breath escaping in groans that sounded like sobs.

'She's bleeding.' Sophie spoke quietly, the words intended only for Finn, as she arrived beside him. 'Let's try and get her into my room.'

Jack was beside Finn. They both supported one side as Jenny made a valiant effort to straighten up.

'Marion?' Sophie still sounded calm. 'Can you take the girls out for a walk for a bit?'

Their receptionist nodded, holding out her hands to the children.

'Come with me, girls. Don't worry... Everybody's going to take very good care of your mummy.'

Jenny seemed to be between contractions again and they'd reached the hallway leading to the consulting rooms. Finn could hear Sophie speaking quickly.

'Liz? Lock the door for the moment. Call an ambulance and then find us as many clean towels as we've got.
Shirley? Do you want to stay in here?'

'What's happening? Is she having the baby? *Now?*'

Finn could feel the weight he was supporting suddenly
getting heavier. They'd only just got inside the door of
Sophie's consulting room and the bed was still several
steps away but there was no holding Jenny up any longer.

'It's coming,' she groaned. 'I can feel something…'
She was reaching between her legs. '*Oh*… I need to
push…'

Sophie squeezed past Jack and Finn. She pulled Jenny's
trousers down. 'I can feel the head,' she said a moment
later. 'Get her down on the floor.'

'Support the head,' Jack told Sophie. 'Try not to push
for a moment, Jenny.'

Amniotic fluid was pooling around their feet as Finn
and Jack gently lowered Jenny. Finn saw the glance that
Sophie gave her father and the way they seamlessly became an instant team. He was crouched behind Jenny,
still supporting her head and shoulders.

'Okay, Jenny,' Jack said. 'Your baby's in a hurry to
get here… You can push with your next contraction…'

Finn could feel the energy building in Jenny's body
and her fingers digging painfully into his arms as she
gave in to the force of the contraction, her chin on her
chest as she pushed as if her life depended on it. He heard
Shirley's gasp as she saw her grandson slide into Jack's
hands. He expected to hear the cry of a newborn in the
next second but instead there was only silence.

Sophie leapt to her feet. 'I'll get the resus kit,' she said
aloud, moving towards a cupboard.

Liz edged past Shirley who was standing, frozen, in

the doorway. She handed one of the towels she was carrying to Jack, who wrapped the baby and began rubbing its skin briskly. Sophie was there seconds later with clamps and sterile scissors to cut the cord. Still, there was no sound of a baby's cry. Finn had to try and help.

'Give him to me,' he requested quietly. He took the limp bundle from Jack's hands and stood up, heading towards the examination couch so he could put the baby down and see what was going on.

Shirley took his place at Jenny's head, wrapping her arms around her daughter, who was shaking violently and sobbing.

'He's had a shock,' Jack was telling her. 'He didn't expect to come into the world this fast, that's all...'

Finn tilted the baby's head to open its airway and reached for the bulb aspirator in the kit Sophie had unrolled on the bed. The baby was making an effort to breathe but its colour was still a bluish grey and, apart from the ribs, its body wasn't moving. Finn could feel the heartbeat but it was too slow. Not much more than sixty beats per minute, the level below which it would be necessary to start chest compressions.

He caught Sophie's glance and saw her fear. He could also see her determination to save this newborn. She had a neonatal bag mask in her hands and he gave a single nod. With his hands around the tiny chest of the baby, he began gentle chest compressions. Sophie covered the mouth and nose, and her pressure on the bag to deliver a breath was just as careful and measured. One puff to every three compressions. It was Finn and Sophie who were the seamless team now and, when he met her glance again a minute or two later, he knew that they both realised a corner had been turned.

The baby was moving beneath their hands, starting to breathe more effectively, and the heart rate was picking up to the point where the skin colour was getting a lot healthier. At the first warbling sound of its cry, Finn could see Sophie blinking fast, as if she was trying to hold back tears. Her lips trembled as she smiled at Finn.

He smiled back as he wrapped the baby in more of the soft, clean towels and then took him to put him into his mother's arms. Both Jenny and her mother were crying. Jack's voice was gruff as he found a warm blanket to wrap around the mother and child.

'The ambulance won't be far away,' he said. 'We're just going to keep an eye on you both and keep you warm until it gets here.'

'Is he going to be okay?' Jenny was holding her baby against her chest, her head bowed so that she could touch his head with her lips.

'He needed a bit of help,' Finn told her. 'He's looking fine now. He's a beautiful baby boy, Jenny. Congratulations.'

She looked up. 'Thank you,' she whispered. 'I can't thank you enough.'

'And Dr Greene,' Shirley added. 'Thank you, Jack. I'm so glad it was you that delivered him in the end.'

Finn glanced at Sophie. Was she offended by her father being the preferred doctor here? But she was smiling.

'Dad delivered Jenny,' she told Finn. 'It's not that often you get to have that privilege for the next generation.'

'And it's a boy.' Shirley had tears rolling down her face again. 'Bob would have been *so* thrilled to have a grandson…'

Marion arrived back with Jenny's older children and their father wasn't far behind them. Then the ambulance crew arrived and took the parents and their new son to hospital. Shirley took her granddaughters home, and Marion and Liz set about cleaning up the clinic so that they could be ready for the late start to the afternoon surgery. Jack went home, saying that Judy would want to hear the news and that he needed a bit of a lie down himself, and Finn followed Sophie back to the kitchen when he saw her brushing tears from her cheeks.

'Are you okay?'

Her smile was misty. 'I'm just happy,' she told him. 'Shirley's been struggling with grief and depression since she lost her husband. This will be a new start for her, I think. Something joyful...'

It wasn't just the relief of a successful outcome to a professional emergency that was shining in Sophie's face right now. It was the shared joy of something positive happening in the life of one of her patients. A member of her community. She cared *this* much...

Sophie Bradford was a very special person and Finn could feel that joy seeping into himself, closing around his heart and squeezing it until it felt as though something was cracking.

Something *was* cracking and he knew what it was. That conviction that he could never trust someone enough to offer them his heart. To love them, as much as it was possible to love anyone. It was different with the twins. He knew he could love them safely because they had simply offered their hearts, the way children did, along with a total trust in him now that he'd proved he wasn't about to disappear from their lives. That other kind of trust, that led to offering your heart to someone that you'd want to be your partner for the rest of your life, was a very different matter, but it was there. And Finn also knew, without a shadow of doubt, that this woman was the only person in the world he was ever likely to feel this way about.

He could actually feel himself falling. Or rather, he could feel the moment he hit a solid surface which, in this case, was the knowledge that he was in love with Sophie. He wanted nothing more than to take her into his arms and tell her. To hold her and kiss her and ask her to share the rest of his life. He knew there was something huge between them that was far more than simply physical attraction. Thanks to the kind of silent communication that happened when they became lost in each other's gazes—as they were right now—it wasn't hard to believe that Sophie might feel the same way about him. It would be so easy to take that step and find out.

But, instead, he forced a smile and a nod and murmured something about how glad he was for Shirley and her whole family. And then he turned and forced his feet to take him away from this space. From Sophie.

It wasn't that he couldn't trust her. He knew just how genuine, loyal and trustworthy Sophie was. If it had been just his own heart on the line, he wouldn't have hesitated to take that step closer, but he had a responsibility that was bigger than his own feelings.

Ellie and Emma.

He had to protect the twins, and he still didn't know whether Sophie could accept them as her own children and be prepared to love and protect them unconditionally and wholeheartedly without any barriers. Imagine if Sophie did feel the same way about him and they started their lives together, had another child and that child became the favoured one? Like Sean had been. It wasn't that he thought that Sophie would do that consciously but he knew how children could pick up on even the most subtle rejection and grow up feeling less important. Less worthwhile.

He couldn't let that happen. Even if it meant sacrificing something this big.

The only reason he'd come here in the first place was to decide what was best for Ellie and Emma's future.

Not his.

CHAPTER NINE

CALLUM MCGREGOR LOOKED older than thirty-eight.

Maybe it was because he was somewhat overweight. Or because of the amount of grey in his rather unkempt hair. He did seem pleasant enough, however. He smiled a lot and laughed often.

'North Cove is exactly what I imagined it to be,' he told Jack as he shook his hand on arrival. 'A nice, sleepy little fishing village. It won't be difficult to find a mooring for a boat, will it?'

'You've got a boat?' Sophie's smile didn't reach more than her lips. 'Is that why the Cornish coast is attractive to you?' She led their guest towards the kitchen. His interview wasn't actually scheduled until tomorrow but he'd dropped in, he'd said, just to say hello, because he'd flown into Land's End and was heading to his hotel in Truro. It seemed only polite for Sophie and her father to offer him a cup of tea.

'I don't have one yet.' Callum grinned. 'But it's one of the first items on my "to do" list when I get here. Don't suppose you'd know someone that was selling one?' He laughed then. 'Of course you will. Everybody knows everybody and everything in a place this size, yes?'

Finn was in the kitchen, stirring a mug.

'Sorry,' he said. 'I'll get out of your way.'

'No need,' Sophie responded. 'This isn't a formal interview or anything. Callum's just popped in to introduce himself. Callum, this is Finn Connelly. He's helping us out as a locum until we find our new colleague.'

'Good man.' Callum nodded. 'I hope it's my chair that you've been keeping warm. I'll have a tea, if you're making one. Milk and three sugars, thanks.'

He sat down at the table. 'I knew it would be nice and quiet,' he said. 'I'm loving this place already.'

'It's not always this quiet,' Sophie said. 'You've caught us on our lunch break. We let our receptionist and practice nurse get out for half an hour or so but one of us is always on hand, in case of emergencies.'

'Don't suppose you get many of them?'

'You'd be surprised...' Finn was arranging more mugs on the bench. 'We had a precipitous birth here a couple of days ago. And Sophie and I dealt with a major accident on the beach recently. A young lad that got crushed by a boat.'

Callum's eyebrows rose. 'Goodness me... Ah, well... I imagine the ambulance service is up to scratch? You've got hospitals nearby?'

'Yes. One in Penzance and the larger one in Truro. And, yes, our ambulance service is very good, but of course we're always first on the scene.'

'No problem. I did a stint in A&E when I was in med school.' Callum was smiling at Sophie. 'I love that you work with your dad. This is a real family practice in more ways than one.'

'Mmm...' Sophie's glance caught Jack's briefly. 'My mother has been the practice nurse here for many years as well, but we're thinking of offering the position to the person who's also helping us out at the moment.'

'Oh? Has your mother retired now?'

'Not exactly.' Sophie's glance caught Finn's now as he put a mug of tea in front of her. 'She's…um…busy with other things.'

Finn didn't seem to be in a hurry to leave the room yet. 'So you're currently in a practice in Glasgow?' he asked. 'This would be a big change.'

Callum didn't look up. He was still smiling at Sophie. 'Change is always good. I have a feeling this one might be the best ever.'

It was impossible to miss the admiration in his gaze. Sophie could also feel a sudden tension in the atmosphere and it seemed to be emanating from Finn. Had he taken an instant dislike to this potential practice partner? She couldn't really blame him. She wasn't too sure she liked Callum herself.

'What sort of on-call hours are you used to?' Jack asked.

'Sorry, what?'

'After hours,' Jack added. 'With only two of us here, it's a fifty-fifty split. Not that we get too many night or weekend calls but we have to be available.'

'Haven't done that for a while,' Callum admitted. 'We use an after-hours service in Glasgow.' He shrugged. 'I'll cope.' He patted his stomach. 'Do me good to have a few nights a week without a beer or two to unwind with.'

'And house calls?' Jack's tone was neutral enough to let Sophie know that he wasn't too impressed.

'House calls?' Callum blinked. 'I didn't think any medical practice did them any more.'

'We're old-fashioned,' Jack said. 'Many of our patients

are elderly and we cover a wide area with some rather isolated farms.'

'And this isn't just "any" practice.' It was Finn, who sounded as if he was keeping his tone deliberately controlled. 'It's a very important part of a rather special community. A very close community.'

Callum drained his mug. 'I'm going to have a look around,' he said. 'And then I'd better find my digs in Truro.' He stood up. 'I don't want to take up any more of your lunch break but I'll look forward to a proper tour and chat tomorrow. Five p.m., isn't it?'

'Thereabouts.' Jack stood up to see him out. 'It will depend on how busy the afternoon surgery is. So you're staying in Truro tonight?'

'Yes. I couldn't find any hotels here online.' Callum's voice was fading. 'Can you recommend any good restaurants in Truro?'

There was a long moment's silence in the kitchen. Sophie finally turned towards Finn.

'He's looking for an early retirement, I think.'

Finn held her gaze. 'And someone to share it with, perhaps.'

That made Sophie roll her eyes. 'Not in a million years.'

'What, as a colleague?'

'As anything.' Sophie sighed, getting up to put her mug in the sink. 'Back to square one, I suspect. I don't suppose we can cancel his formal interview tomorrow. He has come a long way.'

Not far enough, Finn decided as he rinsed the mugs. And, the sooner he went back to where he'd come from, the better.

Callum McGregor was clearly unsuitable for the position here at North Cove's medical centre and he was very relieved that Sophie seemed to agree. He was even more relieved that she hadn't been flattered by his blatant admiration and that was a little disturbing.

What man wouldn't be attracted to Sophie? Okay, maybe Callum wasn't going to be offered the position here, but what about the next candidate? Or someone else amongst the new people she would meet during tourist season or when she was in a bigger place like the hospitals in Penzance or Truro?

He was jealous, that was what it was. Jealous of the man who would arrive in her life without any baggage or complications and who would sweep her off her feet and have the privilege of sharing his life with this amazing woman. Jealous and…frustrated, because it could never be him? He couldn't even admit to how he felt about her because it could influence whatever decision she was going to make about the place Ellie and Emma were going to have in her life. If she genuinely wanted to be their mother, there was a chance that he could be a part of that new family. If not, he would have to do whatever it took to protect his nieces.

It wasn't a battle between head and heart, exactly. More like an internal struggle that was heart versus heart. Whatever it was, Finn was feeling distinctly out of sorts by the time he'd put the mugs back into the cupboard and walked out of the kitchen. Afternoon surgery was due to start soon and it sounded as if more than one patient had arrived early or unexpectedly. But when he entered the waiting room he found it wasn't any kind of urgent appointment.

Jenny was there with her new son in her arms and everyone was clustered around, admiring the baby.

'He's famous,' Liz was saying. 'I loved that photo of you in the paper. And that Dr Greene had delivered two generations in the same family. And that he's the first baby that's ever been born right here in the health centre.'

'Hopefully, the last as well.' Jack was laughing. 'That was a bit too exciting for all of us.'

'We've called him Jack,' Jenny smiled. 'After you. And Robert, after his granddad, of course.'

Jack was looking distinctly misty. Marion was reaching for her phone. 'We need a photo,' she declared. 'I'm going to put it in pride of place on our notice board.'

For a few minutes, Marion was busy taking photos. 'We need one with you as well as Sophie,' she instructed Finn. 'You were part of making North Cove history here.'

He joined Jack and Sophie to stand beside Jenny and her sleeping bundle. And then Jenny smiled at Sophie.

'Would you like to hold him?'

'Oh…yes please…' Sophie carefully transferred the bundle into her own arms.

'Can you stay for a few minutes, Jenny?' Jack asked. 'Judy would love to see this little man. I'll just run home and let her know that you're here.'

'We've got plenty of time.' Shirley was keeping Jenny's older daughters occupied near the toy box. 'I'd love a chance to catch up with Judy myself. Besides, I've made cake. Have you all got time for a cuppa before the hordes start arriving?'

'For your chocolate cake,' Sophie said, 'we'll make time. Anyone who arrives first can join us. I don't think anyone will complain if we're running a little late this afternoon.'

Finn watched Jack hurry away to fetch his wife. Would he bring the twins back with him? he wondered. What would Sophie think, when she saw her biological children while she was holding someone else's baby in her arms? Would she be aware of any difference in how she felt about Ellie and Emma?

But Jack didn't bring the twins back. It was just Judy who rushed in with a huge smile on her face and hugs for both Jenny and Shirley. And then it was her turn to cuddle the baby. Finn knew he should take the first patient who arrived after that but Maureen Redding waved the suggestion away.

'I want to hear all about this new arrival,' she said. 'I'm sure there's more to this story than went into the newspaper. My blood pressure can wait…'

'I'll put the kettle on,' Liz said. 'Oh, wow…did you really make that cake, Shirley? It looks amazing…'

A little bemused by the party atmosphere that had taken over North Cove's medical centre, Finn propped himself against the reception desk and simply watched.

Sophie was standing beside her mother and both women were smiling down at baby Jack. Sophie would be this child's doctor, he realised. She would monitor his progress and be aware of every milestone that was reached. She would give him his vaccinations to protect him from childhood illnesses and look after him for any that couldn't be avoided. She would watch him grow up and go to school and she'd probably still be practising medicine here by the time this baby was old enough to start his own family. Maybe she would be the one to care for his wife when *she* got pregnant. She might follow in her father's footsteps and be the one to deliver a member of the next generation of this community.

Finn didn't really feel part of this celebration.

But he wanted to.

The pull was astonishingly powerful, in fact, and part of him knew that he would be welcomed. In the same way he'd been welcomed into Jack and Judy's household, along with the twins.

And it felt like part of the same thing.

Home…

Eventually, the afternoon routine was restored when Jenny and her family finally headed home. And then it got very busy as they tried to make up for lost time and see all their patients. It was after five p.m. and the waiting room was almost empty when Judy appeared for the second time that day. She wasn't looking anything like as happy as she had been when she'd arrived to see Jenny's baby, however.

'Are they here?' she asked Sophie.

'Who? Jenny and Shirley? No, they went home hours ago.'

'No…' Judy shook her head sharply. 'Your father… and the twins. I can't find them.'

Finn appeared in the door of his consulting room. 'What's going on?'

'Jack said he was going to take the girls for a walk while I came over to see Jenny's baby. He said something about showing them the rock pools.'

'Rock pools?' Finn was frowning now.

'It's a fair walk. They're in the next cove past the boats. I knew it would take a while but it's been too long. And then I thought he might have come back here first instead.'

Sophie shook her head. 'Have you called him?'

'He didn't take his phone.'

'I'll drive down,' Sophie said. 'Don't worry. They've probably just got totally engrossed, collecting starfish or something.' But she was worried now, too. There'd been more than one occasion, since that dizzy spell he'd had in the clinic that day, when she'd wondered if there was more going on with her father's health than simply fatigue from over-work.

Finn followed the women into the waiting room. Sophie was about to ask him to take over any remaining consultations when someone burst through the front door. He was wearing an oilskin coat and gumboots and looked as if he'd just stepped off a fishing boat.

'Sophie? It's your dad. Someone found him on the beach. Looks like he's had a bit of a fall and bumped his head. He's a bit confused…'

'Oh, no… I'll get my kit…' Sophie turned towards the storeroom.

Finn hadn't moved. 'What about the girls?' he asked. 'Are they all right?'

'Girls?' The fisherman looked blank.

'The twins,' Finn snapped. 'They were with Jack.'

But all he received in response was a headshake. 'There were no kids there. Just Jack lying beside a rock and he got real dizzy when he tried to stand up.'

Sophie had the emergency backpack in her arms, still moving fast, but it felt as if she'd frozen for a moment as her gaze met Finn's. And then she was racing for the door.

Finn was right behind her. 'I'm coming, too.'

He was vaguely aware of what Liz was saying to the only people left in the waiting room.

'Sorry, folks, we'll have to reschedule your appointments… Looks like we've got an emergency on our hands…'

CHAPTER TEN

'Two LITTLE GIRLS. Pink jackets. Woolly hats...'

'I saw them.' It was Ethan's father who spoke up from the group surrounding Jack. 'They came past my boat an hour or so ago.'

'More like two hours, Charlie. I saw them, too. Holding Jack's hands. I asked Fred who they were and he said they were the new doc's kids.'

Finn, crouched beside Sophie in front of her father, who sat shrouded in oilskin jackets, said nothing to correct the assumption.

'And they had buckets,' someone else added. 'Looked like they were planning to collect shells or something.'

'Can you remember anything?' Sophie asked. 'Do you know what day it is today, Dad?'

'Of course I do. It's Wednesday.'

Sophie's gaze caught Finn's. It was Friday. She touched the grazed, egg-sized lump on her father's forehead gently but he pulled back irritably.

'Ouch...' He glared at Sophie. 'Why aren't you at the clinic? It's the middle of afternoon surgery.'

'You knocked yourself out, Dad.' She clicked on the light of her pen torch and tried to check the reaction of

his pupils. 'Can you remember anything? Were you feeling dizzy again?'

'I called to see how far away the ambulance is.' Judy
looked almost as pale as her husband. 'It should be here
in a few minutes.'

'I just tripped, that's all.' But Jack was shrugging off
the coats. 'Where are the girls? He was trying to get to
his feet. 'Ellie? *Emma?*'

'Stay still, Dad.' Sophie had her fingers on her father's
wrist. Was it her imagination or was his pulse not quite
as regular as it should be? Had she missed something as
major as an arrhythmia when he'd first shown symptoms?
She focussed intently for a moment but could now feel a
regular beat beneath her fingertips.

She stood up to talk quietly to her mother. 'Can you
stay with him until the ambulance gets here? And go with
him to the hospital? He's going to need observation for a
while. Possibly a CT scan. Get them to do an ECG, and
keep him on a monitor as well.' She lowered her voice.
'I'm not certain, but I think I noticed some irregularity.'

She put her hand on her father's shoulder as he made
another attempt to rise. 'Don't move, Dad. And stop worrying. We're going to find the girls.'

'We'll help,' one of the group around them called.

'They probably headed home.' People were already
moving away. 'We need to check the boats.'

'And the sheds...'

'There's not that much daylight left...'

'And the tide's coming in...'

'Were you on your way home, Dad?' Sophie had to try
again. 'Or were you heading towards the rock pools? You
told Mum that was where you were going, didn't you?'

Shockingly, her father suddenly looked much older—
confused and unbearably anxious.

'I can't remember,' he whispered. 'Oh, God, Soph…
what have I done?'

She leaned down to hug him. 'It'll be okay.' From the
corner of her eye, she caught the flashing lights of an ambulance pulling up on the road above the rocky beach.
'You go with Mum and get checked out. Do you want
me to come with you as well?'

'No… Go and help find the girls.'

She straightened up and looked at Finn. He was pale,
too. His mouth was set in a grim line and his eyes were
darker than she'd ever seen them. She could read disbelief in them. And fear.

She could feel that fear herself. Two three-year-old
children were wandering alone in an environment that
held any number of dangers. Slippery rocks. Pools of
water. Waves that could knock them off their feet and
pull them out to sea. Attractive, brightly coloured boats
that were rocking against the pier, making it dangerous
to try and climb on board. A nearby road with traffic
that wouldn't be slowing down before it got closer to the
port and village.

People were fanning out over the beach now. Sophie
saw someone shading their face against the light with
both hands, staring out to sea. Looking for the shape and
colour of floating pink jackets?

'We'll go this way,' she told Finn, pointing to the other
edge of the small cove. 'That's where the rock pools are.
Surely someone would have seen them if they'd tried to
go home?'

It wasn't as if her parents' house was actually their
home, anyway. How lost would Emma and Ellie feel

without an adult to look after them? Had they tried to wake her father up after he'd fallen? Just how long had Jack been unconscious?

Sophie was almost running as she headed for the big rock formations that formed the natural end of the cove. Finn was right beside her and then he pulled ahead to scramble over the first smooth boulders. His foot slipped and then he stopped suddenly. Sophie's heart seemed to stop for a beat as well. She knew there was a big pool of water there. What had Finn seen?

But he was turning. Holding out his hand.

'It's slippery,' he warned. 'Be careful.'

Sophie took his hand, aware of how strong his grip was as he helped her over the rocks. And then she was staring down at the pool she remembered so well. So deep she'd been able to swim in it when she'd been a child. So clear you could spend a long time admiring the sea anemones, starfish and the tiny, real fish that flashed from one hiding place to another.

So clear it was instantly obvious that there was nothing in the water that shouldn't be there. The relief was enough to make her let her breath out in a sound that was almost a sob. Finn still hadn't let go of her hand and she could feel his grip intensify to the point it was crushing her fingers. He knew what she'd been afraid of seeing. He must also have realised that this wouldn't be the only pool of water amongst these rocks.

They only paused for a second or two, but it was enough for the surface of the pool to start rippling. The very end of a wave had crested the rocks on the sea side and was beginning to refill the pool. At high tide, it would be completely covered, and getting any further around the coast would be impossible.

They kept going. Scrambling over smaller rocks. Squeezing between taller ones. Passing shallow pools beside the cliffs and deeper ones where they had to wait for waves to pass before they could check the depths. How far could two small children go?

'Maybe they didn't come this way,' Finn said. 'They're smart kids. If they were scared they would have tried to find someone to help. They would have been looking for their nana…'

Sophie had to squeeze her eyes shut for a moment. Her mum would be beside herself right now. Worried about Jack. Terrified of what could have happened to the two little girls she loved so much now.

Her granddaughters…

'Oh, *God*…'

Sophie's eyes snapped open. 'What?'

'I can see something. Over there…'

It was a flash of colour on dark rock. Rock that was darker than it had been even a few minutes ago. They would be losing daylight soon. A swift glance behind them showed Sophie that there were already beams of torchlight flashing on boats. Someone would have alerted the coast guard by now. There would be local search teams that would have powerful lights, but they had to find the girls before dark. If they were still exploring or trying to find their way home, the lack of light would make it far more dangerous to navigate over rocks or keep out of the way of incoming waves.

And maybe they were close to finding them… Sophie scrambled to keep up with Finn as he raced towards what he'd seen.

It was a small plastic bucket. Bright red. Shaped to help create the perfect sandcastle but just as good to fill with treasures like shells or pretty stones. This one had had shells inside it. There was a pile beside where the bucket had been dropped.

'*Ellie?*' Finn's shout was loud and clear. '*Emma?* Can you hear me? Where *are* you?'

The only sound in response was the crash of a larger wave cresting rocks further out to sea. The foam kept rolling in. Far enough to make Sophie step back. Far enough to catch the little red bucket and send it closer to the cliff wall. The land curved at this point in the cove. When they climbed over this tumble of rocks, they would be out of sight of the harbour and the village. Finn was standing on the highest point now, staring ahead.

'I can't see anything,' he said, an edge of desperation in his voice. 'They can't have come this far, surely? I think we should turn back.'

Sophie climbed up to stand beside him. 'I used to come here,' she told him. 'There are caves. It would be easy to be somewhere we can't see from here.'

And it had been *so* exciting when she was little. An adventure that was irresistible. These children had half her genes. Would they have felt the same kind of pull towards that excitement? Taken advantage of their freedom from adult supervision to find out what else their new world had to offer?

Sophie reached for Finn's hand. Did she want to offer the comfort of touch, or did she need it herself?

'The whole village will be out looking for them around the harbour and in the streets but we're the only ones close enough to check this area. It's going to get cut off by the tide any time now.'

As if to emphasise her words, a new wave washed completely around the rock they were standing on. It reached as far as the bottom of the cliff and sent a spray of icy water into the air. Sophie felt the chill right into her bones. The fear was even more freezing.

She wouldn't be able to bear it if something *had* happened to Ellie and Emma. She had to find them. She would give anything to be able to gather them into her arms right now. And never, *ever* let them go...

'Show me,' Finn demanded. 'Where are the caves?'

Sophie kept hold of his hand as they climbed down and then moved as fast as they could over the flatter area of rocks, keeping close to the cliff face. They still got their feet wet as one wave and then another rolled in.

'How high does it get?'

Sophie didn't want to tell him that it would be well over head-height for two small children. That nobody would attempt to cross these rocks for hours on each side of high tide. She knew they wouldn't be able to get back themselves by the time they reached the caves. That some of the smaller caves would also be under water within the next few hours. At least the smaller hollows at the base of the cliffs were easy to check. Their voices echoed from the walls.

'Ellie?'

'Emma?'

It was the largest cave that had been the goal of generations of North Cove children. It had a sandy base that made an exciting picnic spot and a cool place for teenagers to hang out. They'd all grown up with the rules drummed into them, though. You never, ever came here this far into an incoming tide. The water was already reaching its wide opening and the light was low enough for the interior of the cave to appear totally black.

'I can't see a thing,' Finn muttered. 'Ellie? Emma? Are

you here?' He was reaching for his phone as he called and, a moment later, he had a bright beam glowing from his torch app.

Sophie watched it play over damp sand and rake rocky walls, her heart in her mouth.

Nothing.

But Finn wasn't giving up. He started again, more slowly this time. Methodically covering every inch of this huge space. There were rocks dotted on the sandy base of the cave and, as he shifted the light past one group of large rocks towards the back of the cave, he suddenly stopped and took it back.

'There...'

And, this time, Sophie saw it, too. A flash of pink.

They both ran. Sophie didn't realise she was still gripping Finn's hand until she had to let it go to hold out her arms towards the huddle of two small, frightened girls who were sitting in a gap in the middle of these rocks.

'Oh...*sweethearts*...come *here*....'

It was Ellie who crawled out first and threw herself into Sophie's arms. Emma came next and it was Finn who scooped her up. But the twins didn't want to let go of each other for more than a second, and reached for each other as well, so it became a group cuddle with all four of them in contact with each other.

It was the most intense moment of Sophie's life. She was holding Ellie's little body so close she could feel the beat of that small heart against her own, but she had her other arm around Emma as well and, somehow, Finn had wrapped his arm around both herself and Ellie. And, in the wash of that overwhelming wave of emotion, she found her gaze locked with Finn's. Tears were rolling, unchecked, down her face and her throat was far too tight to find any words but she knew she didn't need to. She knew that Finn could see that her life had just been saved because she could see the reflection of exactly how she was feeling in *his* eyes.

But they couldn't stand here hugging each other. Time was running out.

Holding the girls, Finn and Sophie turned towards the cave's mouth, only to find a wave rolling right in through the entrance, its final energy only fading inches from their feet.

This time, Sophie could see her fear reflected in Finn's eyes.

'We need to get higher,' he said quietly.

'I want to go home,' Ellie said. 'I'm hungry…'

'I know, sweetheart.' Sophie cuddled her closer. 'But we have to stay here a bit longer, I'm afraid. Just until the tide goes out and the waves go away again.'

Finn was using his torch. Shining it at the back of the cave and up the walls. He held it on a place where the colour of the rocks seemed to change.

'That's the high-tide mark, yes?'

'I think so.' Sophie's heart sank. It was probably high enough to reach her waist. Even if they could hold the twins above water level, she could guess at the kind of currents produced by the wash of the ocean in a confined space.

'Look…' Finn moved the beam of light higher. 'There's a ledge.'

'Can we get to it?'

His gaze met hers steadily and his words were calm and quiet. 'We have to.'

And, somehow, they did. Finn climbed first to find secure footing and then Sophie held up one twin and then the other for him to take and position safely. Then he took her hand and helped her up. Once, twice and then they were all on the ledge, several metres above the sand and well out of range of any sea water. Hopefully, also out of range of any spray, because it was already cold and it was going to get a lot colder.

'There's no signal in here,' Sophie told Finn. 'I can't let anyone know that we're safe. Mum will be worried sick.'

'I know. I'm sorry…you must be worried about your dad, too.'

Sophie could only nod as she tried to swallow past the lump in her throat. 'I'm sure he's going to be fine.'

'So are we.' Finn's voice held a smile. 'Cuddle closer. We'll have to keep each other warm.' He bent his head to where Emma was snuggled on his lap. 'Are you sure nothing hurts?' he asked. 'Can you wiggle all your fingers?'

A small gloved hand appeared, fingers wiggling.

Sophie cuddled Ellie even closer. 'Are you okay?' she whispered. 'You didn't fall over on the rocks?'

'I'm hungry,' Ellie said.

'Me, too,' Emma added.

'Me, too,' Finn said. 'Let's decide what we're going to have for breakfast when they come and rescue us. I think I want toast…'

He was looking straight at Sophie, above the twins' heads. 'With raspberry jam,' he added softly.

Oh… If he was trying to send her a message that the children wouldn't realise had any significance, he couldn't have chosen anything more powerful. It took her straight back to the night they had made love. Was he saying that he wanted it to happen again? That, next time, it wouldn't be a one-off, but the start of something far more meaningful?

She swallowed hard again. 'Me, too,' she whispered.

Yes… She watched the expression on Finn's face change and a smile like one she had never seen before play with his lips. It felt as if she was seeing this man—a part of him, anyway—for the first time.

Barriers had gone. Her own or his? Possibly both…

'I want fish fingers,' Ellie said. 'Like Nana makes.'

'And ice-cream,' Emma added.

'You can't have ice-cream for breakfast,' Ellie said firmly.

'Tomorrow you can,' Finn promised. 'Tomorrow you can have anything you want for breakfast.'

'Will Nana be there?'

'Yes,' Sophie said. 'Nana will be the first person who wants to give you a cuddle in the morning.'

'And Poppa?' Ellie's face was pale in the last of the light the cave was offering. 'He fell over. He went to sleep on the beach.'

'I know. But there's lots of people taking care of him now. You can see him tomorrow.'

Emma's voice wobbled. 'But who's going to take care of *us*?'

Finn and Sophie both spoke at the same moment.

'*We* are.'

For the next hour or more, Finn was constantly aware of every wave that rolled in and broke beneath them, each one coming a little further and breaking a little higher. The sound of the water hitting rock was magnified by the enclosed space, and it could have been a lot more alarming if Sophie hadn't been dredging up every nursery rhyme or childish song to try and keep the twins distracted. They huddled together on the ledge that was quite wide enough to keep them safe but he wasn't about to let go of Emma, any more than Sophie was about to let go of her hold on Ellie. Even better was the solid weight of Sophie leaning against him, her head on his shoulder whenever she bent to peer at the face of the child she was cradling.

'She's sound asleep,' she whispered when Finn had lost track of time. He didn't want to waste the already low battery of his phone by checking it too often.

'Emma's been out like a light for a while,' he said. 'And no wonder. Having an adventure like that must have exhausted them.'

'Maybe they'll sleep until daylight. I don't expect Search and Rescue will come looking for us before then.'

'How long before low tide?'

'About six hours after high tide. But I can't tell if it's completely in yet.'

'It must have been coming in when we came along the beach.'

'We were almost too late,' Sophie reminded him. 'Locals know that it's only within a couple of hours each side of low tide that it's safe to come here.'

'So it might be safe to get out in less than six hours?'

'It'll be pitch black. I wouldn't want to be carrying Ellie over those rocks in the dark.' Finn could see the way Sophie squeezed her eyes shut. 'Unless the Search and Rescue guys decide to come looking in the dark, I just want to sit here and keep her safe. Keep them both safe…'

He was still watching her as she opened her eyes again.

'You love them,' he murmured. 'You *really* love them…'

Sophie was silent for so long that Finn wondered if

she was trying to think of how to tell him that she might love these children now but she still couldn't see herself as their mother. When she did speak, her voice was raw.

'I was so scared of loving them,' she said softly. 'But that was nothing compared to how terrified I was at the thought of losing them.'

And that fear had been enough to smash the barriers that Sophie had built and kept in place ever since life had knocked her down so hard. Finn could understand that. He tried to find his own barrier that he'd kept strong for so many years. The one that made it impossible to trust someone absolutely.

He couldn't find it. Not here. But he'd already known that, hadn't he? That it would never be there between himself and Sophie.

'You're not going to lose them,' he told her.

'You can't know that.' Sophie sounded as if she was close to tears. 'Nobody knows what's going to happen. There are things that none of us has any control over.'

'I know.' Finn gently slid one hand free without disturbing Emma and used it to cradle Sophie's cheek. 'And I know how much your life changed when Matthew had his accident. But you were able to get through that and change your vision for your future, and you knew you'd make it work because you loved each other.'

'But it *didn't* work. I lost him. I lost our baby...'

'The love did. The trust.' Finn let out a slow breath. 'And, yes, it's a risk because we don't know what life has in store for any of us. But if we *don't* trust, or take the risk to love...' He had to close his eyes for a moment to try and find the words for what he wanted to say. 'It takes something huge away from what life can be. Maybe the most important part.' He shifted his body enough to be able to bend his head and kiss Sophie gently. 'You know something?'

'What?'

'I just realised that I've forgiven Sean.'

'For stealing your girlfriend?'

'Yeah. I understand what happened for both of them. I get that you can find someone and fall in love and just know that they are the person you want to be with for the rest of your life. The *only* person.'

Sophie's eyes were shining. 'I get that, too.'

'Of course you do. You had that with Matthew.'

'No…' She shook her head slowly. 'We loved each other. So much. But it was never a lightning bolt kind of "falling in love" thing. We grew up together and it was just the way things were. It didn't feel like… I don't know…a choice.'

'But you can choose now.'

'I can…'

Finn couldn't look away from that glow in Sophie's eyes. If she was choosing what he hoped she was choosing, life was never going to be the same. It was going to be so, so much better. As perfect as you could ever hope life was going to get.

'I choose *you*,' Sophie whispered. 'I know now that I love Ellie and Emma with all my heart and I'd fight, if I had to, to keep them. But I don't just love *them*. I… I love you, too, Finn. But you know what?'

'What?'

'It doesn't feel like a choice now, either. It feels like something that was just meant to be. I was terrified that I was going to lose the twins but I can't imagine my life without you in it, either. I love you as much as it's possible to love anyone. With all my heart *and* my soul.'

He had to kiss her again. 'I couldn't have said that better myself.'

'But…'

'But what?' Did Sophie need reassurance that they were going to get through this ordeal safely? That a few hours in a dark cave, holding onto two small girls that they both loved so much, was not going to be their only chance to be a family?

'But you're going to say it, anyway?'

Finn smiled. 'I'm going to say it every day for as long as I live. I love you, Sophie Bradford. You are the person I want to wake up beside for the rest of my life. The only person I could ever trust to give my heart to. My soul mate. I want to keep you safe and love you for ever.'

For a long, long moment, they simply held each other's gaze. When Finn cradled her face so that he could kiss her again, he could feel the contrast between the warmth of her mouth and the chill of her skin.

He spoke with his lips still brushing hers. 'And…and the sooner we're out of this damn cave, the better…'

'I know…it's freezing, isn't it? It's just as well Dad wrapped the girls up so well for their walk. If we keep holding them, I think we're safe from hypothermia.'

Finn gathered Sophie and Ellie even closer, to share the space between his arms with Emma.

His girls…

His family…

He could feel Sophie's shivering ease after a while. 'I'm starving,' she said, then.

'Same. I'd kill for a piece of toast.'

Sophie peeped up at him. 'Me, too.'

'With raspberry jam?'

'Oh, yes…' Her smile was the most beautiful thing Finn had ever seen. 'Always…'

She fell asleep in his arms eventually but Finn stayed awake. He was guarding his family and he would stay awake as long as it took. Even as he noticed that the waves were receding as the tide ebbed, he wasn't about to wake Sophie and risk carrying the girls across slippery rocks in the dark. He would wait until the first fingers of dawn touched the mouth of the cave and then it would be the time to lead them all back to safety and the beginning of their new life.

But it was still dark when he heard the faint sound of voices between waves. And it wasn't dawn that brightened the mouth of the cave but beams from powerful torches, held by people that were equipped with everything they needed to make sure they would all be safe.

'In here…' he called. 'We're up on a ledge…'

Sophie jerked awake in his arms but the twins just snuggled closer.

For an instant, he could see fear in Sophie's eyes as she blinked in the beam of light playing on them and heard the commotion beneath them as the Search and Rescue team got organised to bring them down.

'Let's make a chain,' someone said. 'We'll lift the children down first…'

And then Sophie's eyes locked on to his own and Finn saw the fear melt away to be replaced by relief.

Trust.

Love.

Joy, even, because she knew they were about to take their first steps into a totally new future.

Together…

EPILOGUE

THE GROUP OF women standing on the sand of North Cove's main beach were wearing summery dresses.

And hats.

Against the backdrop of sunlight shimmering on the bluest sea possible, an archway had been placed, covered with bright flowers. There were roses, daisies and sunflowers—there wasn't a garden in the village that hadn't contributed some of these blooms. A strip of white carpet had been laid on the sand and it was being sprinkled with rose petals from baskets that two small girls were carrying proudly as they walked towards the man waiting beside the archway.

'They're so adorable,' Shirley murmured.

'They're the spitting image of Sophie when she was that age.' Maureen Redding tapped the side of her nose. 'I knew they were her girls before anything got said about that egg donation she'd made.'

'Of course you did,' Colleen Murphy murmured. 'But it's Dr Connelly we have to thank for bringing them here, isn't it?'

'Oh, look at that…' Shirley reached into her handbag for a handkerchief as they saw Finn crouch to gather the flower girls into his arms for a hug as they completed their mission. 'He loves those girls as if they were his own.'

'They are,' Maureen said. 'I heard that all the necessary paperwork for official adoption was completed before they even started planning this wedding. And, what's more, I know that they call him Daddy now. And they call Sophie Mummy. Jenny Thompson told me. She met them at the park when she was there with her girls and young Jack.'

Shirley blew her nose but she wasn't watching the twins any more. Like everyone else, she had turned her head to wait for the arrival of the bride. Sophie was standing at the end of the white carpet, one arm linked with her father's and the other with her mother's. Jack looked like the proudest man on earth. Judy was clearly blinking back tears. Together, they walked through the centre of the crowd gathered on this beach. Virtually everyone who lived in North Cove was here today and, with it being summer, there were plenty of tourists standing at a respectful distance to watch this joyful occasion.

Sophie was wearing a simple white dress that brushed the sand. She wasn't wearing a veil but that glorious, curly hair of hers was studded with pretty flowers—just like the ones in the twins' hair, except that theirs were pink to match their dresses.

'I remember her first wedding,' Maureen whispered. 'In the church. This is…different.'

'Better,' Colleen whispered back. 'Sophie deserves every bit of this happiness after everything she's been through and, the more people that can celebrate that, the better.'

Any tears from Sophie's mother seemed to evaporate with the smile that was on her face as she gathered Ellie's and Emma's hands to lead them to where they were going to stand for the ceremony.

'I've never seen Judy so happy.' Shirley needed her hanky again.

'Jack, too,' Maureen agreed. 'I've been saying for years that it was past time for him to retire. Who knew that he was risking his life to carry on as long as he did? He could have died that day on the beach.'

'But he didn't. And he has a pacemaker now. He told me that he reckons he's got at least another twenty years to make the most of being a granddad.'

'We're all going to miss him at the clinic, mind you…'

'But who better to take his place than Dr Connelly? That's exactly what North Cove needed—what we've always had. A family team.'

'He's doing shifts at the A&E in Truro. Judy told me he wants to keep up his skills in emergency work.'

'A good thing, that.' Colleen nodded. 'Think about what could have happened that day if he hadn't been there for young Ethan.'

The women glanced behind them. Ethan was helping Joe to set up the long trestle tables where the barbecue reception that Joe's Shack was catering would be held very soon. He was still walking with a bit of a limp but that was hardly surprising. It was only eight months since he'd had that terrible accident and it was a miracle that he was still here at all.

Silence fell as the couple began exchanging their vows. It was a bit hard to hear what was being said from where this group of friends had gathered, especially with the gentle wash of the waves behind them and the occasional screech of a seagull overhead, but it didn't really matter. You could see how much love there was between Finn and Sophie just in the way they were holding hands and staring into each other's eyes. And, when it came to the kiss, the cheer that went up from the crowded beach was loud enough to drown out any sea birds.

It was time for photographs to be taken and a chance for the guests to mingle before sharing the village party that this reception was intended to be. This particular group of friends wasn't quite ready to mingle just yet, however.

'I do love a happy ending,' Shirley said. 'Has anyone got a tissue? My hanky's got a bit damp.'

'Oh, look… Judy's coming this way. I must go and say hello. Did you know that her and Jack's wedding present for Sophie is that they swap houses? She says her cottage is far too small for a family but just perfect for a pair of grandparents.'

Shirley was blowing her nose again. 'That old house and garden is just perfect for a family, that's for sure. And don't they make the perfect little family?'

'Hmm…' Maureen was smiling. 'I wonder how long it will be before it's not so little?'

Shirley and Colleen stared at her.

'Not that I'm one to gossip…'

'Of course not.' Shirley and Colleen shared an amused glance. 'But…'

Maureen lowered her voice. 'Well, Enid from the pharmacy told me that Sophie came in to buy one of those test kits the other day. You know…pregnancy test kits?'

'Maybe she needed it in the clinic.'

'That's what I said. But Enid said that Sophie was blushing like a teenager. And that she'd never seen her looking so happy.'

The collective sigh from the women was also a happy one.

'Wouldn't that be perfect?' one of them murmured.

They all turned to where a photograph was being taken of Finn and Sophie, framed by the flowered archway, stealing another kiss. Ellie and Emma were holding hands, looking up at their parents, and, as if they became aware of their audience, Finn and Sophie broke their kiss. Their smiles radiated joy as they both crouched in the same moment to gather the little girls into their arms. Then they rose and all four of them were framed by archway. Ellie and Emma were beaming at the camera. Finn and Sophie were beaming at each other.

It wasn't just Shirley reaching for a tissue this time.

'Perfect,' Maureen sniffed. 'It's all perfect. I knew it would be.'

* * * * *

A NURSE TO
HEAL HIS HEART

LOUISA GEORGE

MILLS & BOON

To my amazing editor, Flo Nicoll, who shares
my love of the wild and wonderful Lake District.

Thank you for saying yes when I came up with
the idea for this story, and for all your wise words
and support over the years. (And, most importantly,
for conjuring up famous celebrities
at opportune moments!)

I'm so lucky to have you xx

CHAPTER ONE

THERE SHE WAS AGAIN.

The third day in a row she'd marched past his house, rattled through the farm gate bordering his property and walked up onto the hill path. He wouldn't have noticed—Joe generally took little interest in the steady stream of day-trippers and hikers walking past his foothills cottage—only for the bright multi-coloured hat and lipstick-red knitted knee-length coat more suitable for shopping than hiking.

It was the hat that had first caught his attention. Oranges and yellows and something he was sure his sister would call *umber* or something. Like a sunburst, or sunrise. A fresh vibrancy in the Lake District early autumnal grey they'd been having for the last few weeks. But wearing a wool coat and no decent wet weather gear? Downright foolish. She was probably one of those ill-equipped flakes he heard about too regularly, that had Search and Mountain Rescue out in the dark, risking their own lives.

Should he tell her about today's forecast? Run after her like a busybody and tell her to wrap up warmly and get back down before dark and the threatened downpour?

Like hell. He'd promised himself he wouldn't get so involved these days—live and let live. Get Katy ready for school, then go to work, come home. That was his life now: rinse and repeat.

But there was something about the brightness that compelled him to watch her. She'd stopped along the path and was looking out over the hotchpotch of grey stone and whitewashed buildings in the village. From this vantage point at the kitchen sink he had a closer view of her profile. Fresh pink cheeks. Long white-blonde hair cascading down her back as she shook her head from side to side and stretched her arms out wide, raised a leg. Such joy and energy in her movements, she waved her arms in the air and breathed deeply, maintaining her single leg balance. A yoga position?

She was doing yoga on a mountainside in sleepy Oakdale.

Yeah, it took all sorts.

As if she knew he was looking, she turned to him and smiled. Something about the openness of her face, of the soft yet bright eyes, had him instinctively smiling back. Enough of a rarity these days that it made the muscles around his mouth feel stretched and strange.

He made a snap decision—hell, he was just doing his civic duty—and found himself on the path running towards her. It hadn't started raining yet, but the wind was cruel and cold. He liked it that way. It bit through his skin, reminding him that he had once been a man who felt things instead of just numbly going through the motions.

'Hey.' He caught up with her. Close up, she was… well, she was beautiful. English rose complexion, pretty smile and that long hair moving round her shoulders like a languid river as she turned to look at him. Beautiful indeed. It had been a very long time since he'd been struck enough to think something like that about a woman. He cleared his throat, raised his voice above the wild whip of wind. 'It's going to rain.'

'I know. I checked the forecast.' Her voice was soft, like velvet. A purr. Her eyes a curious amber colour. Something he'd never seen before. Or at least hadn't noticed. A hint of an accent, definitely southern. Not from around here, so no understanding of how quickly bad weather could creep up.

'But still no raincoat? No waterproof trousers? Gaiters?' She didn't even have a rucksack and he'd take bets on her not having a drink or snack in those cosy pockets in case of emergency. Wool? In the rain? Hypothermia would hit her before she had the chance to call the Oakdale team out. Didn't she know how stupid that was? 'I hope you're not going to be out for long—it's dangerous to be dressed like that out here. The weather changes very quickly at the top of those mountains and you could get caught out. People would have to risk their lives trying to find you if you got lost or hurt—imagine that. Imagine if someone got hurt because you didn't plan your hike properly. You're not remotely prepared for the conditions. Any conditions, to be honest.'

Her sunny smile fell as she looked at his collared cotton shirt then down at his leather work shoes. 'Neither are you, but I wouldn't dream of being so rude to a stranger.'

'Rude? I was trying to help.' *Thanks for nothing.*

Her eyebrows rose and she looked at her legs then back at him. 'Do I look as if I need help?'

Anything but. She looked vibrant and strong. Long limbs encased in black Lycra tights. Pink-cheeked. Well, actually red-faced now. He shrugged. 'Okay. Suit yourself. Get wet.'

She tipped her head and looked at the blackening clouds. 'I like rain.'

She really was a flake, then. Rain might have been good for crops, but it wasn't good for ill-prepared hikers. Or car drivers... He pushed that memory away, along with the accompanying ache in his heart. 'Good, because you're going to get a soaking today. Fill your boots.'

'I intend to.' At least she had sturdy shoes on. That was something. Gold eyes flashed with irritation. Warm-coloured pupils with a cold fleck of anger. She held his gaze.

And he held it right back. So much for being the Good Samaritan. He'd know better next time.

'Daddy? Dad! What are you doing out here? What's for breakfast? Can we have pancakes today?'

His daughter's voice jolted him back to reality. Behind him, Katy was shivering on the path, dressed only in her pyjamas. Nothing on her feet.

'Quick, inside—you'll get cold out here.' He ran back to the house, cursing to himself. *Idiot.* That was the last time he'd try to be helpful. 'Sorry, darling. No pancakes on a school day. I'm making porridge and there's a banana for afterwards.'

'Aww. Not fair.'

'Keep complaining and it'll be two bowls of porridge,' he quipped, trying to make her smile while making a deal.

Katy's bottom lip protruded in her well-worn, years-old way of appealing to his soft side. 'Granny makes pancakes every day when I'm there. Why can't we have them every day too?'

Joe bit back the healthy eating lecture that seemed to form the basis of their communication these days.

His beautiful, playful toddler had turned into a demanding little Miss recently and he wasn't sure why. Growing pains? Not for the first time—and definitely not the last—he wondered how different things might have been if Katy had had two parents around to bring her up. And with that thought he slopped the porridge into a bowl, the altercation with the woman still infiltrating his mood. Thank God he'd never need to speak to her again. Tomorrow, if she went past, he'd keep his mouth shut. Good luck to her.

He slid the bowl over to his eight-going-on-eighteen-year-old. 'Hey, you'll thank me when you still have lots of energy to run around at playtime.'

'Ugh. But I don't like it.' Katy really did look dismayed and Joe's heart pinged. Guilt lingered around the edges. Work was too damned busy at the moment; two staff down had made them all fraught, working extra hours to keep up with demand. Which meant less time with Katy. But now, as she watched his reaction, she grinned so easily, turning from heartbroken to heartbreaker with the simple upturn of her lips. 'I have lots of energy. All the time. And I really, really like pancakes. They're the best thing ever and if I have them I'll smile all day. For ever.'

For ever. He wished he could somehow stop time and preserve her like this, so innocent and so easily pleased by little things.

'Okay, we can set the alarm for earlier tomorrow and try making some pancakes. But you remember what happened last time?'

'You just threw it too high. We know better now. Granny's shown me how to flip them properly.' His daughter looked up at the sticky patch on the ceiling that he hadn't quite managed to remove with normal detergent and water. 'I'll show you.'

'Okay. Pancakes tomorrow. Now, eat up the porridge.' And there. He'd given in to her again. How could he not? She was the light of his life, the reason he got up in the morning. Things could have been so different…

As he tipped the rest of the sludgy breakfast into his own bowl his gaze drifted outside again. Thick clouds darkened the sky as heavy raindrops pelted the windows. See? She'd be getting soaked right about now. Rude? No, sensible. Unlike sunburst hat woman, who had disappeared and taken what little was left of his good mood with her.

The irritation lingered with him for the rest of the morning. His sister would have told him he had a choice and that he could *choose* to be jovial. But now he was running forty minutes late and was choosing to be quietly efficient and, okay, he might well have come across as gruff to the patient who complained about being kept waiting. Jovial and work-smart didn't figure in his picture right now. He was a man, after all; he couldn't multi-task.

And as if he needed more proof of his inability to focus, every time he tried writing up his notes he stared at the screen and the image of sunburst hat woman filled his head. *Gah.* He'd been rude and she'd called him on it, rightly. But it had been for her own good. At least that was what he kept trying to convince himself. And those eyes… The memory of that unusual colour had lingered as long as his bad mood. Why had he gone outside to talk to her when women were off his agenda these days?

'You want a cuppa?' Maxine, his trusty receptionist, called through his open office door.

'Brilliant. Yes, please, in my takeaway cup though, because I'm just heading out on the home visits.'

Maxine hobbled in on her arthritic legs. One day, too soon, she'd retire and he'd never find someone to truly replace her. She wasn't just the face of Oakdale Medical, she was it, heart and soul. 'You'll come through to the staffroom first, though, Joey? The new locum nurse has popped in for a walk-through before she starts properly tomorrow and I want you to say hello.'

There was a glint in her eye that made him nervous. He wasn't sure why. Maybe, because Maxine hadn't had a glint in her eye for a long time. 'Oh?'

'We've got her for a month so we've got some breathing space to fill the vacancy. Be nice—I don't want you scaring her off.'

'I'm always nice.'

'Hmm… No comment.' She smiled and he remembered his sister saying Maxine needed a medal for putting up with him these last few years. No doubt she was right. He hadn't exactly been a bundle of laughs recently. 'Come and say hello at least.'

He probably should, and be thankful someone had turned up at all, given the scarcity of people wanting to work here in the middle of nowhere, but he had patients who needed him to visit them. 'Would it be rude if I said no, and that I'll meet her tomorrow? I've got too much to do before the afternoon clinic.'

'Right you are. I'll tell her. She's lovely, so I'm sure she'll understand. Actually, there's something about her that seems…' As she shook her head her nose crinkled. 'Oh, nothing really. Just me being silly.'

'Seems what?' He didn't want anyone upsetting his

staff. But there he was, jumping to conclusions before he'd set eyes on the woman.

'I don't know...familiar, I suppose, although I've never met her before. She's nice. Got a nice manner. Friendly.' As she turned to leave she stopped short and inhaled sharply. 'Oh. Oh.'

His gut clenched. 'Everything okay, Maxine?'

She hunched forward and rubbed at her chest. Frowned. 'Nothing. Don't fuss. Just indigestion. I told David not to put onions in my sandwiches, but did he listen? No. And I ate them anyway, too quickly for my own good.'

'You sure you're okay?' Pulse prickling with concern, Joe was halfway across the room, assessing her pallor and breathing rate. 'What kind of pain is it? Come and sit down; let me look you over.'

She threw him the same look she'd been giving him for the last five years or so. 'Since that accident you've been on a mission to save the world, Joseph Thompson. And you can't. You've got to stop worrying about everyone and everything.'

'I care about you, so sue me. Let me check you over. Sit down.' He didn't want to be reminded about the accident and his overwhelming need to protect those he cared about. 'Please, Maxine. It won't take a minute.'

But, woefully stubborn as usual, she straightened and waved him back to his seat. 'I'm fine, Joey. Don't go bothering about me. I'll pop the kettle on. The closed sign's up, Jenny's out on calls, Alex is still on annual leave and the nurses are at a vaccination update over at the community hub in Ambleside, so it's tea for two. Oh...three if we count Rose.'

'Rose?'

Maxine's voice wafted down the corridor and he could picture her rolling her eyes, just so. 'The new nurse.'

The one he was choosing not to see. Right. Too bad. She'd understand once she saw his task list and inbox. He checked the clock on his computer screen as he finished writing up the last patient's notes. Five minutes before he was due at his first house call—a fifteen-minute drive away. Today, he was destined to run late for everything. Maybe he'd take a raincheck on that cup of—

'Quick! Someone? Dr…er…er…?' The woman's voice, assertive but breathy, came from Reception. 'Someone? Hello? Er… Crash call! Now.'

Crash call? *Damn.*

It took him less than five seconds to run up the corridor, but his heart rate trebled as he saw Maxine lying on the floor and a woman with white-blonde hair in a messy ponytail tilting his lovely receptionist's chin back…about to breathe for her?

What the hell? 'Maxine?'

'She collapsed. Cardiac, I'm sure. She was clutching her chest.' Amber eyes turned to him, then narrowed. 'Oh. It's you.'

'Joe Thompson. Dr Joe Thompson.' He nodded, then knelt next to Maxine with no hint of recognition or memory of their altercation this morning.

'And I'm Rose.' *Great.* He was the doctor she'd come to work with? The guy from the hill? The kind of pompous man she'd left behind, along with her old life. Still, if he was a stickler for the right walking gear he'd be picky about getting CPR technique right too. She just hoped they wouldn't need it. 'Faint carotid pulse. Dyspnoea. I caught her as she fell and lowered her to the floor, so no head or other bony injury.'

She looked down at the sweet woman who'd been showing her round the medical centre only a few minutes ago. They'd been getting on so well before this; Rose had been looking forward to working with her. She had a nice nature Rose had been instantly drawn to, and she also knew her way round the medical centre like an old hand. Maxine's eyes flickered open and she winced. 'Pain. Arm. Chest.'

'Okay, Maxi. We'll sort you out. Don't worry; we've got you. It'll be fine.' The doctor's face softened with affection and concern as he examined their unexpected patient. 'Those damned onions, right? I'll have to have a word with David.'

Onions? No. Rose blinked up at him and shook her head. It was some sort of cardiac problem. Clearly. What the hell kind of doctor was he? It was obviously cardiac and if anyone knew what that meant she did. She felt her own chest constrict and the long scar down her ribcage prickle in sympathy. 'Er…the pain is central chest and radiating to the left and down her arm. She's short of breath and has a weak pulse. It's not gastric—'

He looked at her as if she'd spoken out of turn. 'I am well aware of the symptoms.'

Yeah. Pompous was one thing, but misguided? Wrong, actually. 'You alluded to it being gastric, and it's not—'

Ignoring the rest of Rose's input, he pointed down the corridor, his voice all business as he spoke. 'ECG machine, portable oxygen and defibrillator are on a trolley in the treatment room. Down there. Second right. Bring it all here then call 999. Our full address is by the phone behind you, but shouldn't be necessary as they know where we are.'

She gritted her teeth and did as requested as efficiently as she could, given she'd only had a brief whip round the place in preparation for a full induction tomorrow. But it gave her enough time to ruminate on her impression of her new colleague and boss. Bad enough that he'd taken umbrage at her clothing choices this morning, but he was also one hell of a grumpy dude at work too.

It was just a shame he was so damned good-looking and she would have to endure looking at those soulful blue eyes for the duration of her stay. Never mind the impressive height and shock of blond hair—had Vikings ever made it this far west? If so, here was their long-lost son. Dr Joe *Thor* Thompson.

Tall. Pompous. Sexy eyes. A tick list to avoid if ever there was one. Been there, done that. Not happening again.

By the time she got off the phone the doctor had managed to assist Maxine onto a gurney Rose had dragged up from the treatment room along with the resus trolley, assessed her blood pressure and oxygen saturation, fitted an oxygen mask over her face and was attaching a twelve lead ECG to her chest. 'Breathing any better?'

Maxine shifted the mask so she could speak. 'Bit.'

Thor leant in and spoke gently. Which seemed incongruous on such a gruff big man. 'Your oxygen levels are a bit low, but once they come up we can take the mask off. How's the pain? Out of ten?'

'Eight.'

He nodded. 'Then I'll give you some pain relief. Nurse? Can you attach the leads while I do the needles?'

'Sure.' But then she wished she hadn't agreed, because

it was always difficult doing something for the first time in a new environment and her hands shook as she peeled back the sticky paper and placed the pads onto Maxine's chest. She willed her own heart rate to slow and the trembling to stop, but no dice. Her body was betraying her today, and all the time she felt Thor's eyes on her, assessing. Why was sticky paper so damned sticky? It wouldn't drop from her fingers as she shook them. It attached itself to the wires and got in the way of…everything. She looked up and caught his gaze. 'I'm sorry, it's—'

'Sticky. Yes.' He didn't move, didn't blink, barely breathed as he waited. But she felt his irritation swaddle her like a cloying cloak and she wished the ground would open up and swallow her. Finally, she managed to get everything in place and she felt him sigh.

Clamping down her own frustration, she closed her eyes briefly and took a deep breath. She would not let another man make her feel…*less*…ever again. She was good at her job. She was a great person, actually. She knew that, and it had been a long, hard journey to finally believe it.

But none of that was important right now; she had to work with this man regardless, and Maxine needed them both to get along if they were going to successfully care for her.

Their patient reached for Joe's hand as the last lead was clipped on. The ECG machine bleeped and whirred, then traced her heart rhythm onto an LED display. Not good news: Maxine was in the middle of an acute cardiac event and needed urgent treatment and admission to hospital.

Joe nodded as he looked at the read-out. 'Okay, sweetheart, it looks like you're going to have to make a trip to

Lancaster General because your heart isn't doing what it should do. So, I need to get a drip in your arm so we can start the treatment here and some aspirin will help make the blood flow a bit easier. But first, pop this tablet under your tongue. Bad news is, I don't think it was the onions after all.'

Maxine seemed to have diminished a little. 'Me neither. But I didn't want to bother you.' She pulled the mask away again and let Joe place the tablet under her tongue. Wincing, the older lady looked up at him and choked back a sob. 'I don't want to die, Joey.'

'Shh. Let the tablet dissolve. You're not dying here, that's for sure, not on my watch.' Once he'd secured intravenous access into her arm, as if it was the easiest thing in the world to do on an anxious woman with poor cardiac output and *refusenik* veins, he squeezed Maxine's other hand, his voice an altogether different tone to the one he'd used with Rose. 'We're going to make you comfortable.'

'But, what if I do die—?'

'No, Maxine. Do not even go there. Save your energy for getting better, not thinking the worst.' He drew up some morphine with very steady hands, handed the ampoule to Rose to check with barely a second glance at her, then he injected the painkiller into their patient.

When he'd finished Maxine struggled to sit up. 'Call David.'

Joe nodded. 'I will. And I'll tell him to meet you at the hospital. Now lie back and start getting better.'

But she tried to sit up again, her hand trembling as she grabbed his arm. 'I'm sorry. We're short-staffed as it is.'

He gently eased her back against the pillow and

stroked her hair. 'Please, relax. Stop talking, stop think-ing about everyone else and save your energy.'

'Tell Katy I love her.' Her voice was strained and thick with emotion, which seemed to take Joe aback.

'Of course, but she knows it well enough.' His eyes filled, but he shook his head, determined. One thing Rose realised now was that she'd grossly underestimated him. Yes, he was grumpy, but he had more than enough affec-tion and compassion for this woman. 'Don't go talking like that. You hear me?'

'And find someone to make you happy. Please. You need that in your life, Joey.'

What? A zillion questions fired in Rose's brain. That was an odd thing for his receptionist to say.

He blinked. Shook his head again, his gaze sliding quickly to Rose and then back to Maxine. Clearly he hadn't wanted her to overhear this conversation. 'Right. I think I can hear sirens. Any minute now we'll have the Lake District's finest bursting through the door.'

And they did. And when they saw who the patient was there was a flurry of activity and a very quick turnaround with a promise of having her back behind the reception desk—as she was demanding—in no time. Joe wanted to accompany her in the ambulance but Maxine flatly re-fused, saying he was needed here and to just phone her husband. So he did, breaking the news in that soft, con-cerned voice he seemed to reserve for friends and not for new staff—but then, why should he?

And then there was just the two of them left to clear up the mess of syringes and sticky papers, and tidy up the reception area, which they did in silence because Rose didn't know what to say that wouldn't receive a terse reply.

Thank goodness the medical centre had been closed for lunch and the incident hadn't played out in front of a clinic full of patients. She looked at the empty chair behind the desk and felt a chill shudder through her. They'd played the scenario down, but acute heart attacks were dangerous. Fatal in lots of cases, even if the patient survived the first bout of treatment. Hearts were tricky things and needed lots of looking after—physically and emotionally.

That was why she was here, after all, to make hers better.

Eventually, Rose couldn't cope with the oppressive silence any more. She wanted to talk about Maxine, even if he didn't. Talking about stressful things was a good thing, so the counsellor had told her. 'She's so sweet. I hope she'll be okay.'

Thor turned and looked up from the desktop computer, as if suddenly remembering she was there. Steely blue eyes narrowed. 'Yes.'

'You're going to miss her.'

'Yes.' He paused, looking as if he was working out what to say. 'She's my receptionist, but she's also my mother-in-law.'

Oh. No wonder he was so concerned. Oakdale was a small community, so of course there'd be family members all working together, unlike at the big London hospital she'd trained at. People there were from all over the world, strangers working with strangers, mostly. She'd come here because the small community had appealed. That, and a weird comforting feeling she'd had when she'd read the description of the place. It had sounded magical, idyllic and just the thing for a broken heart.

A new start, fresh air and lots of exercise to exorcise her past.

But why was his mother-in-law telling him to find someone to make him happy? That made no sense at all.

As if he could read her mind, he shook his head. 'People say things they don't mean when they're in a panic.'

'She was scared. It's understandable. You think you're going to live for ever, then something like this hits you out of the blue. It makes you rethink everything.'

'Right, yes.' He was nodding, but there was little emotion there. She expected a big sigh, at least. A rub of those skilled hands through his blond hair. A raised eyebrow or some sort of shared agreement that it had been really hard working on a friend. A discussion, maybe…some sort of virtual group hug that they'd done the right things in the emergency. Anything they could have done differently, better, things to be worked on for next time. But, no, nothing.

It was like talking to an automaton. But he was only like this with her, Rose noticed. With Maxine he'd been soft and sweet. Maybe she just needed to get to know him…or he needed to get to know her, before they could have cordial work relations. Maybe she just needed to hightail it back to the agency and demand to be placed somewhere else.

Instead, she took a deep breath. Because he must have been shocked by what had just happened; what else could explain his gruff manner? 'Hey, why don't you take a few minutes to debrief? Have a cup of tea or something? It's okay to feel blindsided by this.'

He looked at her as if she had two heads. 'I'm not

blindsided. I'm short-staffed. And I'm running very late for my home visits. Again.'

And with that he was gone.

CHAPTER TWO

THE NEW NURSE was still there when he got back from his home visits, despite her not being due to start work until tomorrow. And every time he came into the waiting area throughout the afternoon to call a patient into his room, there she was, sitting on Maxine's chair, chatting to the patients and other nurses as if she belonged there.

Her blonde ponytail bobbed as she laughed with Dennis Blakely, making the dour old man smile for the first time in living memory, those amber eyes sparkling as she shushed a crying newborn to sleep like some sort of baby whisperer. No longer wearing the orange hat or the red coat, she was dressed for work in a high-necked top and slim black trousers. Smart. Professional.

He wished she was still in the hat and coat… inappropriate for walking or work, but they matched her vibrancy.

As he watched her, Joe had the same feeling he'd had when he'd seen her on the mountain—as if something inside him was starting to wake up after a very long hibernation—he *noticed* her. And that in itself was the strangest thing, because he hadn't noticed much these last few years. He'd been swimming through a fog of survival and grief so deep he'd barely managed to function, drowning really, spending all his energy on making sure Katy got through this well-adjusted and, above all, happy. As happy as she could be. As happy as he could make her.

So did noticing a pretty woman mean he'd moved on?

Panic hit him with force, like bullets pelting his body—his heart, his gut, his throat. He wasn't sure he wanted to move on. Mostly, he didn't want to forget.

But, regardless of what *noticing* her meant, he needed to apologise for being rude. Twice. Probably more. Maxine would have a fit if he didn't and word got round he'd scared the new staff nurse away.

'You still here?' he asked her as he dropped blood forms and paperwork onto the large uncluttered desk, the last of the patients having just left. 'I thought you didn't start until tomorrow?'

'After Maxine's incident I wasn't going to leave you so short-staffed, was I? I just helped out, learning the ropes.' She looked up at him, her tone defensive, with little warmth in the amber gaze. 'Dr Jenny said it was all right for me to stay on. Apparently, they'll have someone to man the desk in the morning.'

'Yes, of course.' Good old Jenny—if it hadn't been for her, Maxine and Alex, the place would have buckled under Joe's flagging leadership and the mire of fog engulfing him. But the fog was lifting now, apparently, if noticing lovely eyes was anything to go by. Which was interesting and very inconvenient because he didn't want to find her—or any woman for that matter—attractive. Especially one who was here on a temporary contract and destined to leave when her time was up. He'd already had his world blown apart by the loss of one woman and he had no inclination to open himself up to that again. 'It's fine by me.'

'Good, because I'm not sure how you'd have got on with no one to cover the front desk during a busy afternoon clinic.' She nodded. 'Actually, it's worked out well, because now I know how the place runs.'

'I'm glad someone does.'

It was meant to be a joke, but it had been so long since he'd made one he wasn't sure it hit the mark. It shocked him that he wanted to see her face light up the way it had this morning as she'd stretched her arms out wide and breathed in the fresh morning air on his mountain.

But she just nodded, all business. 'It's actually very straightforward. Maxine's got systems in place for everything.'

'I know. She's a star and runs a very tight ship. I was… er…joking.'

'Oh. I didn't realise you knew how.' This time she did smile, although it was a little hesitant and didn't warm her eyes and he knew it was because all she knew about him was that he was bad company.

So now was his chance to make amends. 'Look, can we start over? I'm sorry about this morning.'

'Which bit?'

'What do you mean?' Wasn't a blanket apology enough?

Clearly not. She started to count his misdemeanours off on her fingers. 'The comments about my clothing choice for a super quick walk up the hill.' *Forefinger.* 'The dismissal of my input with a very sick patient.' *Middle finger.* 'Outright rudeness when I tried to be compassionate to you…' *Ring finger.* Which, he noted, didn't have a ring, but it did have a barely discernible white line which meant…which meant he was noticing more than he should. Her terse voice made him focus. 'Which are you apologising for, Doctor?'

Those lovely eyes settled on his face. A little warmer. Drifted to his mouth, back to his eyes, and he had the distinct feeling she was sizing him up.

That made him stand taller. So, she wasn't going to pussyfoot around him. This was new, and he wasn't sure what he thought about it. But he definitely deserved it. Maybe he'd been too protected by his staff, who'd all taken the reins when he'd begun to sink, and probably let him get away with too much self-absorption in the process.

'Good point. I'm sorry for everything. Absolutely everything I did, and pretty much everything I didn't do too… The fact that the Tooth Fairy isn't real, the extinction of the dinosaurs, and mostly for *The Birdie Song*.'

Her eyes twinkled at that and she started to laugh. Which made him notice her even more.

She put her hand up, signalling that he'd said enough. 'Okay. Don't get carried away. But…oh, my poor heart… the Tooth Fairy? Not real?'

'I know. I took it hard too. For God's sake, don't tell my daughter; she'd never forgive me.'

'My lips are sealed.' She did a zipping action with her forefinger and thumb across her mouth. Pouting it a little. It was a nice mouth. Full lips. The kind of smile that made you feel as if you had a pool of light in your chest. Seemed it wasn't just his head but his heart noticed her too. Something in his blood started to fizz.

It had no right fizzing. He cleared his throat. 'So, let's start again. I'm Joe Thompson. The patients know me as Dr Joe. Maxine calls me Joey. But I also answer to *hey you*, *oi* and a whole lot of things I can't say in polite company…and that you've probably muttered under your breath more than once today.'

A wry lift of her eyebrow. 'I stopped counting when I got to fifty-seven.'

'That bad, eh? I'm sorry and even though I didn't show it I'm very grateful you're here, particularly today.'

'You're forgiven, but only just, and you're now on a caution.' She nodded, satisfied. The smile stayed in place, hinting he was on the right track with being civil. 'Any more of that grumpy nonsense and you'll be in a lot of trouble. Life's too short to be a huge pain in the ars—'

'Indeed.' As he knew, well enough. But he'd been stewing in his bad mood for five years and he'd thought he might be stuck there.

'Anyway, I'm Rose McIntyre. Locum nurse extraordinaire.' She stuck out her hand, long feminine fingers.

Which he took and shook, trying to ignore more fizzing, this time over his skin as her fingers slipped from his. He caught her gaze and wondered whether she'd felt it too.

No. No hint of any kind of fizzing on her side. Why on earth would she? He dragged his eyes from hers and tried to be more professional. 'So, from somewhere down south, judging by the accent?'

She nodded and two small dots of pink bloomed on her cheeks. 'Born and bred in London.'

'But…?'

'But what?' The pink intensified.

'There must be a *but* if you've moved away from your home to little old Oakdale in the middle of nowhere.'

'It's so beautiful here.' But her demeanour changed,

the openness in her eyes shuttered down. 'I just needed…
wanted a change.'

'Bright lights and big city getting too much?'

'Something like that.' Her gaze slid away from him
and she picked up her handbag, signalling the conversation about her was over. She wasn't going to tell him
anything personal, that was for sure. He didn't even know
why he wanted to know. They'd had other locums and
he'd never asked about their reasons for coming here.
She shook her head as if brushing off a thought and the
smile was back on her face. 'So, anyway, how were the
pancakes? Laced with arsenic? No? Too bad.'

'I wouldn't blame you if you slipped some into my
sandwiches tomorrow. I'll make sure I don't label them
so you won't know which are mine.' He laughed. Actually laughed. It felt strange, muscles working in his belly
that were usually only taxed by exercise. 'No pancakes
today. I made her eat porridge, but I was bribed to do
pancakes tomorrow. Don't be surprised if I come in covered in batter. That happens.'

She smiled. 'Bribery or batter?'

'Both. Too often.'

'Kids, eh?' The way she said it gave him pause. Wist-
ful? Sad? There was a gentle raise of her eyebrows, a
shrug. *That's life.* But she'd already closed down enough
at the remotest hint of a conversation about anything too
personal, so he left it.

Suddenly serious, she closed down the computer and
stood up. 'Hey, did you check on Maxine? Have you heard
how she's doing? I mean… I know I'm not a relative or
anything and I barely know her, so I hope you don't think
I'm prying, but—'

'But you probably saved her life and for that I can't

thank you enough.' If Rose hadn't been here God knew what might have happened. 'I just spoke with the cardiologist at Lancaster; she's comfortable enough and they confirmed a myocardial infarction. She's going to be in for a while.'

'Next time you speak to her, give her my regards, please.'

'I'm going over to the hospital tonight, so will do.' He checked his watch. Time was marching. He really shouldn't be standing here doing this, no matter how much he was enjoying trying to make amends. Thank God the rain had stopped a few hours ago. The roads would be dry and clear so…he steered his mind from where it usually went when he thought about rain and driving, and reframed things…so it wouldn't take too long to get there and back. An easy drive of fifty minutes each way.

She frowned at her watch. 'Really? All that way? It's getting late.'

'I'll take Katy, my daughter; we'll just pop in for a quick visit.' It would have to be a very quick visit if he didn't move soon. But his mouth started to run away on a different tangent. 'You enjoyed your walk this morning? Except the part where a bad-tempered bloke bawled you out?'

She brushed her hand along her hair, smoothing some wayward wisps, and nodded, an ironic smile at the memory. 'Well, yes, apart from grumpy men commenting on my inappropriate, but very lovely, cardigan it is beautiful up there. I can see why you live in that house—the view's amazing and it's such a quaint cottage.'

Pippa had loved it too, the second she'd set foot on the land. More than enough bedrooms, the perfect garden, a kitchen with the best view in the county. He'd bought it for her, for their future and the big family they were going to have...

And just like that his dead wife slipped so easily back into his brain. A familiar tight ache settled under his rib-cage. Maybe he hadn't moved on as much as he'd thought. 'Yes. On a clear day you can see as far as Morecambe.' His voice was tighter, as if his throat had been rubbed with sandpaper.

If Rose noticed she didn't make it obvious. 'Someone told me you could see all the way to Ireland, but I think they were pulling my leg. I only walked up to Craggy Gill and back this morning. Just a quick stretch of my legs before I came in here.'

Fifteen minutes from his house. 'I should have asked you where you were headed then. Lesson learnt.' But the thought of Pippa reminded him of everything he should be doing instead of standing here trying to make a pretty woman smile. 'Right. I have to go.'

He didn't want to. Something about her made him want to hang around and chat. But... Katy. Maxine. *Pip. Sweet Pip.* The hollow in his chest expanded.

Was he moving on? Could he? There was that panic again, deep inside.

Rose headed towards the door. 'Great, I'll come with you.'

'No.' He had to get his head sorted. And collect his daughter, then drive to Lancaster Hospital.

'Just outside. That's all.' Rose blinked. Twice. 'I don't know how to lock up.' She wiggled her fingers. 'No keys?'

'Right. Yes.' What had he been thinking? That she'd somehow want to come with him? Home? To the hospital? Anywhere? What a ridiculous idea. Almost as ridiculous as wanting to make her smile, instead of reminding himself how futile that would be.

'Are you taking your medications?'

'Of course. Not something I'm about to forget, right? They keep me alive.' Rose sighed inwardly and shook her head. It was lovely that her mother was so concerned, but really…sometimes the concern was beyond suffocating.

'Why are you so breathless? What's the matter? Are you ill? Have you got an infection?'

'I'm climbing a mountain, Mum.' Despite the pride at being able to achieve something she'd never imagined possible a few years ago, Rose felt her mother's anxiety shimmering down the phone all the way from London. It didn't matter how many miles she put between them, there was no escape when she was only a phone call away. Still, she couldn't pop round unannounced like she used to do, not without a lot of planning. Rose tried to steady her breathing, but that wasn't easy on the uphill. 'Please don't worry about me. It'll make you sick again. I'm fine. Really.'

'You're climbing a mountain? In the dark? Why on earth would you do that?'

Good question. Rose stopped for a minute to catch her breath and take in the view. A cloudless sky, lit by a silvery moon, more stars than she'd ever imagined there could be above her. And then, below that, a horizon of dark shadows of the mountains surrounding the village, and the orange lights in the Oakdale houses illuminating the foothills like glow-worms.

Magical. Breathtaking. Peaceful. So peaceful. No one to challenge her, to compare her to how she used to be, no one to tell her how much she'd changed. No one to nag her, to fuss. No one to trouble her.

Except for a certain grumpy doctor she couldn't stop thinking about… That was troubling. She'd only spent one day in his company but he intrigued her, probably a lot more than he should. From that whole Nordic vibe he had going on to the full body tingle she'd had when they shook hands.

Tingling wasn't on her agenda. She'd come to lick her wounds and start afresh, have an adventure with a big emphasis on not getting involved with another man for a very long time. She'd had enough of being told what to do and how to act…and, after being in hospital for so long, everyone had been an expert on how she should behave.

Not any more!

Besides, Dr Thor had a mother-in-law, ergo he was married. He had a child. He was so off-limits he might as well have been in Outer Mongolia or… Norway.

Breathing in the cold fresh air, she tried to still her mind the way she'd been taught. In. Out. In. Out. *Feet on the earth. Breathe the scents of wildflowers and grass. Listen.* Up here it was completely silent, apart from the wheeze in her chest at the unusual exertion. And the palpable panic from her mother. 'Rose? Are you still there? Why are you up a mountain?'

'Oh. Yes, sorry. I'm just dropping something off at someone's house.'

'Whose house?'

Thor's. She smiled to herself. He really did have nice eyes and a smile that transformed his face, when he remembered to do it. When he allowed himself… There was something locked up inside him; she could see that. Something had happened to make him so tetchy and reserved. She just didn't know what. Didn't want to know, really. Because everyone had something, right? 'Just the boss's house.'

'What kind of boss brings you out at night in the dark? Walking up a hill? Does he know about your heart—?'

'No.' Rose cut her mother off. At some point she'd realise her daughter wasn't an invalid any more, but it hadn't hit home yet. 'There's no reason to tell him, okay? Why would I? The job agency only ask if there are any medical issues that interfere with my ability to do the job. And I don't have any. I'm healthy. Healthier than a lot of people my age. I get lots of exercise, I eat well. I take my tablets and I get regular check-ups.'

Mostly, she didn't want all the questions, the *Oh, I'm so sorry* or… *You're so lucky* and, worst of all, *What happened to the person who died?* Once upon a time she'd loved being the party girl and centre of attention, but not now. She hated all the interrogation and prying into her life.

Unfortunately her mother hadn't got that particular memo. 'I'm worried about you, Rose. I still don't under-stand why you went into nursing…all those infections in hospitals. You could catch something, or worse…'

'Please, Mum, we've talked about this so many times. I'm fine. Dr Lee said nursing would be fine as long as I was careful.'

'You had a lovely job at Red Public Relations. They were nice people. Our kind of people.'

Your kind of people. Not mine. Not any more. 'Not this again, please. I love nursing.'

'And I don't know why you had to move so far away from everyone who loves you.'

Because of conversations like this. 'I'm just trying to

make my own way, Mum. It's so lovely here; you should come and visit.'

'I just might.'

Give me three years' notice to prepare myself mentally. 'I've rented a place with two bedrooms, so come any time. Just give me some advance warning so I can get time off to show you round. We could go to Beatrix Potter's house; you'd love it.'

'What about Toby?'

'What about him? I don't think he's interested in Jemima Puddleduck. Far too boring for Toby.'

The terrain had evened out a little now as she got closer to Thor's house, but her heart was hammering at the exertion. And at the mention of her ex-boyfriend. 'Please don't bring him with you.'

Her mother sighed. 'I'm sure if you came home and talked to him he'd take you back.'

Rose stopped outside the doctor's house. No car. Which meant they were still out. Good—she'd just leave the food here then head back home. Stupid idea in the first place; God knew why she'd suddenly decided to bring it. Or why they had to talk about her pathetic love life and ruin this lovely evening.

'Toby dumped me, if you remember. Because I'm not the fun-loving girl I used to be, apparently. Because I decided to do something to give back.'

And mainly—although she hadn't had the heart to tell her mum this—because he couldn't cope with the fact that there was still a good chance Rose's life would be cut short. He didn't want to back a lame horse when he could marry a perfectly normal woman with all her own body parts and an uncomplicated life expectancy.

'You could give back in lots of other ways, darling. A

little charity work or something.' She cleared her throat and Rose waited for the *Don't let your one chance slip through your fingers* talk. 'Don't miss out on your chance with Toby Fletcher just because you're stubborn. He said he didn't mind that children were out of the picture.'

'He didn't want them in the first place, Mum.' Rose had been the devastated one when they'd been told that.

'That's good then, isn't it? And he'd look after you, financially at least.'

'For God's sake, Mum, he didn't want me, okay? Besides, are you saying I should marry a man just because he's rich? Do what he says? Fit in with who he wants me to be? Try to be someone who I'm not?'

'Rose?' A man's voice behind her. Gruff.

'Oh!' Her poor heart damned near thumped out of her chest. 'Joe! You're home? I didn't realise. Got to go, Mum. Bye.' Flicking her phone into her pocket, she turned to meet steady and distinctly unamused blue eyes. 'No car here…'

His mouth twitched. A little wary. 'It's in the garage.'

Of course it was. She looked over at the dark shadow of a building on the left-hand side of the house. There was the garage. A faint smell of petrol in the air. She looked down at the plastic container in her hand and shrugged. Now she just felt stupid, like a kid trying to be teacher's pet or something. She'd just planned to leave the container and a note and then go back to her cottage, not have an actual conversation.

And now there were tingles again and she was pretty sure her heart should have stopped bumping after he'd made her jump, but it was still rattling away. 'I wasn't expecting you back so soon. How is Maxine?'

He shrugged. 'As I expected. Tired and still very

poorly, so we literally just popped our heads round the door for a brief chat and then came home. The doctors are doing more tests but she's scheduled for a bypass once she's stable. Katy's just happy to have seen her.'

'It's a long journey; you must be tired.' Clearly they were all very close.

He nodded. 'Worth it, though. She said to say thank you and that she owes you a lot.'

'Seriously, she doesn't owe me anything. Anyone would have done the same.'

'Ah, but you get the Maxine tick of approval. That's usually hard-earned. But you'll see, if she takes you under her wing you'll have the whole village eating out of your hand.'

He stood aside and indicated for her to walk into his house. Exhaustion etched his eyes and she ached to press her hand to his face and get him to lean against her. To take some of his stress away. But why? She couldn't understand what this weird feeling inside her was…unsettled, yet excited.

'So, did you want something other than to talk outside my window about marrying rich men?'

'I—er…' He'd heard? Her stomach twisted into a tight knot. Marrying anyone was the last thing on her bucket list.

'Don't, by the way. Don't ever try to be someone you're not.' A small smile that tugged at her gut. He was trying to be nice. 'Just be you.'

'God, I'm sorry you heard that.' She was still working out who she was. For her, time was split into before she got sick and after the operation. With a blur of pain and panic and dread, and a zillion promises that if she survived she'd do some good in between. But somewhere along the line she'd lost herself, and it was only now she was finding out what she wanted out of life and who she truly was. Today, it appeared to be blithering idiot with a dash of good neighbour. She held out the still-warm container. 'I'm just dropping off something for you to eat.'

His eyes narrowed. 'Why?'

'Because you probably didn't get the chance to cook anything before you dashed to Lancaster. Unless Mrs Thompson's cooked for you…but I assumed she'd go with you to see her mum. So, just in case you were all starving, I thought I'd—'

'There is no Mrs Thompson.' He cut her off, jaw tightening as he looked at his feet. An awkward silence dropped, heavy and thick, around them.

Oh. What to say now? His abruptness was disconcerting. Was it just with her? It seemed to be. With everyone else he was soft and friendly.

And what the hell had happened to his wife?

'What's that?' The girl from this morning skipped into view, eyes zeroing in on the plastic container. Hair in messy lopsided pigtails and with gaps in her teeth and a very sunny smile, she was adorable. 'Is that for us? I'm starving. Daddy said we're not allowed takeaway 'cos it's unhealthy.'

And Rose could have kissed her for breaking the uncomfortable atmosphere. Joe looked over at his daughter and his whole demeanour transformed: his eyes softened, his hiked-up shoulders dropped. Love for her was stamped in every gaze, every movement.

Rose smiled at the girl. 'Kale and chicken pasta bake.'

'What's kale?'

'The devil's work.' Brighter now, or putting on a show for his daughter, Joe lifted the lid and sniffed. 'But it smells delicious. It is very late so I was going to do beans on toast, but this is much better. Go get some plates out, Katy. And say thank you to Rose.'

'Okay, Daddy. Thank you, Rose. You're nice.'

The kid's smile tugged at Rose's heart and she had a sudden urge to run her hand over the top of those messy bunches. Weird. Not something she'd ever wanted to do to a child before. Maybe the fresh air was going to her head?

She followed Joe through to the large kitchen/dining room. 'Cute kid.'

'Yes. Too cute for her own good sometimes. Or maybe I'm just a pushover.'

That was the last thing Rose imagined him to be, judging by his general manner. He frowned and leaned a little closer. The air around her filled with a scent that was light and fresh and yet very masculine.

She had to stop herself leaning into it as he whispered, 'Kale?'

'It's healthy if that's what you mean.'

'In which case you'll want to join us?'

Did she?

She looked round at the comfortable farmhouse kitchen. There was warmth here in the scrubbed, well-used pine table, the overflowing toy box, a cushion-filled window seat that, she imagined, looked out over the village. There was a sense of calm, a familiar smoky smell of wood-burning stove and coffee. A sense of family and love. Scuffed skirting boards and the faint bruises of handprints on the walls…the perfect family house.

On an old wooden dresser leaning against one wall stood myriad framed photos of Joe and a small baby— she imagined to be Katy—and a woman who looked like a younger version of Maxine. The same laughing eyes. Same corkscrew curls that made up Katy's lop-sided bunches.

No Mrs Thompson. Rose's heart began to thud. Because the photos were all from when Katy was little. Not of now. Not of the intervening years. Divorce?

She doubted it. Joe and the woman were staring into each other's eyes, obviously deeply in love with each other and with their child. Rose's heart jerked uncomfortably—she wasn't destined to have that. No children for her…no happy little family.

She had no idea, but she doubted a mother/son-in-law relationship would be so strong after divorce. Toby's mum had distanced herself from Rose the minute they'd split up…or before…when it became apparent that Rose wasn't headed on the path they'd all thought she would.

So…did Mrs Thompson die?

That didn't bear thinking about. A woman so young and clearly full of life and love. And yet it happened, as Rose knew well, through illness or disease or pure bad luck. There was no woman here. No mention of Maxine's daughter going with them to visit her in hospital.

Rose shivered, a strange panicky sensation prickling over her chest. And a sudden deep sadness.

What the hell was she doing here? Intruding on this family?

She found her voice. 'No. Thank you. It's late and I really need to go.'

CHAPTER THREE

THE OFFICIAL FIRST day in her new job wasn't going well.

'I'm so sorry; Maisie doesn't usually act like this.' Janice, the very red-faced mum, apologised, looking in horror at the mess of plaster and water oozing over the trolley edges and glooping onto the floor. Rose's four-year-old patient had stopped screaming and was now all but smiling at the chaos she'd created by kicking over the plaster bowl the second Rose attempted to bandage the broken ankle. 'But she's in pain and the long wait to be seen didn't help.'

Dabbing the floor with paper towels, Rose dug deep for a smile. Because she knew how frustrating long waits were and how hard it was to be nice when pain blurred your edges. 'I'm so sorry for that. The appointment template went down on the computer and it took a while to get sorted out, which meant we had no idea who we were supposed to be seeing next. And in the meantime Maisie's appointment got moved round.' She looked at the water dripping from the trolley and tried to wipe it up, but ended up smearing plaster-infused mess over everything instead. 'And it's fine; it really is. I'll just clear this up. Maybe Maisie's ticklish? Maybe that's why her leg jerked out. I'll be careful. No toe touching. I promise, poppet.'

Janice made soothing noises to her daughter but Maisie started to whimper in such a way Rose knew it would turn into a replay of the roar the child had emitted a few times in the waiting room. 'Okay, new plan. I'll sort the floor in a minute. Let's get that leg in plaster first. That should help with the pain.'

'Thanks.' Janice nodded and started to walk round the end of the gurney. 'And I'll come round that side and hold her good leg down.'

Rose spied a puddle of water that she'd missed on the woman's path. *Damn.* 'Be careful—the floor's wet—'

'Whoa!' Janice jerked forward and disappeared with a thud behind the other side of the gurney. 'Ouch.'

Things were going from bad to worse. Rose pushed the trolley out of her way with more force than she'd intended, sending it hurtling into the door with a crash, and dashed over to help the woman up. 'Are you okay? Oh, my goodness. Let me help you.'

'I'm fine, really. Just a wet bottom.' She laughed as she rubbed her jeans. 'Ouch, though. I damaged my ego more than anything else.'

'It's always a shock. I'm so sorry.' The last thing she needed was another casualty.

'Mummy! It still hurts!' Maisie's promised roar was on the up. And Rose's optimism was taking an uncharacteristic downturn. What had happened to her usual calm? She had a bad feeling she'd left it behind at a certain doctor's house on the hill.

'What the heck is going on here?' Joe stood in the doorway, stethoscope hanging round his neck, frown deep over his eyes.

Just great.

Rose's heart thrummed. She hoped it was out of embarrassment for the chaos happening in the room, and not for any other reason. But every time she saw him her heart did a funny thing. Maybe she should see her specialist and get checked over? Maybe. Maybe she should just admit she had a sneaky crush on Dr Thor, despite all her reasons not to get involved with anyone...especially a family-orientated one, no matter how good-looking. Or how downright grumpy.

'It's my fault. We spilled some water and Janice slipped in it.'

'I am so sorry this happened. Are you okay?' He helped Janice into a chair and did a quick triage assessment. As always, his manner with his patients was impeccable.

'I'm fine, honestly. It's fine. Just get Maisie's cast on and we'll get out of your hair.'

'Yes, definitely.' Rose rolled her sleeves up, took the bowl to the sink to fill it with water but felt the pressure of Joe's gaze on her the whole time. Seemed things were destined never to run smoothly between them, no matter how many times they started over. She turned and gave him a *What do you want?* glare.

Steely blue eyes glowered back at her. His humourless mouth ground out, 'Can we talk?'

She nodded curtly towards Maisie. 'When I'm done here.'

'When will that be?'

She checked the wall clock. 'I have a blood pressure check that was due at eleven.'

'It's now eleven forty-five.'

'I am aware of the time, Dr Thompson.' Trying to

soften her voice so as not to alarm her patients, she turned
away from them. 'After that I have a diabetes check and
a wound dressing. I'm working as fast as I can.'

His nod was sharp. 'When you're free then. Whenever
that's likely to be.'

'Yes. Of course.' She felt as if she was supposed to
snap her heels together and salute. *Sir!* Which was exactly what she'd been trying to leave behind. Oh, what
had happened to the friendly community practice she'd
been promised? Still, she'd only committed for a month
to see whether she liked the locum life or whether she
needed to retreat to the comfort of home. At this rate, the
month could easily turn into a matter of days.

But then, Rose wasn't a quitter.

She was also not afraid to stand up for herself.

For the next hour she worked hard and efficiently and
caught up without rushing her patients. But unfortunately
that meant all too soon she had to go and face Joe and no
doubt the reprimand he'd been planning.

She found him in his clinic room. In contrast to his
lovely home, this space was clinical, bare, apart from a
copy of a photo in his house: him, Katy and that pretty
woman she assumed was Katy's mum.

It was entirely his space. Masculine. She ignored the
little skip in her heart as she walked into his room and
breathed in his scent. Saw the rash of blond hair, strong
hands typing hard on the computer. And, for a brief moment, she wondered how they'd feel around her waist,
tugging her towards him. Or on her face.

Ridiculous. Her cheeks heated at the thought. This
fresh north country air was making her feel strange. Al-
titude sickness? Did that make you a little crazy? Hor-
monal? She made a mental note to look it up later in one

of her medical books. She swallowed. 'Er… You wanted to see me?'

'Rose.' He swivelled to face her. 'About earlier—'

'I know, I know. It was a health and safety issue. The floor was wet—there should have been a sign up.' She sighed. She'd learnt over the years that it was better to hold her hands up and accept there could be room for improvement—that usually took the wind out of the other person's sails. She'd so wanted to give a good impression and it was all going wrong. 'Things have been off all morning.'

His eyebrows rose above those bluest of blue eyes. 'Usually, Maxine—'

'Well, she isn't here and I think everyone's in a bad mood because of it. I get that, I really do.' Rose softened her voice. Of course he knew Maxine wasn't here and how wonderful she was. He was related to her. 'So, we're all trying to do our best out there. Beth's a great stand-in receptionist and she worked hard to get the system up and running as soon as possible but—'

His hand went up. 'Please, stop. Stop talking.'

'Oh.' She clamped her mouth shut, well aware she had a habit of talking rapid-fire when she was embarrassed. 'Sorry.'

'I was going to say, usually Maxine has a welcome lunch for our new staff…but I've been too snowed under to organise it today and now it's almost time for the afternoon clinic to start. Can we do it tomorrow?'

'Oh.' No telling-off. No stern words. Now it was her turn to have the wind taken out of her sails. He'd wanted to make her welcome. Heat radiated from her, she was sure. 'I have sandwiches; it's fine.'

'No, it isn't. We try to make our new staff feel at home

and I know that hasn't happened for you. And I was also going to ask you how it's all going. I think I caught you at a bad moment earlier?'

'Yes. I don't usually try to redecorate treatment rooms with plaster-of-Paris…or drum up extra work by injuring patients' relatives—that's a first, even for me.' That drew a very small smile from him. *Go on. A little more—smiling is easy. It won't break your face.* 'I'm getting to know the ropes but I haven't got a locker or a computer log-on; I'm still using Maxine's.'

'Okay. My fault. Human resources is under my jurisdiction. We share the partner load—Dr Jenny, Dr Alex and I—it's easier if we all take responsibility for one or two things each. So, I'll sort you out a locker and a logon. Maxine would usually do it, but leave it with me. I'll work it out. I'll just have to get the system to talk to me.' His mouth twitched up. 'Judging by this morning's performance, it could be interesting.'

What was interesting was his smile. Such a rarity, but a thing of beauty when it happened. It made his whole face brighter, smoothing away those shadows under his eyes and lightening the blue pupils to a mesmerising colour, like the sky that first day at the top of the mountain. Dazzling. Clear. Endless.

She dragged her gaze from his, all the better to concentrate. 'Do computer glitches happen a lot?'

He shook his head. 'Not for a long time.'

'So maybe it's just me then. I've jinxed the place, clearly.' She laughed; it could be true. 'First Maxine getting sick, then the computers going down and then the water on the floor.'

He laughed too. A deep rumble that had just the faintest smidgeon of joy in it… Then it was gone and she wondered whether she'd imagined it. But he shook his head. 'I don't believe in jinxes.'

'Then perhaps it's pure bad luck, not a jinx.'

'I don't believe in luck either. You do things and they have consequences. Cause and effect.'

'What about magic, make-believe, romance, coincidence? I like to think things happen for a reason.' How else could she explain what had happened to her seven years ago? Getting sick had been overwhelming and near fatal, but it had opened her eyes to how shallow her life had been. That experience had been life-changing in so many ways, she refused to believe it was just something dull like simple maths: one plus one equals two.

'I'm a doctor, Rose. We do science, not romance.' Joe shook his head again. 'And fate? No. I don't believe in that either.'

She sighed; he was a lost cause. 'You don't believe in much.'

'I believe in working hard and making the best of what we've got.'

'Sounds a bit depressing, if you ask me.'

He pushed his chair back from the desk and stood up, sorting through his doctor's bag, stuffing in a wad of notes. He looked directly at her and his eyes darkened. 'It's real, Rose. That's all.'

Something bad must have happened to him, because surely everyone had a space in their hearts and lives for a little whimsy? Mystique. Fantasy. That was what movies and novels were about, right? Taking you away from the mundane. Escapism—everyone needed that. And to dream big.

'Sometimes real can be fun too. I refuse to spend the

rest of my life just working hard and surviving. Living…
that's where it's at. Taking notice of things.'

'Like doing yoga on a mountain…right?' He smiled
at the memory.

'Absolutely. Why not? Why not throw caution to the
wind? Do the unexpected.'

He smiled when he thought of her up there, with her
hair wild like Medusa and her skin being nipped by arc-
tic wind? That was unexpected. She hadn't even realised
he'd seen her doing it, and she wasn't sure she liked the
way her body was reacting to that information, with heat
and giddiness in her stomach.

Joe's head tilted a little to the side as he asked, 'So
what have you done that's unexpected?'

Weird thoughts and sensations when being in the same
room as Thor Thompson—did they count? 'I came here,
for a start.'

'Oh?'

'I was expected to take a job in London, marry the ex
and settle down.' Thoughts of Toby had irritation skittering down her spine, pouring metaphoric cold water
on the adrenalin rush.

'And you didn't do any of that because…?'

Yes, why had she left everything she knew? Come
here, of all places? Because the village name sounded
nice? Because there was something about it that had
piqued her interest…? She couldn't explain it; it just felt…
right. Fate, perhaps. The roll of a dice, maybe. Whatever
that meant.

Although, judging by the way her body was reacting to Thor, she was starting to wonder whether she'd
made a mistake coming here at all. One of the promises
she'd made as she'd lain in that hospital bed contemplat-

ing her death was that, if she was lucky enough to get a chance at a new life, she would live the kind of life befitting two people—a huge life filled with joy and fun and care for others. Training to be a nurse was the start. Oakdale was the next step. After this, who knew? There was a big world out there. Falling for some guy in a tiny village in her own country wasn't on her plan. Falling for a guy at all wasn't. The last thing she wanted was to find someone and then fall sick again.

'I needed to get out of my comfort zone and challenge myself. Plus, you do a good advert selling the place. You know, you should live a bit more dangerously Dr Joe… try some yoga at the top of your hill as the sun comes up. It's good for your soul. So is laughing. You need to do it more. A lot more.'

'Laugh?' Immediately his smile dropped as if he couldn't find a single thing to laugh about.

Okay, she knew she'd overstepped. But she wanted to shake him up and make him take notice of the wonderful things he could be doing, feeling, seeing instead of being blinkered by whatever it was that haunted him and stopped him believing in fantasies and dreams.

'Right. Note to self: smile more. Great.' He blinked. Shook his head. Taken aback by her words, he started to walk towards the door.

'Sorry. I shouldn't have said anything.'

'Actually, you're the first person to call me out on it. Things have been a bit rough these last few years and everyone's tiptoeing around me. I've got used to getting my own way, I suppose, but when you're deep in it you don't have the time or energy to drag yourself out.'

There was something about the way he was explaining it to her, so matter of fact and devoid of emotion, that made her want to wrap her arms around him and hold him tight. 'Sounds like it's been tough.'

'And then some. Things got intense…' He shook his head but smiled. 'I'm out the other side now.' He blew out a big breath, as if he'd been holding it for all those years he was talking about. And something shifted in his eyes. Like a cloud edging away from the sun and letting more light in. His shoulders dipped, relaxing as he reached past her to push the door open. 'Too much information?'

Not at all. Not enough. Nowhere near. So many questions zipped into her head, but asking would probably push him back behind that armoured wall he hid behind. 'No. Honestly. We've all got backstory.'

Eyebrows rose. 'Toby?'

'Amongst other things.'

'Things that you're not going to talk about.'

'No.' She was not going to let her past poison her present. 'I like to look forward, not backwards. That way, you don't get neck strain and you can see where you're going.' As she looked up at him she noticed some gloop on his shirt at her eye level. 'Oops. Is that…did you get plaster-of-Paris on your shirt?'

Frowning, he peered down. 'Maybe. Or, more likely, it's pancake batter gone rogue. Still, most of it stayed in the pan and they were just about edible.'

'And wearable—who knew?' She laughed.

'Not me, that's for sure. You know, not one person has said anything about it all morning.'

'Probably too scared to. I'm the only one with a run-away mouth brave enough to mention it.'

'You probably are.' He smiled as he ran a paper towel under a tap then dabbed it onto his shirt. A stain oozed across his chest as he tutted and dabbed some more, spreading the gloop instead of cleaning it off.

She fought the urge to help him. And also not to look too closely at the press of fabric against hard muscle. 'Not such a good idea to be so upfront with your boss, right? Would you prefer me to tiptoe like everyone else? Is that more likely to keep the peace?'

As he threw the paper towel into the bin he brushed past her. Without thinking, she put her hand on his arm. Then quickly removed it. The contact was too intense. She'd only just met him. This was ridiculous; she was imagining a connection between them when there couldn't possibly be one.

But his gaze snagged hers and something almost palpable zipped between them. Thick and sultry. She got the feeling that tiptoeing around him wasn't on his agenda, but something else might have been. Tiptoeing up to him, perhaps? Tiptoeing to reach his mouth? A shiver of something primal shuddered up through her and she knew it must have been in her eyes, betraying her. There was certainly a flash of heat in his. Something she hadn't seen for a long time in anyone's eyes, not for her. It was shocking. Exciting. But scary.

The room seemed to shrink, claustrophobic and hot. He was too close. So close she could still catch his scent, see the little blond hairs in the 'V' of his chest. The hard muscle under linen.

When he broke the silence his voice was cracked and he took a step back from her. 'Don't you dare let me off the hook, Rose McIntyre. Just be yourself.'

'Which is what? Bad-luck-bringer? Jinx?'

'Refreshing, actually.' He smiled. 'You're actually a real breath of fresh air.'

'Yes, well, you won't be saying that when your treatment room's covered in plaster-of-Paris again, or the next time the computer system dies.' She followed him out into the empty reception area. Afternoon clinic didn't start for another half an hour, but any minute now the early birds would start to appear. She had a lot to organise before that, instead of standing around flirting... Was she flirting?

Surely not? Not with him.

'I think we'll cope.' He shrugged. 'Now, I need to repay you for the lovely casserole you brought us last night. Even Katy liked it.'

'Even Katy? Praise indeed. But really, it's no big deal.'

He checked something on the computer. 'It is, to us at least. We're taking Lila out for a quick spin on Saturday morning before we head down to see Maxine at the hospital. You want to come?'

Did she? He'd said *we* so that meant Katy too—it wasn't a date or anything. And was Lila his girlfriend?

Maybe. Of course. A man like Joe Thompson would be snapped up. So that meant he was just being kind, trying to make up for his grumpiness and the lack of welcome lunch. A drive in the countryside with a group of people. Easy. Fun, even—if she could shake off this attraction to him. A dose of seeing him with his girlfriend would easily sort that out. 'If Lila doesn't mind, that would be lovely. Where are you going? I don't want to intrude.'

'Lila won't mind.' He laughed. 'She's my boat, docked up at the Windermere marina. Have you been there yet?'

Oh. Not a girlfriend. Fizz bubbled in her stomach. 'I haven't had much chance to get around, to be honest. It's on my to-do list.'

'Time to do some sightseeing then. You'll love it. Katy

would love you to join us. And maybe I'll bring a friend for her too.'

A friend… She certainly could do with one up here. Being a locum was very flexible, but it meant continually moving and meeting new people, making and then leaving new friends.

But was she his friend? Should she read anything into this?

No.

And how amazing to see the mountains from the water. 'Okay. Yes, thanks. I'd love to.'

'I'll pick you up—where are you staying?'

'In the new cottages on Berry Street. Number six.'

He nodded. 'Okay. I'll be there at eleven. Bring your swimsuit and a raincoat.'

'Swimsuit?' The happy bubbles in her stomach popped. Stupid, but that hadn't occurred to her. Being on a boat to her meant getting the Greenwich ferry, not getting half-naked in a bikini. She rubbed her palm across her collarbone, dampening down the prickle skittering across her chest. She'd have to invest in a cover-up, a wetsuit that zipped to her chin, if she was going to stop stares and unwanted conversation.

But he didn't pick up on her anxiety. 'It's the Lake District; you're going to get wet one way or another.'

It wasn't the water she was worried about; it was her past, her scar and her heart. Suddenly, spending time with him on a boat—and in very few clothes—seemed like the worst possible thing she could do.

CHAPTER FOUR

A TEMPORARY BRAIN-FLIP. That was the only thing Joe could think of to explain why he'd suddenly invited Rose out on this boat trip. But her bright manner had been infectious and yes, she was right. He needed to smile more… He'd spent the last five years barely surviving. Fun hadn't entered his head. Being a good father to Katy, trying to keep his head above water at work, trying to hold together this community that had nurtured and loved and then lost Pippa. He'd done all of that.

Fun? He couldn't remember what that was.

But when he knocked on Rose's door and she answered wearing her eye-catching orange hat framing two long blonde plaits, a yellow dress that slashed across the top of her collarbone, nipped her waist and flared over her hips, calf-length red cowboy boots and a smile that was as bright as this morning's sun, he had a feeling he was going to be reminded what fun was all about. She looked as if she was going to a rodeo or a music festival, not on his cruiser, but even so his body fizzed just looking at her. 'Good morning, Dr Thompson. Ship ahoy and all that.'

She saluted and clicked her heels together and he found

himself saluting back. Which was…unusual. 'Aye aye. Come on, let's get going—throw your bag in the boot.'

'What are you looking at?' Before she moved, her eyes flickered a little warily and she clutched the handle of her huge blue and white striped beach bag. 'Is something wrong?'

'Nothing wrong. No. It's just that you have a very interesting choice in clothes.' Nothing conventional out of work, clearly. Or appropriate for a cruise on the lake. But then, he was learning, Rose McIntyre was anything but conventional.

'I make it a point of principle that when I'm not working I only wear things that make me happy. I didn't realise there was a dress code for a boat trip.'

Was there? Usually, people wore shorts, shirts and trainers or boat shoes, like he was wearing right now. But why? Why shouldn't she wear what she wanted instead of the usual uniform?

He shrugged. 'I don't suppose there is. As long as you don't slip on the deck.'

'I won't. I'll take my boots off.' Unperturbed, she nodded and climbed into the passenger seat, waving at Katy and her friend Emily in the back. 'Hey, girls. Perfect day for a boat ride.'

'I love your hat, Rose.' Katy smiled a little shyly and Joe's gut tightened. How was his daughter taking this? He'd never brought a woman out with them before. Oh, everyone had told him he needed to date again, but he'd never had the heart to, or the inclination. Never met a woman who he'd *noticed* before. But he was just doing the friendly thing, right? Showing a newbie around the place. Nothing more in it than that.

And if he believed that then he was a fool. Berating himself for the zillionth time for the brain-flip, he threw the car into gear and set off towards Bowness-on-Windermere.

'This is my favourite hat at the moment, Katy. I have loads.' Patting the orange wool, Rose turned and smiled at his daughter. 'I'll make you one. Tell me what colour you love. Any colour at all as long as it isn't a dull one.'

Katy bit her lip and thought. 'Pink, I think. No... purple. But I like the colour of your dress too. It's too hard to decide.'

'How about pink and purple and yellow stripes?' Rose laughed at Katy's wide eyes. 'Okay, too much? Maybe we'll stick with just purple to start with.'

'I love your hat too.' Emily grinned cheekily, obviously wanting to get in on the action.

'In that case I'll make one for you too. And one for Joe. What colour should I do for him?'

'Brown, of course,' Katy said, and as he kept his gaze firmly on the road ahead Joe imagined her rolling her eyes. 'Because that's all that men like.'

'Er...' he interjected, trying to think of a reasonable retort, but his daughter was right—he did prefer colours that didn't stand out. No, actually, he'd never given a moment's thought to what colours he wore. He was a man, for God's sake. A man stuck in a car with three females who had immediately clicked. 'You're probably right. But I do have blue stuff too. Look at my shirt.'

'Pale blue. *Boring.*' Rose eyed Joe and laughed. 'We'll make a huge pointy wizard's hat for you in rainbow stripes.'

She would too, and she'd insist he wore it. No. Way. He shook his head. 'Please don't. I'm beginning to feel outnumbered here. If you really must make everyone you meet a hat then I'm happy with brown. Or grey if I'm feeling…edgy.'

'Edgy? Joe Thompson?' Rose's mouth tipped up as she caught his eye and said in almost a whisper, 'I'd like to see that.'

And I'd like to show you.

Heat slammed through him as his breath stalled in his lungs. *What the hell?*

This was more than taking notice; this was a physical reaction. A hot ache.

He drew his eyes away from her before he crashed the damned car.

This attraction didn't make sense. She was everything he should steer clear of: quirky, passing through, moving on after her month here. And then there was that little bit of reluctance to open up about herself. Was she hiding something or just guarded? He needed honesty and openness in any relationship, not just for his sake, but for Katy's too. And she definitely didn't need someone flitting in and out of her life.

So there was no point even thinking about that attraction, never mind acting on it.

'Can I look at your hat, please, Rose?' Katy's eyes grew wider as she sat as forward as her seat belt would allow, to get a closer look at the hat Rose had slipped off her head and was showing them. 'You made it yourself? Wow.'

'Sure, it's just crochet and very easy to do.' Rose clapped her hands together. 'I know! If you want to learn, I'll show you. And you can make lots of flowers to put on the hats too. The brighter the better, I say.'

Clearly. Joe realised he was smiling, regardless of what his brain was telling him, and it felt as if it wasn't just his mouth but a hot spot in his chest was beaming at her too. But then, anyone who was kind to his daughter deserved a *friendly* smile.

They were just lucky that the sharp tang of lust hadn't almost driven them off the road. And with that thought the heat dissipated, leaving him with an uncomfortable ache in his heart.

What the hell was he doing here with Rose? Really?

After a few more minutes they were at the marina, life jackets donned and then on the water. Joe breathed in the cool fresh breeze as he steered towards the less crowded part of the lake, away from the ferry and busy village. Maybe some of this air would blow some sense into him. Then again, all sense seemed to get lost when he was around Little Miss Sunshine here.

Soon they'd left the busyness behind and the soft purr of the engine and the view on all sides of green and russet mountains soothed his senses.

He could do this.

Rose sat in the cockpit with him and stroked the wooden dash, her eyes dazzling in their vibrancy as they flitted from one part of the cruiser to another. 'Wow, what an amazing boat.'

'Pride and joy. After Katy, obviously.' He'd bought it after Pippa's death—something else to focus on that gave him a brief respite from the grief, and to be able to get out and breathe. To be honest, sometimes he'd wanted to just set sail and never come back, but he'd had Katy to look after, and she deserved so much more than a hermit father.

His daughter looked up from her digital tablet and gave him a smile. Frustration played in his belly. 'Put the tablets down, girls. We're here for fun, not to be stuck to screens. Why don't you go for a swim?'

Katy scowled. 'Okay. But can we have ice cream soon?'

'After swimming in a cold lake? How are you not endlessly shivering?' The bright hopeful smile won him over. 'Okay. Yes. Ice cream after a swim. But stay away from the reeds. Don't—'

Before he'd even finished his list of rules, the girls were jumping into the water.

So, with the backdrop of the girls' happy shrieks, he was left with Rose. Alone.

His gaze slid to her mouth.

How would she taste?

The thought slammed into his brain, along with hot, slick need that prickled through his body. He swallowed, tried to control the rush. But he couldn't stop looking at her, at that mouth…lips slightly parted. A hint of gloss.

Fresh water. Sunshine. Maybe coffee? Toothpaste? Smiles. She'd taste of smiles. Because that was what she did. All. The. Time.

Stop.

He had to stop this. 'Okay, well, as the kids are getting wet, I think you should too. A quick—and cold—induction into Lake District life. You have to do some swimming or water-skiing. No? Doughnut-riding?'

'Doughnut-*eating* sounds a lot less wet and cold.' She bit her lip as her eyes grew wide.

He laughed, an image of those lips covered in sugar from one doughnut bite hovered in his brain. One lick and the sugar would be gone. One lick from him. His gut tightened. 'But not nearly as much fun.'

'Clearly, you don't eat the right doughnuts.'

Clearly, food was the last thing on his mind. 'Come on. Give it a go.'

'Okay, I'll just pop downstairs to put on my wetsuit.' She jumped up, the hem of her skirt flaring a little, giving him a good view of creamy skin and long shapely legs.

He closed his eyes. *Why?* Why did she have to be so beautiful? And so…temporary? Distraction had to be key here. 'Great. I'll call the girls. You can all ride together.'

That way she'd be more than touching distance away… but, given he needed a good sluicing with cold water rather than thinking about chat-up lines that would go nowhere, maybe he should be the one sitting on the water ring.

'Wow! That was amazing!' Having been dunked and sprayed and dragged along behind the boat at what felt like a hundred miles an hour, holding on for her life to a small rubber handle on a ring that skimmed across the water, Rose felt alive. Truly alive.

Every part of her, every sense, every pore vibrated and pulsed with life. And it felt so damned good. She clambered back onto the boat, dripping-wet and shaking from the excitement, and ignoring the way her heart was battering against her ribcage. This was fun. Wild, wet, fabulous fun, not impending doom.

'My face feels as if it's been sandblasted and I'm sure I look hideous, but that was epic.'

She knew she must look hideous anyway, because no one looked good in a full body wetsuit. No one, not even an underwear model. But there was no way she was going to expose her scar and face a zillion questions. The wetsuit zipped perfectly to the base of her throat and kept her secrets under wraps…or, rather, under neoprene.

'You look amazing. Windswept, that's all,' Joe said in a matter-of-fact voice, but his eyes sought hers and there was nothing matter-of-fact about the way he was looking at her. Eyes filled with heat. His body tilted towards hers. His smile. For her.

Her heart tripped and she looked away. Was she imagining it all? Was there interest? Heat? Something?

She chanced another look at him. Yes. She was damned sure there was something. Something that made her feel even more alive. And scared. And hot.

She wasn't sure, but there must be something magical about this place. Everything seemed more vibrant here. The colours more intense. The scent more pungent. The feelings whirling in her gut more effervescent. The tug towards Joe and the growing awareness more acute. His smell in the air, his breath on her neck…

It was stupid to feel this way with the kids milling around. Stupid to feel this way at all, because if he ever got to hear her story he'd run a mile in the opposite direction. That was the effect she'd had on Toby anyway.

But, stupid, or not, the awareness was there.

'Thank you, but I know I look like a drowned rat.'

'Believe me, drowned rats do not look like you. You look…magnificent.' This he said almost in a whisper. This she couldn't interpret as anything other than attraction. But then he turned away. After wrapping Emily in a towel, Joe then rubbed his daughter's arms from blue to pink. How could it be possible that he was any more adorable, when his instinct was always to attend to others?

'How did she do, girls? Any good as a newbie?'

'She nearly fell off!' Katy giggled. 'We had to hold onto her.'

'Not fair, Katy Thompson. You're telling him all my

secrets. I did not nearly fall off.' Rose pressed her lips together to hold back her laugh, then admitted, 'I *may* have had a bit of trouble holding on.'

'You did well.' Joe took hold of the steering wheel—if that was what they were called on boats—and pretended to jerk it hard left then hard right. 'Next time, I'll actually move the boat a few feet and see how you stay on then.'

'You did move the boat. We were going really fast.' If her hair was anything to go by, they'd been through a wind tunnel at warp speed.

'Okay… I did crank the throttle up, but I have to go slow from now on; there's a speed restriction here.' He steered the boat into a little marina filled with white boats and people milling around enjoying the sunshine. Beyond the moorings was a large wooden building with red and white striped umbrellas out front and what looked like a grassy bar area and a sandy bay with a little pontoon just offshore.

As they floated alongside the jetty Joe started to wrap coils of thick rope round an iron bollard. With his pale blue cotton shirtsleeves rolled up she could see the way the muscles contracted and stretched on his arms. Good strong forearms with fine blond hairs and very capable hands. Suddenly, she wondered how they would feel spanning her waist, tugging her to him.

How she would feel pressing her mouth against his.

Then wondered why she'd think such a thing when she'd told herself a million times already that she couldn't be interested in him. Or his hands. Or being tugged to him.

Definitely not interested in kissing him.

Liar.

The giddiness in her stomach intensified and it had

nothing to do with being on the doughnut and everything to do with Joe Thompson. Her gaze travelled from his arms to his face, first seeking out his mouth. Lips slightly parted in a smile that set off fireworks in her stomach. A stubbled jaw she ached to run her fingers along, slashed cheekbones. Back to that mouth that had recently learnt how to laugh and was now embracing it. That smile that transformed him from Thor to formidable.

Thor-midable.

She forced herself not to laugh out loud. She'd invented a word that suited him perfectly. He was so tall and occasionally gruff and a little aloof at times...and she knew now that was because he was juggling so many things, not least bringing up a child on his own. But he was also unbearably sexy and kind and he had a hidden sense of humour that he only shared when he was relaxed.

She liked him relaxed. She liked him like this, all shipshape and rippling muscles.

But all she was aware of, right now, was that mouth. All she could think of was the way it would feel pressed against her own.

She shivered. Maybe she was getting hypothermia. That made you hallucinate, right?

She swallowed, tried to clear her brain from kissing thoughts. 'Um... You need a hand or anything?'

Mid-rope-knotting, he twisted round to face her and once again she was shocked at the force of need humming through her as he met her gaze.

'No, thanks. I'm fine. Girls, we're going to make a stop here. If you want to go get ice creams say now.'

'Now!' Katy screeched, obviously well used to this game. 'Please!'

'Be careful. No running, okay?' Joe's eyebrows rose

as he handed Katy some cash just as she was about to
disappear down the jetty, pink towel flaring behind her
like a flag. 'We'll meet you at the bar in a few minutes.
I'm guessing Rose needs to put on dry clothes first.'

She definitely did. Discarding her life jacket, Rose
wandered over to the door leading down to the lower
deck, but stopped to ask, 'What is this place?'

'It's a holiday park, but it's a good stop-off place for
ice creams and decent coffee. Hey, you're shivering. Take
this.' He came over and wrapped a huge stripy beach
towel around her shoulders. 'Once you're warm and dry
we can pop up to the café and grab something to eat.'

'Sounds great. I hadn't realised, but I'm starving.'

'All that screaming works up an appetite. I hope you're
having fun?'

'Of course.' She could have looked at the bright blue
sky, the backdrop of mountains, the sunshine that gave
her joy. She could have looked at the girls, the umbrellas,
the boats for inspiration for her answer. But she didn't.
She looked right at him. 'It's a perfect day. Just perfect.'

He looked relieved. 'Not everyone would be okay with
a couple of eight-year-olds hanging round.'

'They're gorgeous. Of course I don't mind.' Even
though she faced a childless future, she wasn't one of
those women who stayed away from kids because it hurt
too much to be around them. The better thing, for Rose
at least, was to surround herself with kids of all ages
and dote on them so she didn't totally miss out. 'Thing
is, they're teaching me all kinds of things when surely
it should be the other way round. Am I a fully fledged
country girl yet?'

He shook his head, all kinds of tease with sparkling

eyes and that kissable mouth twitching into a sorry smile.
'No way. You have a long way to go.'

'Looks like I'm going to need more lessons then.'

'I can do that.' The air stilled and she realised he
hadn't taken his hands away from her shoulders. One
of his palms ran down her arm…but not in the way he'd
rubbed the blood back into Katy's skin. And he wasn't
looking at her the way he'd looked at Katy either. Nowhere near.

She hadn't imagined the connection at all. But she
also sensed him holding back, grappling with this connection as much as she was.

'Joe… I…'

Want to kiss you.

If he stood any closer she'd have to know what it felt
like to press against him. She didn't know if she had the
kind of willpower that would hold her back—he was too
close, too temptingly close. How would he react if she
just kissed him? It would probably mean the end of…this.
She didn't want it to end, not yet. So she should probably
go and get changed, but she didn't want to move away
from him. Not for one second, certainly not for the time
it would take her to fight her way out of a wetsuit.

'Um… Tell me about this part of the lake. What's that
hill over there?'

'Which one?' He turned to look and she felt the absence of his breath and his heat keenly. 'Ah, yes. That's
Orrest Head. There's a good walk to the top, and from
there you can see some of the bigger mountains further north: Langdale Pike, Scafell Pike, The Old Man
of Coniston.'

'Is that the name of a hill?' She laughed, her proximity
to him making her coy and yet brave at the same time.

And still her heart hammered. 'Not a nickname for one of your patients?'

'It's most definitely a mountain and an old slate mine, and not one of my patients.' He smiled and looked out into the distance. 'You could do your yoga on any one of those peaks, although some might be a bit steep.'

'If you promise to come and do it with me, I'll teach you some moves.'

'No need. I have moves all of my own.' His finger-tips traced a track up her throat to her cheek, his focus back on her.

'Oh?' She dragged in a breath, stuttered and clipped. Her body hummed with energy...*need*...so much she was practically shaking. She could barely get words out through her tight throat. 'You have moves?'

Show me?

As if reading her mind, his head dipped close to hers and his mouth brushed her lips. Gentle. Tender. But then he stopped and looked at her, captured her gaze and held it with his question. *Is this okay?*

'Yes.' Her whisper was caught by the breeze and she didn't know if he'd heard. So she touched his face with trembling hands, pulled him closer, stood on tiptoe and put her lips to his.

It started as a gentle exploration. Tender. Reverent. But the soft mewl in her throat at his touch was met with a deep groan. Taken aback by the feelings inside her, she tugged away. Swallowed, tried to control her heartbeat. This was good. So damned good. Why had she tugged away when he wanted to kiss her and she wanted to kiss him right back? It was only a kiss.

Too much. Too fast. Too soon.

Somewhere in the recesses of her brain alarm bells rang, but she shoved them away, closed them off.

She would listen another time, but not now.

The second touch was less gentle than the first as she wound her arms round his neck and dragged him against her, need and want rising inside her so ragged and fast it almost snatched her breath from her lungs. Emboldened, she opened her mouth and shuddered as his tongue met hers.

He tasted of sweetness and spice, of something elementally Joe Thompson. Of the heather and wild thyme that scented the air on her early morning walks.

His hands cupped her face as if she were fragile and delicate, but the press of his mouth told her his need was anything but. Her hands explored his chest, then spanned broad shoulders. He was big, this man. Big in body, big in heart.

And he wanted her.

He wanted her as she was. Rose McIntyre. With no preconceptions of who she might have been or who she would be in the future. He wanted her as she was now and that knowledge made her heart sing.

His hands moved down the back of her head to her shoulders, then she lost all track of what and where and when and gave herself up to the kiss. Hot and hungry. All she was aware of was the taste of him. His heat. His strength as he wrapped her close. She fitted there, in his arms. As if this space was meant for her.

When his mouth left hers and found the soft spot on her neck she curled tight against him.

'Downstairs?' His voice was laden with desire.

And *God,* she wanted to go with him, to explore him,

to find out everything about him. But she pulled away before desire took them too far down that path.

Too fast. Her heart beat rapid-fire against her ribcage. Bullets pelting bone. She willed it to slow, hauling in deep breaths.

Thor-midable indeed.

Still shaking, she looked up at those blue eyes that gave away what he was feeling. Right now it was desire. Now, a battle. With his conscience? Now, more desire. Didn't matter how much he liked her or wanted her, he was struggling with the idea of kissing her. So she saved him the worry. 'Not downstairs, Joe. No. We shouldn't do this.'

There was a beat as he processed this, chest heaving with need. He nodded. 'It's all too complicated. And—'

'Neither of us needs anything like that.'

His forehead touched hers in such a sweet gesture it made her heart soften. 'Believe me, in another life I'd be asking to see you again and again. But—'

'But it can't happen again.' She nodded. It was for the best. Even if the best hollowed out her core.

'No.' He looked out and waved at what Rose assumed was the two girls somewhere in the melee of tourists and boaties.

'Because of Katy?'

At the mention of his daughter's name, heat left his eyes as swiftly as if she'd flicked a switch. Reality seeped in and she watched it settle in the hitch of his breath, between his shoulders and in that little wrinkle on his forehead.

'She needs stability, Rose. It was a hard stretch when she lost her mum and we clung to each other to get through. She's never seen me with anyone else. She's never known me date. I don't know how she'd react.'

'You can't live the rest of your life alone.' Although Rose had resigned herself to that kind of future and she'd been okay with it until…until now.

He nodded. 'I know. But I can't risk—'

'Hey, I understand. I'm a threat to everything and you don't want to rock the boat.' She ran her hand across the wooden rail. God knew, she didn't want to upset Katy either, but this feeling, the way her heart beat for him, and his daughter, was too intense. She probably needed some space. And she most definitely was not going to go on another boat trip with him. But somehow they'd have to muddle through at least today. And then for the rest of her stay. And then…what was the saying about mixing work with pleasure? Never a good idea. This was why. Because she'd have to spend the next few weeks knowing what she wanted and not being able to have it. 'Good kiss, though.'

'Damned right. The best. I just wish things were different.' He caught her arm, his gaze sliding from her face to her chest. His finger followed, gently touching just below her collarbone, making her shiver. 'Hey, what's the scar from? Looks like some serious stuff going on.'

No. She turned away, eyes slamming shut. *No. No. Not now.*

Holding back a curse, Rose looked down and saw her wetsuit zip had somehow unzipped, or he'd tugged it, or maybe she had. Showing off the top of her scar. Framing the damned thing.

No. Rule one: don't ask about the scar.

Her heart rattled as she tugged the towel tighter round her shoulders so he couldn't see more.

Please don't think anything less. Not yet.

She'd tell him about the transplant once they knew each other better, some time…never. It was too soon for him to do the whole pitying thing, the tiptoeing to make sure she was okay, like her mother's endless loop of questions.

'Taking your tablets?'

'How are you feeling?'

'Should you have a lie-down?'

Up until now he'd treated her exactly the same as he'd treat anyone else and she didn't want that to change. And it would. Once he knew.

Or maybe he'd never know and she'd leave this place with her dignity and secret intact. No pity. No questions. Just as a fond memory of a woman who'd walked through his life, once upon a time. That way she was in control.

'Ah. A long time ago.' Although he'd know all about scarring and how it aged. He'd see it was relatively new, fading but not faded completely. He'd want to know the details. Why couldn't she be kissing a plumber who had no interest in scars? She tugged the zip up to her collarbone. 'Nothing to worry about.'

He frowned. 'Rose, I'm a doctor. I know they don't open your ribcage because you have a rash or a simple headache. Are you okay?'

Desperately searching for a distraction, she turned towards shore. Somewhere—over by the little beach area—she heard excited squeals. 'Do you think the girls need you down there?'

But he was still looking at her, eyes misted with concern and…*ugh*…pity. 'Mitral valve?'

'I think I can hear them. Seriously, I can hear…' This wasn't a distraction; this was real. They weren't excited screams; they were terrified ones. Pain. Fear. 'Wait. Joe? Are they okay? Is that screaming coming from the girls?'

Tension rippled through his body as his jaw tightened, eyes searching the grassy area where they'd last seen the girls. Two discarded pink towels lay on the lawn. He ran to the jetty, hand clutching his head. Searching. 'Katy? Emily?'

The wails got louder. Then, 'Joe! Joe!'

Rose scanned out into the water. And her stomach gripped tight. 'There. On the pontoon.'

One little girl sat shaking and crying. The other no-where to be seen.

'Where's Katy?' Joe shouted, running along the jetty. 'Katy?'

Emily pointed to the water. To nothing but water. And panic ground through Rose's gut. 'There.'

CHAPTER FIVE

WATER SLUICED INTO his mouth, his nose, blurred his vision.

Katy. Katy. Where the hell…?

Kicking harder, he dived deep, to where the water bit like ice and murky darkness clouded everything.

No. Not Katy too. He wasn't going to lose her.

But he couldn't see her. Couldn't sense her anywhere. He'd know…right? He'd know if she was here. He'd find her. He would. He reached out with both hands, tried to grasp at something, anything, but only water ran between his fingers.

Katy! His whole body screamed her name. *Where are you?*

His lungs stretched and burned as he turned and twisted, reaching and reaching. Nothing.

But it was no use; he needed air. If he was going to find her he needed more air. Kicking hard, he broke the surface and hauled lungs full of oxygen then dived again. He saw fish, reeds, pebbles, stones. Detritus. No Katy.

Determination fed his strokes. He would not lose her. He just wouldn't.

More air.

Air.

As he surfaced he gasped and again, twisting and

turning. Emily on the pontoon, shaking her head. Rose on the grass, calling. He couldn't hear what.

'Katy!' He just wanted to find her. The baby he'd promised to keep safe. But instead he'd been... What did it matter? He hadn't been concentrating on Katy. And now...now she was—

'Katy! Joe!'

He caught Rose's ragged cries and followed the line of her pointing finger. There...a scream slashing her face. 'Katy!'

His daughter's beautiful, beautiful face contorted, just before she slipped back under the surface.

No. Just no.

He powered towards her, caught her waist and lifted her, her body racked with choking and coughing and gasping, above the water. 'I've got you, baby.'

Briefly, she looked at him with shimmering love, then her eyes fluttered closed and her body went limp in his arms.

'No! No. Come on, baby, breathe for me.' They were further from shore than he'd realised, but somehow he eventually found firm footing and carried her to where Emily was now standing with Rose, silent tears streaming down her face.

This wasn't happening. This was his worst nightmare. He should have been watching her... Darkness filled him as he looked at his beautiful girl's face.

He should have been watching her.

'Here, quick. Lay her down.' Rose, still in her wetsuit, knelt and felt for a carotid pulse. She looked up at him and nodded, but her eyes were apologetic, distressed. 'She's tachycardic, but that could just be all the panic. We need to get the water out of her.'

Could be the panic. Could be worse. Air hunger, exhaustion, closed airways.

She helped him put Katy into the Safe Airway Position then rubbed his little girl's back and muttered soothing words. And he kept harsh ones from erupting from his mouth. It wasn't Rose's fault—hell, she was here, working on Katy like the professional she was. God knew what was going on in her head too. But he couldn't think about that or about her.

He pressed Katy's belly, gently at first then a little harder, trying to force the water from her body. He pressed it again and again and...*miracle*...water began sluicing from Katy's mouth and nose. 'It's okay, Katy. Come on, girl.'

'Da...' Sounds came but not words as she spluttered and coughed, her little body shaking uncontrollably. *'Da...'*

'It's okay. I've got you. You're okay now. You're fine, baby. You're fine.'

But she might well have not been. Grief, anger, frustration and relief poured through him and he didn't know which to address first. He made tight fists, releasing the adrenalin coursing round his veins.

She was safe. She was safe and alive and that was all that mattered, but how could she have been so stupid?

How could he? It was his job to be there, to watch her, to keep her safe. A job he'd failed to do properly.

He knelt next to Rose and cradled Katy to his chest. 'You gave me one hell of a fright there, baby girl.'

'Ugh.' Katy turned and vomited more lake water onto the grass, then sobbed quietly, clutching his shirt, clutching his heart right there, almost to breaking point. He wrapped her tightly in her towel and pressed her close, wishing he could rewind to earlier, to yesterday, to the day before Rose had walked up the hill and he'd noticed her.

And Rose watched and soothed and spoke gently to Emily, reassuring her that all was now well.

And he should have been grateful, but he couldn't see past the fact that he'd almost lost his daughter to the depths of Lake Windermere while he'd been elsewhere. Kissing Rose.

She was sitting close enough that he could kiss her again. His eyes found hers and he saw compassion there. Relief too.

Regret? He wasn't sure. It had been a damned fine kiss and it could have turned into more. But thank God they'd stopped when they had.

A few minutes of shocked silence passed and Katy's hold on his shirt started to relax. He leaned back a little and stroked her face. 'What were you doing in the water? You know you should never go in the water without telling me first. You know that.'

Katy looked away, down at her fingers. 'I'm s-s-orry. I was getting hot.'

That wasn't a real excuse. It was a warm September day, but the sun was hardly baking the flagstones. 'I don't care if you were burning to a frazzle; you must always ask me first. I thought you were safe, eating ice cream. I waved at you when you were sitting on the grass.'

'We'd finished eating them and we couldn't see you any more.' Dark eyes turned to him and he wondered if she'd seen the kiss. Worried where the adults had got to. What they were doing. But her mouth clamped shut and he knew her well enough to leave it or all he'd get would be sobs.

But he couldn't, so he tried, he tried hard, to be gentle as he asked her friend, 'So what happened then?'

'We had a race to the pontoon.' Emily snuggled close under Rose's arm. 'I'm sorry, Dr Thompson.'

He squeezed his daughter close. 'Even though you know you're not allowed to go in the water without asking me first? Without a life jacket.' Even he heard the gruff tone and tried to stifle it. Too late. 'I thought I'd lost you forever. Katy, don't ever do that again. Ever, you hear me?'

Katy shook her head, tears still running down her pale face. She scrambled away from him and buried her head in Rose's knees and sobbed as much as her exhausted body could. Joe's heart twisted.

He was saying all the wrong things, handling this so badly, but he couldn't hold back the dread at the thought of losing her too.

Rose glanced over and then turned away. Shoulders hitched. Even with her back to him he knew she was sending him some kind of message. There they were, the three of them locked together in an awkward huddle. And here he was, alone.

She stroked Katy's leg. 'You're a great swimmer, Katy. So did something hurt you? Did you get a pain or something?'

His daughter nodded. 'I g-g-got a funny feeling in my foot and I couldn't move it and I kicked hard with the other one but I c-c-couldn't move properly.' She inhaled shallow breaths and again. Coughed. Joe made a mental note to check her airways and chest the moment they were back on the boat. Thank God he never went anywhere without his medical bag. 'It hurt so badly. And then I forgot to kick and water came into my mouth and I was scared.'

'I know. Me too.' Even to him his voice was gruff. She had to learn she'd done the wrong thing, so she wouldn't do it again. But he'd talk to her later, when everyone had calmed down and he was in a better headspace. *Whoa.* That last thought surprised him… He wasn't usually so aware of how he acted—Rose had made him aware of his imperfections. And yet she'd still kissed him anyway. What did that mean? He filed that thought to come back to later and dialled down the gruff with Katy. 'Don't be scared any more. You're safe now. I love you, Katy.'

'I love you too, Dad.' She wriggled from Rose's knee and came and settled on his. Safe in his hands.

Rose sighed and stood up, helping Emily stand too. 'We need to get her to A&E so they can monitor her for a few hours. Just as a precaution. And get her into something warm before she gets hypothermia. And you too, Joe.'

He hadn't felt cold at all, but now he realised that at some point ice had slid into his veins, turning his hands blue. 'Quick. Let's get the heck out of here.'

Emily slipped her hand into Rose's and Katy held his tight, insisting on walking and not being carried, and they all walked slowly back to the cruiser, a lot quieter and a little more heartsore than when they'd arrived.

After he'd checked and double-checked Katy had no ill-effects from the water so far and pulled up anchor, he powered up the boat again, taking a moment to clear his head.

Cramp.

His eight-year-old daughter had had cramp while he'd

been making out with Rose. Probably in full view of the whole of the holiday resort. And Katy.

That thought knotted deep in his gut. This was why he didn't date, why he focused on Katy and work. Because otherwise bad things happened.

'Hey, there. You okay?' Rose stood in the doorway, back in her sunny dress, hair combed and pulled back into a sleek ponytail.

There was something about looking at her that made him hot and unsettled and yet peaceful at the same time. Like the familiarity of doing minor surgery, but the challenge and adrenalin of something he hadn't yet tackled. Although surgery had never made him hard before. He nodded, trying to find a smile. 'I think my heart's just about recovered.'

'Mine too. I can't imagine how you must feel.'

'I wasn't going to lose her, Rose. That's all I know.' Adrenalin made his hands shake and he turned away. Made clenched fists until he calmed down. He felt her come closer and the ache of wanting to touch her almost overwhelmed him.

'She's safe now, because of you.'

He turned to look at her again. She was right. And yet wrong too. 'She should never have been there. And I should have been watching her all the time.'

'I know and she's sorry for her part in it all.' She ran her hands over the slash top of her dress and his thoughts skidded back to the moments before they'd almost lost Katy. The scar. It wasn't faded enough to be from when she was a child. Mitral valve? Something big; it had to be. No one had their chest opened for something trivial. Something congenital, maybe. Why didn't she want to talk about it?

He didn't want to intrude; clearly she was embarrassed by it, some people were. Pippa had been the same with her caesarean scar, no matter how much he'd said he loved it.

Instead of his gaze lingering there, he made sure his eyes met Rose's. 'Girls okay down there?'

Her shoulders relaxed a little as her hand dropped to her side. She smiled. 'Fine. They're downstairs playing with an app that shows them how they'd look with different hairstyles and colours. Katy's thinking of getting an ombre.'

'A what?' One day he'd understand female language, but right now he needed a translator.

'It's when hair starts dark at the top and gets lighter towards the ends.' Rose touched the top of her head and ran her hand slowly down her ponytail. His hand twitched, aching to touch the silk strands. 'It's all the rage.'

'Not until she's old enough to date. Which will be when she's sixty-seven.' But she was safe at least from the water, if not from growing up too fast. 'I think I prefer it when they're stuck to their screens after all.' He thought back to the hat conversation. 'Hey, thanks for saying you'll teach Katy how to make a hat. It's not something Maxine has ever mentioned doing. Pippa did a lot of that kind of craft stuff, but I'm hopeless. Can't even thread a needle—'

That was half his problem, trying to be both mother and father to a little girl when he didn't have much of a clue what girls did, never mind liked, when they were kids.

'Pippa?' Rose's head tilted a little as she looked over at him. Softly. Gently. The smile a little less carefree but still there imbued with concern.

'My wife. *Late* wife.' Rose's eyes softened as she held his gaze and he felt he had to add something more, to explain. 'She died.'

'I kind of guessed.' She came over and sat next to him, wrapping the hem of her dress round her thighs as she perched on the seat. 'I'm so sorry.'

'Yeah. Me too.' No point being coy about it. The slash of pain in his chest still whipped his breath away at times. Although it was less intense these days.

Sometimes he went whole days—almost weeks—without thinking about it. And sometimes grief still hung around the edges, dulling everything. Because Pippa wasn't here and there was so much she'd missed. Katy, mainly. Their wonderful tomboy daughter who surprised him every day.

Pippa. Guilt rippled through him. Not just about the accident, but about being here enjoying himself when she wasn't. But she wouldn't have wanted him to spend the rest of his life unhappy, of that much he was certain.

Some of Rose's hair had escaped the plaits and spun in all directions in the wind and his only instinct was to hold her tight and smooth his palm over the wayward strands.

That would make him halfway to happy right now. To touch Rose's face. Her skin.

To taste her again.

He couldn't think that. They'd agreed.

'It must have been awful. I can't imagine how you coped. When? When did it happen?' Rose ran her hand across the top of her ribcage. A nervous thing, he thought—she'd done it a couple of times now. He wasn't sure she realised she was even doing it.

Then her hand slipped over his. Cool. Soft. And stoking the very wrong kind of feelings inside him when he was talking about how his wife had died. But it was a comfort to have Rose's skin against his. And a comfort to talk to her.

'A few years ago. Car crash. Katy was in the car too, but I don't think she remembers any of it. At least, I hope not. She does miss her mum, or the idea of her at least. She tells me that.'

Now he was sounding maudlin and not doing enough smiling…as instructed.

But Rose didn't seem to mind, or notice, as her hand was still on his, their eyes locked as the connection between them tightened and tightened.

And he most certainly shouldn't have been holding hands with one woman when talking about another. 'Anyway…it was a long time ago.'

'It's okay to be sad.' She squeezed his hand. 'You don't have to pretend with me.'

'I'm not pretending. I just don't know what else to say.' Because he wasn't going to talk about the argument they'd had before Pippa had hared off into the dark and wet night. Or the way he'd had to make the worst decision he'd ever made. How he'd wished over and over that his life had ended instead of his wife's.

'Katy must have been very young.'

'Barely three.'

'That must have been a struggle, looking after a toddler and working and missing your wife so much. And no wonder you're so concerned for her safety. You've had a rough time.'

It was the first time he'd really spoken about it to anyone other than family, but something about Rose made it easy. She understood. 'Yes, it was, but I have a lot of help.'

'Maxine.' She nodded and then her smile slipped as she remembered what had happened only a few days ago.

Despite all her encouragement for him to find someone new, what would Maxine really think if he started dating again? Would she see it as a betrayal of Pippa's memory?

'Katy's grandparents are very on hand. My mum and sister live in Bowness so they're very much in our lives too, but it's not the same as having a proper mum around.'

'Poor you. Poor, poor Katy.' Rose was back to rubbing her collarbone and frowning. 'I just can't imagine…that must have been so difficult. I'm so sorry.'

So much for trying to smile and laugh more. 'Very.'

'But you can't wrap them up in cotton wool all their lives either. Stuff happens, Joe.'

He gripped the boat wheel with both hands. 'I know that more than anyone.'

Rose blinked, two bright red circles appearing on her cheeks. 'Yes, you've had to deal with a lot. But you're not the only one.'

He thought back to the way she'd attempted to deflect his attention from the scar when he'd enquired about it. To her conversation on the phone about Toby, her desire to leave her family and friends in London and move into unknown territory. Rose McIntyre had clearly been through a lot too. What, he didn't know, but he intended to find out one day. Because knowing only titbits about her wasn't enough. 'That was rude. I'm sorry.'

'At least this time you realised without me having to say so. I'd say you're learning.' Smiling, she put her hand on his shoulder. He caught the scent of something earthy and yet fresh. Some kind of flower? Not one from his hills. It was the same smell that had enveloped him when he'd kissed her and he turned instinctively towards it. His eyes settled on her mouth as his heart lurched into a very unsteady tachycardia. Arousal hit him swift and hard, pushing out all other thoughts as she said, 'So, everyone's safe. The girls sound happy enough down there, but maybe it's time to be heading home?'

'Yes.' He fought for control, not feeling as safe as she did. Seemed everything was slipping out of his grasp today. Katy. His reactions. Emotions. 'We've all had enough excitement for one day.'

He wasn't sure if he was talking about Katy's accident or the kiss. That one highlight of his day that could never be repeated. And if ever there was proof of why they couldn't do it, his gasping, shivering daughter was it.

And yet, despite everything, he still wanted to do it again.

Next time on dry land.

CHAPTER SIX

MONDAY MORNING CAME around too quickly, but a vomiting outbreak at the local high school meant a rush of sick teenagers and worried parents needing appointments, so Rose had little time to think about the kiss. Not that it had been out of her head much over the hours since the boat trip.

In truth, it was all she'd been able to think about once she'd pushed guilt about Katy's accident to the back of her mind. But it wouldn't stay there. She'd kissed him and the consequences of that had blown up his world, she could see. God knew how he must have been feeling.

She bundled the latest of the morning's triaged patients into a special isolation room they'd set up and went back to Reception to call the next one through.

Beth looked up from the computer. 'You okay? You don't want to catch the bug too.'

'I'm maintaining as much distance as I can and doing all the necessary isolation procedures. Chances are I've had this bug before anyway.' She hoped she had, at least. If her mother had any idea she was here doing this she'd be on the first train north. 'Infection control is always my top priority.' For more reasons than one.

The receptionist nodded. 'I've had a look through the protocol manual and found some handouts about how to deal with this kind of outbreak on a large scale. I'll send some over to the school.'

'Excellent. Thanks. You're doing great considering you've only been in the job a few days.'

That made Beth smile. 'Maxine has everything organised in files; it's quite easy to learn. Just good that I was here with my mum when Maxine got sick.'

'And so you ended up with the job, how? Did they put out a call to anyone in the village who fancied stepping into Maxine's shoes?' Small towns fascinated her after living in London all her life.

Beth laughed. 'No. Mum helped out here a lot in the past, when Maxine went on holiday or on courses. She's quite debilitated now, though, so can't stand for long. Rheumatoid arthritis,' she explained. 'She gets a lot of support from the neighbours and the doctors here. But it's not really enough any more.'

'Oh, I see. That's such a shame. But you have to love a village that is so tight-knit.'

The conversation paused as they waved at a mother and very pale son leaving, a big plastic bag clutched tight in his hand. Rose sighed. 'We're going to need some special cleaning solution for that back room once things have died down. And we're woefully low on emesis bags now too.'

'Right. I'll get onto it.' Beth grinned and flicked her hand towards a small but beautiful bouquet of red roses sitting next to her on the desk. 'Oh, and someone has a secret admirer.'

Roses. Her namesake—and the usual kind of flowers

people sent to her. She'd give anything to have something a little less…obvious. Not that she was ungrateful for the gesture, but her hospital room had been full of them and the scent always reminded her of feeling so weak and hopeless. 'They're lovely. Probably expensive.'

'And for you.'

'Oh.' Surely Joe wouldn't have done such a showy thing as sending her flowers to work? And if he had, what did that mean? Maybe an apology? Or a declaration. Of what? What did she even want a declaration of?

She tore open the envelope, her heart rat-a-tat-tatting. An apology, but not from the right man.

Sorry about everything.
We need to talk.
Come home, please.
Toby xxx

The rat-a-tat-tat turned into a slow stutter. *Home?* She didn't know where that was any more, but it certainly wasn't the apartment she'd shared with him. She wasn't going anywhere she was made to feel less or made to put aside her dreams. She threw the card in the bin, unsure whether the bigger disappointment was that they weren't from Joe at all. She managed to keep her smile in place, she hoped. 'You can have them if you like.'

But Beth shook her head. 'I don't want the flowers, hon. I want the admirer. How lovely to get sent roses at work. Must be someone special?'

'No. An old flame in London. Believe me, he's more trouble than he's worth. They all are.' Then she thought about Joe and the kiss and the fact he'd taken her out on a boat trip. And the kiss... The kiss was always at the forefront of her mind. 'Okay, maybe not all of them.'

Beth leaned forward and grinned. 'So you're single then?'

'Yes. And that's absolutely fine by me.'

'Good, because Mum tells me there's a man drought in the countryside—all the eligibles have moved to the city. Although...' Beth had a mischievous look in her eye. 'Not my type, but Joe's nice.'

'Oh.' That was unexpected. Rose played down the butterflies in her stomach. 'I guess.'

'Very nice on the eyes. Must be all that Viking blood.'

'I hadn't noticed. Viking? Oh, the blond? I suppose so.' Honesty was all very well but not at times like this.

'Come on, I see the way you two are together.' Beth fluttered her eyelashes and held her palm to her heart. 'Like two suns circling each other.'

Rose couldn't help laughing at the theatricals. 'You're as bad as Maxine—she was trying to get him to find someone too, even as she was in the middle of a heart attack. Is everyone here trying to hook him up?'

'He is very well loved and so was Pippa. She was a good friend of mine from years ago. It was so sad when she died. Tragic, actually. But at least they had the transplant thing to console them.'

Transplant? This was news. All the tiny hairs on Rose's arms stood on end. 'Transplant thing? What do you mean?'

'They agreed to donate some of her organs.' Beth's hand was on her chest, her eyes misted. 'Don't ask me which, because they wouldn't say. But it was such a beautiful gesture. I don't know if I could have done it.'

Rose's scar prickled as her heart thumped hard. She'd

only known the benefits of receiving an anonymous donor's heart, but Joe had had to face making that decision,
letting his wife go and helping someone else to live—or
at least have a better life.

But maybe he'd understand what she'd been through
then, if he'd been on the other side. And then again, perhaps he wouldn't. No doubt it would bring all the hurt
back for him. Maybe he'd be angry that she'd survived
and his wife had died.

Beth rattled on, interrupting Rose's thoughts. 'Mum
said he must be lonely after all this time on his own. She
takes an active interest in all the doctors' lives. Well, everyone's in the village too, if I'm honest.'

Yes, everyone knew everything here. She had so many
questions about Pippa, but she couldn't risk asking them
here when Joe could walk in on them gossiping about his
loss. She wouldn't do that to him. If it was something he
wanted to talk about, then he would.

She changed tack. 'And so what's your type, Beth?'

The receptionist bit the end of a pencil and thought for
a moment. 'Ooh…insanely good-looking, great sense of
humour and chronically unavailable. At least, that's my
experience so far.'

'Anyone in particular?'

'No. No one.' Although she answered far too quickly,
Rose noted. Something told her Beth had her heart set
on someone, but they didn't have their heart set on her.

Maybe that was preferable to having had a kiss, wanting another one but knowing that would be all kinds of
the wrong thing to do. 'Really, no one?'

'No. I think I need to change my type—actually, I've
been thinking that for a long time. Right, well, seeing as
we're two ladies who are single and ready to mingle, how

do you fancy a night out at The Queen's Arms some time? They have live music night on a Friday and even though the bands aren't always up to scratch, you're guaranteed to have a laugh.' At Rose's hesitation she smiled. 'Look, if I'm talking out of turn then I'm sorry, but you're new here and Maxine would have a fit if we didn't look after you properly. Thought you could do with a bit of social-ising. Beer, music and laughs. What's not to like?'

'That's…well…very kind…' What to say? If she was only here for a few weeks was there any point in forging relationships, only to leave them behind? But then, she hadn't decided to be a hermit either. Life was for living.

Beth's smile dropped and she looked sheepish. 'I mean, I know you're used to London and the excitement of the big city, so if you'd rather not then that's okay. It'll seem really boring here compared to what you're used to.'

Beth was lovely, and a similar age to Rose and, if this conversation was anything to go by, lots of fun. 'Friday night drinks is an excellent idea. I'd love to come.'

Beth's eyes widened. 'Right then. Put on your glad rags. It's a date.'

The thought of a night out lifted Rose's spirits and the rest of the morning flew by. She was in the clinic room scanning the appointments template for the afternoon— also known as daydreaming about a certain kiss—when a sharp tap on the door tugged her back to reality.

'Is it okay to come in?' Joe opened the door and Rose's heart jigged. Memories of how he tasted blurred with her sense of professionalism and the decision she'd made not to get further involved.

It was the only way forward. And she knew he'd come to the same decision too, even before Katy's near drown-ing episode. And definitely after it.

He blamed himself, she knew. Even though Katy had broken a cardinal rule, he should have been paying more attention. 'Of course. Is everything okay?'

'Thought I'd let you know that the school has now reported seventy-two kids and five teachers with the bug. Probably norovirus. They're closing early and sending everyone home. The leaflets we sent over have been handed out and people now know how to manage symptoms. But there are always those who want reassurance.'

'So we'll have a busy afternoon then.'

'Probably.' He nodded and came further into the room instead of dashing back to his in readiness for the afternoon. She was acutely aware of him. Of his size and strength and his scent, and the way the room seemed to shrink with him in it; he filled the space.

She took a steadying breath. 'Anything else?'

She didn't want to admit what she was hoping for. Didn't even know, long-term…but short-term she wanted to kiss him again.

He nodded. 'I wanted to apologise for the way things went belly-up on Saturday.'

Aha. Professional, not overly friendly. Good, that was the way to go. Not kissing. 'It's fine. We all just had a fright.'

He groaned. 'Is an understatement. Thanks for all your help calming them down. I was probably making things worse.'

'You saved her life, Joe.' She would remember for ever the way he'd dived into the lake, ashen but not panicking, focused only on saving his little girl. The way he'd powered through the water, the way he would not give up. The way he strode out of the water in wet clothes clinging to every muscle and sinew, and the way her body had reacted even then, even in the most dire of circumstances.

And then the way he'd struggled to keep his fear under wraps—almost. She'd seen the gruff edge of him emerge but he'd wrestled it back. He was a good man. That was the sum of it. A good man with a good heart. And a very good kisser.

Not to mention the *Thor-midable* sex appeal. A shiver ran down her spine and she tried to cover it up by shuffling bits of paper on her desk. Viking? She hadn't noticed…

He smiled. 'Katy is asking if you still want to teach her how to crochet. She understands you're probably cross with her and may not want to. But I thought I'd ask on her behalf.'

'Got to be safer than swimming, right? A nice safe hobby? Is that where we're at now? Wrapping her up in cotton wool…or, rather, crochet wool?'

Although, she was hardly one to talk about being overprotective; she'd phoned him at the hospital after he'd taken Katy there for a check-up. Phoned him again that evening to make sure all was still fine with the little girl. Phoned him the next day to double-check. And each time he'd thanked her for her concern guilt had rippled through his words like the water he'd saved her from.

He raised both hands in surrender. 'You got me. Although, really, she keeps asking when she's going to see you again. I think you have an admirer. Two, really.'

The shiver intensified and heat suffused her skin. The ache to walk into those strong arms and just breathe him in was sharp and hot. 'Please—don't. We agreed.'

'We did. But I just want you to know that I don't usually invite women onto my boat and then make out with them.' He seemed at pains to let her know this. 'You're the first.'

'Good to hear.' And she could draw a line—or at least try—between her and Joe, but she had made a promise to his little girl that she wasn't prepared to break. 'How about I come round tonight to do the crochet thing? I'll bring supplies so there's no need to worry about getting anything in.'

He shook his head. 'We're going to the hospital and she's looking forward to seeing her granny.'

'That's fine. Another time then.'

'Tomorrow night? If I go on my own to the hospital then I'll be able to have a proper conversation with Maxine and the doctors without little ears listening.' Joe smiled. 'I'll see if Emily can come too.'

Even better that she could keep a promise to Katy and her distance from Joe. Win-win. 'Great. Well, then, we've got a date.'

He shrugged. 'In a manner of speaking.'

She watched the door close as he left, and then breathed out a rush of air.

Two dates in one day. Neither of them with a…what did Beth call them…an eligible. Rose smiled to herself. At least she was starting to feel accepted. Maybe making friends.

Even if *more than just friends* was something her body was interested in where Joe Thompson was concerned.

CHAPTER SEVEN

DAISY CHAINS. EVERYWHERE. Looping across the coat hooks in the hallway, over the door handles, draped over the paintings on the wall. Crocheted yellow and white flowers on strings. Like Christmas decorations, but made out of wool. *What the hell...?* How could they have done all this in the few short hours he'd been away?

Joe pushed open the door into the lounge and heard soft chuckles. 'He's back! Quick! Dad! Look! Look what we made.'

More daisy chains were woven through their loose long hair like little crowns. On the back of the sofa, around the edges of the coffee table, over the television. It was like something out of an impressionist painting. Very beautiful. Very Rose.

'Wow.' He laughed, the sight of his daughter so happy making his heart ache. The sight of Rose making his body ache too.

Chaos. Bright chaos.

And there was the thing. All he'd ever wanted for his daughter—all he'd ever worked towards since she was left motherless—was consistency and stability, but here she was, shining in the midst of mayhem.

She nearly hadn't been. For a moment he was drawn

back to the water, to her limp body. Guilt shuddered through him again and dulled his senses. She was safe, he reminded himself. She was here with Rose and she was safe. 'This is really…something.'

Rose laughed, her soft voice breathing freshness into his stale house. 'Is it too much? We thought it would brighten the place up a bit.'

'Well, it does. But what happened to the hats? I thought you were making me a blue one? Only don't…whatever you do…make me a daisy chain.'

'Aw… You'd rock one.' Rose's eyes twinkled as she teased, 'Not macho enough?'

'No.'

'I'll try to make you a hat next time, Dad. I promise. I'm just learning. Give me a chance.' Katy rolled her eyes and tutted to Rose as if to say *This guy, huh?* He watched, helpless, as the bond between them tightened. And he wasn't sure how he felt about that.

Rose was going to leave. And then there'd be a hole in his daughter's life. For so long he'd organised it so she was supported and nurtured, never having to face such heartache as losing her mother again.

But he couldn't stop her from making friendships in case they didn't work out—he couldn't protect her heart for ever. Life was a natural ebb and flow of people coming and going: friends for a reason, a season… He just had to be there for her when the heartache happened. And for the joy too.

There was a lesson there for him too. Maybe there could be space here for something to develop between him and Rose. *Geez,* it was the first time he'd felt anything for a woman in years and it would be a damned shame to pass it up.

But he needed to be a parent first.

But she was going to leave.

But…

So many damned buts—not one of them enough to ease that physical ache for her.

'You're not listening, Daddy.' Katy held out a fistful of multi-coloured metal crochet hooks and a ball of yellow wool. 'I said, Rose says I can keep these to practice on. I'm going to take them into school tomorrow and show Emily.'

He dragged his attention back to his daughter and away from Rose and her soft lips and mesmerising eyes. 'Shame she couldn't make it; tell her we'll definitely invite her next time.'

'The more the merrier. I'll bring more boring blue and we can do hats.' Rose impersonated Katy's earlier eye-rolling and they laughed. 'One for Dad.'

'Yes, please.' Then Katy yawned and he realised she was up much later than normal; dark circles edged her eyes. He needed to keep a careful watch on those lungs to make sure she didn't get sick after swallowing half of Lake Windermere.

He scrubbed the top of her head with his palm, making sure to miss the flowers laced into her hair. She looked tired. More, she looked happy and that was all Rose's handiwork. 'Hey, you, it's well past bedtime. Scoot, go clean your teeth. I'll come and tuck you in once I've said goodnight to Rose.'

'Okay.' She gave him a quick kiss then hugged Rose, said something that they both laughed at. Then she was gone, hair daisy chains and all.

He watched the door close behind her and breathed out. 'One happy girl.'

'And one tired teacher.' Rose sighed. 'She's a fast learner and very keen. Clearly she has no after-effects from swallowing all that water.'

'She's fine, says she was scared but glad we got her out. I've watched her like a hawk but it's as if nothing happened. Kids, eh?'

'Despite everything she's been through you've got a resilient daughter there, Joe. Well done.' Rose stuffed her wool and more hooks into a large green and pink bag and stood up. 'And now I should go.'

'No. Stay. For a drink, at least…? I need to thank you for entertaining her all evening.' But as he saw the debate raging in her head, then the softening in her eyes, he wondered whether he was doing the right thing. 'No. Stupid idea.'

'Not at all.' She smiled, eventually. 'One drink while you tell me about Maxine.'

He brought over two glasses and a bottle of red, poured and handed her a glass. Then settled next to her on the sofa, with enough space to be considered friendly but nothing more.

'Maxine's bored, to be honest. You know what recovery is like—one step forward and two back and made even more difficult because she's got arthritic knees, which hamper her mobility. She's fretting about Beth doing things properly and has threatened to self-discharge and come back to work just to make sure things haven't gone bad in a week.'

In truth, he seemed to remember a lot of the conversation had been about Rose. Maxine had a keen interest in Joe's love life. Unfortunately. She'd caught a whiff of something he'd said about their new locum nurse, or a look in his eyes, and kept steering the conversation back to her. At least it had given her something else to think about rather than self-discharge.

Rose's eyes grew wide. 'She wouldn't! She had a heart bypass. You have to stay in for a good week or so after that. She deals with poorly patients all the time; she must know how silly it would be to discharge herself.'

'You don't know Maxine.' Getting his mother-in-law to change her mind really was like trying to hold back the tide. 'I wouldn't put it past her.'

'She has to do what she's told. You have to make her stay there, Joe.'

'You can't make Maxine do anything, trust me.'

Rose took another sip of wine. 'Tell her that Beth's doing fine. Really. I'm very impressed.'

'She's fine now, but Alex is away at the moment. When he gets back things might not be quite so…fine.' That was putting it mildly. His business partner and their stand-in receptionist had a past.

'Oh? And this Alex… Dr Alex? Is that who you're talking about? The one on holiday at the moment?' At his nod she steepled her fingers and smiled secretively. 'Does he happen to be insanely gorgeous with a good sense of humour?'

What? A sharp stab of envy hit him in the gut. They might have agreed not to take the kissing further, but that didn't mean he was happy about it or about an interest in another man. He damped down his reaction. Tried to. 'I haven't noticed. He's not really my type. But he's a good laugh, I suppose.'

'And…unavailable?'

'What is this? He's usually got a girlfriend in tow, if

that's what you mean. But they never last long. He's not exactly Mr Commitment.'

Her eyebrows rose. 'I see.'

'Why the interest?' The thought of her kissing anyone else exacerbated the pain in his chest.

She slid him a wry smile and patted his arm. 'Joe Thompson, don't think I'm hanging out waiting for any old doctor to come along and sweep me off my feet. Truthfully, I'm not hanging out for anything. Or anyone. That kiss…? Was the exception, not the rule.'

'I didn't think you were hanging out for anyone. You're the epitome of independent.' He wondered what it would take to sweep her off her feet. Wondered if he had the guts to do it. Decided in that moment that he was going to try.

If he didn't like the thought of her kissing anyone else then he'd better man up and do it himself. Because, hell, he'd already lost one woman and he wasn't going to let this chance slip away. If he was going to show his daughter about living life he had to take a step forward. Some time.

Now. He'd been living in a fog for five years and Rose had shaken him out of it. It was time to let go.

Whoa. He exhaled and scrubbed his hand across his jaw. There'd been times he'd had to remind himself to breathe, because his grief for Pippa had used up every part of him. Now he was thinking about another woman.

Thinking of impossible things, like a future. And kissing Rose again.

But he'd take things slow. He'd bear Katy in mind, always. *Always.* He'd…hell, this was all so damned complicated compared to being young with no responsibilities.

He slid his hand over Rose's. 'I'm the exception… I like that.'

For a moment her fingers were rigid in his, then they relaxed, as did her shoulders. He could see the tension slide away from her, as if she'd found the answer to a difficult question.

She breathed out a long sigh. 'It's just something Beth said about her not having any luck with men and her type being chronically unavailable.'

Ah. He laughed. 'Apparently, Alex and Beth have some unfinished business. No one knows the full story but we all know to keep them apart where possible.'

'Interesting.' Hand still in his, she shuffled her bottom round on the sofa so she was facing him, her bare feet tucked under his legs. She was making herself comfortable around him, with him. That was something.

Threading his fingers into hers, he tugged her a little closer. The skin-on-skin touch sent all thoughts of comfort skittering, replaced by a hot energy which he was struggling to keep under wraps.

'What's interesting is that I haven't seen you on your walk these last two mornings.'

He'd tried not to keep an eye out for that bright orange hat, but caught himself doing so on too many occasions. Her presence was distracting enough, but her absence was too.

She licked her bottom lip and smiled. Teasing. 'There are plenty of other hills, Dr Thompson. You said so yourself.'

'And I said I'd show you them if you showed me some yoga moves.'

The smile was full of mischief. 'I remember.'

'You want to teach me some yoga now? We can move

the chairs and make space.' An image of them tangled on his rug slipped into his head. 'No time like the present.'

'Don't be silly.' She indicated her snug-fitting jeans and high-necked T-shirt. 'I'm not dressed for yoga.'

'We can improvise.' He'd imagined her dressed in only his rug. Maybe those daisies still in her hair. Skin slick from kisses. 'It can't be that hard, surely. Come on, show me. What about good doggy?'

'It's downward dog. But I think you know that really.' As she laughed she leaned even closer, eyes shining, lips glossy. Ripe for kissing. *God,* he wanted to kiss her. All over. So much so he could barely focus on what she was saying. 'I'm no teacher; I just like the way it makes me feel. I'll send you details of a vlog you can watch online. That's how I learnt. It means you can do it any time you're free rather than hanging out for a class.'

Which was so far away from where his mind was it might as well have been outer space. 'A vlog's no good, Rose. I'm a kinetic learner.'

'What does that mean?'

'I much prefer to be hands-on.' He let that sit for a moment. Waited a beat. Watched her cheeks burn red and knew exactly what she was thinking. Wanting. Desire was spurring him on, making him say things he'd normally hold back. No—he wouldn't normally have these thoughts. He wanted her more than he'd wanted anyone. Ever. But he wrestled it under control. Didn't want to come on too strong. Strong enough she knew what was behind his words, but not to frighten her away. They'd both agreed to no more kisses, but they could both *un*-agree that too. 'I'd like to learn purely for professional reasons. I want to introduce some of my patients to mindfulness and the benefits of yoga to help with stress and anxiety.'

'Professional? Really?' The raised eyebrows again. She looked up at him through thick dark eyelashes. 'How can I refuse such a noble cause?'

He shook his head. 'You can't. You have to teach me yoga for the sake of my business. Unless, of course, Roses Man changes your mind.'

'He won't. Never.' Those warm eyes sparkled. 'Wait—Beth told you Toby sent me flowers? Ha. So much for female solidarity.'

'Oh, she didn't tell me any secrets. Not in so many words. The flowers were in Reception. I asked her if they were hers or if we'd suddenly started buying flowers to make the place look nice…because we have to be careful about pollen and allergies and infection control. She said they were yours.'

'And you assumed they were from a man?'

He laughed. 'Yes. But only an amateur would send roses to a woman. A man with a very limited imagination.'

'Oh? So what would you send me? Er…what would you send a woman? If you were sending flowers?' She rested her chin on her free hand and gazed at him. Her smile a killer, megawatt. Her teasing stare a gauntlet. A game. Definitely a flirt. His heart jumped as his gut tightened.

It had been a long time since he'd played this kind of game but he was finding he still knew the rules. He also knew she was confused about all this. That she wanted him—or at least another kiss—as much as he wanted her. Knew she'd been hurt in the past and that she needed careful handling, not to feel rushed, and given every opportunity to stop. On her terms.

Agonisingly slowly, he reached out and touched the crocheted crown on her head and laughed. Careful not to touch her anywhere else. Felt her hand squeeze tight in his. Saw the need in her eyes. Heard the sharp intake of breath.

'Would I send you daisies, maybe? You obviously like them. But then you seem to be able to conjure up enough of those on your own. No, I wouldn't send you flowers in the hope they'd make you want me, Rose. That's not my style.'

'You have a style?' She laughed, her throat moving gently—mesmerisingly—as she tilted her head back. There was a dip at the base of her throat that was perfect for his lips. His tongue.

He ran a lock of her hair through his fingers then tucked it behind her ear, lightly grazing the side of her cheek. He saw the shudder run through her and felt it resonate inside him too. 'I wouldn't hope that flowers changed your mind, Rose. Not if I wanted you back— which I'm assuming was the message. If it was me, I'd drive up here in person to talk to you. I'd listen. I'd find out what you wanted, then I'd do everything I could to give it to you.'

'Even if that was to walk away?' The tiniest of lines appeared on her forehead.

'I'd want you to be happy and if that meant letting you go I'd do that, no matter how much it hurt. If that was what you wanted.'

She looked surprised. But not serious. 'You'd let me walk away?'

'If that was what you wanted. But not without a fight.'

'Oh? You'd fight me? Interesting…' She bit her bottom lip again and smiled. And, God, the last thing he wanted to do right now was fight her. Unless there was make-up sex afterwards. A lot of make-up sex. That he could buy into.

'I'd make it worth your while staying.' His fingers stroked down her cheek to her chin and he tilted her face so he could look into her eyes. Saw the swirl of need there. Then he asked the question, knowing the answer already. 'What do you want, Rose? Right now? Right this moment? Do you want to walk away?'

She swallowed. Licked her bottom lip and he damned near exploded with need. Her voice was hoarse yet soft. 'No.'

'What do you want?'

'This.' She cupped his face in her hands and brought her mouth to his.

She'd been waiting for this. Ever since the kiss on the boat her body had been craving his touch, his mouth on hers. She'd been waiting for this, for him, her whole life. She just hadn't known it until now. Joe Thompson was everything she could ever want in a man: gentle yet strong, honest and kind, with a wicked laugh when he allowed it to spring free. She loved the way he put others first, the way he tried to hide his instinctive need to protect those he cared for.

He kissed like a god.

And every minute she spent with him knocked another chink in her resolve and in her armour.

She kissed him because she couldn't not kiss him.

Sliding her mouth over his, she felt the sweet tang of arousal shimmer through her body like a shining light. Starting at her lips at the first touch, spreading fast through her veins, pooling in her abdomen. Low and deep. Stoking the depths of her desire, setting fire to her need.

His hands cradled her head as his tongue slipped into her mouth on a tight groan. 'God, Rose.'

She curled against him, into him, her hands gripping his shoulders, holding on, holding tight to this. To him.

He tugged her onto his lap and she straddled him, feeling his hardness under her thighs. The pressure against her core was almost too much to bear, and yet not enough. She ground against him, wanting him there. Fingers, mouth, everything.

But she had plans for that mouth, his taste so addictive she couldn't bear to break from him. The lightest touch of his skin making her reckless and needy and hungry for more. She kissed him hard, and fast and long and slow.

After who knew how long he drew back, drew breath, the way he looked at her making her feel as if she was the most beautiful woman in the world. As if there was nothing to fear, nothing to lose, nothing to remember except this beautiful kiss in a landscape of handmade daisies.

As if she was home. His home.

Then his mouth was at her neck, her skin wet with kisses. His hand slipped under her T-shirt, fingers stroking her side, then beneath her breast. Over her bra, under her bra. He pushed her T-shirt up. And she froze.

The scar.

He was going to undress her and he would see the scar fully.

Not yet.

She didn't want this beautiful spell to be broken but it had to be, so she put her hand on his chest and broke away from him. *Hot damn.* 'We said we weren't going to do this.' She heard the strain in her own voice, the desperation and need.

He pressed his forehead lightly against hers, kissed the top of her nose and smiled. She could see so much in that smile: lust, friendship, affection. Everything she wanted, everything she felt too. There was laughter and a groan in his throat. 'Doesn't matter how many promises I make, when you're around I can't stop myself. I want you, Rose. Crazy as it sounds.'

'I don't even know where this came from… There's something here, right? Happening between us? Something intense?' But she had to know… How would he be when he learnt the truth? Would he stay or would he leave? Would he think less of her? Or more? Would it change anything? Everything?

'I can't stop thinking about you, Rose McIntyre. You're in my head all the time. Even when I'm at work. I need to see you. Smell you.' He put his nose to her neck and sniffed, laughing. 'I think I'm going a little crazy.'

'Glad I'm not the only one. But I…er…' She looked across the family room to the photos of Pippa, the way they were looking at each other, the love captured in black and white, and her heart constricted. She'd got a heart from someone like Pippa—she'd got her life back and Pippa hadn't. And, with her history, she couldn't give him what he wanted, needed or deserved: a family, a certain future.

'Is there something wrong?' He followed the line of her gaze and sucked in air. 'Pippa? Is that the problem?'

So many things made her feel as if what they were doing was wrong. Yet it felt so right too. 'I feel bad doing this, knowing how much you loved each other. I feel bad knowing Katy's close by and you don't want her to be upset by you finding someone else who isn't her mum. Mostly, I'm just confused. This wasn't meant to happen. I came here for some space, not to make out with a guy I barely know.'

He nodded and leaned back. 'You want to know more…ask.'

'What? It's going to be that easy? A question and an answer?' And a route to falling in deeper than she wanted to go.

'Sure. Why not? You ask one question. I'll do the same. No judging. No pushing beyond what's comfortable. Just getting to know each other.'

Would he push, though? And what would she say? But the more she found out about him the more he appealed on every level. She unwrapped herself from his legs and settled next to him. He slid his arm round her. Held her as she said, 'I don't even know what to ask. I understand you had a deep love for her and you may not want to talk about it. That's fine.'

She wasn't sure she wanted to hear how much he'd loved Pippa, but then how wonderful would it be to find a man capable of such great love that he'd mourned hard for so long?

Joe twisted a little to face her, but kept his hold on her. Over her. 'We met at med school and discovered we'd grown up in neighbouring villages, but our paths had never crossed. Funny how life works out. I came back here to be with her. We had Katy and then…' He paused. Smiled sadly. 'She died. I thought my life was at an end, but now I'm here doing this. Doing something I didn't know I was even capable of.'

She knew how that felt. How you thought you could

never feel whole or hope again. Then she'd been given her second chance too. By someone just like Pippa.

He stroked her hair. 'But you're not Pippa and I'm not the same man I was five years ago. I don't want you to think I compare you to her—ever. Because I don't. I don't want you to be her, or to replace her. This...what we have is different. *Good* different. I like you because you're Rose McIntyre and, truthfully, it sounds crazy even to me after such a short time. Days, really... I can't comprehend it. But there's definitely something...yes.'

Which was not what she'd wanted to hear really. A quick fling, perhaps...mindless sex with no strings. Not that he felt as crazy about this as she did. One of them needed to stay sane here.

'I'm sure it'll wear off.'

'Maybe it will. But right now I'm enjoying the way it feels and I think you are too. Maybe that's just what we should do...enjoy it. Get to know each other. See how we fit.'

She smiled and placed her hand on his chest. 'I'm the goddess to your grump.'

'I'm the...' He thought for a moment and then laughed. 'The wise to your wacky.'

She flicked her hand lightly against his arm. 'Hey, watch it. I'm wise too. I'm just on a different journey.'

'Ah, yes. Passing through onto bigger adventures.' He was quiet for a moment then he asked her, 'D'you think you'll ever do the family thing? Settle down. Kids?' His voice was tentative, as if he was trying hard to be nonchalant. Too hard.

She didn't know how to answer, because whatever she said would be loaded. 'I...er... I love kids.'

'Something about your tone tells me there's a *but*…
You don't want them?'

'It could be difficult.' At his raised eyebrows she gave
an indifferent shrug. At least she hoped it was indifferent.
This was getting way too deep. 'Long story.'

'I'm listening.' His head tilted slightly to one side and
he smiled gently. How easy it must be for his patients to
tell him everything.

'Trust me, you don't want details.'

'What kind of men have you been around to make you
so wary of talking?' His eyes darkened. 'Don't answer
that. I know what kind of men. The ones that send you
roses instead of being here in person. I'm sorry about
that, Rose. You deserve so much more.'

'Not your fault. Not his really, either. Or mine, for
that matter.'

'So what happened? I've given you an overview of my
past, now it's your turn.'

What to say? She tried to keep to the facts rather than
dwell on her medical history. 'With Toby? We were together a few years. I met him at the PR agency I worked
at before I trained to be a nurse. Got engaged and we had
our life mapped out. But…things happened.'

There was a pause. He was waiting for her answer,
she knew it. And when she didn't say anything he asked,
'What happened, Rose?'

'I no longer fitted into his expectations of how a
woman should be or act. I think he felt betrayed that
we'd made decisions about our future and then…then
I wanted to do other things.' Reconcile herself to the
fact she couldn't have kids. Grieve. Breathe. After facing and then cheating death she had to take stock. She

wasn't old Rose and she didn't know who new Rose was, what she wanted.

Joe squeezed her hand. 'Was it something to do with the kids question?'

'That and other things.'

'Well, I can't say I'm sorry if it means we get to do this.' He fingered the daisy chain round her head. 'I can't imagine you in some high-flying PR job. You're the furthest thing from corporate I've ever seen. Although I wouldn't say no to seeing you in sky-high heels.' His fingers traced a slow track up the back of her leg, calf, knee—making her squirm and giggle—and to her thigh. 'And a short skirt.'

'Typical man.' But she liked the way his fingers stroked her leg, even through her jeans.

'Hey, it's every guy's fantasy. Although orange hats get me too… Every. Single. Time.'

She laughed and then found his mouth on hers again and she didn't pull back. She went wholeheartedly into this kiss. That was the problem right there: Joe wanted her for her quirks. He wanted her. He *liked* her. And she liked him back, a whole lot more than she was prepared to admit. She moved against him.

Maybe she would tell him about her transplant. Maybe he'd understand. Maybe it wouldn't matter to him— because he'd seen it from the other side and knew what a precious gift it had been.

But then she would have to tell him everything on the flipside too. How her heart might fail again and she'd die anyway. How her anti-rejection drugs could stop working any time. How she grasped every day because it could, truly, really, honestly be her last.

No matter how amazing this was, she couldn't make

him want things she couldn't give him: a family, the future he wanted. And, despite what he might be saying now, he wanted more than fun. He was that kind of guy—solid, dependable, a one-woman man.

He wouldn't want her. Not when he knew the truth.

His finger trailed her collarbone, down to her chest bone. He whispered in her ear, 'A low-cut blouse…low enough that I can get a teasing glimpse of—'

'I can't…' She pulled away from him. Wanting more, so much more, but wary about taking more and how that would open her to hurt.

This was getting too deep too fast. She ran her fingers down his jaw. 'I'm sorry, Joe. I have to go.'

His forehead furrowed and he leaned back. 'What, now?'

'Yes. Now. I need to think.'

'But—I don't understand.' Neither did she. How could her heart and her head be at such odds? How could she let herself walk away from this chance?

He stood and followed her towards the front door, his voice endlessly understanding, which made her feel so much worse, 'Hey, stay and talk. What's going on, Rose? One minute everything's fine and you seem so happy, the next you're running away. What's the matter?'

'It's all so intense—you, me, this. I'm so, so sorry. Please don't feel badly about me.' She hugged her coat tight across her chest. Then hurried out of his house.

Running away the minute things got difficult.

So much for living a big life.

CHAPTER EIGHT

'BETH SAID YOU needed me?' Rose steamed into his room, brisk and efficient and with no obvious sign of embarrassment or tension about the way she'd run off a few nights ago. But it was there. In her eyes. In the stiff stance. No one would have noticed but him.

Their paths had barely crossed for three days—whether by design or not he didn't know, but even eye contact had been brief and she'd always rushed past saying *busy, busy*—and he'd been left to ruminate on why she'd made such a hurried exit. When it came to reading signs Joe clearly had it all wrong. Signs with women, that was. It had been so long since he'd dated he'd all but forgotten the rules, and he was pretty sure he'd been following them. But obviously not, if he'd scared her away.

And now she was interfering with his head at work too. Truthfully, the last thing he needed right now was her.

He swallowed a sigh. He'd asked for any of the other nurses or even Jenny to come and help him because what he needed was another pair of hands. He looked down at the semi-conscious young girl on his examination couch and tried to relay the urgency without actually telling Rose to hurry the hell up.

'Can you grab a glucometer?'

'Sure thing.' Her eyes slid over to seven-year-old Molly, one of Katy's friends and usually bubbly and outgoing and obsessed with gymnastics. Today she was vomiting, lethargic, on the verge of systemic collapse.

As Rose left the room he continued his assessment. 'How long has she been vomiting?'

Alli, Molly's mum, shook her head. 'A few days. I was going to come yesterday, but I thought she'd get better.'

'And she will.' No fever. Heart running a little fast and thready. 'Anything else unusual happening?'

'Mummy. Drink?' Molly raised her fingers then flopped back onto the couch again.

'She's thirsty. All the time recently, and never off the toilet. She even...' Alli mouthed the words *wet the bed*. 'Is she okay? Please, Joe. What's wrong?'

'I need to do some tests.' He touched the little girl's hand. Despite all the drinking she felt dry, a little dehydrated. 'You know what? I think we should hold off on the drink just for a little while. How's your tummy feeling, Molly?'

'Hurts.' Molly grimaced.

'And your head?'

She nodded, her eyes slowly closing. There was a sweet smell about her, like ripe fruit. The giveaway. *Bingo.* The good thing about medicine was that it was based on logic and science. Two things he did understand. But he had to work fast, and not assume anything. Because it seemed he was starting to second-guess himself on everything these days. 'So, not long back at school after the holidays. Who's your favourite teacher? Molly?'

Molly's eyes were closed and her breathing was becoming laboured.

Her mum squeezed her hand and the little girl's eyes opened. 'See. She keeps nodding off and it's hard to wake her.'

Ketoacidosis. Risk of diabetic coma. Not there yet—she was still conscious. Just. But they needed to test her blood sugars and urine and get her to hospital if his hunch was right.

'Molly, listen. I'm just going to take your blood pressure with my machine.' He reached for his sphygmomanometer, keeping watch on the girl's reactions. Her eyes fluttered open and she grimaced, then turned onto her side.

A groan. A look of shock. And then his trousers were covered in vomit.

Molly's mum jumped backwards, mouth open in shock. 'Oh! Goodness. I'm so sorry.'

'Occupational hazard. Don't worry at all.' It was the last thing he cared about right now. He threw paper towels onto the floor and stepped over them to get to his desk.

'Hey. How are we doing?' Rose bustled in carrying the glucometer. He watched as she assessed the situation, eyes flicking from patient, to mother, to the paper towels on the floor. As her gaze met his, her cheeks coloured dark red. 'Do you want me to do the finger prick test?'

'What's the matter? What's wrong with her?' Alli again. Guilt edged her eyes, and worry. And love. He knew all about the emotional trifecta of being a parent and his heart went out to her.

'Once we've done the finger test we'll have more of an idea, Alli. Also, a urine sample would help too.'

Rose looked up from assessing Molly. 'Glasgow coma score of twelve.'

When the little girl had come in it had been fifteen. He needed an ambulance here now.

He watched as Rose talked soothingly to their patient, getting her to agree to having her finger pricked as if they had all the time in the world. How she told her how brave she was and that she'd be feeling better soon. Watched how she put her hand on Alli's and reassured her that everything would be okay and that she'd done the right thing by bringing her daughter in.

Easy to do the medicine, not so easy to do it with such grace and gentleness. Unlike his gruff manner.

When she showed him the LED display of the very high blood sugar reading he nodded and explained to Alli what they were going to do, trying not to spook her with the news her daughter was very sick right now.

'Molly's blood sugar is very high at the moment and we need to bring it down. It's not something we can do here; she needs to go to hospital and be monitored. So I'm going to call for an ambulance to take her there now. I can put in an IV and some saline to keep her hydrated for the journey and she'll need a bolus of insulin to start dealing with the sugar levels. The paramedics will keep a good eye on her.'

'Will she be okay?' Alli's face was as pale as her daughter's and her hands were shaking.

Rose took them both in hers. 'If she has got diabetes she's going to need to have medicine—injections or a pump—to keep her blood sugar stable. It'll be a lot to take in at first and it's a steep learning curve for everyone, but there's no reason why she can't have a perfectly wonderful life.' Rose's arm was now round Alli's shoulders as if they'd been friends for years. She had such an easy way with her, attracting everyone to her like a bright flower. But he also knew the sting of her rejection too—even if she did it in the nicest way. 'It's amazing how quickly kids adapt. And you will too. I promise. It's amazing what we can deal with, honestly.'

She said it with such heartfelt meaning that he knew she was talking from personal experience. What had she dealt with?

In all the times he'd seen her, every day for the last couple of weeks, she'd worn something tight at the base of her throat: a scarf, a high-necked blouse, buttoned collar, zipped wetsuit. He assumed she used them to hide the scar she refused to talk about, but for him the accoutrements just drew his eye to the area and made the questions loom larger in his head. Why wouldn't she talk to him about it? What the hell had happened?

And every time he saw that cover-up his heart constricted. She'd obviously surmounted odds and survived whatever had caused it. But she'd made it clear she didn't want to talk about it and he wasn't going to harp on about something that made her feel uncomfortable.

But she'd had open heart surgery, that much he knew. Why wouldn't she talk about it?

After the paramedics drove away with Molly and her mum Joe wandered back to his room with Rose and she helped him clear up. At least, they seemed to silently agree that he'd wipe the floor while she sorted the sharps and neither of them spoke. But the tension between them was as thick as fell fog on a winter's morning.

This couldn't go on; they had to work together. 'Rose?'

'Yes?' She looked up from washing her hands and all the connection he'd felt the other night steamrollered into him again. He wasn't imagining it. He hadn't taken a misstep. If the mist in her eyes was anything to go by, she wanted to kiss him just the same. But she had her reasons and he had to respect them.

'Thanks, you were a great help. I can take things from here.'

'No problem.'

There was so much more he wanted to say, to ask. He wasn't angry, just confused. But, in the end, she was only here for a short time and then she'd be off being a locum somewhere else. Perhaps she was making the wisest choice? Better not to get involved when she was moving on anyway.

When she'd dried her hands he expected her to go but she didn't. She just stood there and smiled and, regardless of what was for the best, he couldn't deny the tug to her getting tighter and tighter.

'Er...sorry to tell you this, Doc, but you smell bad. Better not go see Maxine in those.'

He looked down at the sticky patches on his trousers and pawed at them with another paper towel. 'I'm going to go home and change right now.'

'Wait. I know you're busy.' Her teeth worried her bottom lip as she chose her words. 'But can I apologise for running away the other day?'

He shrugged. 'Hey, I'm a big boy—I can take rejection. I just read things wrongly. My fault.' He was impressing himself with how nonchalant he sounded when he felt anything but. But the last thing he wanted to do was make her feel bad about being in a situation where she wasn't comfortable.

'Not your fault. I'm sorry. You didn't read anything wrong. I wanted to kiss you. I still do. My head's in a bit of a whirl. I've had sleepless nights going over everything. But...oh, God.' She shook her head. 'I'd rehearsed what I was going to say but now I don't know. But I think…you'd understand. I want to tell you—at least I owe you an explanation. But please don't freak.'

'What is it? What's the matter?' Gone was the usual vibrancy in her eyes and in its place was something Joe could only describe as anxiety—which was so unlike her he almost did a double-take. Whatever she was going to say was clearly going to take guts, but one thing he knew about Rose was that she had them aplenty. He opened the door. 'You want to go outside? For a walk?'

She covered his hand and tugged the door closed. 'No. I still have paperwork to do and one hell of a grumpy boss if it's not finished.'

'I'm sure he'll let you off.'

'Can't take that chance. I need him for a reference.' There she was, pointing out she was moving on. Yes. That was why she'd left. Must have been. She breathed deeply, fingering the fabric of her blouse, right over the fading purple line. He waited. She said nothing.

He waited some more then couldn't help asking, 'Are you married or something? Or in some kind of trouble?'

She laughed and shook her head. Then took his hand and walked him over to his desk. They sat down opposite each other, as if in a consultation. And he wished they were anywhere but here at work.

'No, you idiot, of course I'm not married. And yes… I think I'm in a lot of trouble where you're concerned. I just want you to know what the scar is for. I don't want it to be a secret… I was just… Oh, it's hard to explain. But it is important. You'll understand. I hope.'

'Okay.' This *was* a big deal. An important step for them. For her, at least. She'd shied away from talking about it last time. And…was that what the other night had been about?

'So…' Her eyes sought his, reading his reaction even before she said any more. Then, 'I had a heart transplant.'

'Okay. So not mitral valve.' He kept his reaction steady, although the words had his own heart reeling as images skittered through his head. Pippa. Tubes. A form. A dotted line. The reassuring beeps by the hospital bed. Then no beeps, just silence. Then later…much, much later…a letter thanking him for the gift of life. A letter he'd cast aside because he wanted his wife back, not pieces of paper.

He shook the thoughts away. This was Rose. She was alive and vibrant and here and needed him to be present and kind. Not regretful or distracted. He reached out and stroked her hair. It wasn't an issue she had with him, or them, after all. It was just something she needed to get out there. A huge deal. 'And just look at you. I would never have guessed. You look amazing.'

So many questions ran through his head. When? Where? Why? All the medical stuff. And the sudden realisation that there were ramifications too: issues with carrying children, shortened life expectancy, how her body could reject this heart at any time.

This was a very big deal.

'Thank you.' Her shoulders relaxed a little and she smiled softly. 'Once people know they either run a mile or shoot the pity line, which I hate. I'm not sick now; I'm very healthy.'

Her skin glowed, energy resonated from her even now when she was sitting so close to him. 'Yes. You are.'

'I probably should have said something sooner, but

when's the best time to introduce it into a conversation? First meeting? *Hi, my name's Rose and I had a heart transplant.* That's just weird, especially if you're never going to see that person again.' Her eyebrows rose. 'First date? We haven't really had one, have we? When is a good time to tell someone you're not exactly in pristine condition and should perhaps be put in the seconds bin for a cheap sale?'

He frowned. 'Rose. That's not how it is at all. You're not in any seconds bin. It's a second chance. It's wonderful.'

'And not something I'm keen to talk about usually. Because I'm more than the sum of my working parts, right? I don't want to be treated any differently. Please—' she palmed his cheek '—stop looking at me like that.'

'Like what?' *Pity?* He'd never pity her. He tried to straighten out his features. 'You are more than anyone I've ever met, to be honest. But…how weird that…er… nothing.' He ran his fingers over his scalp. *Heart transplant.* The coincidence was weird, but not necessarily startling. Transplants happened most days in this country. He found his gaze straying over to the photograph on his desk. A copy of the one Rose had been looking at the other day. Every step forward he took away from his past seemed to glue him back there again. His own heart tightened, then he drew his focus back to the woman opposite him. 'Sorry. I shouldn't keep bringing Pippa into conversations, but it's just weird that we donated some of her organs.'

'It is such a coincidence. It feels as if we'd understand each other more somehow.' She was right; there was a connection of understanding that no one else could possibly have with him. Rose knew. She knew what he'd been through because she'd been there too. On the other side. Waiting, probably hanging onto life. *God.* What she must have been through. The anxiety in her eyes melted away and all that was left was a kindness that was mirrored in her soft voice. 'What did she donate?'

'Heart, a kidney and corneas. It was the best thing we could do, considering. It was what she wanted. What we all wanted, in the end.'

'That's so amazing and very comforting for you, I'm sure. I know how difficult that must have been. But thank you. From every single donor recipient ever. Thank you so much for what you did.'

Outside he could hear Beth chatting away, the phones ringing. Everyday humdrum life and in here Rose was baring her soul. He bit back questions about her medication.

Rose knew what she was doing. And he wanted to be—what did he want to be? Her lover, not her doctor. Her lover. Yes, that was the idea he'd been chasing before. Did knowing this about her change that? His head ran through the ramifications again. He knew it shouldn't change things but he thought it might. Certainly that need to protect her was fiercer. *Hell.*

'It feels as if things have… I don't know…come full circle in some ways. You're well? You take your meds?'

He had to be sure. Lover perhaps, but always a doctor.

Her hands hit her hips and she scowled. 'Do I look well, Joe? Yes? Can I run up your mountain? This is exactly what I mean by too many questions… I can manage myself just fine. I don't need any special treatment. I'm not broken. Well, not much. I make sure I'm well. I look after myself. I live every single day as if I may not be here tomorrow. I try to live big, Joe.'

All the jigsaw pieces slotted into place. 'The bright colours and the yoga—'

'Give me joy. Life really is too short to do anything except live big.'

'That explains so much about you. But this is so weird. I don't know what to think, how to feel. I'm relieved you're so well but...' His wife had died. She hadn't made it. But she'd given other people the chance to live. People like Rose. This brought it all back to him. It was hard to get his head around.

Seemed Rose knew exactly what he was thinking. 'It's sad that someone like Pippa had to die, right? I know. I live with that guilt every day. Trying to be a better person. A bigger person, trying to live two lives.'

'Do you know who the donor was?' He'd often wondered who had Pippa's heart, kidney, eyes. And so it came back round to her again. No matter how much he tried to wrestle free, he found himself being pulled back to her somehow. 'Sorry...just being ghoulish probably.'

'No. I wrote a letter thanking the family. I should have written more but you never know whether to bring it up with them. You don't want to open the raw pain again. But every year on the twentieth of March—my re-birthday I call it—I send a thank you up to the sky and hope they feel it. Lucky me to have two birthdays, just like the Queen— What's wrong?'

'The...when?' The blood in his veins slowed to icy sludge. Surely this was just a coincidence. There were hundreds of transplants every year in Britain. This was just a very weird coincidence. 'The when?'

He was aware he'd raised his voice. She blinked. Twice. Scuttled back a little on the chair, making more

space between them. Her voice was barely a whisper.
'The twentieth of March.'

'When?' Louder and more insistent, he knew and he
struggled to control it. 'Two years ago? Five? Ten? Decades? *When*, Rose?'

'Five years ago.' She put her hand on his and shook
her head. 'I'm so sorry, Joe. This must be so hard for
you. I shouldn't have said anything. I was in two minds
about it because I don't want to drag up all that upset for
you again. But I figured I needed to be honest about why
I might seem to be acting hot and cold. I was rejected
once because of it and I don't want that to happen again.
And…well, you know there are consequences. I don't
know how long I have…'

Upset? She didn't know the half of it. His mind
whirred. His gut clenched. His fists closed tight. This was
too weird. Too bizarre. 'Where? Where was the transplant, Rose? I need to know.'

'St Mary's in London. Why? What's the matter?'

London. A fist of pain tightened in his gut. There'd
been a helicopter waiting to fly some of Pippa's organs
to London. He hadn't thought to ask specifics—they
wouldn't have told him even if he had. The storm that
had caused her car crash was still raging in the south and
they hadn't been sure the chopper would make it safely in
time to save the recipient's life. Was Rose the recipient?

No.

No. No. No. Impossible. Surely? Highly unlikely.
Crazy. Weird. And, if impossibly crazy and weird, then…
'Is this some kind of joke?'

'Sorry? What?' Her fingers worried the blouse fabric
now and confusion ran across her features. Confusion and

surprise. 'It's not a joke, Joe. What? Why would I joke about something like this? I don't understand.'

'Why are you saying all this then?' Because surely he was doing the maths and getting the wrong answer.

'Because it's true—wait. When…oh, no.' Her hand went to her head and all colour drained from her face. 'When did Pippa die?'

'Don't you know? Didn't Beth tell you that?' At the shake of her head he squeezed the words out. 'The twentieth of March. Five years ago.'

This changed everything.

He'd distanced himself from her physically, but she'd watched the emotional barriers rising too with every second. She had seen the moment he'd realised. The shadow scud across his face. The fast shake of his head. And it had taken her a few moments to catch up.

Now her chest constricted tight. Too tight. This had to be a mistake, surely?

There are nearly two hundred heart transplants every year in England.

There was no way they could be connected. It would be bizarre. Too coincidental. She believed in some sort of fate, but something as spooky as this? No way.

But why else had she been attracted by the sound of Oakdale? Why had it felt so right to apply there, so exciting when she'd been given the temporary job? And what about this strong attraction to Joe and Katy? And the immediate connection with Maxine? Pippa's mother.

The mother of the heart now beating in Rose's chest? Was that real? Even possible?

Wow.

Wow.

Could it be possible?

'You think I came here on purpose? I'm not allowed to know who my donor was. And I had no idea until Beth told me that Pippa had donated her organs.'

He rubbed a palm across his forehead, eyes wide. 'If you really didn't know then…what the hell? I can't get my head around this.'

'You and me both.' The life-affirming muscle in her chest beat hard against her ribcage. Hard and fast. She pressed her palm against her scar and rubbed gently. Even now it prickled, oddly, when she was anxious or upset. A psychological thing, the counsellor had said. But it still took her breath away.

Rose hadn't wanted to know who her heart had come from. Truly. Because then she'd feel obliged, and sad and, as always, so very grateful to someone who'd died and so she'd lived. Why them? Why her? Survivor's guilt. But, on the other hand, she'd wanted to let the donor's family know they'd done a good thing so she'd sent a letter via the organ donor scheme. Anonymous, to protect both sides.

'It doesn't make sense. Do you…did you want to have her life or something? What's going on?' He was still shaking his head, as if he could erase this conversation by doing so. He'd shut her out and wasn't listening.

'No way, Joe. Please listen to me… I did not know. We still don't know. I don't want her life; that would be bizarre. Pippa had nothing to do with me coming here.' She looked over to the photo on his desk. Such happiness. Such love between Joe and his wife. Such pain now too. 'I'd never heard of her until I met you.'

He stood. Shaking and shaking his head, and looking at her as if she was some kind of monster. 'I feel sick.'

She reached a hand towards him, then drew it back. 'You and me both.'

He paced across the floor, stopping at the door, the furthest point away from her. 'Do you want to find out?'

She didn't know. 'Do you?'

His palms raised. 'No. No, I do not want to know if my wife's heart is in your chest. That would be too weird. It's all bizarre. Too bizarre to comprehend. Geez, Rose, have you any idea how many times I've walked down the street scouring people's faces, wondering…just wondering? *Is it you? Is it you? Could there be part of my wife that's keeping you alive?* That hope kept me going; it got me through the worst part of my life. But I don't want to know now. No.' Laughter in Reception had him glancing away. Then his eyes grew wild. 'What about Maxine? Katy? It would break their hearts if this isn't true. It could break their hearts if it is. How can I tell them anything about this?'

In a community so tight she imagined them broken by the grief of losing one of their own. She had no idea how they'd respond, what she'd even say.

'I don't know, Joe. I just don't know. And I'm so sorry. I wouldn't have come to Oakdale if I'd known. Honestly. I'm not some weird stalker or anything. I don't want to impose on your grief—hell, I didn't know anything about you or the village before I came, apart from the beguiling description you put in the advert. It sounded so lovely… and it is. But I had no idea that Pippa had ever existed.' In the end, should it matter whose heart beat for her, just as long as she had one and put it to the best use she could?

But it did matter. It mattered to her and it very definitely mattered to him.

Rose had had a lot of reactions to her transplant story

but this had to be the one that hurt the most. None of this was exactly her fault. She hadn't pursued this; she hadn't chosen this. This was what she'd been given and she was trying to make the most of it.

'You know what? I should leave.'

His eyes finally settled on her, such pain and anguish. 'Yes. We both need time to process this.'

Everything was falling apart when all she'd wanted to do was feel whole again. Would she ever feel completely whole with this foreign heart in her chest?

She gathered her things together and walked towards him. He opened the door wide and she couldn't help thinking he was desperate to get rid of her. The memory of his kisses fresh on her lips. 'I mean Oakdale. I should leave here.'

'That's not going to help one damned thing.' Then the door closed behind her and she was standing alone, her heart hurting, breaking, splintering inside her.

CHAPTER NINE

How could this be possible? *What the hell?* Joe stalked up the cobbled road towards his house. His and Pippa's house. His family's house. Was this some twisted nightmare he was going to wake up from soon? *Please?*

None of this made sense. How could she come here and do this to them? To Katy?

He'd thought he was up against someone who was as wary of relationships as he was and who'd decided to travel a while before settling down. Normal things. Standard issues.

He'd thought he was up against his own damned issues of trying to live with the guilt of living and moving on when his wife was in the ground.

Not this.

He couldn't even compute.

It was a wild idea. Despite what she'd denied so vehemently, had Rose come here knowing she might have his wife's heart?

He'd liked her. A lot. Maybe too much. She was fun and beautiful and she'd won over his daughter's heart. And his own.

Now he had to collect Katy from his sister's house and be normal around his nosy family. Be normal? A cold laugh came from his throat. He didn't know what that was any more.

Be normal around Maxine. God, how could he even begin to tell her that Rose had her daughter's heart?

His phone rang and he paused outside his house. *Katy.* 'Dad? Can I stay at Aunty Kathy's a bit longer? We're going to do some baking.'

'Great. Make extra for me.' He tried to keep his voice upbeat, but knew it wasn't working. Rose had been walking round with Pippa's heart and he hadn't sensed it. He hadn't felt closer to Pippa. He hadn't felt her presence. He'd just been consumed by lust. That was what it had been. He'd been bewitched by Rose's brightness. As had his daughter. She'd be heartbroken, confused if she ever found out.

'Thanks, Dad. And can you tell Rose I tried doing the hat like she told me, I even watched a video online, but it got messed up and I need some help.'

He cursed silently. Rose and her damned online videos. Rose and her damned…lies. No, she hadn't told him a lie. She'd just withheld the truth until she'd drawn him in. Hook, line and sinker. How would he even be able to look at her at work, never mind speak to her?

He'd have to. Hell, he'd brought her here through the agency, ticked the boxes and said yes, she sounded perfect for the role. He'd brought her here to destroy the world he'd carefully constructed.

'I'll tell her at work tomorrow.'

'Can I see her tomorrow? I said I'd make you a hat. I promised, Dad, and now I can't do it.'

'I'm not sure if she'll be free.'

'It's the weekend. Of course she'll be free.' He imagined his daughter rolling her eyes, with no idea as to what she was asking of him.

So he tried hard not to get irritated, but it came over in his voice, he knew. 'We have things to do, like going to see Granny and chores. Laundry.'

'Aw... Not fair. Chores are boring. Rose isn't boring.'

Hell, no. Rose was anything but boring. She was chock full of surprises. 'Leave it, Katy.'

How could he tell her that Rose wasn't the person they'd all grown to like?

Suddenly she'd become so important to them all. But that was before...before he knew who she really was.

The evening crawled by, pierced by hurt and confusion and, frankly, disbelief. The rest of the weekend too. She'd locked the door and not ventured out on her walks in case she might bump into him or his daughter. Turned down Beth's offer of a drink at the pub, feigning a dicky stomach and the possibility of having caught the norovirus.

Because she couldn't just pretend to be happy, and she certainly couldn't make sense of it all. And she had a feeling if Beth asked her what was really wrong, she'd blurt it all out. So she'd stayed home alone.

Coward.

Never mind. She'd turned down the agency's offer of extending her contract here. She'd be gone by the end of next week, regardless. All this would be a memory.

But until then she had to get on with her commitments. Get ready for a new week at work. Walk down the hill to the clinic. Because she'd have to face him. She couldn't let the practice down. She wouldn't run away. Not this time—at least, not immediately. She was big enough to finish her contract, but the minute she could leave Oakdale she would.

Putting on mascara was difficult. Not least because of her shaking hand, but also because of the rogue tears that splashed down her face willy-nilly. Damned tears. They'd made too much of a show for the last few days.

She was making her packed lunch when a loud hammering at the door made her jump.

Joe? It had to be. No one else would knock at her door at this time in the morning. Surely? She ran to it. Not knowing how to feel. Whether to hope. Or whether he was here to tell her to pack her bags.

Panic swirling in her gut, she swung the door open.

'Oh.' The sight of him made her heart almost break. There he was, eyes swimming with tears. Jaw clenched. He was pale. Still shocked. And so many emotions swam in his features he was clearly in torment. 'Rose—could it be…?'

'I don't know. I just don't know.' She shook her head, holding back more tears of her own. She'd done this to him and there was nothing she could do to make it better.

'May I?' He stretched a hand towards her.

'Of course.'

He tugged her to him. His breathing hitched and he blew out a long breath, blinking, opening and closing his fist. Looking the most unsure about anything she'd ever seen him.

Then he pressed a shaking palm against her chest. Above her heart. Took another breath, kept his eyes on hers, searching for answers, for the truth.

She didn't speak. There was nothing to say. She knew he had to feel this to reconnect somehow. To believe it could be possible.

He nodded slowly in time to the rhythm of her heart-beats and as he did so she watched his features soften, the press of his lips, as if holding in a thousand screams. The way his eyes flickered closed as if holding back a river of tears. And her heart swelled for him and his loss, for her survival. For this moment.

Whatever happened, there would always be this connecting them.

When he eventually looked at her again he was still shaking. Just a little. 'Do you want to find out, Rose?'

'No.' She'd made that decision. It was kinder to them all if they just didn't know. 'I don't. Do you?'

'No.'

Her throat was raw and burned with more unshed tears. 'I'm so sorry.'

'No.' His voice was gruff but she put it down to all that emotion. 'Don't be sorry that you lived, Rose. But this is the most bizarre thing I've ever heard. I can't wrap my head around it.'

'I didn't know, Joe.' Would he believe her?

'I can't stop thinking about it. Katy said I was back to being grumpy again.' Half his mouth turned up in a very wary smile. 'Did you pay her to use those words?'

She managed a weak laugh. 'No. But she's a very wise girl.'

'She is. She also asked me to ask you if you could help her with something she's making. I said you were busy—'

'You don't want me to see her? Is that it?' That hurt.

His forehead wrinkled and he shook his head. 'I thought it would be for the best.'

'Best for who? You?'

'For all of us.' But he looked shame-faced. 'I don't want her to get hurt.'

'And you think I do? Joe Thompson, you think the worst of me, really. Don't you?'

'No. Rose, I don't.' But they both knew he was lying.

She lifted her chin. 'Tell her I'm free any time.' Fact was, she was free every night until the contract ended.

'No, Rose. It isn't fair.'

'What's not fair? Breaking my promise to help her? What's that going to teach her? That adults are unreliable? Or punishing her for something that's not her fault. I said I'd help her and I want to. She's not stupid, Joe, she'll think she's done something wrong if I don't help her. This isn't her fault.' *Or mine.*

His jaw fixed as he thought about it. 'Okay.'

Good. At least he put his daughter front and centre of everything he did. 'So, where do we go from here?'

'Come up to the house. Six-thirty tomorrow. If that's okay? I'll make sure I'm gone as soon as you arrive.' A sharp nod of his head. Decision made. He'd conceded to her but he wasn't happy about it.

She caught his hand. 'I mean us, Joe. What happens now?'

'Oh, Rose.' He shook his head and let her hand fall into nothing. 'I don't know. I just don't know.'

If she hadn't actually felt his hand on her heart and breathed his scent in, committing that precious moment to memory, Rose wouldn't have believed Joe had been at her house this morning. At the surgery he was back to being the grumpy doc from the first day she'd met him.

And she wasn't the only one to notice.

'What's eating Joe today? He bit my head off a few minutes ago,' Beth asked, between mouthfuls of chocolate they'd been given by a grateful patient.

'How would I know?' And truthfully Rose didn't know where to begin so she didn't even try. The whole scenario sounded so improbable she couldn't put it into words.

Beth shrugged. 'I just thought you two were…you know…part of a mutual fan club.'

'No.' Rose chose not to go any further down that route. 'Can we confirm the date the flu jabs are arriving? I'm fielding questions and don't have any answers.'

'Two weeks away, I think. Apparently we do an advert and call-back for all the regulars, which I'm in the process of sorting out now.' She swivelled in her chair and caught Rose's eye, straight on. 'What's the matter, Rose? You're like a bear with a sore head today too.'

Rose put down the forms she was sorting through and sighed. Seemed like there was no hedging today. 'I'm fine, honestly.'

'You're not, neither of you are, so I can only deduce that the man's clearly done something. Or not done something. And therefore he's an idiot.' Beth's words were barely audible, but they made Rose smile. They'd both done and said stupid things and yet, somehow, knowing they shared this secret made her feel closer to him on some level. She was still reeling from the idea, so God knew how he must have been feeling.

A shriek had her turning to Beth and then to the front door. 'Maxine!

'Hello, love. Hello, Rose.' Maxine walked gingerly into the clinic and made her way over to the reception desk, waving her hand away at any offers of help. She'd lost a fair bit of weight and her walking was definitely easier than it had been before, but she was a little stooped and obviously in some pain.

Rose dashed over to take her hand and help her to a waiting room seat, refusing to accept her protestations of being able to do it herself. It was her job, her promise to herself and to whoever had given her this heart that she'd do good. Although, recently, she had to admit, all she'd done was unwittingly cause chaos. And a small part of her wondered why she'd been so drawn to Maxine in the first place. Now she had a suspicion where her heart had come from would she ever have faith in her intuition again?

'What are you doing here? You've only just been let out of hospital. You should be resting at home.'

Maxine shook her head. 'Just thought I'd come in and check that you're all coping without me.'

'Barely.' Beth smiled and winked at Rose. 'But we'll manage until you feel fit enough to decide whether you're coming back to work.'

'The doctors said I need to take it easy, but who takes any notice of them? I knew Alex when he was in nappies, so he can't think he can tell me what to do when he gets back from his holiday. And as for Joey...' His mother-in-law's eyes settled on Rose. 'Well, he's just a work in progress.'

'Tell me about it.' Beth rolled her eyes, but Rose laughed, hugged Maxine and gave her a quick visual check-over that no one would have noticed unless they were a medic. Respiration rate was fine; she had colour in her cheeks. She wasn't wheezing or struggling; her ankles weren't swollen— *Oh.* Both women were still looking at her expectantly.

Joe.

Yes. She'd tried hard not to focus on that particular topic of conversation, but thought back to the way he'd been when she'd met him. He'd changed so much…so had she. 'Seriously, he's come a long way.'

'Not far enough, knowing that boy. Anyway, I'm glad to be out of that hospital and I couldn't wait to see you to say thank you, my dear. If it wasn't for you I wouldn't be here at all.'

Rose felt her cheeks pink. 'I did what anyone would have done. I was just lucky to be here at the right time.'

'Thank God you were. And thank you for waking Joe up. I know he's still half asleep, but he's getting there.' Maxine gave a little satisfied nod. 'I haven't seen him smile so much in a long time. I know you must have something to do with it.'

Great. Everyone really did know your business here. 'Right. Yes, well. He's a nice guy. Let me go get you a drink. Coffee? Tea?'

'I fancy a gin, to be honest. Too early? What a shame.' At Rose's hurried shake of her head Maxine laughed. 'I'll have a black coffee and no sugar…apparently. We'll see how that goes, but—oh. I had no idea. Snap!'

She pointed to Rose's chest and the exposed scar. It was the first day she'd decided not to hide it because she was done with hiding who she was. All that had done was cause problems. But she hadn't expected to see Maxine today…of all days.

Maxine popped two buttons on her flowery blouse and showed off the very new, very raw, line down her chest. 'Scar twins. What's yours for?'

Rose paused, open-mouthed, unsure as to what to say. The truth, but not all of it. She had to be kind to the woman whose daughter had given up her heart—maybe to Rose—and she had to be gentle.

'Maxine, I see you're ignoring medical advice as usual.' Joe strode across the room and gave her a hug.

Rose's heart hammered. How long had he been there? Had he heard he'd been the subject of their conversation? Had he heard Maxine's questions? Did he know how much turmoil Rose had in her heart right now?

'Hello, Joey.' Maxine gave him a quick peck on the cheek. 'I need to know you're all okay, and then I can rest. Now, Rose and I were just comparing scars.' She turned inquisitive eyes back to Rose. 'What happened, love?'

A big deep breath.

'I had a heart transplant. A few years back.' She tried hard to sound casual, as if it was no big deal, and that she talked about it all the time.

Please don't ask more. Please.

Biting her lip, she looked to Joe.

Please. Help. Please. I am so sorry.

He breathed out slowly, his eyes flickering closed for a beat. Then he opened them and smiled. 'And doesn't she look great?'

She saw the soft look in his eyes, the struggle that was still there, and she ached to just run into his arms. And yet she knew there was a very difficult path for both of them to get through this. If they ever could.

But Maxine was still looking at the scar. 'Ooh. That must have hurt, love. But look at you—so well. Which hospital was it? Don't tell me it was Lancaster, because that's too much of a coincidence. When did you have it?'

'It was down south, a long, long time ago. Well before I trained as a nurse.' A few details. Not enough for anyone to draw any conclusions. She couldn't give this woman any kind of stress, either happy or otherwise, given she was recovering from a heart operation herself.

'My daughter… Pippa…she was a donor, you know. When she died.' Maxine inhaled a stuttered breath and for a moment Rose thought she was going to cry. She dug very deep. Made sure she didn't rub her scar even as it prickled, the way she usually did.

Pippa. Always Pippa.

As it should be.

If she stayed here it would always be Pippa.

She couldn't stay; it would be too much for them to deal with.

'Yes, I heard. That must give you some small comfort. It was a wonderful thing for you to do, all those lives saved.' She stroked the woman's hand. Because who knew what had really happened in the end? The only real truth here was that her daughter had been the hero in all of this.

Maxine's smile was sad and small. 'I wish she was still here. I wish it every single day, but it does help to know there's someone, somewhere with her organs, hopefully living a good life. Just like you.'

Blinking back tears, Rose looked up at Joe and saw he was watching her intently with a strange look on his face. She felt her heart squeeze tight and forced the words through a thick and raw throat. 'Yes. Yes. I always said I'd live a big life, fitting both of us. For me and the donor.'

'Do you know who it was?' As Maxine was getting animated, Rose watched to make sure she wasn't getting too upset by it all. 'Have you made contact?'

'At the time I wrote them a letter to say thank you. I don't want to dredge up any more pain. I know how hard it is to lose someone.'

'It's unbearable.' Maxine shook her head.

'It is, and you think you'll never get over it. But somehow you carry on. Right? With a lot of help.' Joe reached forward and put a hand on both their shoulders. Like a shield, a wall protecting them from further pain. Then he gave them both a dose of his wonderful smile. 'And now, Maxine, you've discovered we're all up to your standard so you have to get home and put your feet up. Let's get you outside. I presume David's waiting in the car?'

Their unwitting patient shook her head. 'But Rose was going to make me a coffee and I was going to get stuck into the filing.'

'David can make you a drink when you're sitting in front of the TV.' Taking absolutely no notice of her cries of *Just a bit of filing,* Joe helped her up and walked her slowly to the door. 'No way. No way are you working until I say you're well enough. Now, let's get you home, so these guys can get ready for the afternoon clinic.'

Saved by Thor. Rose could have kissed him.

Trouble was, she wanted to, so damned much...and the sad, sorry part of it all was that she never would again.

CHAPTER TEN

'Is this right?' Katy asked Rose, clearly struggling with whatever she was making, sticking out the tip of her tongue as she concentrated. 'I keep losing a stitch. Who taught you to do this? Was it your mum? Or a friend? Or the Internet?'

Joe had let himself in and was watching them through a chink in the door, working hard on their crochet projects, heads so close together, completely oblivious to his presence. He didn't want to disturb them and break that spell.

Rose took hold of Katy's work, checked it and nodded. 'Good work, Katy. The person who taught me was a very old lady who was in the bed next to me when I was poorly in hospital. I loved all the bright colours of the wool because the hospital walls were so dingy…a horrible snot-green colour.' Katy giggled at that. 'She said it would help me relax, and it did—apart from when I had to undo it a million times to try to get it right the first few times.'

Joe's gut contracted hard. He hadn't even asked Rose about her time in hospital. He'd just barked at her and walked away. She'd been facing death—she must have been if she'd needed a new heart. She'd have been fright-

ened and weak and fighting for every breath...she'd survived and brought light into his house and his heart and
his only reaction had been to throw accusations at her.

Idiot. Damned selfish idiot. He'd been so concerned
with his own hurt, he hadn't considered hers.

'Did you keep doing it wrong, too? Like me?' Katy
took her work back, looked at it and grinned. No blue,
Joe noted. Just yellows and oranges.

Rose smiled at his girl. 'We've only pulled a few
stitches out. You're doing really well. You'll have it finished in no time.'

He watched his daughter's chest puff out a little and
made a mental note to give more compliments if that was
the effect they had. She was blossoming right under his
nose, and it was Rose's magic that was doing it.

His body still ached for her, even though his head
knew it was never going to happen. Working with her
was his worst kind of nightmare—*look but don't touch.*

And, deep down, he believed she hadn't come here
for any reason other than she'd liked the sound of the
village name. But had she liked it because of some kind
of muscle memory? From Pippa? Did Katy like her...
hell, did *he* like her because there was a part of her they
connected with subconsciously? A part that was more
Pippa than Rose?

And now he knew, would he ever be able to separate
all this in his head? Pippa. Rose. Two women. One heart.

Hell, he didn't know. He just knew he'd liked Rose
from the second he'd met her...okay, maybe not the second...but he'd noticed her, he'd kissed her, all before he'd
found out about the transplant.

Suddenly his daughter chirped up, 'How old was the
lady? Even older than you?'

'Hey, cheeky.' Rose nudged Katy and laughed. 'I said very old. Like, ancient.'

'Like Granny, then.' A small silence fell as they both went back to their crochet and he was just about to walk in when Katy said, 'I was in hospital once.'

'Oh?' Rose put her crochet down and looked intently at his little girl.

Joe stilled again, waiting to hear what came next. Katy never talked about this to him. 'I was in a car crash and Mummy died.'

'Yes, I heard about that.' With a soft sigh, Rose looked over at the photograph of Pippa. He followed her gaze. Lovely Pippa—he missed her. But he missed Rose too. Missed the fun they'd been developing, and how good they were together. Rose put her hand over Katy's and gave her a gentle smile. 'It must have been very sad.'

'Yes. Why were you in hospital? Were you in a car crash too?' So easy for her to slip seamlessly from one thing to another. From the past to the present. From old hurt to new fun. Joe marvelled at his daughter's resilience and wished he'd got an ounce of that too.

'Not a car crash. I was very sick. I had a bad infection in my—' Rose jumped at Joe's cough. He missed her, but he was unwilling to stand and watch this play out any further, so he strode into the room.

'Hey. Having fun?'

'Oh, hi, Joe.' The way she looked at him damned near crushed his heart. Wariness edged her eyes. Hurt shone from her features. 'We're just finishing up.'

Whatever else he knew…he liked to watch her, liked to talk to her, loved the way she laughed. 'No need. I can sit and watch until you're done.' If he was honest with himself he could sit and watch her all day, all night too.

But...but he didn't know how to fix this. Even if he could. There was a lot to get over.

He was aware Katy was watching the interaction, looking first at him, then at Rose, and her eyes narrowed as if she was trying to work out a puzzle.

Rose smiled, but it wasn't warm. 'It's fine. Actually, I think we're getting tired now. And we're at a good place to stop.' There was a determined tone in her voice. The same way she'd been with him at work these last two days. Emotionless. Empty almost. But she smiled warmly to his daughter. 'I'll email you the links to the best videos, Katy.'

'Thank you.' Katy jumped from her seat, gave him a swift hug. 'Hey, Dad, can Rose come with us to the cave on Saturday?'

Rose looked surprised as she stood and gathered all her things into her bag. 'What cave?'

'It's only—' He wasn't sure she'd want to be in the same room as him, never mind a cave. He wasn't sure he wanted that either.

'I know it's meant to be just our secret,' Katy admonished him. 'But I want Rose to come too. Will you? Please, Rose?'

'A cave?' Rose looked at Joe, for guidance on how to reply, he assumed. For a reaction. But, as far as Katy was concerned, he had no reason not to ask her. And, in fact, the thought of seeing her again made his heart thump harder.

It would be good manners to show her round the place before she left.

Before she left. 'Yes. Come with us.'

But when he walked her to the door she lowered her

voice. 'I'm sorry she put you on the spot. I won't come; I'll find an excuse.'

'Don't.' His gaze connected with hers and he saw the wariness, he saw the hurt, he saw the attraction…all three things warring in her head. And, no matter how hard he tried to deny it, the ache for her was still there in his chest, the sharp tang of need and desire washing through his body…but now it was fed with a deeper understanding of what she'd endured and who she'd become. 'Come—it'll be fun showing you the cave.'

'Are you sure?' She blinked up at him, confusion on her brow.

'Yes.'

She nodded, clutching her large woolly bag to her chest. 'Okay. For Katy's sake.'

No, he was surprised to find himself thinking, *for mine.*

'Ready?' He was standing at her front door with a rucksack on his shoulder. His hair ruffled by the autumnal breeze. His blue eyes tentative but still so damned sexy.

And, as always, just the sight of him was enough to make her legs feel wobbly. Was this a good idea? It was hard enough to pretend at work that things were okay, but around a bright, bubbly, intuitive eight-year-old? She looked behind him towards the car. No little girl waving madly from the back seat. *Oh?* 'Where's Katy?'

He shrugged. 'She cried off at the last minute and went to play at Emily's, but she was adamant I still take you. So, here I am.'

Okay. This was worse. Being alone with him, in a cave? Torture. Temptation. Trouble all round. Better just to keep a distance and give them all time to heal. Time she didn't have in Oakdale. 'We can do a rain check if you like?'

He tapped the rucksack. 'I have a picnic here and it's too much for one. Even me.'

Ever the romantic. *Not.* She imagined what Beth would have to say about that. 'Why? Why do you want me to come?'

He looked at his feet, then back at her. The one thing she knew about Joe was that he was the most honest person she'd ever met, but today even he was struggling to get words out. 'Katy will kill me if I don't take you to the cave. She seems as hooked on keeping promises as you are—only she didn't seem to think it mattered that she wasn't coming too. Kids, eh? But really...we need to talk, Rose. We can't keep avoiding each other.'

No matter how much of a coward she was, wanting to hide away and pretend they didn't have a problem was not the best idea. He was right; they did need to talk and try to clear the air. 'Well, with that kind of invitation, how could a girl resist?'

Truthfully, the prospect of talking filled her with dread, but he smiled and that settled something inside her. So she slipped into step with him and they walked up and over Oak Top, across two green fields sliced in half by limestone walls and then down into a steep ravine with jagged edges. Rounding a corner, they came to the yawning mouth of a cave, half-hidden by a cluster of oak trees on the seasonal turn, their leaves a beautiful rusty orange.

'In here.' He pointed to a slash in the rock, flicked on a torch and started to walk into darkness.

But she hesitated, unable to see further than five

feet. 'Really? You want me to trust you enough to walk into there?'

After you didn't trust me...at all?

'I do.' He nodded. 'It's worth it. Come on. Honestly, you'll be fine.'

'I'm not sure I'm ever going to be fine again.' But something about his enthusiasm for her to see whatever it was he wanted her to see piqued her curiosity. So she inhaled deeply, swallowed her misgivings and followed him. Sloshing through ankle-deep water, they dodged stalactites and stalagmites with the constant drip of water their only accompaniment.

Finally, he came to a small outcrop of rocks and told her to lean against the wall. 'I'm going to turn the light off now for a few seconds. Don't be scared.'

'I'm not scared.' So why was her body trembling and her heart pounding? It wasn't for the caves; it was for him. For what they'd broken...something that could have been so good.

But then they were plunged into total darkness. She blinked and blinked and tried to see...anything, but thick blackness pressed her against the damp wall. Into it. Panicking, she flailed her hand in front of her. Couldn't make out her fingers. Anything. 'Joe? Joe?'

Stupid woman. It's just a cave.

But she wasn't scared of the dark; she was scared of the overwhelming feelings inside her. The anger at his reaction to her transplant story. His pain, his hurt. And hers, which was buried deep inside her. She was scared of her strength of feeling. The way she still damned well wanted him, even after his reaction. But fear made her brave. 'I am so bloody angry at you, Joe Thompson.'

'Is this really a good time?' He laughed. He damned well laughed and it echoed in the dark space.

'At least this way I don't get to see you and keep on wanting to kiss you every time I look at you. Either that, or wanting to kill you. I haven't decided which yet. It's too close to call right now.' She paused. He waited. She decided it was better to be honest now than have things unsaid. And, funnily enough, just saying them into the dark was wonderfully therapeutic. 'You didn't trust me, Joe; that's what hurts the most. I did not choose all this. I didn't want this to happen. If I could change anything, I'd have told you that first day, before we got so involved.'

'I know.' A quiet voice.

'It could have been good. It could have been so damned good, Joe.'

'I know, Rose.' He was so close and she wanted to touch him, to hold him. Wanted him to hold her in his arms the way he had done before and tell her it didn't matter. But she had no idea how they could move on from this.

'I spoke to the locum agency, and you'll be pleased to know I'll be gone at the end of next week.'

'So it's definite. You're not going to stay. Why would you think I'd be pleased? Why do you think that?' His voice echoed in the cave, hurt all over again. 'And why the hell run away?'

'I don't want to hurt anyone by being here. Least of all you. But I don't fit here—I can't possibly ever fit. It was never going to be permanent. I promised I was going to travel and have fun and this—' *Was breaking her in two.* 'You know the score. I don't know what's round the corner.'

'Neither of us do.'

He'd had his share of heartache too. More than anyone should endure. But it wasn't her fault and she hadn't
come to rub it in his face.

'Can you put the torch back on? I want to go.'

'Look up,' he whispered. 'Just look up.'

So she craned her neck and blinked and blinked
around her, wondering if she was dreaming. Because,
above them, next to them, all round them, tiny lights
started to appear, as if hundreds of teeny switches had
been switched on. As if there were a thousand stars…
inside.

Wow. 'Glow-worms?'

'Yes.'

It was beautiful. The anger melted enough for her to
see that it was such a Joe thing to do: bring her somewhere that took her breath away. Again. 'Well, aren't you
full of surprises?'

'Not as many as you, but I try my best.' He laughed.
'I think you win in any surprise war, Rose.'

And his laugh was so infectious she couldn't help but
join in, because if it wasn't so damned sad it would be
funny. And suddenly she felt connected to him again—
not like before—but there was some hope. 'You keep
showing me these wonderful things.'

'It's a great place to live. I want you to see it all.'

Before I go.

'Why are you being Mr Nice Guy?'

'Because I reacted badly. I just have to get my head
around a whole lot.' She heard his exhale. The silence.

'Yes. Me too.' She stepped forward but lost her bear-
ings, tried to right herself, blindly reached out to grab
something to steady her. Anything. Her hand brushed
against his and for the briefest of beats their fingers

entwined. Squeezed. Her heart jolted and her body strained. 'Joe.'

This was so hard. So damned hard.

'Rose.'

She waited. For more. More words. More kisses. Anything. Just more.

But he let go of her hand and the cave filled with torchlight again and the moment was gone.

'You do a good picnic, Dr Thompson.' They'd stumbled out of the cave, blinking into the lunchtime light, back up to the top of the hill and over to a small grassy area.

He'd laid a blanket out and stretched out those long legs of his and settled down to eat chicken pie, coleslaw, dips and bread and a glass of rosé wine.

But he wasn't eating and just watched as she picked at her pie. 'I'm sorry I behaved so badly, Rose. I should have stayed and talked to you. I should have listened. I should have been kinder after everything you went through, but I was blindsided by it all.'

'I know. Me too.' Having screamed at him in the cave, she felt calmer now and glad he'd apologised. Truth was, they were both reeling from the shock. 'It's…it's strange but… I don't know…wonderful to think I may have brought her back to you, at least for a little while. I'm sorry if it brings back all the hurt for you and your family, but I hope it gives some peace too.'

'It doesn't hurt, Rose. It's just… I can't even put it into words.' A silence fell as they ate—she tried to, but her throat was thick and sore and swallowing was difficult. And then he said, 'You're very different to Pippa, but there's something about you that is so like her. It's hard to describe but it's in the way you look at Katy. Your sense of fun. The way you use your hands when you speak. But what's to say you weren't always like that? I wish I'd known you before...but then, if things had been different, I guess I'd never have got to know you at all.'

'I've read about organ recipients whose eyes change colour after transplant. Who start liking food they never liked before, or discover a talent they never had—like being able to paint, or play the piano. I've never really believed it.'

But to fall for the same man? The same community? Family? Even though she didn't know for sure, the co-incidence was remarkable.

If it came to it that by some wild miracle she stayed here, she didn't want to be in Pippa's shadow for ever. A constant comparison. 'I don't suppose she had a thing for orange hats?'

'No.' He looked at her head and her favourite hat on top of it and laughed. And she got the feeling that the smile was for her and not for some memory of his dead wife's clothing choices. At least, she hoped. But how would she ever know now? Was he smiling at Rose? Or at the thought of Pippa's heart beating so close by? 'She just wore regular things.'

'Instead of irregular ones?' She pointed to her purple T-shirt that was covered in a mass of bright yellow flowers and that even she thought might have been just a little...loud. But it had lifted her spirits this morning when she saw it in the drawer, so she'd worn it.

'Extraordinary ones.'

His gaze slid back to her and she saw the struggle he was having. The need for her was still there, the pull to her. The way his body tilted towards her, the way his eyes slid to her mouth as if he ached for more kissing, the way she did. She saw too the confusion as he tried to make sense of what they'd discovered and what that meant for them all.

As his eyes strayed from her face he blinked. 'I'm glad you decided to stop covering up the scar.'

She tugged down the neck of her T-shirt and looked at the silvery line bifurcating her chest. 'No more hiding.' If she was going to be the Rose McIntyre upgraded version, she was going to embrace what she'd been through. 'I am who I am, Joe. I always said I'd live a big life for two people and I'm not doing that if I hide parts of me away.'

'You are extraordinary, Rose.' He looked at her then with a real affection that had been missing these last few days. 'And we've been lucky to have you here.'

'Are you sure, even after all this?'

'Yes, Rose. Hell. Yes.'

But last week he'd have pulled her to him and kissed her senseless until the sun went down. Now, he just looked away.

CHAPTER ELEVEN

WORKING ALONGSIDE ROSE every day was torture. But no more so than having been rostered on with her to visit the local high school to give a talk on hygiene management to the staff, as a follow-up to the norovirus outbreak.

A roster, he had a feeling, that had been engineered by Beth or somehow influenced by Maxine. If it wasn't Katy organising dates to the cave and then ducking out at the last minute, it was others trying to matchmake. They'd all fallen hard for Rose in such a short time and clearly thought he should do the same.

If only they knew.

So now he was stuck in the car with his muddled head, raging awareness of her scent and her body, and still too many things unsaid. He pulled the car into the school grounds and parked.

Her eyes lit up at the eco-friendly roofing that seamlessly melded into the lush background of heather and grass. 'Wow, aren't they lucky to go to school here, in the middle of the countryside.'

'I reckon they just think everyone goes to a school nestled in between two mountains.' It occurred to him then that he didn't know much about Rose's background.

He glanced at his watch; they had a few minutes to spare. 'Where did you go to school?'

'A private girls' school in central London. Very lovely. With a special focus on the arts. Basically, I spent a lot of time at the theatre and in stuffy museums. My parents are lawyers so they thought it would be good for my cultural education,' she explained, her nose wrinkling as she gave a half-grimace, half-smile and, hell, that turning up of her mouth did something to his already overwhelmed senses.

He was struggling to put distance between them even though he knew it had to be the answer. Every part of him ached to touch her, despite…everything. That was the most curious thing of all—how much his body was ignoring the signals from his brain to keep away, to protect himself and his daughter and protect everything they'd worked so hard to build over the last five years.

Her coming here had blown everything he thought he knew and had reconciled wide open. But the need to learn more about her was insatiable. He was fast running out of time. 'They didn't mind you not wanting to follow them into the profession?'

'It was expected. My brother did, so at first they were disappointed…you know, in a way only a parent can be. But then I got sick and they just wanted me to be alive. Mum's been a bit…how shall I put it?…overcautious ever since.'

There was a big difference between what his family had gone through and what hers had but he felt the acute connection, the common fear. The pain of loss. 'Every parent would be.'

She laughed, looking square at him. Knowing him. 'You would be.'

'She cares about you and what you went through.'

'I know.' The laugh faded and she turned away.

She cares and you don't was the message. So much hurt in her eyes. He'd rejected her, pushed her away when she'd been at her most vulnerable with him, taken by surprise with knowledge that could change her life. Accused her of doing something calculated when she was pretty much the kindest person he knew.

Prize damned idiot. If they couldn't get round the Pippa issue he wanted to make her smile again, at least, but she was already pushing open the car door.

'Okey-dokey. Time to teach these teachers a thing or two about hand-washing.'

Her long legs swung out of the passenger seat, her back straightening as she started to walk to the entrance, leaving the soft scent of her perfume in her wake. And he wondered how many times he would watch her walk away until he had no more chances to haul her back into his arms.

Whether he could. Whether it would even be possible.

She was leaving. He'd always known that, but she was going to leave with such anger and hurt in her heart for him and for his village—and he'd caused that.

An hour later they climbed back into the car, flushed with success and full of carrot cake laid on by the PTA. He turned the ignition and drove the car onto the main road back towards Oakdale. 'It went well, I think.'

'Now, every time they sing *Happy Birthday* they'll think about germs. Not sure that's how I want to be remembered, but hey, that's how it goes.'

They'd given the infection control spiel, Rose had made them laugh and she'd been welcomed like an old friend.

Next week she was leaving—how would he be remembered by her? He didn't even want to think about that.

Outside, the sun was starting to dip behind Orrest Head, bathing the landscape in hues of orange and yellow. Rose's colours.

An idea bloomed first in his head, then quickly grew roots to his heart. *Why the hell not?*

Otherwise, he would drop her off at home tonight, there would be awkward conversation. They would bristle past each other at work. They would never resolve anything. Then, too soon, she would leave and who knew if he'd ever see her again? The way things were going, he doubted it.

'Rose, fancy taking a detour? It won't take long.'

Frowning, she turned to him. 'Don't you need to get back for Katy?'

'She's got a play date with Emily.'

A hesitant nod. 'Okay, I suppose. If it doesn't take long. I have a hot date with a ready-made frozen lasagne.'

'Excellent.' He swung the car to the side of the road and climbed out. 'Come on.'

She followed, peering at the path leading up and up and up to the top of the hill, winding first through woodland and then out into open country. Another frown. 'I sincerely hope we're not climbing that.'

'Yes, we are.'

She pointed to her work blouse, trousers and the low-heeled black boots. 'I'm not really dressed for it.'

'Hey, you walked up my hill in a wool cardigan when rain was forecast and that never bothered you. Seriously, you'll be fine. It'll take twenty minutes to get up there and I have a spare fleece if you get cold. Then, I promise, you can get back to your cosy date with a tasty Italian.'

'Yummy—' she pretended to swoon '—I can't wait.'

Heat and—*ridiculous!*—jealousy sprang from nowhere and slammed into him. He didn't want her to have
a hot date with anyone. And yes, he knew she was talking about food, but he had an image in his head now of
her kissing someone else and his gut tightened.

She looked up the hill then back at him and shook
her head, but there was a faint smile playing on her lips.
'Can't you just do something normal, like take me out
for dinner and a glass of wine?'

'Really?' With her multi-coloured clothes, not caring
about convention, her living big ideas? 'You wouldn't
settle for that, now, would you?'

'No. I don't suppose I would.' She gave him a full-
blown smile then, and it gave him hope that perhaps they
could at least find some common ground while climbing up a hill.

'It's not quite dark yet and I have these.' He handed
her one of the head torches he kept in his car for emergencies. 'The path's very wide and it's a clear evening.
It'll be fun.'

'Are you sure?' Her eyes darted to the top of the hill.

He held his hand out to her, not sure what this step
meant. Wondering if he really was going mad. 'It's fine.
You're perfectly safe, Rose.'

Although he wasn't—nowhere near.

Safe? Far from it. She was on very dangerous ground
here. But Rose grabbed the head torch with one hand
and his outstretched palm with the other and they strode
up the hill to the very top, where there was a grey stone
plaque identifying all the hills and mountains in front
of them. She leaned against it and caught her breath, en-

joying the exhilaration of exercise, the beads of sweat. Still amazed that having been so very sick she could do this now.

And with him. The reality was, despite the attraction and affection, they had too much to work through. If they could even get over the transplant problem there were too many residual issues stemming from that.

It was impossible.

Still, whatever else, Thor was as good as his word. He'd promised to take her up a mountain and that was what he was doing...wind whipping her hair as she watched the very last rays of the sun dip under the horizon in a blast of oranges and reds. A patchwork of clouds scudded over them, stained in peach and gold, brighter even than her wool stash. In the distance sat the little town of Bowness, hugging the lake shore, to her left and right the green and purple mountains and, below, the shimmering, beautiful Lake Windermere, slicing the countryside like a thick silver ribbon.

She was going to miss this.

'Rose.'

Her heart lifted at his voice. She was going to miss him too.

She turned to look at him and nearly fell over. 'What the hell...?'

'You promised. And I promised.' He was standing at the highest point of the hill, lifting a bent leg and clamping it to his knee. Determination was written all over his face, and laughter too, as he placed his hands together over his head. It was a woeful attempt at tree pose, but he was doing it.

And laughing so much she thought he was going to fall over. 'See? Nothing's impossible.'

Healing just could be. But she loved that he was trying to make her smile. 'Joe Thompson, you win the award for surprises now.'

'The next surprise—although it probably isn't—is that I am never going to do this again. I much prefer hiking to standing still. Yoga is definitely not my thing.' And then he wobbled, put both feet on the ground and marched them across to her. Before she could register what was happening, he was pulling her to him and kissing her. Kissing her so hard, but not enough.

Never enough.

There was no fight left in her, no reason to fight. She kissed him because she couldn't stop. Because they were entwined in something that seemed bigger than the sum of them. She wound her arms round his neck and leaned into him. And in that kiss she learned how much she wanted him, despite her anger and confusion, and how much he still wanted her. How little resistance she had and that she didn't care. She wanted to explore him, explore what could be possible, if only for a few more moments.

His hands slipped under her blouse until he touched her bare skin, and he groaned into her mouth. And she pressed against his hardness, her hands connecting with the taut muscles of his belly. Want rippled through her as his tongue danced with hers. The wind dropped away to a whisper of breath, the world reducing to just this moment of two people trying to find their way back to each other.

She pulled away, breathless, aching. 'What does this mean?'

'It means I'm sorry. It means I want you.' He touched her face. 'It means… I don't understand but maybe I don't want to understand.'

But his phone rang and he huffed away, shaking his head. 'Katy. She needs picking up. It's getting late.' He looked out over the darkening valley and his features smoothed from lust to uncertainty.

He was torn in two, she could see. His body burning for kisses and more, his head with his daughter. He would always be torn between being a father and taking time for himself; that was only natural and she would always, always encourage him to prioritise Katy.

And maybe he'd always be torn between his loss of Pippa and finding someone new. Maybe he'd be different if that new person wasn't Rose McIntyre with a dicky heart that belonged to someone else.

To Pippa?

And even though she ached so much for more of his kisses, she make the decision easy for him. 'Then that's what you'll do. Katy must come first.'

'And this—?' He ran a thumb down her cheek, over her lip.

She pressed her palm to his cheek. Because she didn't have any answers. Plain and simple. 'Katy needs you.'

It had been a long week and emotionally exhausting. Rose was glad for the kiss at the top of the hill and for Joe's attentiveness but there were no answers to an impossible puzzle. So she was beyond glad when she closed the clinic door at the end of the week and sought refuge with Beth. A drink, some laughs and a local band would put her spirits back in shape again.

'Thank God it's Friday. I so need this.' Beth pushed open the door of The Queen's Arms and stepped back for Rose to go in first.

'Me too. You have no idea.'

'I think I do,' Beth said, laughing. 'But you can confess all over a wine.'

The half-full pub was softly lit and a gentle murmur of conversation ran through it. In the far corner was a small dance area and what looked like a four-piece band tuning up.

'I think we're early; it's usually heaving for band night.' Beth waved at pretty much everyone as she walked towards the bar. Clearly a local and well-loved and Rose felt a tinge of envy that her friend so easily slotted into everyone's lives here.

Once the drinks had been bought Rose found them a free table. It was easy to fall into conversation with Beth; she was that kind of open and friendly person. 'What did you do before you came back to Oakdale?'

Beth grinned. 'I'm a vet.'

'Oh, how lovely. Do you have a practice somewhere waiting for you to go back to?'

'I had a job in Glasgow and loved it, but Mum needs me for the time being, so I had to give it up.' She shrugged. It clearly had been a difficult choice for her.

'You could get some work here then, maybe in Bowness? I'm sure there's a practice; there must be. There are a lot of cows and sheep around here, so there must be vets too.'

'And dogs and cats and hedgehogs and snakes…' Beth laughed. 'I'm sure I could. I did some volunteer work at Cooper's in Bowness in my university holidays; I'm sure they'd know if there were vacancies anywhere. But it depends how long I need to stay around and how much Mum needs me. I don't know. I'm keeping my options very open.'

A woman after Rose's heart. 'I know that feeling.'

'I'll drink to that!' Beth chinked her glass against Rose's and took a good long sip of wine. 'So what's the plan for when your contract is up?'

'There's a job in Plymouth that sounds perfect. Just a fill-in for a couple of weeks to cover someone's holiday, then I'll move on somewhere else.' The reality hit her. She'd grown to love Oakdale and she was leaving just as she'd started to put down roots.

'Wow, you're a better woman than me. Not sure I'd like to be moving on and moving on all the time.'

'It's my big plan, you see. Travel the world.' While she was still healthy enough to do it. 'One GP practice at a time. See how I like being a locum here and then taking it abroad, maybe Australia, New Zealand, Canada.'

Before she'd come here she'd been ready to conquer the world. Now she was sad to be leaving this tiny village in the north of England, her world after only a matter of weeks. Was she going completely crazy? She'd been totally derailed.

'Okay, well, to be honest, you don't looked thrilled about it.' Beth smiled. 'And what about the lovely Dr Joe?'

It was Rose's turn to shrug, not wanting—and yet wanting—to talk about Joe. She didn't know how much to confide in her new friend, who was fun but could ask too-difficult questions. In her old PR job everyone knew everyone else's business and sometimes that didn't work out well. Gossip ran through her social life like wildfire. But she had a sense that Beth, though lively and outgoing, was also well versed in confidentiality. It came with the medical professional territory. 'To be honest, it's complicated.'

'Isn't it always? What I'd give to just skip the hard bit

of finding The One and just fall in love and live happily ever after.' Beth's eyebrows rose. 'Fairy tale, yes?'

'Probably. Although I do believe you should make your own fairy tale.' Rose admitted to herself that she wasn't making a good fist of it right now. 'But where men are concerned, that's not always easy.'

'That's why I love working with animals. They're so uncomplicated and always pleased to see you. Maybe I should just get a puppy.' Beth giggled.

'Sounds like a plan to me.' Rose dug deep into her wine and thought how nice it would be to be settled enough to have a pet. And then remembered she was going to have a bigger life than just settling. Whatever that meant. 'Although not great for moving from job to job.'

Beth leaned forward as more people piled into the pub and the noise level started to rise. 'You do fancy him? Joe, I mean.'

No point lying if her cheeks were going to betray her anyway as they burnt hot. 'Yes. I do.'

'We're going to need someone over winter; it gets very busy. You could stay here a while longer and then go travelling. Come on, Rose? It's fun having you here.' There was a mischievous look in Beth's eyes. 'And you could get very busy with Dr Joe.'

'It's all too hard.' Rose fiddled with a beer mat, ripping off the top paper and squeezing it into a tight ball. 'It's better if I just leave and don't look back.'

'Want my advice? Don't analyse it too much. I thought I was going to live in Glasgow my whole life, I even bought a house there, and now look at me. Back home with my mother.' Beth grimaced. 'God, that sounds bad. And I do love her to pieces, but it's not where I imagined

I'd be at thirty. I'd say you should go with your gut. Forget what's going on in your head and just go with your feelings, see where they take you.'

'I can't...' This was getting depressing. She might as well tell Beth as not. 'There isn't any future in it. There can't be.'

'Why not?' A frown and a shake of her head. Then she joined up the dots. 'The heart transplant? Is that a big thing? Should it matter?'

'It means I probably can't have kids. I could get sick. I mean... I have a fabulous life, and I'm so lucky to have had it. But—I can't promise a big future.' If he even wanted it with her after everything.

'Maybe he just wants some fun too? You ever asked him that?'

'No. It's just too...difficult.' It was one thing to grasp and live her life with no regrets, and entirely another to drag someone into a relationship with a time limit on it. Especially if that someone was Joe Thompson.

Beth shrugged. 'Maybe not. He's already had a full-on love-of-his-life thing.'

And didn't Rose know all about that? 'Pippa.'

'So maybe he just wants to dabble, you know...nothing heavy. So why not? Just have a good time. Go on. Use him for sex.'

'I am not that kind of woman.'

'You should try it. You might enjoy it.'

Could she? Could she put all this behind her and just have some fun?

As she laughed, Beth looked up over Rose's shoulder and her cheeks bloomed a puce colour. The laughter died in her throat. 'Oh, great.'

Rose turned and felt her own cheeks colouring too. So

much for a relaxed girls' night out. Because, making a beeline right for them, was Joe, who turned briefly and said something to a tall man ordering at the bar.

Before Rose could pretend she hadn't seen them, Joe waved and arrived by her side.

But he spoke to Beth first, looking a little sheepish—if a big man could ever look that. 'Hey, Beth. Sorry—I know this is awkward. Alex arrived back from holiday and said he needed a drink. I tried to convince him to go to the White Hart but he likes this place as it's walking distance. Plus, it's live band night and always worth a laugh. Or a cringe.'

Beth shrugged. 'Hey, it's a free country.'

'You want to sit with us?' Rose shuffled sideways to make room to pull another chair up, because it would be rude to do anything other than offer. It was only then she saw Beth shaking her head. *Ah.* Of course she wouldn't want them to sit here if there was unresolved past history. *Oops.* Too late. Joe nodded and dragged a chair over and squeezed into the tiny space between her and the next table.

Her heart beat just that little bit more frantically when he was near. 'Where's Katy?'

'At my sister's. Friday night sleepover. Nice to have a break.' He smiled and when he looked at her like that she felt anything could be possible.

'And pretend you're footloose and fancy-free and actually have a life? Dream on, kiddo.' The tall man put two pints onto the table and stuck out his hand towards Rose. 'Hello. I'm Alex.'

'Hello.' Beth was right. He was handsome, very athletic, with short dark hair that seemed a little unruly. Nice eyes. Nothing like Joe's, of course. A paler variety of blue as far as she was concerned. Not as tall or as *Thor-midable*. Not nearly as impressive as Joe at all, but Rose knew she was very biased. She could see why Beth would think him gorgeous. He was textbook magazine model where Joe was real, rugged and raw. She took Alex's firm hand. 'I'm Rose. Just a locum nurse.'

'No *just* about it.' Joe grinned and explained, 'Rose saved Maxine's life, and then our bacon, by stepping in and working above and beyond. In fact, both Beth and Rose just about single-handedly controlled a norovirus outbreak and prevented any of the staff or other patients getting it. Very efficient.'

'At least no one else has caught it…yet.' Beth managed a smile, although she still looked embarrassed and uncomfortable. More so as Alex bent to kiss her cheek in a swift *hello* gesture, then sat down next to her on the overstuffed banquette.

'To our two lifesavers then.' Alex picked up his glass and tapped it against the other three in turn, his gaze lingering just a little longer on Beth than on the others, Rose noted. *Interesting.*

And so the bubble of intimacy between Beth and Rose was burst by clinic gossip, the weather, Alex's recent holiday and back again, the men having an easy banter that showed a history of solid friendship.

But Rose wasn't listening. In the snug pub things were starting to get cramped as more and more people poured in to listen to the band. She could feel Joe's knee pressing against hers. Wasn't sure if he was doing it on purpose. But when she glanced up at him his face was impassive as he paused to watch the lead singer strutting about as if he was at Wembley Arena and not in a tiny pub in the Lake District.

Behind them was standing room only and more people pressed forward, making Joe shuffle closer. And closer.

The more she felt Joe's heat against hers, the more she wished everyone would just fade into the background and she could start the fling—if that was what they were going to do.

Beth caught her eye and she gave her a quick reassuring wink. *Go, girl.*

Then the music kicked up a gear and all chance of conversation was blown away by an electric guitar and a lead singer just a little off-key.

After a few minutes of that Beth raised her hand a little and waved to Rose, leaned closer and shouted, 'We're just going outside for a chat… Can't hear a damned thing in here.'

'Okay.' Rose thought for a beat then mouthed, 'Is everything okay?'

But they'd disappeared into the crowd, leaving her and Joe alone, in the glare of a zillion Oakdale gazes that made her feel a little like she was in a goldfish bowl. Sometimes an anonymous hospital where no one knew your business appealed, but she wasn't going back there.

Just where was she going?

In a brief lull in the music she asked him, 'How's Maxine?'

'She's feeling a lot better.' He grinned. 'I popped round to see her and she told me to leave her alone and get my ugly face busy with someone else's business.'

'Charming.' Rose had a feeling she would never tire of looking at him. The swift changes from serious to light and back again. The clefts and dips of his cheeks, the blue of his eyes that burnt for her.

'That's our Maxine—obviously she's feeling better if

she's talking like that.' He smiled. 'So you're a big fan of country glam rock fusion music?'

'Oh, um…yes.' She looked over at the ageing singer wiping sweat from his bald head, in his tight leather trousers and checked shirt unbuttoned to his…*ugh*…podgy navel, and laughed. The whole band was very amateur but kind of kitsch in an off-tone kind of way. 'Isn't everyone?'

Joe finished his pint. 'I was counting the days until they came back to do this gig. Couldn't wait.'

'You said you wanted to go to the White Hart.'

'Ah. Yes. To be honest, I was trying to avoid these guys as much as I could. Trouble with being the doctor here is that I know most of the crowd, and the band. I happen to know that Dave, the singer, is a mortician by day. Owns a funeral parlour in Bowness.'

'Maybe he should stick with what he's good at then. And it certainly isn't singing in a band on Friday nights at The Queen's Arms.' She laughed, relaxing a little, but wanting to slide her hand into Joe's or just curl into his arms, knowing how good that would feel.

'And this isn't quite the Friday night I had planned. I think my ears will bleed if I hear any more.' He looked as if he was about to stand up. 'You want me to walk you home or are you going to stay a while? If your ears can take it?'

She knew he was trying to do the right thing by not pressuring her into any decision or conversation about staying or kissing. She put her hand on his arm. 'One more drink?'

'I don't think—' His eyes were all questions.

Which she answered with her best smile. 'Let's kick back and have some fun. Just some fun, Joe. It's Friday night after all.'

He shrugged then and went to the bar for more drinks. When he came back he was smiling. 'Phew, it was a wrestling match just to get to the bar. I think it's only going to get worse.'

'So let's head off after these drinks and find somewhere quieter.' Beth would be proud of her taking the initiative here.

'Sure. If that's what you want?'

'Friday night fun.' She hoped being flippant might temper the feelings she had in her chest and her gut. The hope and the excitement superseding her caution. For now, at least.

His gaze caught hers just as the guitarist struck up a note and her voice was drowned out. So she tutted and shook her head and smiled. And he smiled back and held her gaze for even longer than Alex and Beth's hot meaningful looks. And Beth's words came back to her.

So Rose went with her gut and pressed her leg more firmly against Joe's as she slid her hand onto his thigh. He closed his eyes briefly but when he opened them again his gaze was filled with so much heat she wondered how he'd managed not to self-combust. He covered her hand with his and squeezed it tight, moved closer so she could smell him, see only him and desperately want to touch him more, all over.

And she wished they'd decided not to have this second drink and got out while they'd had the chance.

Next to them, one of the crowd watching the band started to sing along. Loudly. He was standing, waving his hands in the air with gusto, and everyone turned to watch and cheer him on.

'Better than the band!'

'Someone give him the mike!'

'Brian,' Joe mouthed. Then did a hammering action.

'Builder?' Rose guessed.

Joe touched his nose and pointed at her, grinning. A game of charades ensued as he then mimed other people's jobs and she tried to guess. Teacher, soldier, accountant—which took a while to work out—meanwhile the singing and the band drowned out all attempts of being heard. And all she could do was laugh at Joe's attempts at milking a cow, because most of the clientele in here were farmers. And, judging by his acting, he most certainly wasn't.

She wondered how he'd react if she mimed kissing. Or, even better, just did it. Right here and now. Showed him that her intentions were completely and utterly dishonourable.

But Joe was well known in this community and news travelled fast. She didn't want Katy or Maxine hearing things that could upset them. Didn't mean she didn't want to do it though.

Suddenly Brian lurched sideways as someone shuffled past him. He teetered close to Rose, pint in hand spilling over Rose, but was stopped from falling onto her by Joe's hand. 'Whoa. Watch it.'

Joe stood, holding the guy at arm's length, then straightening him up. 'Maybe find a seat, eh, Brian?'

Brian swayed. 'Sorry, Doc. Just a bit wobbly.'

'Sitting's good then. Just try to keep away from the tables.' Joe's hand was on her back, stroking softly. 'You okay, Rose?'

No. She wanted his hands all over her. 'I'm fine, honestly. It'll wash out.' She stood and wiped drips of beer from her top.

Joe turned to her. 'Let's get out of here.'

'Yes.' Feeling a little wobbly herself, she stood and grabbed hold of Joe's hand as Brian started to jump up and down, a fist in the air, singing along to the track. She tried to squeeze past him, losing Joe's grip in the melee, and the next thing she knew, a sudden heavy weight was pushing her forwards and down to the floor with a crunch.

CHAPTER TWELVE

'ROSE!' JOE PUSHED back through the drunken crowd the minute her hand left his. His heart ripped at the sound of her wail as she disappeared from view. When he found her she was splayed on the ground, surrounded by people just standing staring. No one moved. Except him, and he was by her side in a second. Still too long as far as he was concerned. Didn't matter what she'd said; it seemed that his instinct would always be for her. He helped her to sit up. 'Hey, are you okay? Let me check you over.'

'I'm fine. Just a bit shaken.' She rubbed her hip and grimaced. 'Nothing broken.'

Brian bent down to speak to her, breathing fumes into their faces. 'S...sorry, love. I lost my balance. I'm a bit... wobbly, I think.'

And even though she was saying she wasn't hurt and the danger was over, Joe couldn't hold back a snap. 'Back off, Brian. Okay?'

'Hey, cool it.' Rose shot him a frown, then turned to Brian. 'It's fine, honestly. I just want to leave, okay?'

This time the crowd parted as Joe took her hand and led her outside into the fresh autumnal air. He took a deep breath, filling his lungs and trying to dispel all the feelings inside him, not least the ones of shock as he realised the whole pub—and therefore most of the village and beyond—had seen him react like some kind of Neanderthal and then hold Rose's hand walking out of the pub.

That would get the gossips talking.

Ugh. Katy. Maxine. They were bound to hear about it from someone. Things could get messy from here on in. Things were already messy enough.

But she stopped short, tugging him to a halt. 'What's the matter, Joe? You were so rude to Brian. He's just had a bit too much to drink, that's all. I'm sure he didn't mean to knock me over.'

'He should have been more careful.'

She tapped his nose. 'You've gone back to Dr Grump again. Where's my nice Joe gone?'

'You have any idea how it feels to see someone you care about get hurt?' So, yes, he cared for her. It was more than lust. It was shockingly intense and yet somehow effortless and radiant at the same time and holding it all in was increasingly difficult.

She blinked. Thought. 'Recently, yes. I was there for Katy, remember?'

And she cared for his daughter. A fist of something hot and fierce settled in his chest. 'Then you'll know how I felt when I saw you on the floor… Thank God it wasn't serious, because it could have been. There's a lot of glass in there…'

'I'm fine. Or would you prefer me to just stay home and play with wool too?' She blinked, slowly. Sighed and put her hands on his chest. 'Sorry. I didn't mean that. It was cruel.'

He took a chance and held her fingers in his. 'You think I'm over-the-top with Katy and now with you.'

'Yes. No. I think you had a terrible thing happen and you don't want it to happen again.'

'Too right I don't.'

'But you have to loosen up. Okay? Take a risk and let others do the same.' She gave him a small smile. 'Here's me with my big brave words when underneath this bright, confident exterior I'm really the most scared person in the world.'

After all the battles she'd fought? The way she approached everything with optimism and a sunny smile. 'No way. You're the bravest. You're like a bright star.'

'You don't know the half of it, Joe.' She looked away and shook her head. Then she looked back at him and smiled. 'But Friday night is all about fun. Right?'

He wanted fun and serious, the whole package. 'I want to know everything.'

She curled her fingers into his and nodded. 'What I've learnt is that bad things can happen but good things happen too. Wonderful, amazing things.'

Was this a signal she wanted to take things to the next level? 'There's a whole lot of good things I want to do to you and with you.'

Her smile was teasing. 'Really?'

He looked at her mouth, her throat, lower, and his fingers tightened around hers. 'You have no idea.'

'I can guess.' She stood on tiptoe and pressed her lips against his cheek. And God, he wanted to kiss her, and so much more, but she had to lead.

'Come for a walk with me?' Because he still had no idea where they stood and if he deposited her at her door she might close it behind her. And he wanted a few more moments with her. Alone.

She was leaving. He couldn't reconcile that. All he knew was that he wanted more of her.

'A walk? Now? In the dark?' Her eyes, wide and dancing.

'Why not? Feet can move any time of the day or night. That is…if your hip's not sore.'

'I'll survive. Really, it was just a little slip, Joe. Where are we going?' Rolling her eyes, exactly like Katy, she shook her head. It was uncanny the way they'd clicked too, the way they shared mannerisms that made him laugh. He shoved away comparisons to his dead wife. Rose was Rose was Rose.

'An adventure. Give it a few minutes and a short hike. Because that's when it's at its best.'

'What's at its best?'

'Wait and see.' He started to walk down the path leading west from the village and she skipped up to him and put her hand in his.

'Where are we going?'

'To Oak Top.' Up ahead there was just enough moonlight to see a shadow looming large up in front of them.

She laughed hard. 'You didn't say we'd be having another workout.' When they reached the top of the little hill she was glowing with effort and a light sheen of perspiration. But, as always, she was smiling. 'Great view of…blackness.'

'Your eyes will get used to it. See how we're facing away from the village now and there's no artificial light? Come here, sit down. And we can wait.'

His coat was big enough for her to lie on so he threw it over a soft smattering of heather and tugged her down to sit. Then he lay on his back, tiny soft purple spikes caressing his head. Giggling, she followed his lead and looked up and around her, searching. Her head close to his.

'What are we waiting for?'

'The clouds are in the way. Wait…wait…wait for it…' The shadows floated away, carried along by a soft southerly breeze, and there it was, a bright slick of silvery violet slicing across the sky as far as anyone could see and more stars than any one person could count. Large, small. Some twinkling, many still. All beautiful. 'There. The Milky Way.'

She put her hand to her mouth, which he took as a good sign. And inhaled sharply. 'Wow. Oh, wow. It's amazing. I've never seen anything like it. Stars, yes, obviously, tons of stars, but not like this. So many. So pretty. They stretch out so far, pointing to forever.'

'You city people don't know what you're missing.'

'Truth is, we probably just never look up. Too attached to our devices or sheltering from the rain or just generally watching our step. Always too worried about the next step to stop and look around us. But this is so, so beautiful. Thank you for showing it to me.'

'Hey, it's a free show. Open every night. Available to all.' He loved it that she laughed then, a gentle giggle bubbling from her throat. Loved that she was as enthusiastic about the simple things, like nature and outdoors, as he was. There weren't many women who'd lie on a bed of heather in the middle of the night and gaze in wonder at the sky. 'I don't believe in a lot of things, Rose, but I do believe in the magic of this.'

And now he wasn't sure if he was thinking about the night sky or this single moment with her.

But was showing her this the right thing to do? He used to bring Katy here and tell her Pippa was up there, in that lush slick of stars, shining down. They used to wave to her. Katy blew her kisses and sent them into the wind to find her. He couldn't remember when they'd stopped doing that. When Pippa had become just a memory rather than being actively remembered in Katy's daily life.

Still, if Pippa was up there…if he chose to believe that…he wondered what she'd be thinking right now. Would she be devastated he was here with Rose? Or would she think he was doing the right thing? Moving on with his life, as she'd have wanted.

It occurred to him that thinking of Pippa was still sad and beautiful, but a comfort rather than a hurt. She was then. This…this was now.

This was now. He watched Rose's radiant face as she followed the strip of stars and all thoughts of the past were wiped. 'We're the lucky ones, Rose. You can't see it in the city, but imagine all that energy above us and around us—that's why you fit in so well here. All that crackling energy you have in spades.'

'On a good day.'

'Seems to me you don't have many bad ones.'

'It depends who I'm with.' Laughing more, she turned to face him and propped her head on her fist. In the dim light he could see the soft focus of her eyes, the smile that made her more beautiful than a clear sky at midnight.

He stretched out onto his side to face her. The wonders of nature giving him nowhere near the thrill he got from just being with her. He would not think of next week and saying goodbye. 'It's been intense.'

'That's one way of describing it.' Her voice died away and her eyes settled on him.

Not knowing what to say next, because he didn't want to fill his need or the soft silence with pointless chatter, he just looked at her. Took in her gentle features. That smile.

She looked back at him. First to his eyes, then his mouth, then away. But her chin lifted and her gaze slid back to his again. The atmosphere around them was charged; a soft breeze brought scents of wild thyme and heather and the faint sounds of laughter somewhere down the valley.

And the smile fell from her face to something far more serious.

And still he said nothing and did nothing but held her gaze, and the seriousness was stoked by sensuality, her eyes doing the talking. She wanted him—that hadn't changed. Palpably, her body buzzed for him. Her hitched breathing led the rhythm as she reached her hand to his face and stroked his jaw with the back of her fingers.

In the end, he spoke as softly as he could. 'I'm glad you're here. I'm glad you didn't hotfoot it out of Oakdale the first chance you got.'

'Me? I'm not a quitter—in fact the doctors said I was quite the fighter in the end.'

He caught her fingers in his. Kissed the tips, watched as she softened at his touch. 'Tell me? Tell me, Rose. I want to know.'

Her eyes flickered closed as if she was holding in all the fear and pain she must have endured, and he wondered if he'd asked too much, too soon. She opened her mouth, closed it. Seemed to be trying to find words, debating what to say. In the end she sighed and shook her head.

'I was sick for two years, getting weaker and weaker, and I knew what was going to happen. I was so scared, Joe. You cling to anything—a single word, a look in a doctor's eye…anything that might give you hope. *Anything* at all. And then they tell you there is nothing more they can do and you'll die within weeks without a transplant and you're faced with no hope at all.'

She breathed out. Swallowed. 'You think of all the things you didn't do. The chances you didn't take. You think of all the love you have left to give. So much love in here.' She ran her palm over his chest, above his heart. 'And you ache for the lost chances.'

'I know.' He'd felt the same thing. 'How many times you wish you'd said something different, done something different. How much giving you still had inside and nowhere for it to go. How damned hard it is to let go.' He was back there for a moment, all the pain tightening inside. But this time it was for Pippa *and* for Rose.

'Let go?' Rose's eyes filled. 'No way. I wasn't ready to let go at all. I held on so tightly. So damned tight, Joe. I don't think I'd have made it if I hadn't.'

'I wish I'd been there somehow. I wish I could have helped. Held you. Fought for you.' *Loved you.*

He wanted to love her. That much he knew now. No more raging or confusion. No more fighting this attraction; it was more than that. Deeper.

He wanted her. *God*, how he wanted to take care of her. He imagined her, weak and small in a sterile hospital bed with tubes and machines keeping her alive. He thought of the fear of saying goodbye, wondering if this was going to be the last time she saw someone she loved. He imagined the thoughts that flitted through her head in the dark and lonely nights and his heart cracked for her.

So he wrapped her in his arms the way he would have done five years ago if he'd been there. He stroked her hair, kissed her head, her cheek, stroked her hands, kissed her fingers one by one and told her with his kisses and his caresses, as best he could, that he would have taken care of her, no matter what.

Then he slid his mouth over hers and kissed her, pouring everything he had into that connection. It was the kind of kiss he'd read about. It was the kind of kiss that blurred his thoughts, filled his heart. And all he wanted was more. And more. But he wanted to hear her voice. And her story. Because he'd never given her that chance. 'And after?'

She gave him a sad smile. Because they both had their suspicions about the part in between the before and the after. 'I can't even describe—it was the best gift, Joe. So, so precious. Heartbreaking and yet life-giving. It's so hard to get your head round. I decided I had to do some good in return. Pay it forward, live big. See and do everything possible. Experience everything I could. Because I owed it to…' she paused, eyes cautious again '…to them and to me. I was alive. I'm alive! Look at me. I can breathe, move, dance. I can climb mountains. I can kiss, Joe. I have enough energy and breath to kiss again, and you have no idea how good that feels.'

He ran his hands down her arms and tugged her closer. 'I know how damned good you feel.'

'You too.' She edged even closer to him, aligning her body with his. Her breathing came fast and he could almost feel the need rippling off her. Her scent filled the space between them.

He could feel the outline of her breasts against his chest. The soft press of her thighs as she arched against him.

'So do you want to shut me up or should I keep on talking until the sun comes up?'

He brushed his hand over her cheek. Ran his thumb to her lip. Bent to her mouth and whispered so, so close to her lips. 'I like the sound of your voice, Rose. But I really do love it when you moan.'

'Yes.' Her pupils dilated and she sighed his name.

And he needed no other encouragement than that sweet sound.

She wanted him.

Rose wanted him inside her, on her. To touch him, kiss him, to feel his hands over her, everywhere. For ever. There was enough light—just enough—for her to see his beautiful, rugged face filled with desire, his startling blue eyes. And the need. Such need. Shimmering there in his gaze. Molten liquid heat.

His kiss was deep and hard and mirrored the hunger in her, fed it, stoked it until she thought she might burn out with desire. Not one cell in her body thought this was a bad idea. She knew, deep inside her, that everything would be better after sex with Joe Thompson, during sex with Joe Thompson.

And then…? Then she didn't know.

His fingers were under her T-shirt, stroking below her ribcage, and this time she didn't flinch as he went to her breast. She cared only for more touching, more kissing. Her T-shirt went skimming across the moorland, her bra in the opposite direction, and when he sucked in her nipple she thought she might scream in ecstasy or die or both. When he cupped her breasts she fisted her hands into his hair, but it wasn't enough; she wanted to feel his lips against hers again. Always. Mouth-to-mouth, skin-to-skin. So she hauled him back to face her, planted wet kisses on his lips and stripped off his T-shirt.

Mouth sliding against his, she traced her fingers down over a tight abdomen and covered his hardness through his jeans, feeling him jump under her touch. He put his hand over hers, sucked in air. 'Rose. Wait.'

'I don't want to wait.' She was emboldened by her misted senses, drunk on lust for this man. And yet scared she'd lose her nerve in a tumult of questions and encroaching doubts.

His mouth traced a trail of kisses down her throat, her neck then he stopped and ran his thumb across her scar. 'I am so sorry you went through that.'

She pressed her hands to the sides of his head. 'Don't be sorry. Please don't. Make me glad for it. I want you. Joe.'

'I want you.' He made her moan just the way he said he loved, one hand on her breast, one over her scar. Protecting. Caressing.

Her hands trembled as she undid his jeans zip and took him in her hand. He was so hard, so ready for her. And she was so ready for this, for all of it. But as he slid out of his jeans and helped her off with hers he smiled, long and slow. 'First, you. Then, us.'

She didn't realise what he meant until the beautiful, sharp scrape of his stubbled jaw bruised her abdomen. Her hip. Her thigh. And he made a space for his fingers, then his mouth at her core.

She lay back on the heather, the prickles at her neck a dim observation. Her senses were already overwhelmed by his mouth. His heat. The stars. His scent. His fingers, pulsing against her. The heather. His heat. The stars.

Joe. Joe. Joe.

Then he was saying her name over and over and she bucked against his fingers, clamping tight around them.

She was almost there, so close, so close…but she wanted him there too. So she tugged away from his hands and put her palms to his face again. 'Joe. Now. Please. I want you inside me.'

He shook his head. 'Hell. I am so sorry. I don't have a condom.'

She bit back a curse. She was so close. So damned close to everything being perfect. 'You're a bloody doctor, Joe Thompson.'

'Who hasn't had sex in a long time.' He shrugged and went to pull her back into his arms, but she grabbed her purse and pulled out a foil.

'Well, it's lucky I'm a forward-thinker then.'

'Okay, so now I do believe in luck.' He laughed as she sheathed him. 'Unless that's one you've crocheted, in which case…no. I can wait.'

'Well, I can't. And I'm pretty sure this is one hundred per cent condom.'

But the grin fell as he pushed her hair back from her face, achingly gentle. 'Honestly, are you sure about this?'

Was she?

Live big. With no regrets. She would never regret this. 'I have never been more sure of anything in my life. I just don't know what happens after this. Between us…'

'We can make it up, make our own rules. But I want you to know this is important, Rose. To me. I don't know what tomorrow will bring or the day after. Next year. Next lifetime. But, right now, I want you. So damned much. And you want me…?'

'God, yes, I want you. This. More. All of it.' Her heart was beating…*hard and fast, hard and fast, hard and fast* against her ribcage. Pulsing out her need, shaping its rhythm to this, to him. To them.

And then he was sliding inside her and her eyes flickered closed at the sharp press, the gentle push, at the too-sexy groan coming from his throat as he filled her. *Whole.*

He kissed her then, slow and languorous, and his rhythm matched—*their* rhythm matched—slow and deep. But when she opened her eyes he captured her gaze and looked at her as if she was the answer to everything.

She pressed her fingers hard into his skin, wanting to sear this moment into her memory and into her soul, pulling him hard against her, urging his strokes to go deeper. To take all of her.

His breath hitched, his angle changed and she was right back on that edge. He rocked against her over and over, cradling her face with one palm, locking her against him with his other arm. Tight. Hard. Close. Hard. Fast. Deep. What he didn't say she already knew. He was hers. She was his.

Then, with her name on his lips, raw in his throat, he groaned and thrust and took her with him. And the millions of stars were outside her body and inside her head and she was with them and with Joe, reaching out to forever.

Words failed him.

For five whole minutes Joe couldn't think of a single thing that would ever match the magic of what had just happened. He couldn't let this go, not now he'd found it. Somehow he'd make it work. Slowly. Rose's pace. This pace.

Was she going to stay? Could it work? Was he taking a huge risk, only to lose another woman he'd fallen hard for?

Fallen? Already? Hell, he was racing ahead of himself.

'You okay?' Rose curled tight into him and he wrapped his body over her to shield her from the breeze. Hell, they'd made love on the top of a bloody hill.

Shoving the doubts away, he laughed. With her around he was doing that more and more these days; that was a good thing, right? 'I'm great, but I think you need to get dressed—it's getting cold.'

She reached for her T-shirt and dragged it close but snuggled her bottom against him and pulled his arms tighter round her. 'What happens now?'

He was completely clear on this, even if he wasn't on anything else. He wanted to spend the night with her. In a bed, preferably, and not on a bunch of woody flowers. 'We go home.'

'To my place?'

'Yes.'

She twisted to look at him. 'Not to yours? Is that because of Katy and Pippa?'

No. Yes. No. 'Because it's closer and you're shivering.'

'From too much excitement, that's all.' She grinned. 'I like you, Joe Thompson, very much. But what the hell did you do with my jeans?'

'Hmm…' He reached behind him. 'Not sure.'

'And my underwear?' She knelt up, rummaged in the dark, completely unembarrassed about her semi-nakedness now. And God, what a powerful punch to his heart that was. 'Oh, my God. If they've blown away you're giving me yours to wear. I can't walk through the village with no clothes on my bottom half.'

What the hell? He laughed, the sound rumbling through the air, probably as far as Bowness. Lancaster.

London. 'And I can? I'm the doctor—it's grossly unprofessional; they'd have a fit.'

'Not if they got a glimpse of that gorgeous body. Come on…' She tickled his belly. 'Live a little. Skinny running?'

'I do know a shortcut.' He nuzzled his nose in her hair. 'I can get you there in about five minutes, without going down the main street. Besides, half-naked means… easier access.'

'To what?'

'You, of course.' He palmed her breast and she arched against him, soft sighs leaving her throat as he kissed a path from her mouth to her neck.

'Joe Thompson, I'm seeing a very different you these days.' She reached behind her with her hand, patted the earth. And again. Sighed out a laugh. 'Wait. Here they are. Yes. Jeans at least. Oh…silky, yes. Underwear.'

'That's a shame. I much prefer you naked.' He was hard again already.

She stroked down his midriff, inhaled as she gently squeezed him. Kissed him full on the mouth, hot wet kisses. 'Yes, please. How long did you say to get to the cottage? Five minutes?'

'Three if we run.'

It took too long to get the key in the lock. Too long to push open the door.

Once inside he backed her against the wall. His lust a fever he couldn't fight. Too long to undress her again. Would he ever have enough of her? *No. Just no.* 'I don't think I can make it upstairs.'

'Good.' She was breathless, ragged, limp with desire,

arching and pressing against him, fumbling with his zip. Cursing. Giggling. 'I've got a damned fine sofa and I'm not afraid use it.'

CHAPTER THIRTEEN

SOME TIME LATER, in the small dark hours, she lay awake in her bedroom listening to him breathing, the rhythm disturbed. He was awake too and she wondered if he was going through the what-ifs the way she was.

'Joe, am I the first since Pippa died?'

'I haven't wanted to…' a long moment of silence '…until now.'

'You okay with this?'

His arm over her belly, his voice at her ear. A whisper. 'Of course.'

'Only… I know it's a big deal. And I can't imagine what you're thinking or feeling.'

'Just good things, Rose. About you.'

She stroked his arm. 'I thought you said you'd be honest with me.'

A soft rumble of admission. 'My head's a bit messed-up. Not about you,' he added with certainty.

'About Pippa then?' Of course he'd be feeling all kinds of things right now, just like her, because they'd both brought so much baggage.

He sighed. 'Do we have to talk about her?'

'Tell me what happened.'

'Why the hell would you want to know about that? Please, Rose. Can't we leave her out of this?'

She turned over to face him. 'I want to know everything about you. What your favourite colour is, what you like to eat. Where you go on holiday. All those things. But I also want to know about the woman you loved.' And whether he still loved his wife so much he didn't really have the space he was saying he had for Rose.

Whether he was trying—in some way—to find Pippa again. She remembered the way he'd looked when he'd felt her heartbeat and she had to know he was ready to move forward with Rose McIntyre.

Because, even over these last few hours, this had gone into a deep intimacy that she desperately wanted to believe in, and jump into wholeheartedly. It could work. She could keep well. People did. She could stay here. Perhaps. Or at least come back to him. Love him. She could love him, she thought, suddenly hopeful. But she needed to know he was free to do that too.

'That night. What happened?'

'I don't want to go there, Rose. Not now.'

'Then when? Ten minutes? Ten days? Ten weeks? Ten years? Who's counting?' Did she have ten years?

'You're talking in years now, Rose?' At her shrug he looked a little less wary.

'I want to know. You know everything about me, Joe. Everything. No secrets.' Her heart hammered. This could be it. This could be her chance for a bigger second life filled with love. Despite her misgivings, he could fall for her. Despite all her problems. She could jump in and not be so afraid on the inside, with all her veneer of bravery on the outside. She could be herself. She could live a life befitting two people here in Oakdale. But she had to rid herself of this spectre of Pippa.

'Okay.' He rolled onto his back, arms under his head, and stared at the ceiling. It was a few moments before he spoke. 'Five years ago. Sometimes feels like yesterday, sometimes like another lifetime ago. We were at a conference in Bristol. I was there giving a paper and she and Katy came down for the weekend. But we had a fight. Just an argument, stupid. We said stupid things.'

'About what?'

He shook his head, rubbed his temples, glanced over to her. 'Having more kids, would you believe? We'd been down the IVF route with Katy and it had taken a toll on us both, but on her mainly; she'd reacted badly to some of the meds. She wanted more kids and I wasn't sure we should try again. God, yes, I wanted more; we both did. We'd always talked about having a football team of children but we had Katy. It had worked for us once; who knew if it would work a second time? And we needed to focus on being the little family we'd been blessed to be.'

'I've heard that story a lot. IVF is wonderful, but it can be a hard journey for all involved.' He wanted more kids. He wanted to share his life. For the long term. For ever.

He nodded, scrubbed his fist across his head. 'She told me she'd made an appointment and was going whether I liked it or not.'

'Sounds feisty.'

He gave a rueful smile at the memory. 'She was. But things got out of hand. I accused her of being selfish. She said the same about me. So she packed her bags and said she was going home to think. I was giving a paper on working in a rural practice so I had to stay, but I couldn't make her and there was no way she was going to let Katy stay either so she bundled her into the car too. Locked the door and refused to let me in.' He hauled in oxygen. 'Last time I saw her she was crying as she drove the car out of the car park into lashing rain.'

His face was bleak.

She stroked his jaw, closed her eyes, knowing what was coming.

'Ninety minutes later there was a policeman at the hotel door telling me they were on their way to hospital after a head-on collision. That the family I had was falling apart.'

'Katy? Traumatised? Hurt?'

'Just a few scratches and a lot of tears.' His eyes flickered closed and he swallowed. 'You know the rest.'

'I do.' She hugged him close, knowing a lot more now. That his dreams had been snatched away, that he wanted the things she couldn't give him.

He reached for her and pulled her tight to him, his naked body pressed against the length of hers. 'No more now. That's it. I'm done with all this talking about the past.' He kissed her. Twice. Came up smiling. 'Time for some sleep, Rose McIntyre.'

'Indeed.' So she wrapped her arms around that broad back, entwined her legs with his and snuggled close to his chest. But she couldn't get rid of the sadness, the despair, the deep and raw love shining in his eyes.

How could she be sure any of it would be for her?

'Hey, I've got some very good news.' Joe slipped his hand into hers and they started to walk up the hill towards his house after a busy afternoon clinic.

The last few days had flown by in a blur of boat rides and crochet lessons for the girls and happy lunches and dinners filled with laughter. Rose had slotted into their timetable, loving the closeness father and daughter had and not wanting to miss out on spending precious time with them.

And, at the same time, always, *always* Joe was attentive and kind and funny and sexy with Rose, as if a weight had been taken from him and he was freed up somehow. But he still had a long way to go. They both did. They needed time and they just didn't have it.

They hadn't talked about what next. Because they both knew she had a contract somewhere else and things were fragile. Beautiful, but fragile. But the spectre of her leaving threaded through their kisses and lovemaking like ribbons, tugging them closer and tighter and taut.

'Oh? Let me guess.' She leaned against him. 'The new vomit bags have arrived. About time too. I ordered them ages ago.'

'No.' He guffawed. 'Better news than that.'

'Okay then… We've identified the person who eats all the chocolate gifts from the patients. And don't say it's Beth because I know it's you, Dr Thompson.'

'Nowhere close.' He stopped and took her face in his hands, kissing her right there on the main street. When he pulled away his eyes were shining. 'The agency rang to say they've managed to find someone to take over from you, but I told them we didn't need them and to cancel your contract in Plymouth. So it's all sorted.'

Ice prickled down her spine. He'd fast-forwarded them into a space she didn't want to be. 'What? You cancelled my contract. I thought only I could do that.'

'Well, yes. There's paperwork involved but I thought you'd want to stay on. You could stay longer. Stay, Rose.'

'But that's for me to decide.' Her mind was trying to

keep up with the happy flip in her heart that he'd even done such a thing. And then the downward flip at the impossibility of it all and the fact he'd not even consulted her.

He shook his head again. 'It's not a marriage proposal, Rose. And I don't want you to do anything you're not comfortable with. I thought we could take things slowly. Get to know each other. You said yourself this connection was intense, and it is. You said you had too many missed chances. Let's have some fun and a chance at something good.'

It had taken a lot to get him to this point, she knew. She'd seen his struggle. Seen how hard it had been for him to let go of his past.

And oh, she wanted him, wanted to stay here so badly, to make what was left of her life a good one right here… It could be three years, or thirty, and she couldn't think of anywhere she'd rather be than in his arms. She'd thought it would be easy to stop herself from falling from him, but it hadn't worked.

She'd been going to conquer the world, save all those lives, make her own life worth something while she could. She was going to grasp each day and make it count. She was going to have a big life befitting two people. She wasn't ever going to fall for another guy, but Joe had made her feel as if she could risk it all for a second chance at love. She wanted a future; she wanted to be loved for however long she had. But, to take that risk, she had to know he was available and that would take time and she'd already started packing.

Because what if he wasn't? What then for her heart?

'Is your silence a yes? You'll stay on?' He pressed his mouth on hers.

One more time.

Her throat thickened with tears, her heart beat fast to his rhythm and her tummy contracted with need. Clutching her hands to his neck, she kissed him back.

If only. If only. If only.

He pulled away and kissed the tip of her nose, her eyes, her cheeks, breath coming fast. She could see desire in his eyes, in his face. Could feel it in his body.

But wanting to love her was not enough. 'We haven't talked this through, Joe. It's a big step. It's my job. My future.'

'*Our future.* I want to make this work, Rose. See how we go. We can take it slow.'

It was almost a promise. Almost enough to make her think it could work. But there was too much at stake—not just her heart, but his and Katy's. 'And Pippa?'

He blinked at the name. 'It's enough to know she saved someone's life and if that person is half as good as you then it was worth it. In the end. And if it really was you, then this is a gift. A beautiful, precious gift. If it was true it would be beautiful.'

'And if it isn't true?'

He thumbed her bottom lip. 'It's still beautiful, Rose. You're beautiful.'

'You make me feel as if I am.' This was so damned hard. 'But listen, Joe, I can't be the person you want me to be. I can't give you the family you want and deserve. I can't give you a promise of forever because I don't know how long I have.'

His eyes darkened. 'What matters is having you here, Rose.'

'Things are so muddled for us both and we need to work it all out, with space. I have made my decision, but it isn't to stay, Joe. I'm sorry. It's all too complicated here. I can't be what or who you want me to be.'

'I want you to be you, Rose McIntyre.'

'Do you? You want a family. You want someone to grow old with. That's what you deserve. I don't know if that's going to happen.' She touched his face, ran her fingers over that beautiful, stubbled Viking jaw. 'Maxine said I'd woken you up, but you're not fully awake yet—you're dreaming of something we can't have. Of something with someone who isn't like me. Of a second chance with Pippa, maybe?'

He snapped upright. 'This isn't about her. Please believe me.'

'It's about everything. I don't want to catch you looking at me, wondering if there's part of her that you're clinging to. I don't want you to resent me for being alive when she isn't.'

'I wouldn't do that. Ever.'

'You need to be sure. More than that, I need to be sure.' Love wasn't about holding on; it was indeed about letting go and she had to do that. She remembered the way he'd looked when he'd felt her heartbeat. That softening, that hope. 'Can you tell me, honestly, that knowing I may have Pippa's heart hasn't made a difference in any way?'

There was a silence then as they walked slowly along the path. She had her answer. Because, above all, she knew he was honest. It made a world of difference. 'I'm sorry, Joe. So sorry.'

That wasn't even the beginning of how she felt. Every cell in her body yearned for him, tugged towards him.

He stopped again. 'No, you're not sorry—you're running away. I never would have thought that of you.'

Anger fed her voice as she tried to defend what she knew were excuses. She was scared of being hurt, of being rejected in the end. Of saying goodbye again for the last time. 'Perhaps I am. Or perhaps I'm being true to my overall aim of having some fun and seeing the world.'

'You can tell yourself lies all you want, Rose, but I won't believe them. You like it here. You like Katy. Hell, I think you even like me. So your living big talk is falling on deaf ears. You don't think I've been hurt? You don't think I haven't lain awake at nights wondering what the hell I'm doing letting myself get involved again? Allowing Katy to get close to you?'

'I know it's been a big step for you both.'

'Big? Big? You have no idea. Katy looks at you like you're some kind of movie star. And me… I've taken the biggest risk of my life here. I lost the woman I loved and for five long years I didn't think I'd be able to ever feel anything again. Then along you came and I finally started to feel something. To have fun. To look forward with hope.'

Rose's heart contracted. She was being selfish, but sometimes that was what you had to be. Call it self-preservation. 'Thank you. Thank you for everything. I adore Katy and I'll keep in touch with her.'

'Thank you? What the hell? She doesn't want an occasional email and the odd Christmas card and neither do I. Thanks for the memories? Yeah. Back at you.'

'Joe. Please.'

Please don't do this. Don't make this hard. Don't break my heart.

But it was already too late. This time she'd broken it herself.

He caught her arm and crushed her to him. 'I've never

met anyone like you before. You make me believe in the crazy. You make me believe in luck and magic and fate—because what if you were meant to come here? What if we really are meant to be together?'

If only. If only. If only.

A sharp pain gripped her chest. Heartache.

She wanted Joe. Wanted to be with him, more than she'd wanted anything before.

A thought—a realisation that was as frightening as it was inevitable—slid into her head, recognising the emotions swimming in her body. She loved him and she had to go, for all their sakes.

She loved him.

She'd already taken that risk without knowing. Her heart was one step ahead but her head...her head knew that they couldn't rush this. She couldn't make promises and neither could he.

If only love didn't hurt so damned much.

'Oh, Joe.' She cupped his cheek then pressed a kiss there. Tears forcing their way down her cheeks, no matter how much she tried to stop them. Fisting them away, she took a deep breath. Better to believe in something than nothing at all. 'If we're meant to be together then we will be. Some time. Somehow. But not now.'

There was no changing her mind. He tried. All the way back to her cottage. When he took her to her door. Before she closed it. After she'd closed it, making her open it again. Her face was wet with tears, eyes red, lips swollen from their kiss. So beautiful and vibrant and bright. But he could see the strain and wished he could do anything to take it away. 'You are so damned determined and independent.'

Her chest heaved and she dragged in air. 'I thought it was a positive.'

'It is.' Even begging wasn't beneath him, but he knew he wouldn't change her mind. 'Just not when you do it with me.'

'I have to do it for us both then. And for Katy.' The smile she gave him was so damned sad it was a swift blow to his gut. 'Look, I can't talk about this any more. It's so hard. Too damned hard, Joe, but it's the right thing to do. I have to go now and do more packing.'

'So it's all worked out? That's it?'

'That's it. I'm heading off on Friday after work.'

That was enough to give him caution. 'I'll drive the damned car. I'll drive you to Plymouth.'

'No, you won't. I have to do this. You'll understand. I have to get away from here, from you and Katy, so I can think straight.'

He wanted her to stay. He wanted to love her. God, yes, he wanted to. So damned much. Did the fact she might have Pippa's heart make a difference?

No. He was pretty sure it didn't. He wanted to believe it didn't. Wanted to believe he'd moved on. Was fighting to move on, but it seemed he was mired in the past even without wanting to be.

'Does it have to be complicated?' He needed to make her believe 'Stay, Rose. It can be just as simple as that. Stay. We can work anything else out later.'

'No. No, Joe. And I'm not going to argue about this. It's too hard and it's breaking my heart.' Then she was closing the door and she didn't open it again, not after he knocked. Twice.

So he was left standing in the middle of a cobbled road with the wind slicing him in two. He looked up at

Oak Top, where they'd made love only days ago. He'd thought his life was getting back on track and yet here it was…woefully derailed again.

By a woman in an orange hat with the best kisses in the world, who tasted of smiles and looked like sunshine.

Who had melted his heart and now snapped it in two.

CHAPTER FOURTEEN

'WELCOME TO WHITSTABLE Medical Centre. I'm sure you'll enjoy it here and thanks for coming at such short notice.' The efficient head practice nurse gave her a nod and a sharp smile. 'The last one went off sick and we're a bit stuck.'

'Not a problem. Glad I could help.' Rose's voice was filled with enthusiasm, but her body wasn't feeling it. Four weeks since she'd left Oakdale and she'd moved halfway across the bottom of the country, starting in Plymouth and now on the south-east coast. Seemed she just couldn't keep still, couldn't settle. Not when her heart wanted to be elsewhere.

From the medical centre's window she could see the sea throwing an autumn tantrum. Far from the sunny south she'd been promised, she'd seen nothing but wind and rain since she'd arrived. But hell, she hadn't exactly been a ray of sunshine herself.

She wondered what the weather was bestowing on the Lake District. She loved it when the wind howled and nearly blew her off Joe's hill, when it was calm and still with a gift of heat. She even loved the fog. She missed the place.

And she missed Joe. Missed him as if a part of her

had been amputated. Missed Katy and Oakdale and the friends she'd started to make there. And here she was, starting over every few weeks—lonely and lost. Not knowing anyone, not making friends because she was moving on and it was too damned hard to start caring for people and then leaving them. That was a lesson learnt. Hardly the big life she'd promised herself.

Still, she'd got the distance she'd wanted.

Be careful what you wish for.

The morning plodded on and she learnt the new systems, the little quirks of the practice. Each had their own way of doing things. The receptionist was nice and she didn't appear to be about to keel over, so that was a bonus.

But she wasn't Maxine. Or Beth. Lovely Beth. And the doctors weren't grumpy at all. Which should have been a bigger bonus, but they weren't Joe.

Her head and her heart kept sliding back to him.

She managed the morning, where she was polite and efficient and didn't spill plaster-of-Paris or annoy anyone—she didn't think. And she was just buttoning up her coat to go for a lunchtime walk when a bunch of the biggest daisies she'd ever seen appeared at the front door. Carried by… 'Rose? Rose. Thank God.'

His voice settled at seeing her.

Joe was here? Her heart danced at the sight of him. Because even though the daisies were huge they still looked small in his grip. She fought back the urge to tear them out of his hand and jump into his arms. Because…

Because she had to hear what he was going to say.

But daisies. Not roses, she'd noted with a smile. 'Whoa. They're huge.'

'Cape daisies. The biggest ones I could find.'

'They're…amazing.' As was he. He was looking at

her as if he'd found gold. As if he'd found his home. And she wanted to believe they could go forward. But what if they couldn't? 'How did you find me? The agency? They wouldn't give out my personal details…' But he had been her employer, after all, so maybe they had.

He grinned, looking so proud of himself. 'I looked your mother up online. Gave her a call—'

'At work?' Oh, my God, she could just imagine how that went.

'Yes. I told her I needed to see you. Life or death. And so, here I am.' He handed her the flowers. Didn't kiss her cheek. Didn't come close to hug her.

A smile swelled from Rose's chest. 'You told my mother? About…us?'

He nodded. 'She seemed a little excitable. Will she be okay?'

A sharp shrill beep came from her phone. She took a peek. *Mum.*

'Is he there? What's he saying? Are you okay? Do you need to sit down?'

Rose laughed. 'You may have just given her a heart attack. But once that's over she'll calm down.'

Then the fun fizzled from her gut and she just looked at him, drank in every detail. Those bluest eyes. That scruff of blond hair. *Joe.* Her lovely Joe.

Here.

She wanted to kiss him. To lie in his arms in the heather, in a bed. But he had to be sure. So did she. If the last few weeks had taught her anything it was that she didn't want to spend her life on her own.

'What…why are you here?'

He stood tall and proud. Steady and still. And put his hands out. 'This is me fighting for you. I should have done it when I had you with me but I messed up that opportunity. I said I'd make it worth your while staying. I didn't. I should have done more.'

She thought about the Milky Way, and the glow-worms and the boat ride. About the picnic and the slow way he made love. And the fast way too. Mostly, she thought about how he'd captured her heart. 'It was lovely.'

'But not enough.'

She shook her head. 'I wanted to stay. I wanted to believe it could work...once we'd got through the transplant stuff. I really did, Joe. I just didn't want you to believe it was something we could do for ever. It's not fair on Katy or you.'

He took a step forward and took her hands in his. 'I don't want to count the days with you, Rose. I want to make every day count. I want forever to be as long as we have.'

'As long as I have, you mean? I'm the one with the dicky heart.'

He shook his head. Tipped her chin so he could look deep into her eyes. 'I already promised one woman I'd be with her for ever and look how that ended. You said yourself, stuff happens. I want any stuff that happens to be *with* you, okay? Not without you. You made me believe that amazing things can happen and maybe it is fate that brought you to me... I don't know...but I want you stay by my side. For ever...however long that is.'

His mouth was so close to hers and she wanted, so much, to slide her lips against his. 'Joe... I want to. I really do. I just don't...' Want to say goodbye again. In any way possible.

His mouth was against her cheek. 'You said you

wanted a big life. So what's bigger than falling in love? Wholeheartedly. Completely. For ever.'

'Nothing's bigger than that. But I need to know it's me, and not some idea of me, that you want. Because I asked you before if my heart made a difference and it did.'

He'd said *falling in love*. Did he love her? Had he fallen?

His arms spanned her waist and pulled her to him. She could feel his heart thumping against her chest. 'I wasn't ready to face that, Rose. But I've thought long and hard about this. In fact, it's all I've thought about. I just want to see you, be with you. I love *you*, I miss *you*. I want *you*. Not the memory of someone else, not a dream of something else. You. Me. Us. Your orange hat, your red cowboy boots, your smile. Your heart. Whoever had it before doesn't matter. It is yours, Rose, yours alone. And I love it. And you.'

She sighed against his throat. 'After everything?'

'Maybe even because of everything. I really didn't want to, I didn't think I was capable of it, but I fell in love with you that first day up the mountain when you growled at me.'

'Hey, you growled first.' She laughed. Maybe it was possible. Maybe it didn't matter how long forever was, just as long as she spent it with him. He loved her. She loved him. What could be bigger than that?

'That love grew when I saw your choice of boating clothes. The way you treated my daughter with such care. The way you kiss and taste. Do you want me, Rose?'

She kissed him then. 'Yes. I love you. So much you can't imagine.'

'I think I can.' He stepped back a little then and she

realised she didn't ever want to be even this distance from him again. 'Will you come home?'

'I have a contract here.' She looked at the reception desk and wished she'd never set foot in here, but she had and she wasn't the kind of person to renege on a contract.

And he knew that and understood her. 'When it's done I'll bring you home.'

'Yes, Joe. Bring me home.'

Six months later

'There is no way I'm allowing you to wear that for our wedding.' Rose grabbed the blue hat from Joe's head and he grabbed it back.

'You made it, so I'm wearing it.' He kissed her then pulled it back onto his head.

'We made it, Dad. Me and Rose.' Katy twirled in her white silk dress and ballet shoes. Luckily for Joe, there were no woolly clothes on either Rose or her best brides-maid. They'd all crammed into Joe and Rose's bedroom to make use of the full-length mirror and some more family time—just the three of them—before they made it official.

But Joe shook his head. 'And I love it, so it will stay on my head.' Then he tied his tie, turning sharply at a knock on the door.

Maxine walked in and smiled. 'Sorry to bother you. Oh, don't you all look lovely.' She put a hand to her chest as a tear edged down her face. 'Joey, can you and Katy go downstairs? The photographer wants a picture of you together. Rose, you have to wait five minutes, then it's your turn for photos.'

Rose noticed her…what was she?…mother-in-law-in-law?…no, *friend*, that would do fine…her friend's mascara was starting to smudge. She grabbed a tissue and put it in Maxine's hand. 'Here you go. Don't spoil your make-up.'

'Thank you, I can't help myself.' She watched as Joe and Katy left the room. Then she leaned close and tucked one of Rose's curls behind her ear. 'That's better. Look, love, I know I shouldn't say this, but you're a lot like her. There's something, I don't know, I can't put my finger on it. Mannerisms, maybe, your voice, the way you look at Joe. I don't know what, but you are like her. And I know you two would have got on. She'd have been a firm friend of yours.'

Pippa. Rose smiled, her throat filling. 'I wish I'd known her.'

'But then…' Maxine looked at her full-on, giving nothing away in her expression. 'Then maybe you wouldn't be here, would you?'

'I—' Rose was speechless. Had Maxine worked it out? Or was it an educated guess, just like Rose and Joe had made? Two halves made a whole, but what if…what if they didn't? What if they made more than that? 'I honestly don't know.'

Maxine's smile didn't slip. 'Anyway. She'd approve of you and Joe and that's all I can say. Now, come on, let's go join the others.'

With that kind of blessing it had to be a good day. And it was. Rose walked up the aisle holding her father's arm, but had to force herself to slow down before she ran straight into Joe's arms. And he waited for her, tall and strong and ever so Viking, love for her shimmering in his eyes.

The little church was so full it seemed as if the whole

village had turned out—they probably had. And there was such joy on everyone's face as she walked back down the aisle as Mrs Thompson. She didn't think she could ever be happier.

She had a daughter of her own to love and cherish, and a very full heart—whoever it belonged to in the past didn't matter. It was hers now.

And Joe's, of course. For ever.

* * * * *

MILLS & BOON

Coming next month

ISLAND DOCTOR TO ROYAL BRIDE?
Scarlet Wilson

'What do you think of Corinez so far?' She could hear the edge of uncertainty in his voice.

She took a step closer and put her hand on his arm. From here she could smell his aftershave, see the shadow starting to show along his jawline. 'I like it,' she replied honestly. 'And I want to find out more.' She licked her lips and moved even closer. 'And I like it even more that I can see how passionate you are about your country, and how much you want to make things better.'

He looked down at her, his hand sliding behind her waist. 'That's exactly how you are about Temur Sapora.' He lowered his head so his lips were only inches from hers. His breath warmed her skin, 'Maybe it makes us a good match.'

'Maybe it does,' she agreed as she moved closer until her lips were only millimetres from his. She couldn't help but smile.

'I sense you might be trouble,' he teased.

'I think you might be right.' She smiled as his lips met hers. Every cell in her body started reacting. All she cared about was this moment. Her body melded to his. She was already tired and somehow leaning against him made her instincts soar.

She didn't even notice when the elevator doors slid open.

What she did notice was someone clearing their throat. Loudly.

They sprang apart and Philippe stiffened. 'Luka.' He nodded to the dark-suited man at the door. 'You're looking for me?'

The man started talking in a low voice, his eyes darting over to Arissa and giving her the most dismissive of glances. She was instantly uncomfortable. She waited a few seconds then slid out of the elevator before the doors closed again and started walking down the corridor, praying she was heading in the right direction.

Her heart was thrumming against her chest, part from the reaction to Philippe and part from the adrenaline coursing through her body in annoyance.

She turned a corner and sighed in relief as she recognised the corridor, finding her room quickly and closing the door behind her. She took off her jacket and shoes and flung herself down on the bed. Her head was spinning.

Last time she'd kissed him he was just Philippe, the doctor who was helping at the clinic. This time she'd kissed Prince Philippe of Corinez. Did it feel different? Her heart told her no, but her brain couldn't quite decide. And as she closed her eyes, she still wasn't quite sure.

Continue reading
ISLAND DOCTOR TO ROYAL BRIDE?
Scarlet Wilson

Available next month
www.millsandboon.co.uk

COMING SOON!

We really hope you enjoyed reading this book. If you're looking for more romance, be sure to head to the shops when new books are available on

Thursday 24th January

To see which titles are coming soon, please visit

millsandboon.co.uk/nextmonth